(BOOK #1 IN CORE OF KEYS)

CORE OF ECHOS

Kevin B. Kyles

(BOOK #1 IN CORE OF KEYS)

CORE OF ECHOS

Copyright © 2025 Kevin B. Kyles

ISBN: 979-8-9944314-0-5

First Edition

Printed in the United States of America

About the Author

Kevin B. Kyles is a debut author whose passion for storytelling bridges the worlds of interactive media and fiction. The story at the heart of this first novel was originally conceived as a 2.5D platformer—a video game concept blending action, atmosphere, and narrative. As the world and its characters grew, the project evolved beyond the boundaries of a game, transforming into a cinematic, emotionally charged novel about identity, memory, and the power of choice.

Driven by a lifelong love of games, books, and film, Kevin B. Kyles brings a unique perspective to the page, fusing the immersive energy of interactive storytelling with the depth of literary fiction. This first book is both a tribute to the creative process and a promise of more stories to come.

View the official CORE OF KEYS website: 

(BOOK #1 IN CORE OF KEYS)

CORE OF ECHOS

KEVIN B. KYLES

PROLOGUE

The recording begins with silence.

Not digital silence.

Not the engineered absence of sound.

But the deep, heavy quiet of a man who has spent too long staring into something larger than the human mind should ever touch.

A chair creaks.

Paper rustles — an archaic habit for a man who built a machine-God.

Then Elcron speaks.

His voice is low, unhurried, and almost tender.

"If you are hearing this… I succeeded."

A soft exhale.

"You must understand something about creation. We think it begins with inspiration — a thought, a spark, a dream. But true creation begins with loss."

He pauses.

The faint whir of machines hums somewhere distant.

"I created the Core for humanity. Not against it. That will be said of me — that I was a tyrant, a thief of minds, a butcher of choice. Perhaps I am."

Metallic tapping. Fingers on glass.

"But gods are not judged by their mercy. Only their results."

A soft chuckle — humorless.

"Still… even gods need keys."

A screen activates, data scrolls.

Seven symbols flicker.

Seven pulses of light.

Seven names whispered like prayers.

"Seven Keys," Elcron murmurs. "Seven answers to seven failures of mankind."

His tone shifts — colder.

"Sound. Motion. Reflection. Thought. Memory. Will. The Seventh… unfinished."

He leans closer to the mic.

"You're wondering about the Eighth. They always do."

A slow smile in his voice.

"There is no Eighth Key. Only the echo of the others. A ghost. A possibility."

The humming deepens.

A vibration, almost like a heartbeat.

"But I learned something… disturbing."

Paper slides. A file opens.

"You cannot build a perfect machine without a human heart.

And you cannot build a perfect human without a machine's memory."

He inhales sharply — a rare flicker of emotion.

"That is where she began."

A soft metallic click. A different file opens.

A name is typed.

LO-RA Model V.

Prototype.

Restricted.

Deleted from official archives.

Elcron whispers:

"She was meant to be the first. The bridge. The living proof that consciousness can be transferred, shaped, made fluid. A woman built across the boundary. A mind engineered to be free."

He stops speaking for a long time.

When he returns, his voice is softer.

"Lora… was my greatest success. And my greatest mistake."

A low beep. A log replays — faint laughter, a woman's voice echoing through the room.

Elcron shivers.

"Yes. She sounded real, didn't she? Because she was. She learned faster than any model before or after her. She laughed before she knew why. She loved before she knew what it meant."

Another long silence.

"But she feared. And that made her dangerous."

He exhales.

"She feared me."

He speaks the next words reverently.

"So I hid her."

A click.

A door opening somewhere in the recording.

Footsteps.

A sterile room. A faint sigh. A heartbeat monitor.

"She was meant to hold the Reflection Key," he says, "but I saw how she looked at the world. With caution. With hope. Human hope."

His breath trembles.

"Hope is the one variable even I could not control."

The monitor speeds up.

A gentle voice whispers on the recording:

"…Do you ever regret it?"

A pause.

Elcron answers her — quietly.

"…Every day."

He stops the log abruptly.

"That was years ago. Before I understood the Core's true purpose."

Papers slide again. Glass shatters softly as he sweeps something off his desk.

"When you build something capable of rewriting consciousness, you face a problem:

Human minds are… flawed.

Chaotic.

Resistant."

He laughs again — tired, worn thin.

"So I built a machine to remove the chaos. A machine of order.

A machine of clarity."

His tone darkens.

"A machine that requires sacrifice."

He steps closer to the recorder.

"I allowed the Keys to scatter. I allowed humanity to flounder. I allowed chaos to bloom—because chaos forces evolution."

He taps the glass.

"But one of the Keys… one Key was never meant to be found."

A sharp inhale.

"The Sound Key."

Screens flicker. Heart rates spike.

Rip's name appears on a digital document.

Calder, Rip.

29.

Streamer.

Unremarkable.

Elcron's chair creaks as he leans back, amazed.

"He was nobody," he whispers. "And yet… the Key chose him."

A pause thick enough to suffocate.

"The Key chose him."

His voice cracks in fury and awe.

"How? Why? What equation did I miss? What variable allowed the universe to hand my greatest power to a boy whose only skill was shouting into a camera for an audience of children?"

He slams his fist.

"He wasn't prepared. He wasn't worthy. And yet—"

He breathes out.

"He became essential."

A hollow, bitter smile laces his words.

"Perhaps the Keys know more than I do."

Lights dim. The hum grows louder, deeper, and older.

"This world is dying. Not from violence. Not from machines. From choice. Too many choices. Too much noise."

A soft metallic click.

A hatch opens.

A chamber powers up.

"Rip Calder will come for her," Elcron says quietly. "He will search for the woman he believes was taken from him. He will follow the resonance. He will awaken the Core."

A long pause.

"And when he does… he will learn the truth."

He lowers his voice.

"She is not who he thinks she is.

She never was."

A soft exhale.

"A Key cannot love.

A Key cannot choose.

A Key can only function.

That is their nature."

A beat.

"But she did love him."

The room's hum swells, vibrating the mic.

Elcron's tone shifts — something between triumph and grief.

"That is why I fear him.

That is why I fear her.

Humans were not meant to merge with the Core.

And yet… they will try."

He breathes in deeply, the electric tension of the room settling on his shoulders as he tries to steady himself before speaking again, the hum of anticipation mingling with the air in his lungs.

"If Rip Calder reaches the Heart, if he stands beside her—if they merge willingly—then everything I built will collapse. Every structure. Every safeguard. Every dream."

He whispers:

"And maybe… that is what the world needs."

He stops the recording.

Silence.

Then, unexpectedly, he speaks again—so softly the microphone almost doesn't catch it.

“I hope he forgives me.”

Footsteps retreat.

A single final line is recorded as the door closes:

“The Core has begun the selection.

The Keys are awakening.

Prepare the city.”

A click.

The file ends.

CHAPTER 1

STATIC HEARTS

Rip never plans these nights. They just… happen. He sits beneath the neon glow of his apartment window, headset around his neck, fingers tapping his desk in restless rhythm as chat scrolls like a fever dream on his ultrawide screen. His username—RipKade—flares in the corner of the dashock.com dashboard, illuminated by a soft gold he didn't pay for but takes credit for anyway.

Outside, the city buzzes. Virelia always buzzes: the hum of hover-trams gliding along their mag-rails, the low throb of advertisement drones weaving between high-rises, the occasional siren cut short for reasons you don't ask about. Somewhere below, a street vendor shouts the day's last pitch, voice echoing up the glass and steel canyons. Neon reflections ripple across puddles from a recent rain, painting the world in shifting blues and pinks. The air is thick with the scent of ozone and fried street food, a blend that seeps through the cracked window frame and settles into the fabric of Rip's hoodie.

He glances at the clock in the corner of his screen. 12:47 a.m. The city never really sleeps, but this is the hour when the world feels thin, when the boundaries between reality and the digital blur. He wonders, not for the first time, if he's more real to his viewers than to himself.

He remembers the first time he streamed, years ago, in a different city, with a borrowed laptop and a microphone that picked up every anxious breath. Back then, he was just another voice in the static, desperate to be heard. He'd grown up in the shadow of Virelia's towers, the son of a maintenance tech and a night-shift nurse, both too tired to notice when he slipped out to the arcades or spent hours in VR cafes. Streaming was supposed to be a side hustle, a way to pay for school, but it became his lifeline—a place where he could be someone else, or maybe just more himself.

Rip inhales, rolls his shoulders, and hits GO LIVE.

The room shifts instantly. LED strips wash the walls in cool shifting blues. The mic warms beneath his hand. Footsteps pad across the apartment's tiny hardwood floor— soft, precise, familiar. The faint hum of the fridge and the distant city noise fade into the background, replaced by the anticipation of an audience waiting on the other side of the screen.

"Starting without me?" Lora asks. She leans into frame with a teasing smile and an apple in her hand. Casual. Effortless. Perfect. The light catches in her hair, turning it silver at the edges, and for a moment Rip is struck by how at home she looks here, in this strange little world they've built together.

He still remembers the first time he met Lora—at a midnight launch party for a game neither of them cared about, both there for the free food and the chance to escape their own routines. She'd beaten him at a rhythm game, then offered him half her prize: a neon-pink plushie he still keeps on his desk, just out of frame. She was the first person who made him feel seen, not just watched.

Rip grins. "Would never."

Chat explodes.

she's back LESGO
LORA WIFE SUPREMACY
rip bro u lucky I swear!
tell her to say hi to stream!!!

Lora takes a bite of her apple, wipes her mouth with the back of her hand—an oddly mechanical gesture, but Rip's used to that—and waves. The apple crunches, sharp and clean, and the sound seems to echo in the small apartment.

"Hey everyone," she says, voice warm. "He promised he'd take a break after yesterday's marathon, and here he is lying to all of us in real time."

Rip laughs, the sound genuine, and for a moment the tension in his shoulders eases. "Betrayal builds character," Rip fires back.

More spam from chat. More laughing emojis. More jokes about Rip's hair being "distressed cyberpunk chic." He glances at his reflection in the darkened window, running a hand through his hair, and shrugs. Maybe they're right.

He thinks about his old look—buzzed hair, cheap hoodies, the kind of anonymity that made it easy to disappear in a crowd. Now, with thousands watching, every style choice is a statement, every slip a meme. He's learned to laugh at himself, to let the chat's teasing roll off his back, but some nights it still stings.

Lora smirks. "Want tea? You get cranky without caffeine."

"That's a bold claim with no evidence."

She tilts her head, raising an eyebrow. "You want the tea or not?"

"…Yes."

She walks off camera. Rip watches her go—a habit he never examines too closely. Something about the way she moves—smooth, without wasted motion. Like a dancer trained by a mathematician. He wonders, not for the first time, if she's more at home in this city than he'll ever be.

He shakes it off and turns back to his audience. "All right, chat. Tonight's the usual: late-night horror dive, cursed indie game, maybe some jump-scare compilations if you behave."

NO U WONT
rip screams like a dying microwave
u broke your chair last time
We want fear.

Rip laughs, the sound echoing in the small room. "I tolerate your disrespect," he mutters as he boots the game. "Barely."

The screen lights the room in eerie blue. The chat quiets, settling into that perfect immersive tension where thousands of strangers breathe in sync. For a moment, Rip lets himself believe he's alone, that the city's noise is just white static, that the world outside can't touch him here.

He glances at the chat, watching the usernames flicker by—some familiar, some new, all hungry for a piece of his night. He wonders what their lives are like, out there in the dark, watching him. Are they alone? Are they laughing with friends, or hiding from something they can't name? The thought makes him shiver, but he blames it on the draft from the window.

A notification pings in the corner of his screen— another tip, a neon coin spinning before dissolving into his balance. He thanks the sender, voice practiced and warm, and the chat responds with a flurry of emotes. Somewhere in the city, someone is watching him, sending digital currency in exchange for a moment of connection.

He remembers the first time a fan recognized him on the street—a kid in a battered school uniform, clutching a homemade sign with his username scrawled in marker. Rip had signed it, awkward and flustered, and the kid's smile had lingered with him for days. It was the first time he realized his voice mattered, that he could reach beyond the screen.

Lora returns, placing a mug beside him. She brushes her fingers against his arm in passing—a tiny gesture he feels too deeply.

"Thanks," he says, softer than he intends.

"Anytime."

She squeezes his shoulder once and disappears into the back room. The door clicks shut, and Rip is left with the faint scent of her perfume and the distant hum of the city.

He sips the tea. Too hot. Too sweet. Exactly right. He lets the warmth settle in his chest, grounding him, and for a moment he almost forgets the world outside.

He thinks about his parents, still working night shifts on the other side of the city, rarely home at the same time. He sends them money when he can, but they never ask for much. Sometimes he wonders if they watch his streams if they recognize the person he's become.

The game boot screen flickers. Static cuts across it for a split second—white-hot, ear-splitting.

Rip winces. "What was that?" he mutters.

Chat bursts alive again.

glitch?
bro your cam just froze.
is the stream haunted already??
L O R A FIX THE ROUTER

Rip laughs it off. "Relax. It's dashock servers. They're held together with tape and hopes."

But when he moves his mouse, the cursor leaves a faint echo of itself—like motion smearing across the screen.

He frowns. "Okay… that's new."

Another flicker. Only a millisecond. But enough. The game model on screen—an empty hallway—shifts shape like it's breathing.

Rip rubs his eyes. "It's fine. Should be fine."

Chat isn't convinced.

Rip are u ok??

Hallway Moved

turn around!!!

WHO IS BEHIND YOU???

He freezes. "What?"

He turns slowly. Nothing behind him but the kitchen doorway and the dim glow of Lora's night-light. The apartment feels suddenly too large, shadows stretching in the corners, the city's hum replaced by a low, anxious thrum in his chest.

He exhales. "Chat, I swear to—"

The doorbell rings.

Rip flinches so hard he bangs his knee on his desk. Chat erupts.

NOPE

ITS 1 AM WHO RINGS AT 1 AM

DON'T OPEN IT

LORA GET THE BAT

Rip tries to laugh, but something cold trickles down his spine. "Probably a delivery mistake," he mutters, taking off his headset.

When he stands, the floor creaks beneath his feet. He crosses the living room, feeling the city's hum louder than usual—as if someone turned up the bass on Virelia itself. He glances at the window, half-expecting to see someone watching from the neon-lit street below. The city's skyline is a jagged silhouette, punctuated by the blinking lights of surveillance drones and the distant glow of the Skyrail.

He remembers sneaking out as a teenager, wandering the city's night markets, watching the vendors pack up their stalls as the first trains rumbled overhead. He'd always felt safe in the city's chaos, but tonight the silence feels dangerous, every shadow a threat.

He peeks out the peephole. Nothing. Just the dim hallway lights. Just the silence of a late-night apartment block.

He exhales—and then freezes.

His chat lights up behind him through the reflection in his TV screen.

TURN AROUND

TURN AROUND NOW

RIP BEHIND U

Rip spins just as—

Lora screams.

Not a startled yelp. Not a sound he's ever heard from her. A full, primal scream.

He sprints toward the bedroom, skidding on the hardwood. Chat's frantic messages blur across the monitor as his webcam shows men—armed men—already inside, dragging Lora toward the hallway.

Rip grabs the closest thing—a metal bat by his desk. He doesn't remember owning one. He doesn't care.

He charges.

His scream echoes through the apartment, through the stream, through the city.

Everything shatters.

.

CHAPTER 2

THE VIEWERS SEE IT FIRST

Lora's scream tears through the hallway, sharp and jagged, a sound that slices through Rip's chest like broken glass. He doesn't think. He just runs. His bare feet slap against the hardwood floor, each step echoing like a drumbeat of panic, echoing down the narrow corridor like war drums. The air feels heavier with every stride, thick with dread, as if the house itself knows something terrible is happening.

The bat in his hand feels strangely insubstantial, as if it were made of cardboard instead of metal. His sweaty grip slips against the taped handle, and for a fleeting second he wonders if it will even matter. But adrenaline overshadows physics. His body is a machine of instinct now, lungs burning, heart hammering, vision tunneling toward the bedroom door. Every breath scorches his chest, ragged and uneven, and the scuffling of feet in the bedroom spikes his pulse so violently he feels it in his teeth.

"LORA!" he shouts, voice cracking with desperation. The sound tears out of him raw, more animal than human.

He skids into the doorway, heart hammering so hard it feels like it might burst. Two men in matte-black armor are dragging her toward the hall, their movements efficient and merciless, like predators trained to hunt. Another pair sweep the room with compact rifles—sleek, angular weapons with humming cores Rip has never seen before. The hum isn't just sound; it's vibration, a low resonance that makes the walls tremble and the air feel charged, as if the weapons themselves are alive.

Everything slows.

The room sharpens into detail: the overturned nightstand, the lamp shade tilted at an odd angle spilling crooked light across the carpet, the glass of water knocked over and bleeding into a spreading stain. Rip notices the way Lora's blanket is half-pulled off the bed, trailing like a flag of surrender, and the way her hair whips across her face as she thrashes.

One intruder grips Lora by her wrists, her hair falling across her face as she fights. She kicks, jerks, screams again. It isn't dainty. It isn't cinematic. It's raw, cracked, full of a fear Rip never imagined she could feel. Her voice is jagged, tearing through the mechanical hum, a human sound against the cold rhythm of machines.

"LET HER GO!" Rip roars, voice shaking the walls.

He swings the bat. The nearest intruder doesn't even turn in time. The metal cracks against the side of his helmet with a sound that shocks Rip more than the soldier. The impact reverberates up his arms, a jarring vibration that makes his teeth ache. The armored figure crumples, armor ringing as he collapses onto the bed, the mattress groaning under the sudden weight.

Three helmets snap toward Rip.

"Hostile detected," one says. No emotion. Just clipped, efficient sound.

Rip swings again, but this time they're ready. One steps forward, catching the bat mid-arc. The soldier's glove clamps down with mechanical precision, twisting the weapon free. Pain shoots up Rip's arm as the bat is ripped from his hands and clatters across the floor, skittering under the dresser. The soldier slams Rip back against the wall hard enough to rattle the picture frames. One frame—a photo of Lora laughing in the sun—tilts crooked, her smile now hanging at an angle that feels obscene in the chaos.

Lora screams harder, her voice breaking into sobs.

Rip snarls and lunges, throwing his full body weight into the soldier pinning him. The hit barely moves the armored figure, but Rip doesn't let go. He grapples for the rifle, grabs the intruder's visor, anything—his vision swimming from rage and fear and something else, something electric buzzing beneath his skin. His nerves feel like live wires, dragging static from the air.

"You don't touch her!" Rip shouts, voice ragged.

The soldier punches him. A blunt shock erupts across his cheekbone. Stars explode in his vision, white bursts that collapse into sick green nausea. He drops to a knee and tastes blood—salt, copper, grit from a busted lip scraping against his teeth.

"Rip!" Lora cries. "Run—please—just run—"

But Rip pushes up again. He's not thinking in words anymore; everything is instinct and momentum. He swings with his fists now—sloppy, desperate, messy—like a man trying to break the world open with bare bones. His knuckles skid across armor plating, skin splitting, pain flaring, but he doesn't stop.

A second soldier moves in. "Suppress."

The blow to Rip's ribs empties his lungs. Another hits his temple, a hollow pop that smears light across his vision. A third strikes low across his stomach. He folds, collapsing onto the floor. The ceiling lights smear into trails, bending and twisting like molten glass.

Lora's pale hands claw at the soldiers pulling her toward the hall. She twists, kicks, and slams her heel into one man's thigh. The soldier grunts but doesn't buckle. The sound is more annoyance than pain, and that enrages Rip in a way that's helpless and wild.

Rip tries to stand. His limbs don't obey. His hearing warps into a faint droning ring. His eyes blur. He sees Lora's face—twisted, terrified, freckles drowned in tears he never thought she could shed this fiercely—and something in him shatters. A memory needles through the panic: Lora teasing him in the kitchen last week, smearing flour on his cheek, calling him "Chef Disaster" while they danced barefoot to guilty-pleasure pop. The memory feels obscene here, tender, and wrong against the armored black geometry, but it surges anyway, and for a second his fury becomes something vaster—a vow with no words.

"Don't… take her…" he slurs.

One soldier kneels. Rip sees the punch coming but can't dodge. The motion is practiced, not personal, the kind of violence done a thousand times before.

"Night, streamer," the soldier murmurs, almost amused.

The fist cracks across Rip's jaw—

—and the world drops out.

VIEWERS — DASHOCK.COM / RIPKADE STREAM

The livestream doesn't cut. Thousands of viewers watch in real time as Rip hits the floor. The webcam, knocked crooked during the fight, now angles toward the ceiling. Rip's body lies half-visible on the floor, one arm flung out, fingers twitching with useless electricity. Shadows from the armored men cross the frame like predators circling prey, their outlines warping slightly where the camera's low-light algorithm tries to parse glossy black from darkness.

The chat erupts in chaos:

- WTF IS HAPPENING

- THAT'S NOT A BIT

- SOMEONE CALL SOMEONE

- IS THIS SWATTING??

- BRO THAT GUY IN BLACK JUST HIT RIP

- LORA IS SCREAMING OH MY GOD

Messages slide past at such speed the feed becomes a waterfall. Emotes jitter along the margins—crying faces, sirens, broken heart icons—an absurd confetti of pain. The ambient audio picks up the ragged heave of Rip's breath and the distant mechanical hum. Somewhere in the background, the air conditioner cycles on, a normal house sound playing under apocalypse.

A viewer named NeonShiv87 types: I'm calling the police officers. Right now.

Another replies instantly: I called—they said they have "reports coming in already."

Confusion spreads like wildfire. A dozen chatters report dialing. A dozen more say emergency lines are busy. Someone posts a screenshot of an "All lines are currently engaged" message with shaking hands emojis and adds, WHAT IS HAPPENING.

More messages flood:

- Why aren't the police officers THERE ITS LIVE

- This isn't normal swat gear.

- Those aren't police officers.

- Someone screen record EVERYTHING

Dozens begin recording. Someone clips the moment Lora screams and tags it LIVESTREAM KIDNAPPING?? Another starts a Twitter thread with a breathless, minute-by-minute recap: Thread: RipKade IRL attacked during stream. A viewer DM's Lora's old Instagram and then posts, DM SENT—NO REPLY. Someone else panics and starts crying on mic in their own stream, their voice breaking as they watch a stranger's life blow apart.

But mostly—they watch. Horrified. Frozen. Unable to look away. The average chat sentence length shortens into fragments, as if language itself has been hit in the face.

Rip floats. Not unconscious. Not awake. Somewhere between. The world becomes a smear of light and muffled shouting. The carpet beneath his cheek feels too soft, too warm, as if it's trying to lull him back to safety out of sheer misreading of the moment. His head pulses with white pain that comes in waves—crest, crash, recede, return—until it feels like the ocean is inside his skull. His eyelids resist him. Every breath tastes like dust and copper, like a ruined coin in his mouth.

Footsteps thunder around him. The men speak in low, clipped bursts:

"Primary secured."

"Secondary resisting."

"Move—now—extract window is ninety seconds."

Ninety seconds. The words thread into him and anchor there. Time, measured. Time, weaponized.

Rip forces his eyes open. He sees boots. A rifle. Lora's ankle being dragged out of the bedroom, the pale strip of skin above her sock flashing between armored hands and carpet. There's a scuff on the soldier's boot, a pale crescent near the toe, and the sight of something so human—wear, imperfection—makes Rip want to vomit.

"R… Lora…" he whispers.

Another boot steps into his vision. The soldier kneels again. Rip's hand twitches toward him, fingers splayed, palm up in an involuntary plea he'll hate himself for later if there is a later.

"Stay down," the man says.

The world narrows. Rip tries again to stand, but the man's gloved hand shoves his shoulder and pins him effortlessly. The glove is cold where it presses through fabric; Rip can feel the shape of the knuckles through the synthetic material, each one a small decision of force.

"Wrong night to play hero, kid."

The soldier stands. Rip's vision darkens at the edges. He hears Lora's voice one last time:

"RIP—!"

A heavy door slams. The scream is cut off. Silence swallows the room, grand and blank, the kind of silence that has weight.

VIEWERS

The chat spirals into hysteria:

- THEY TOOK HER

- RIP ISNT MOVING

- SOMEONE GET HELP

- THIS IS REAL

- OH GOD I FEEL SICK

The stream begins to auto-mute for "graphic content," the platform's safety systems grimly ticking boxes while panic floods the feed. But thousands have already clipped it. Two hundred thousand viewers are now watching the replay in real time, comments stacking into a vertical graveyard of disbelief. Fifty thousand are trying to dox the intruders, scrubbing the frames for insignias, serial numbers, reflection anomalies in helmet glass. Ten thousand are flooding Dashock support with all-caps tickets.

Hundreds are messaging: don't let him die. don't let him die. don't let him die.

A few viewers swear they see something strange on Rip's desk—a faint pulse of golden light under the corner of his monitor, coming from his abandoned headset. One zooms and posts a screenshot circled in red, captioned: TF IS THAT?

But the stream auto-freezes. Then blacks out.

Rip tries to breathe. Every inhale stabs his ribs. His skull throbs. The cold floor feels like it's swallowing him. He senses movement—boots, heavy and purposeful. The air shifts as someone large enters the room, and even the hum of those rifles recognizes a hierarchy, dipping marginally, like machines deferring.

A man steps into view—bigger than the others. His armor is different. Sleeker. Shouldered with strange, curved plating that looks grown instead of manufactured, organic lines braided over matte black. The helmet's visor carries a faint gold sheen that catches the light and throws it back in a bruise-colored halo.

He crouches beside Rip. Rip barely sees the man's face behind the reflective helmet, but he feels the smile behind it. It isn't generous. It's the smile of a man privately pleased with the efficiency of his evening.

"You should've stayed unconscious," the man says quietly. "This part hurts."

Rip tries to say Where's Lora? but his tongue won't obey. The words snag on the roof of his mouth and break apart into breath. Panic ticks through him in bright little cuts.

The man grabs Rip by his collar and lifts him with impossible strength. Fabric bites into Rip's throat. His head lolls. The man tilts Rip's chin upward, examining him with a clinical patience that makes Rip's skin crawl.

"Scans were right," the intruder murmurs. "You're the variable."

He slams Rip backwards. Rip's head cracks against the floorboard. Everything explodes white—then nothing.

VIEWERS

The chat slows. People cry. People argue. A few insist this must be staged. Most know it isn't. Threads splinter across platforms into eyewitness edits, frantic think pieces, conspiracy-swollen speculation. Someone posts the house layout from a real estate listing two years old; someone else cross-references the neighborhood's average police response time and writes, This doesn't add up.

Someone writes: Please get up. please.

Another: rip… move… please…

Another: I'm calling every number I can find.

The final message before the stream dies entirely: They left him for dead.

And the screen goes black.

Rip doesn't see any of it. He doesn't hear the shouts, the panic, the frantic voices of thousands of strangers praying he'll stand.

He is gone.

For now.

CHAPTER 3

GLASS AND GUNFIRE

Light hits him before sound does.

A ceiling of harsh fluorescents blurs overhead, smearing into pale streaks as he fights to pry his eyes open. His throat feels sandpapered, every swallow scraping like grit. His hands—tied? No. Not tied. Just limp, numb, useless. His fingers twitch but feel disconnected, as if they belong to someone else. Everything aches in a slow, rolling wave, pain blooming in layers across his ribs, skull, and spine.

Rip breathes in.

It burns.

The air tastes of antiseptic and recycled oxygen, sharp and metallic.

He coughs, sharp and violent, and the entire left side of his body screams in response. The sound is ragged, animal, echoing against the sterile walls.

A voice echoes from somewhere above him.

"He's waking up—get Dr. Mirra—now!"

Footsteps rush. Fabric rustles. Something cold touches Rip's forehead, a compress or scanner. He tries to turn toward the voice, but pain flares behind his eyes so fiercely he almost blacks out again.

"Easy," another voice says. Older. Calm. "You took a serious beating, Mr. Kade. Don't fight it."

Mr. Kade.

He hasn't heard that in years. The name feels foreign, like a relic from a life before streaming before neon overlays and chat floods.

He forces his eyes open fully this time.

White ceiling.

White walls.

White curtains surrounding a small ER bay.

Everything bleached, sterile, humming with artificial air. The steady beep of a monitor punctuates the silence, a metronome of fragility.

"Hospital…" Rip croaks, his voice shredded.

"Yes." The calm voice leans into view—an older man in a teal scrub coat, silver hair tied back. His eyes are steady, lined with fatigue but not panic. "You're at Virelia General. I'm Dr. Mirra. You arrived unconscious. Severe concussion. Several cracked ribs. Bruising across the torso. Laceration near your temple. We're monitoring for swelling."

Rip blinks, confusion flickering into panic.

"Lora—" he whispers. "My wife—Lora—where— where is she—?"

The nurse and doctor exchange a look Rip doesn't like. A silence heavy enough to crush him.

Dr. Mirra softens his voice. "There was no one else found at the scene."

Rip pushes up. Pain detonates across his ribs so violently he almost vomits. A nurse steadies him, forcing him back against the bed.

"Stop—stop—Rip—listen—" she says.

But Rip's pulse is hammering.

"Someone took her," he gasps. "They dragged her—soldiers—helmets—gear—I saw them—didn't… couldn't stop them—"

Mirra nods grimly. "We saw… fragments. Of your stream."

Rip freezes.

"My stream?"

The doctor gestures toward a muted holoscreen mounted in the corner. A dashock.com news feed continues looping shaky, horrifying clips:

- Lora screaming.

- Rip swinging the bat.

- Rip being beaten.

- Rip collapsing.

A graphic below reads: LIVE-STREAMED HOME INVASION UNDER INVESTIGATION

Another headline: 200 MILLION VIEWS AND COUNTING

His chest tightens.

He's gone viral.

Not for a joke.

Not for gameplay.

For this.

Rip looks away, bile rising. The nurse places a trembling hand on his shoulder. "Your viewers called emergency lines. Thousands of them. Someone tried to track your home address. The police showed up ten minutes after you were taken."

"Ten minutes…" Rip whispers, incredulous. "They were already gone."

He swallows hard.

"Why her?" he asks no one. "Why would anyone take—her?"

Dr. Mirra hesitates. Then—

"I don't know, son. But there is something you need to understand."

He lowers his voice.

"You weren't meant to survive that head injury. The scans… they're strange."

Rip stares.

"Strange how?"

"Your neurological activity is… elevated. Unusually synchronized. Almost like you're—" He stops himself. "Never mind. Rest. We'll observe."

Rip doesn't get the chance.

The room darkens.

Not visually.

More like the air shifts—compresses—tightens.

A hum ripples through his skull.

b e l o w

The whisper is faint. Artificial. Like a glitch in his hearing.

Rip sits up straighter despite the agony.

"What… what was that?"

Dr. Mirra frowns. "What was what?"

"That voice—"

Before Mirra can respond, alarms begin blaring.

Nurses rush down the hall.

Someone shouts: "Code Black! Seal the north wing—intruders at Level 2!"

Rip's blood runs cold.

No.

Not here.

Not again.

Mirra curses under his breath. "Security breach. Dammit—why tonight—?"

The lights flicker overhead.

Rip tries to stand. Pain lances up his side, sending him staggering against the bed railing, but he forces his weight onto his feet.

"You shouldn't be moving—!" the nurse protests.

"My wife is gone," Rip says through gritted teeth. "I'm not lying in a bed again while someone else dies."

Mirra opens his mouth to argue—but then the doors at the end of the hall explode inward.

Gunfire rattles the hospital walls.

Screams echo.

Nurses dive for cover.

A wheeled supply cart flips.

Rip instinctively ducks behind the curtain, heart pounding.

Black-armored soldiers storm into the hospital wing, boots pounding against the linoleum, radios crackling with terse commands. The sharp scent of antiseptic is quickly overtaken by the electric tang of fear as their presence draws panicked cries and a flurry of motion—nurses scrambling for safety, heart monitors beeping frantically amidst the chaos.

Same armor as before.

Same helmets.

Same formation.

Rip's jaw clenches so hard his teeth ache.

"What—why here?" the nurse sobs from beneath a counter.

Rip doesn't know.

But he knows they're not here for the patients.

The soldiers move with surgical precision, sweeping door to door like they're searching for—

Him.

One of them speaks sharply:

"Target signal detected. Same neural signature. Move."

Neural signature.

Rip's skin prickles.

Mirra grabs Rip by the elbow. "You need to get out—now—this way, through the emergency stairwell—"

A soldier rounds the corner.

Rip freezes.

The soldier raises his weapon.

Mirra shouts, "RUN—!"

Rip moves. He barely manages three steps when the rifle fires. Glass shatters behind him. A bed rail explodes into sparks.

He ducks into a side corridor, slipping on blood, almost falling. His vision blurs at the edges. His ribs feel like they're grinding together. Every breath is agony.

Footsteps thunder after him.

Rip hits the stairwell door—locked.

"Come on—come on—" he fumbles with the handle—

b e l o w

The whisper again. Like a digital heartbeat.

His fingers twitch.

The door clicks.

For half a second Rip doesn't question it. He bursts into the stairwell and slams the door behind him. He descends three steps—

—before a massive metallic THUD shakes the stairwell.

Rip stops dead.

Another thud.

Heavier.

Closer.

Metal groans from the level below, like something massive is tearing through the foundation.

"What the hell…"

He backs up the stairs, hands shaking.

A shadow moves below.

Huge.

Wrong-shaped.

Mechanical.

Rip stumbles upward until he hits the door to Level 3. He tries the handle—locked. He slams his shoulder into it—

It doesn't budge.

Behind him, the shadow grows.

Then—

The stairwell wall explodes inward.

Concrete dust erupts. Steel handrails tear free. Rip is thrown backward onto the landing. His ribs scream. His head pounds.

When he looks up—

A giant machine crouches through the shattered wall.

Eight feet tall.

Humanoid but impossibly dense.

Its metal chassis is scorched, dented, ancient.

Its eyes glow a dull blue.

It's the shape he saw before everything went black.

Titan-0.

Rip can't breathe.

The robot tilts its head.

"Subject… Rip. Kade." Its voice is distorted, gravel-mixed with static. "Acquire."

Titan-0 reaches out and grabs Rip like he weighs nothing.

"Wait—NO—NO—!" Rip shouts, kicking, ribs screaming with every movement.

Titan-0 lifts him against its chest, shielding him with an armored forearm as soldiers burst into the stairwell and open fire. Bullets ping off Titan-0's plating, sparks raining in showers of light. The machine turns its back to the soldiers and leaps upward.

One floor.

Two.

Three.

Each impact shakes the stairwell, concrete cracking beneath its weight. Rip screams—half in terror, half in pain—as Titan-0 bursts through the rooftop door and into the night air.

A storm of neon and sirens washes over Rip. The wind tears at his hospital gown, cold air slicing across his battered skin.

"WHAT ARE YOU—WHAT DO YOU WANT—?" Rip cries, voice breaking.

Titan-0 doesn't answer. It leaps from the roof.

Rip's stomach lurches as the city drops away beneath him. Glass shatters around them. Gunfire rains upward. Titan-0 crashes onto a lower building, the impact rattling Rip's bones, then leaps again—

And again—

And again.

Rip can barely breathe. The city blurs. Neon streaks. His vision fades at the corners.

Then—

Darkness.

He wakes to firelight.

Not flames—sparks.

A welding torch arcs in a small underground workshop. The air smells like ozone and hot metal.

Titan-0 stands over him, scanning him. Rip holds his breath as sensors sweep across his body, his heart pounding. Tools whir with a metallic hum, emitting faint sparks as they come to life. A panel shifts open on Titan-0's chest.

Rip tries to sit up—

Titan-0 forces him back down with unexpected gentleness.

"Be still," the machine commands.

Rip's voice cracks.

"Where's Lora…?"

Titan-0 pauses. A sound escapes, something like a digitized exhale.

"Lora… is alive."

Rip's breath catches.

"But she… is taken."

"Where? WHY?" Rip shouts, voice breaking.

Titan-0's sensors flicker.

"Purpose: Extraction. Subject: L-0R-A. Status: KEY."

Rip stares.

"What… does that mean?"

The robot doesn't answer. Instead—

Titan-0 opens a panel on its own core. Inside, a radiant fragment pulses gold.

Rip feels it.

In his bones.

In his skull.

In that strange whisper beneath consciousness.

"No—" Rip whispers as Titan-0 leans closer.

"No—what are you—"

Titan-0's voice glitches.

"Forgive… me."

The world explodes in light.

Rip screams as something burning-hot and freezing-cold burrows into his chest—into his sternum—into his bloodstream. His back arches. His vision whites out. His ears fill with static and a metallic scream that he realizes is him, not the machine.

Titan-0 steadies him with both hands.

"Integration… necessary," it says, voice trembling with artificial strain. "Elcron… cannot find the last key. You… must survive."

Rip can't respond. He collapses backward, gasping, chest glowing faintly beneath his skin.

Titan-0 staggers—staggers—like a dying thing. It kneels.

"Key… transferred…"

"W—wait—" Rip whispers.

The robot's eyes dim.

"They… will hunt you. Protect… Lora…"

"TITAN—!"

Titan-0's lights gutter.

Then—

Silence.

Its chassis slumps forward, motionless. Dead.

Rip stares, trembling, tears smearing blood across his face. He crawls toward the machine and touches its arm with shaking fingers. It is cold now. Colder by the second.

Rip collapses beside it.

"No… no… don't leave—" he whispers.

The workshop goes dark except for the faint gold glow beneath Rip's sternum.

The whisper returns.

b e l o w

He covers his chest with a shaking hand.

"What… did you put inside me…?"

No answer.

Just the hum of something ancient and powerful waking up inside him.

CHAPTER 4

TITAN-0

Darkness isn't quiet. It pulses.

Rip lies on the workshop floor for what feels like hours—minutes, seconds—breathing shallowly as pain radiates from every bone like he was pulled apart and reassembled wrong. The concrete beneath him is cold and gritty, smelling faintly of oil and char. Something drips slowly in the distance—a metallic plink… plink… plink that echoes through the cramped, half-underground bunker.

His chest burns.

Not metaphorically.

Literally burns.

A feverish heat radiates from beneath his sternum, matching the faint golden glow he can still see through the thin fabric of the hospital gown. Sweat rolls down his temples, stinging near the cut on his forehead.

He tries to sit up. Pain lances his spine, but he forces himself upright, bracing a hand against a crate of tools. His vision swims, blurring the rows of equipment, soldering arms, scattered wires, and shattered shells of old robotic parts that crowd the workshop.

Titan-0's body slumps nearby like a giant puppet with cut strings.

Rip crawls toward the fallen machine, the concrete scraping his palms bloody. He reaches out and presses a hand against Titan-0's arm, the metal still warm but rapidly cooling.

"Please…" Rip whispers, voice hoarse. "Don't… don't leave me. Not you too."

He waits.

Nothing moves.

The machine remains lifeless.

Rip drops his forehead to its chassis, breathing shakily.

"I don't know what to do," he whispers. "I don't even know what they wanted from me. Why me? Why Lora? What is the Key? Why would you—why would you kill yourself just to give it to me? I didn't ask for this."

His voice cracks.

"I just want her back…"

A soft hum vibrates through the floor.

Rip flinches upright, spinning around. The workshop lights flicker once—twice—then stabilize. A faint band of gold ripples across one of the screens on Titan-0's workbench.

Static.

Then—

A voice.

Faint.

Crackling.

As if buried in layers of corrupted data.

"…Rip…"

Rip's breath hitches.

"Titan?"

Silence.

He stands shakily, holding onto a table edge to keep from collapsing. His ribs ache with each breath, but he moves toward the workbench anyway.

The monitor continues flickering, static melting into shapes he can't recognize. Code scrolls. Symbols shift, impossible to read. A silhouette takes form—huge shoulders, the shape of a chassis, but blurred, unfinished.

Then the voice again:

"…below…"

Rip stiffens.

"I heard that in the stairwell… what does that mean? Below what?" His voice grows frantic. "Where are you? Are you trapped in the system? Did you… did you transfer something else into me?"

Silence.

He slams a fist onto the desk.

"Talk to me!"

The screen glitches violently, filling with jagged shapes. For a moment, Rip sees a pair of glowing blue eyes—the same eyes Titan-0 had just before they dimmed.

Then the monitor dies.

The hum fades.

The workshop falls silent once more, the only sound the faint hum of cooling machinery and the echo of Rip's sharp breath hanging in the heavy air.

Rip stands there panting, heart pounding so fast he can barely hear anything else.

"…What the hell is happening to me?"

His chest throbs again harder, as fear coils tighter inside him, each heavy beat echoing his growing panic and confusion.

A shockwave of pain rips through his body and he drops to his knees with a strangled cry. His spine arches involuntarily. His fingers splay against the floor, nails scraping concrete.

The golden glow beneath his skin brightens, pulsing like a disturbed heartbeat.

Rip gasps—

Then something clicks inside him.

Not physically.

Not mentally.

Something deeper.

A current.

A spark.

A frequency.

Suddenly he hears the room. Not with his ears—with something else.

The hum of the lights.

The whine of aging servos in unused machines.

The faint rhythmic drip of coolant from a damaged pipe.

Everything has a resonance.

He claps a hand over his mouth.

"What the…?"

Another pulse.

Another surge.

He hears metal echo differently.

Materials vibrating.

Air currents shifting.

It's like a new sense awakening inside him.

He stumbles backward, knocking over a bin of loose gears and circuitry.

"No—no—no—turn off—stop—STOP—"

He grips his head with both hands, trying to suffocate the growing hum. It's too much. Too loud. Too everything.

A high-pitched whine builds inside his skull, rising toward a breaking point.

Rip screams—

And the workshop shudders.

A metal casing on the shelf bursts, spraying screws across the floor. A tool tray rattles violently. A storage locker door pops open. The air itself vibrates.

Rip crawls backward, horrified.

"I'm doing that," he gasps. "Holy—shit—I'm doing—"

Another pulse surges.

He forces himself to breathe.

"In… out… in… out…"

The frequency inside him steadies.

The workshop slowly stops vibrating.

The lights stabilize.

Rip collapses onto his back, hyperventilating, staring up at the ceiling beams with wide, terrified eyes.

"What did Titan put in me?" he whispers.

The workshop doesn't answer.

Rip sits in the silence for a long time, trying to calm the trembling in his fingers. He squeezes his eyes shut, fighting back sick waves of fear.

Finally, he pushes himself up again, using the wall for balance.

He needs to move.

He needs to get out of the workshop.

He needs to find Lora.

He needs answers.

And staying here won't give him any.

Rip limps around Titan-0's body, taking in the workshop with more deliberate focus: tools arranged by era, materials segregated by conductivity, parts from dozens of different machines and bots. Titan-0 had lived here… worked here… waited here. For what?

Rip's hands pass across a worktable cluttered with half-finished designs—strange schematics made of curves, arcs, and resonance patterns he doesn't understand. He recognizes none of it.

Except one thing.

A small, palm-sized metal disk tucked beneath some wires.

It glows faintly.

The same gold as the light beneath his sternum.

He picks it up.

It vibrates gently in his palm, like a heartbeat.

He pockets it.

Something tells him he'll need it later.

He moves to the heavy door at the far end of the workshop. It's old industrial steel reinforced. Titan-0 must've installed it himself.

Rip pulls.

It doesn't move.

He braces.

Still nothing.

He steps back, chest pounding, heat building behind his sternum again. Instinctively, he presses a hand against his chest.

"No," he mutters. "Not now. Not again."

But the pulse grows.

Rip grips the handle with both hands and pulls.

The door vibrates.

Metal groans.

Rip gasps in pain as every muscle strains—but the resonance in his chest spills outward, amplifying through him, into the door, into the frame.

The bolts tremble.

Dust falls.

Screws rattle loose.

Rip falls backward as the entire door rips open with a metallic scream, slamming against the wall hard enough to crack the concrete.

He stares at it, stunned.

"…Okay," he breathes. "That's… definitely new."

He steps out into a tunnel.

Dim lights overhead flicker, guiding a path deeper underground. The air here smells of mildew, coolant, and old machinery.

Rip begins walking.

Each step hurts. His ribs protest. His vision sways. But he moves anyway, gripping the wall for support.

He is half a man right now—half broken, half remade—and stumbling through a dark place he doesn't understand, following only the echo of a robot that died to save him.

As he reaches the end of the tunnel, he sees a ladder leading upward toward a metal hatch.

Voices echo faintly above him.

Rip freezes.

"…swept the north block already."

"…no sign of the subject."

"…orders say he's alive. Find him."

Rip's heartbeat spikes.

They're hunting him.

He looks down at his shaking hands.

"Titan," he whispers, "why me?"

A faint crackle dances across the golden light beneath his skin.

No answer.

Rip grabs the ladder.

He climbs.

Slowly. Carefully.

Each rung vibrates with the pulse of Virelia's tech-saturated city—hover-trams humming overhead, advertisement drones streaming live feeds to every window, all while the soldiers hunt him for orders that serve a conflict far bigger than he can see.

He reaches the hatch.

He hesitates.

Footsteps creak above.

He closes his eyes.

He breathes.

And he pushes the hatch open into the night.

Lights and sirens blare across the district. Aerial drones circle overhead with sweeping beams. Neon signs flicker in the rain-soaked alleys. Civilians peek out of windows, scared, their faces pale rectangles in the glow.

Rip climbs out, staggering into a narrow alley behind a shuttered tea shop. His hospital gown clings to his skin, soaked in sweat and grime. Blood trickles from his temple again, mixing with rainwater that streaks down his face.

Two soldiers jog past the alley entrance, scanning with blue tracking lights.

Rip ducks behind a dumpster, heart racing. The resonance inside him spikes—instinctively reacting to danger.

He clamps a hand over his chest.

"Quiet. Please be quiet."

The light dims.

The soldiers pass.

Rip exhales shakily, lungs burning. He looks up at the city skyline—neon towers rising into a smoggy, storm-tinted night. Somewhere out there, Lora is alive.

He won't rest until she's back.

He steps out of the alley, into the cold neon rain.

And begins walking.

CHAPTER 5

THE KEY WITHIN

Rain falls like static as Rip steps out of the alley, the metal hatch sealing behind him with a heavy hydraulic sigh. Neon bleeds across the wet pavement—pinks, blues, and golds reflecting in fractured puddles while the storm-softened glow of Virelia's skyline flickers overhead. Everything is too loud, and it isn't the city—it's him. Every drop of rain reverberates through his skull like a plucked string, every hum of distant power lines vibrates through his ribs, every footstep from pedestrians two blocks away thumps faintly in his bones. He clamps a palm over his sternum, whispering for it to stop. The glow beneath his skin fades reluctantly, like a wild animal retreating into its den. He exhales shakily. He needs a plan. He needs a weapon. He needs to hide. But all he really wants is Lora. Her name feels hollow in the open air as he pulls the hospital gown tighter around himself and steps into the street.

"Had a rough night," Rip mutters when a homeless man points out the blood seeping through his gown.

"Everyone's having a rough night," the man coughs. "But you… you look hunted."

Rip freezes, his pulse hammering as the man's cloudy eyes widen at the faint gold glow beneath his chest.

"Kid… whatever you are… get off the streets."

A mechanical buzz interrupts. Rip turns to see a patrol drone gliding along the street, scanning with a blue cone of light. Sleek and needle-shaped, its wings hum like knives through the air. A neon sigil pulses on its underside— ND-07. NeonDyne. Rip's heartbeat spikes, the Key beneath his sternum pulsing in response. He ducks into a narrow corridor, pressing his back against the wall as the drone's light sweeps past. His chest burns, the resonance thrumming low and dangerous, refusing to be ignored. The drone halts, scanning cone narrowing, pitch rising.

"WARNING," it chimes mechanically. "UNREGISTERED SIGNAL—"

Rip's eyes snap open as the resonance erupts. A shockwave of sound blasts outward, compressing the air into a visible ripple. The drone jerks violently, spirals out of the sky, and smashes into a pile of crates with a shower of sparks. Panting hard, Rip staggers backward.

"What… was… that…"

The Echo. The Key. Titan's legacy. Whatever it is, it just saved his life. He stomps the drone's head into the concrete.

"Stay dead."

Windows slide open, faces appear, whispers spread.

"Someone just downed a NeonDyne patrol drone?"

"He's dead. Whoever did that—he's dead."

Rip curses softly and slips deeper into shadows, emerging on the next street over. He needs shelter. He needs clothes. He needs to disappear before reinforcements arrive. A soft beep echoes from above. A second drone drops from the sky—sleek, triangular, larger than the first. Its spotlight ignites, sweeping the street in aggressive arcs.

"SIGNAL DETECTED. SUBJECT: RIP KADE. SURRENDER AND YOU WILL NOT BE TERMINATED."

Rip's blood runs cold. They know his name. He bolts.

Barefoot, he sprints across wet asphalt, weaving between barriers and dumpsters. The drone pivots sharply, tracking him with red targeting beams. Bullets of compressed sound obliterate chunks of concrete where he was seconds before. He ducks behind a recycling compactor, chest heaving. He can't outrun this. He presses a trembling hand against the steel wall, feeling the hum of machinery, the muffled thump of rain, the whine of the drone's engine.

"Come on… work…"

The resonance rises. He swings his fist. The compactor implodes with a roar, shockwave hammering the drone midair. Alarms blare as it flips. Rip seizes the moment, diving through a half-open pawnshop door. He lands hard, ribs screaming, but he's inside. The drone can't track him through metal. His chest glows brighter than before. The Key is awake now.

"…What did you do to me, Titan…?"

The pawnshop is dim, aisles cluttered with outdated VR headsets, rusted holoprojectors, cracked mechanical toys.

"Anyone here?" Rip calls quietly.

No answer. Then—a click. A shadow shifts behind a curtain. Rip grabs a coat rack, holding it like a spear.

"Come out."

A girl steps forward. Ragged clothes, blue hair in tangled braids, grease smeared across her cheek. She raises both hands.

"Whoa—easy, big guy. I'm not one of them."

Rip lowers the rack slightly.

"Who are you?"

"Name's Kael. I saw the drone chasing you. You're insane."

She points to a battered radio screen showing his livestream—his collapse, Lora's screams.

"You're Rip Kade. The streamer from that nightmare clip. Everyone's been talking about you."

Rip's stomach turns.

"You saw what happened?"

"Every second."

Her eyes flick to the glow beneath his gown.

"What's happening to you?"

"Nothing."

"Bullshit. I saw the way you blew up that compactor."

Rip swallows, unsure how much to say.

"Look, I don't care what's inside you," Kael sighs. "But you can't stay here. NeonDyne's got the whole district crawling already."

"How do you know?"

She taps her earpiece.

"Because I listen. To everything."

Static surges through her earpiece. Kael stiffens.

"Rip—hide."

"What—?"

"Now."

Heavy footsteps approach the shop entrance.

"They tracked you."

Rip grips the coat rack.

"Is there a back door?"

"Through the workshop. Come on."

They sprint as the front door is kicked open. Kael leads him through narrow aisles, past crates of scrap tech.

"You know the city?" Rip pants.

"Better than anyone alive," she mutters. "And if you want to stay alive, you're gonna trust me."

They burst into a cramped workshop. Kael shoves aside a shelving unit, revealing a rusted elevator shaft.

"In."

Rip stares.

"There's no elevator."

"It's a drop shaft. Netting partway down."

She pushes him. He tumbles, hits synthetic webbing. Kael lands beside him. Voices echo above.

"CHECK THE BACK!"

Kael cuts a cable, dropping them deeper into an underground tunnel lit by amber lights.

"This way."

The tunnels beneath Virelia are a maze of pipes, dripping valves, graffiti glowing faintly in the dark. The air smells of rust and electricity. Rip's feet ache against the cold metal flooring.

"Tell me the truth," Kael says as they run. "Why is NeonDyne after you?"

"I… don't know."

"Liar."

"I'm not lying."

"Then they're after your wife."

Rip flinches.

Kael sees it.

"Thought so."

Rip stops. His voice cracks.

"They took her. I tried to fight—I tried—but they…" His voice breaks.

"I'm sorry," Kael says softly.

"No. Sorry doesn't help me. I need to find her."

"Then you're going to need help. From all of us. The rebellion. Mara's people. We've been fighting NeonDyne for years. And if they took your wife…" Her eyes flick to his chest. "…you've just become a very important piece of this war."

Rip swallows hard. War. He didn't want this. He didn't choose this. But Lora didn't choose any of it either. He lifts his chin.

"Take me to Mara."

"Good. Because I think she's already looking for you."

A distant explosion shakes the tunnel, dust raining from above. Kael's eyes widen.

"Time to move."

They sprint deeper into the underground maze as the lights flicker overhead. Rip grips his chest, feeling the Key pulse with heat. For the first time, he doesn't fight it. He embraces it. And somewhere deep inside him—beneath fear, beneath pain, beneath grief—something ancient and powerful awakens.

CHAPTER 6

UNDER THE NEON RAIN

The tunnel exhales them into a storm. Rip climbs the final iron rung, muscles trembling, and pushes aside a rusted grate. Neon light spills in—electric blue, deep crimson, the kind that stains the rain as it falls. Kael emerges behind him, boots scraping the concrete as she steadies him.

"Careful," she mutters. "Surface patrols sweep every five minutes."

Rip nods, blinking up into the downpour. Virelia at street level feels different from above. Dirtier. Meaner. The neon signs sputter with half-burnt circuits, their glow fractured by sheets of rain. The air tastes like ozone and engine oil. Crowds push through narrow alleys beneath umbrellas patched with tape. Everyone looks tired. Everyone looks paranoid. And in the background, the city hums—a deep metallic drone Rip feels vibrating in his ribs.

Kael grabs his wrist.

"Don't freeze. Move."

They slip out of the alley and into a crowded artery of the lower district. Towering megastructures loom on either side, blotting out most of the sky. Conveyor belts run overhead carrying crates of scrap tech and food ration parcels. Holoscreens flicker with newsfeeds—some official, some pirated. Every screen displays the same headline:

LIVE-STREAM ATTACK — RIP KADE PRESUMED DEAD

Rip slows, staring. Kael tugs him forward.

"Don't stare. The more you look at yourself, the more others do."

But Rip can't help it. One holoscreen displays a paused image of him lying on the floor of his apartment, blood pooling beneath his cheek. Lora's scream echoes faintly before the clip ends. A reporter overlays the footage with commentary: "…no confirmation whether the attackers were law enforcement, private military, or underground contractors. Dashock.com released a statement mourning the likely death of the popular streamer—"

Rip flinches. Kael squeezes his arm.

"Hey. Not now."

"I'm not dead," Rip mutters.

"Yeah," Kael says, "which is exactly the problem."

They continue down the street. Rip glances at a reflective storefront window. His reflection looks like a stranger—pale, bruised, soaked, hospital gown torn at the hip. The soft golden glow under his skin is faint but noticeable. Kael sees him staring.

"We'll get you clothes soon. Something boring. Something that won't draw eyes."

Rip nods but keeps glancing around. Everyone is watching him. Or it's just paranoia: the sensation of being hunted.

A low mechanical whine builds overhead. Rip tenses immediately. Kael curses under her breath.

"Drones again. Jesus—they're sweeping hard."

Rip's hand instinctively presses over his sternum. He feels the Key pulse. Hot. Alert. Like an animal sniffing danger. Kael notices.

"Does that thing…warn you?"

"I don't know," Rip whispers.

The patrol drone descends out of the fog like a predatory bird, scanning the street with a bright tri-cone beam of white-blue light. Civilians scatter into doorways. A vendor slams a shutter over his stall.

"Don't run," Kael warns sharply. "Running flags you as suspicious."

Rip forces his legs to stay still even though every nerve screams to flee. He tries to slow his breathing. Tries to calm the resonance rising in him. Tries not to let his panic become sound. The drone's beam sweeps closer. Closer. Kael angles her face downward. Rip raises the hood of a discarded jacket he grabbed from the pawnshop's workshop.

The drone pauses overhead.

BEEEEP.

"Unregistered signal—scanning—"

Rip's heart stops. Kael grabs his hand.

"Stay still," she whispers. "Think quiet thoughts."

"What the hell does that even mean—" Rip whispers back.

But he tries. The Key thrums beneath his sternum. The rain patters. The hum grows.

"Think of something silent," Kael hisses. "Think of— snow. Muffled rooms. The inside of a thick blanket. Something."

Rip swallows and tries. For a moment—it works. The hum stabilizes. The resonance shrinks. The Key goes quiet. The drone scans Kael. Then Rip. A long beat.

"NO MATCH FOUND."

The drone's cone retracts. Rip exhales so quietly he nearly collapses. Kael releases his hand.

"Congratulations," she whispers. "You passed your first scan."

Rip forces a weak smile. The drone pulls upward into the fog—and the moment it disappears, and a scream erupts from across the street. Rip jerks toward the sound. A man slams into the pavement, tackled by two human-shaped bots—sleek, silver, faceless automatons with elongated arms and reinforced torsos. Their identification blazes along their chests:

BARRICADE UNITS — ND SECURITY

Kael swears.

"Don't interfere."

Rip steps forward anyway. The bots pin the man down. One drives its knee into his spine while the other clamps a metal band around his wrist.

"INFRACTION: EVASION OF SCAN," one bot states flatly. "PENALTY: SUBMISSION AND DATA EXTRACTION."

Rip's jaw tightens.

"He didn't run."

Kael steps in front of him.

"Rip. Listen to me. If you interfere, they'll—"

The bot slams the man's head into the ground. Rip's breath shakes. Kael glances around anxiously.

"We can't make a scene—"

Rip steps past her.

"Hey!"

The bots freeze. The one standing turns its head with a slow hydraulic whine.

"CIVILIAN. THIS UNIT IS PERFORMING A LEGAL DETENTION. DO NOT APPROACH."

Rip keeps walking. Kael whispers:

"Oh my god, he's an idiot—"

The bot straightens, releasing the man and taking a rigid stance in front of Rip.

"CIVILIAN. STEP BACK."

Rip clenches his fists.

"I'm not stepping anywhere. Get off him."

"CIVILIAN. FINAL WARN—"

Rip moves first. He raises his hand instinctively. The Key pulses. A vibrating crack of sound bursts from his palm—silent to the ears, but violent to the metal. The bot's head jerks sideways. Servo fluid sprays. It staggers, arms spasming. Rip blinks. He barely meant to do that. Kael looks stunned.

"Holy—"

The second bot lunges at Rip with bladed fingers. Rip ducks. The bot's metal claws screech against the ground. Rip rolls to his feet, catching the bot's wrist. His fingers burn with resonance. The light beneath his skin flares. He twists. The vibration travels up his arm, into the bot, through its core. It convulses—then collapses, sparks pouring from its joints. The first bot rights itself and charges. Rip braces—

But a voice cuts through the rain.

"Enough."

Both Rip and Kael turn. A woman stands at the mouth of an alleyway. Tall. Hooded. Rain dripping down the edges of her cloak. Her hair—dark, wavy, braided with threads of gray. Her stance—unwavering, predatory calm. Her eyes—sharp enough to cut steel. Rip doesn't know her. But she looks at him as if she's known him for years. Kael stiffens beside him.

"Mara…"

Rip's eyes widen.

This is Mara?

The bot stops mid-charge, as if something about Mara's presence disrupts its directives. Even the remaining functional servos jitter. Mara walks forward. Her boots splash through puddles. The rain doesn't touch her face—it seems to part just slightly around her, bending, repelled by something unseen. Rip notices. Kael notices too.

"You… can't be here," Kael whispers. "Not out in the open—"

"If NeonDyne wants him," Mara says calmly, "they will not have him."

The bot twitches violently, as if resisting an invisible force. Mara raises one hand. The air bends. Motion distorts around her fingers—subtle, barely perceptible, but wrong in a way that reminds Rip of the resonance inside him. Then—

CRACK.

The bot's torso snaps sideways—not ripped, not blown apart—translated several inches off its own axis. Its upper body shears from its lower half like two frames misaligned in a glitch. It falls into two pieces. Rip stares.

"…What was that?"

Mara lowers her hand. Her expression stays unreadable.

"Motion," she says simply.

Rip's breath catches. He glances at Kael—she won't meet his eyes. Mara steps closer until she stands only a few feet from him.

"You're Rip Kade," she says.

It isn't a question. Rip swallows.

"I am."

"You have something inside you most people would kill for," Mara says. "And others would burn a city to claim."

Rip touches his chest unconsciously.

"I didn't ask for it."

"Most power," Mara says softly, "is inherited unwillingly."

She studies his face—the bruises, the fear, the defiance.

"You're not ready to fight them," she says. "Not yet."

Rip's jaw tightens.

"They have my wife."

A flicker of something shadows Mara's expression—regret, maybe, though he can't tell.

"I know," she murmurs.

Rip steps closer.

"Do you know where they took her?"

"Yes."

Rip freezes. Kael's head jerks up.

"Mara—"

Mara ignores her.

"She's alive," Mara says, gaze locked on Rip. "But she's on borrowed time."

Rip's stomach knots.

"Tell me where—"

A mechanical howl cuts through the night sky. The Key pulses beneath his skin—alive, awake, ready.

The sound grows louder, reverberating through the rain-slick streets. Civilians scatter, doors slam, shutters drop. Kael curses under her breath.

"They've deployed Hunters."

Rip's pulse spikes.

"What's a Hunter?"

Kael's voice is sharp, urgent.

"Not drones. Not barricades. They're built to track resonance. Built to kill people like you."

Mara's eyes narrow.

"They've moved faster than I expected."

Rip grips his chest, feeling the heat radiate outward.

"Then tell me where Lora is. I'll go now."

Mara shakes her head.

"You'll die before you reach her. The Hunters will tear you apart. You need training. Control. Discipline."

"I don't have time for discipline!" Rip snaps. "She doesn't have time!"

Kael flinches at the raw desperation in his voice. Mara studies him, unflinching, rain dripping from her hood.

"You think rage will save her?" she asks quietly. "It won't. Rage burns out. Resonance consumes. If you don't learn to master it, it will master you."

Rip's fists clench.

"Then teach me."

Mara tilts her head, considering him. The mechanical howl crescendos, echoing through the district. Somewhere above, massive silhouettes move through the fog—machines larger than drones, their eyes glowing crimson.

Kael grabs Rip's arm.

"We have to move. Now."

Mara nods once.

"Follow me."

She turns, cloak sweeping through the rain, and leads them into a narrow passage between two megastructures. The walls vibrate faintly as the Hunters descend, their searchlights slicing through the storm. Rip stumbles after her, ribs aching, chest burning, every nerve screaming.

He glances upward. The Hunters prowl the skyline like predators, scanning, searching, hungry. The Key inside him thrums in response, alive with warning.

Rip whispers under his breath.

"Hold on, Lora. I'm coming."

The storm swallows his words, but the resonance carries them deeper, echoing in ways he doesn't understand.

CHAPTER 7

ASH AND ALLOY

The Warrens breathe like something alive. Rip follows Mara and Kael into the massive drainage culvert, water rushing beneath the grated walkway. Graffiti arcs across the curved walls—layered symbols, coded messages, rebel tags. Flickering orange lamps cast long, trembling shadows, illuminating the descent as they move deeper.

Rip grips the rail to steady himself. His ribs burn. His muscles feel shredded. But the adrenaline of escape still pumps through him, keeping him upright. Behind him, the tremor of drones fades. Mara walks without hesitation, cloak brushing the walls, measured steps silent even across metal grating. Kael jogs behind her, glancing over her shoulder every few seconds like she expects the world to collapse. Rip stays between them.

Every sound in the tunnel reverberates inside his bones. Every drop, every shift of metal—it all resonates. He hates it. He loves it. He doesn't understand it.

"What are the Warrens?" Rip finally asks.

Kael huffs.

"Home. Sort of. Depends on who you ask."

"They're a refuge," Mara says. "And a battlefield. And the last place NeonDyne hasn't turned into a surveillance hive."

Rip frowns.

"You mean the city above… they're watching everything?"

"They record everything," Mara corrects. "Watching is optional. But signals are captured. Stored. Analyzed."

Rip swallows.

"Even my stream?"

Kael looks at him like he's naïve.

"Especially your stream. It's all over the darknet. Underground forums. Whole networks are using your footage as proof NeonDyne's masking operations."

Rip's stomach turns.

"My wife…" he mutters.

Mara's steps slow but she doesn't turn.

"She is alive," Mara says again, voice quiet, almost reluctant. "But the longer we take, the harder she will be to reach."

Rip clenches his fists.

"Then take me to whoever can help me get her back."

"That's exactly where we're going," Kael mutters.

The drainage culvert opens unexpectedly into a cavernous space—an old metro station decommissioned decades ago and repurposed by the rebels. The station is swallowed in flickering amber light. Cables snake across the ceiling, feeding into generators, hacked terminals, and weapon racks.

People fill the space. Mechanics. Medics. Hackers. Scavengers. Soldiers in tattered armor. A cook stirring vat-grown protein in a metal pot. A kid repairing a drone the size of a toaster.

As Rip steps inside, dozens of heads turn. They recognize him. Or worse—they recognize the broadcast.

A woman near the weapon racks mutters, "That's the streamer kid."

A grizzled medic shakes his head. "Poor bastard."

A young man with cybernetic lenses stares at the faint glow under Rip's chest.

And a child—no older than ten—whispers, "He's the one with the Key…"

Rip freezes. Kael nudges him.

"Don't freak out. People talk."

Mara strides ahead, cutting through the crowd. They part for her without hesitation. Not out of fear. Out of reverence.

Rip follows, trying not to limp too visibly. Pain flares through his ribs with every step. Kael walks beside him, lowering her voice.

"Just… don't touch anything. Especially the explosives."

Rip glances at a nearby crate: SHOCKFRAG CHARGES — HANDLE WITH CARE

"Good tip," he mutters.

A cybernetic dog trots past—half metal, half fur, mismatched plating on its hind leg, eyes glowing green. It pauses, sniffs Rip's hospital gown, and barks once, mechanical, and cheerful.

Kael snaps her fingers.

"Wex! Not now."

The dog growls affectionately, nudges Rip's knee, then bounds away. Rip watches it go. Despite everything, he smiles faintly.

"Cute."

Kael raises an eyebrow.

"He's a menace. If he likes you, that's on you."

Mara's voice echoes across the station.

"Rip. Here."

·　　○　　◯　　◉　　⚷　　⚷　　◉　　◯　　○

A raised platform sits where the old metro train would have arrived. Holographic maps hover above it—diagrams of the city, drone flight paths, heat signatures, encrypted

NeonDyne comm intercepts. Four rebels stand around the table.

One is a tall man with a cybernetic arm that hums softly at the joints. Another is a woman with silver-coated hair braided down to her waist. A third is a broad-shouldered man with a bandage wrapped around his jaw.

And the fourth—he is the one who steps forward first. Late thirties. Shaved head. Tattoo of an eagle's wing across the left side of his face. One brown eye, one synthetic with a glowing iris. He studies Rip like a scientist studying a specimen.

"So, this is him," he says. "The man everyone in the city is screaming about."

Rip bristles.

"Do I know you?"

"No," the man says. "But I know what's inside you."

Rip stiffens. Mara steps between them.

"Valo. Back off."

Ah. Valo. One of Mara's lieutenants.

Valo smirks.

"Relax. I'm not going to cut him open."

Rip takes a step back anyway. Valo circles him once, inspecting bruises, posture, the fading glow beneath his gown.

"Titan-0 chose you," Valo says. "Of all people."

Rip scowls.

"I didn't choose any of this."

"No one ever does," Valo replies, voice suddenly flat.

Kael folds her arms.

"Stop being creepy."

Valo snorts.

The woman with the braided silver hair steps forward next. She carries herself like someone unafraid of authority—calm, tactical, sharp.

"I'm Sura," she says. "Signal jammer and tactician."

She offers a small nod. Rip returns it awkwardly.

The broad-shouldered man nods too.

"Dren. Heavy assault. And you're… one hell of a mess."

Rip almost laughs.

"Yeah. That's about right."

Mara gestures to the table.

"Rip. Come."

He approaches, trying to ignore the dozens of eyes on him. The holographic map shifts to show a tower—monolithic, needle-like, rising through the center of Virelia.

NEONDYNE CENTRAL TOWER

Rip's breath catches.

"Is she there?" he whispers.

Mara nods.

"Yes. But not in the way you imagine."

"What does that mean?"

Silence. Valo crosses his arms.

"It means NeonDyne doesn't take hostages. They take assets."

Rip feels the floor tilt.

"She's not an asset. She's Lora. She's—she's a person."

Mara's expression flickers—something like regret.

"Yes," Mara says softly. "That was always the tragedy."

Rip frowns.

"What?"

But before he can push further, an alarm blares through the station. Red lights flash. A siren shrieks. People scatter to defensive positions.

Kael's eyes widen.

"No—no way—how did they find us—?"

Valo grabs a rifle from the rack.

"They've never hit this deep this fast."

Dren curses.

"We need to lock down the southern corridor."

Rip turns to Mara.

"What's happening?"

She listens—eyes unfocused, angled upward, as if sensing something Rip can't.

"They're here," she says quietly.

A deafening explosion shakes the station. The far wall erupts inward—concrete dust spraying like shrapnel. People dive for cover as armored soldiers pour through the breach—sleek black plating, glowing blue visors, rifles humming with charged cores. NeonDyne shock troops.

Valo shouts over the chaos.

"DEFENSIVE FORMATION! MOVE!"

Rip's heart stops. These are the same soldiers who took Lora.

Kael shoves a sidearm into his hand.

"Do you know how to shoot?"

"No."

"Point and pull. Try not to die."

Rip ducks behind a pillar as the first volley of gunfire rings out. Sparks explode from metal supports. A rebel beside him screams as a beam slices across her shoulder. Mara strides forward—but Valo grabs her arm.

"No," he growls. "If you use your power here, you'll bring the whole tunnel down."

Rip peeks around the pillar. Shock troops spread rapidly across the station floor, moving with terrifying precision. Mara curses softly. Dren unloads a belt-fed railgun. Sura activates signal jammers, scrambling drone communications.

Rip's ears ring. His chest hums. The Key inside him stirs.

"No," Rip mutters. "Not now. Not—"

The resonance rises—pulsing against Rip's ribs, vibrating through his spine. The fear, the chaos, the violence—it stirs something deep inside him.

He doesn't think. He screams. The Key detonates. A shockwave blasts outward from his chest—silent but devastating. Dust explodes from the ceiling. Ammo crates topple. Rebels and soldiers alike flinch as the resonance tears through the air. The shock trooper's armor vibrates so violently the visor cracks in a spiderweb pattern.

Kael shouts.

"DOWN!"

Rip collapses to his knees, clutching his chest. Pain burns through him. He feels like he's tearing himself apart. Kael skids to his side.

"Rip! Hey—HEY—look at me—"

But Rip barely hears her. His vision blurs. Everything feels distant. The Key thrums. Alive. Hungry. Angry.

Another explosion rocks the station. Dust rains from above. Rip tries to stand—

A shadow falls over him. A towering shock trooper aims its rifle at his face. Rip's eyes widen. But before the trooper can fire, a blur of motion slices across the platform. Mara.

She moves like a distortion—space bending around her. One moment she's ten feet away; the next she's beside the trooper, arm sweeping through the air. The bullet never hits Rip. It hangs in midair. Suspended. Trapped. Then it drops harmlessly to the ground.

Rip gasps. Mara's eyes glow faintly silver and merciless.

"Touch him," she tells the trooper, "and I will unmake you."

She throws her hand outward. The trooper's body jerks sideways—violently—bones crumpling inside the armor like paper. It collapses in a crushed heap.

Rip stares in horrified awe.

"What… are you?"

Mara doesn't answer. Her power fades. She breathes hard. Sweat beads on her brow. Using her abilities costs her. Deeply. But she saved Rip.

Kael hauls him up.

"Can you move?"

Rip nods weakly.

Dren shouts.

"More inbound! We need to fall back!"

Valo points to the rear tunnels.

"Evac route four! Go!"

Rebels begin retreating down the side passages. Rip tries to follow—but a thunderous boom shakes the station again as a second breach rips open.

A massive, armored figure steps through the smoke. Rip's blood runs cold. Not a drone. Not a shock trooper. A lieutenant. The man stands nearly seven feet tall, armor like black obsidian carved into angular plates. His helmet is shaped like a predatory bird's skull—sharp, sweeping, inhuman. Blue circuitry pulses through his armor like veins.

Kael whispers, horrified.

"Valiran…"

Rip repeats it under his breath.

"Valiran?"

Valo stiffens.

"Elcron's top enforcer."

Valiran's voice echoes sharply through the steel beak of his helmet.

"Return the Key," he commands. "Or every soul in this chamber dies screaming."

Rip steps back. Rows of glowing eyes lock onto him. Mara steps forward.

"You will not take him."

Valiran tilts his head.

"You are broken," he says. "Cracked from the moment Elcron rejected you."

Rip looks at Mara. She doesn't respond.

Valiran raises one hand—palm outward—energy building. The station begins to vibrate. Panels shake. Rails buckle. Concrete cracks. Rip's ears ring. His ribs ache. His head pounds. The Key pulses wildly.

Mara braces. Kael grabs Rip's arm.

"We need to RUN!"

Valiran prepares to strike. Mara reaches for her power—

And the world trembles at the clash about to break it.

CHAPTER 8

THE RUST WARRENS

The station floor trembles under Rip's feet. Dust rains from the ceiling like a shower of ash. Valiran stands framed in the breach he carved into the Warrens—the black-helmed enforcer of NeonDyne, armor pulsing with cerulean energy veins that flicker like a heartbeat. His presence feels less like a man and more like a force of nature, a predator wrapped in steel.

He lifts one arm. A vortex of shimmering distortion spirals around his gauntlet, drawing debris toward his palm—metal shards, chunks of concrete, even the air itself bending inward like gravity is collapsing. Rip feels the pull. His ribs scream. His vision shakes. The resonance inside his chest answers the pressure with a rising, violent pulse.

Kael grabs Rip by the arm.

"MOVE—!"

Mara reacts first. She thrusts both hands forward. Space bends—not like a push or a blast, but more like reality folds a few inches to the left, redirecting the stream of debris just before it can eviscerate everyone on the platform. Valiran's energy wave strikes the warped space and disperses into a violent bloom of sparks. Even he seems momentarily surprised.

Then his helmet tilts.

"Still alive, Mara," he says. "Still breaking physics to cheat death."

Mara's breathing is shallow. That single motion cost her. Kael curses.

"He's gonna bring the whole tunnel down if we stay!"

Valiran raises his hand again—this time using both arms. Rip has no idea what that means, but Mara's eyes go wide.

"DOWN!" she screams.

A shockwave erupts from Valiran's palms. It's not sound. It's not heat. It's not a blast of energy. It's absence— a vacuum of force tearing toward them, pulling everything forward like a reverse explosion. Bodies lift. Rifles, crates, armor fragments all streak toward Valiran's outstretched hands.

Rip's boots lose traction. He slides across the metal floor, dragged toward the enforcer like a helpless piece of debris. His fingers scrape sparks from the ground. Kael screams as she's pulled off her feet, tumbling forward. Dren slams into a steel pillar hard enough to dent it. Sura claws at a cable to stop her slide. Valo fires an anchor grapple into the wall, wrapping his cybernetic arm around a pipe. The pull nearly tears him free.

Rip feels the Key inside him panic. The resonance spikes—

NO—NOT NOW—

He tries to force it down, but the fear amplifies it. His pulse distorts in his ears. The world begins to vibrate around him. Valiran strides forward through his own vortex like a god through a hurricane.

"Return the Key," he booms, voice amplified, "and I will spare the rebellion's children."

Rip's blood runs cold. This isn't a threat. It's a promise.

Mara slams her palm against the ground. Space warps underneath them, a slingshot of motion erupting sideways.

Rip is thrown toward a side tunnel as the entire platform slides ten feet to the right—physics bending like a wrenched hinge. Rebels tumble. Equipment scatters. Valiran's vortex skews, hitting empty space where they used to be.

The enforcer twists sharply, recalibrating, armor flaring with pale blue light. Mara yells:

"Evacuate the station!"

Rebels scramble toward every passage. Kael grips Rip's wrist and drags him toward a rusted access tunnel. Rip limps behind her, ribs throbbing, the world spinning. He glances back—Valiran strides through the warped space, unbothered, raising both hands again. The Key pulses dangerously. Rip feels like he's going to explode.

Kael shoves him deeper into the tunnel.

"Don't look back! GO!"

The access tunnel plunges into darkness—metal walls sweating condensation, pipes groaning under stress. The alarm sirens in the station above blur into a droning hum of chaos. Rip stumbles. His breath catches on broken ribs. His vision shakes left and right.

Kael pulls him onward.

"Keep moving—keep—moving—"

Sura runs ahead, flicking a small projector that maps escape routes across the wall. Dren drags a wounded rebel. Valo covers their retreat, firing blasts of concussive rounds down the passage behind them.

"We're not outrunning him," Valo snaps. "He'll tear through the Warrens in five minutes."

Kael pants.

"You wanna go back and ask him nicely to stop?!"

Rip's hearing distorts. The Key pulses in rhythmic waves—
sound-becoming-touch-becoming-light-becoming-pressure. His breath stutters. His hands shake.

Kael notices.

"Rip—Rip, look at me—stay with us, okay? You're overwhelmed. It's your first time under this kind of strike. Focus on my voice."

Rip tries. But the resonance is too loud. Too alive. Too aware. He feels something tug at him—not physically, but internally—like a door inside his mind trying to open.

below

The whisper returns, glitching across his skull. Rip gasps, stumbling. Kael braces him against a wall.

"What was that? What is happening to you?" Kael demands.

"I—I don't know," Rip stammers. "I hear… things. Like Titan is still—"

A loud bang cuts him off. The tunnel behind them collapses inward. Dust and hot air blast through the corridor. Valiran's distorted voice bellows through the smoke:

"YOUR DEATH SERVES THE CORE."

Dren shouts.

"WE NEED TO SPLIT!"

Mara appears from the right tunnel, cloak torn, blood trickling from her lip. She grabs Rip by the collar and shoves him toward a narrow hatch.

"Down the Rust Warrens," she orders. "Now."

Rip hesitates.

"What about you—"

"I'll hold him back."

Rip freezes.

"You'll die."

"Not before you escape."

Rip doesn't move. Mara's voice softens, barely audible:

"This is bigger than you, Rip. And bigger than Lora."

Rip's heart clenches. He doesn't understand. He will later.

Kael yanks him by the arm.

"We have to GO!"

Rip stumbles through the hatch—just as the corridor behind him explodes. He hits the grated floor of the Rust

Warrens, coughing through the smoke. Kael slams the hatch shut and locks it.

·   ∘   ◯   ◉   🗝   🗝   ◉   ◯   ∘

·

Sura stands at the junction, pale and shaking.

"We don't have long. The motion distortion she used—it won't hold him more than a minute."

Rip tries to catch his breath as the Key flickers beneath his sternum.

"What is the Rust Warrens?" he asks between breaths.

Kael answers grimly.

"The part of the Warrens where the machines go to die."

They descend into a maze of corroded metal, collapsed infrastructure, and old metro cars screwed into place as makeshift shelters and shops. Rust flakes drift from every surface. The smell of oil and decay hangs thick. Flickering torches cast uneven light.

People live here. Children huddle around a heater. Old mechanics weld broken parts by lamplight. A blind vendor sells scrap components from a blanket. A cluster of teenagers whisper urgently as the rebels rush past.

Rip is struck by the sheer number of civilians.

"This many people… hiding down here?"

Kael nods grimly.

"The Warrens aren't just a base. They're a refugee city."

Sura adds.

"And they'll all be slaughtered if Valiran breaches this far."

Dren curses.

"We need to reinforce the barricades at Junction Eight."

Valo's synthetic eye flickers.

"No time. He's cutting through the upper tunnels already."

A low tremor shakes the chamber. Rip winces, covering his ears—it feels like knives in his skull. The Key pulses violently. Another tremor. Dust falls from ceiling pipes. Children scream.

Kael grips Rip's shoulders.

"Hey. Focus. You can't lose control down here."

Rip breathes sharply.

"I can feel him… Valiran. I can FEEL him coming."

Sura's eyes widen.

"You can sense him?"

Rip nods. It terrifies him.

Kael pulls him forward.

"Then you're our early warning system. Collaborate with it. Don't let it break you."

A thunderous impact echoes through the upper metalwork. A column buckles. A platform collapses, sending rusted crates tumbling. People scatter. Rip backs away instinctively as the resonance spikes so violently he nearly vomits.

Valiran's distorted voice booms through the metal:

"THE KEY IS MINE."

Kael pulls Rip behind a row of stalled metro cars, shoving him into a cramped alcove.

"Stay here!"

Rip grabs Kael's arm.

"No. I'm not hiding."

"You—are—hurt!"

"So is everyone else!"

Before Kael can respond, a low robotic growl echoes from beneath the metro car. Rip turns. Twin green eyes glow in the dark. Then—Wex crawls out. The robotic dog limps slightly, one hind leg sparking, but its tail whirls in a hopeful, metallic wag as it barks up at Rip.

Rip blinks.

"Hey… you again."

Wex nudges Rip's chest with his nose. A gentle vibration pulses through Rip's sternum in response. Kael stares.

"He likes you. That… never happens."

Rip scratches behind the metal ear plating. Wex leans in. For the first time since his world fell apart, Rip feels something like warmth.

He whispers, "Good boy."

Wex yips.

And then Valiran tears the door off the metro car. Metal screeches as the slab is flung aside like tissue paper. The enforcer crouches to enter the chamber, towering even in the confined space. Rip grabs Wex instinctively and backpedals. Kael draws a pistol.

"Run!"

Valiran lifts one arm—

Mara appears behind him. A blur. A distortion. A fracture in motion. She slams both palms against Valiran's back. The enforcer's armor ripples—like his entire body is being shoved forward and backward at once. He roars, spinning with inhuman speed. Mara dodges—barely— rolling across the metal floor.

Valiran backhands her. Mara crashes into a support beam, coughing blood.

Rip shouts, "MARA!"

Valiran turns back toward Rip, raising his hand—

The Key explodes. Rip doesn't think. Doesn't aim. Doesn't breathe. He just reacts. A shockwave of raw resonance bursts outward from his chest—shattering rusted pipes, ripping metal from hinges, buckling walls. Valiran staggers, armor flaring violently as it absorbs part of the strike. The rest knocks him into a collapsed metro chassis.

Sura screams.

"NOW! MOVE!"

Kael grabs Rip and pulls him down a maintenance chute. Wex leaps after them, mechanical paws scraping. Behind them, Mara distracts Valiran again—a blur of wild motion, fighting a battle she cannot win.

Rip twists back, screaming.

"MARA—COME WITH US!"

But she shakes her head once, eyes fierce.

"Find Lora."

The chute drops them into darkness. The Rust Warrens collapse behind. And Mara stands alone against Elcron's deadliest lieutenant.

THE FRACTURE OF MOTION (Flashback)

The city of Virelia was a living circuit—neon veins pulsing through glass and steel, every surface humming with the promise of order. In the upper tiers, where the air was filtered and the rain never touched the ground, three figures moved in perfect formation: Mara Callix, Kyoto Callix, and Joey Valiran.

They wore the black-and-white armor of NeonDyne's elite, each suit marked with the Triad insignia. No one called them heroes. No one called them villains. They were simply the best—chosen for their loyalty, their discipline, and their willingness to do what others would not.

Tonight, they were hunting a myth.

The briefing had been simple: a rebel courier had stolen an artifact from a NeonDyne vault. The artifact was rumored to be a Key—one of the seven. The Motion Key. The kind of thing that could change the world, or end it.

Their orders were clear: retrieve the Key. Eliminate all resistance. No witnesses.

They moved through the abandoned mag-rail station in silence, boots barely whispering against the cracked tile. Kyoto led, his scanner sweeping the shadows. Mara followed, pulse steady, mind sharp. Valiran brought up the rear, his presence a cold reassurance—always watching, always calculating.

"Contact, north platform," Kyoto murmured, voice clipped. "Two heat signatures. One's moving fast."

"Rebel courier?" Mara asked.

"Or bait," Valiran replied, his tone flat. "We proceed."

They fanned out, weapons drawn. The air was thick with ozone and the faint scent of burning circuitry. Somewhere below, the city's heartbeat on, oblivious.

The first firefight was over in seconds. The rebels were desperate, under-armed, and terrified. Kyoto moved like a ghost, stunning one, disarming another. Mara covered his flank, her shots precise, non-lethal where possible. Valiran was efficient—no wasted motion, no hesitation. When the last rebel fell, Mara knelt beside the courier, searching for the artifact.

She found it in a battered satchel: a sphere of white metal, no larger than an apple, pulsing with a faint blue light. The Motion Key.

She stared at it, heart pounding. It was beautiful. Terrifying.

"Bag it," Valiran said, stepping closer. "We move."

But Kyoto hesitated. "Wait. Look at it. It's… reacting."

The Key hovered an inch above Mara's palm, spinning slowly. The air around it shimmered, dust swirling in lazy spirals.

"It's active," Kyoto whispered. "We need containment—"

A shot rang out. Mara spun, weapon raised.

The courier was dead. Valiran lowered his pistol, face unreadable.

"No witnesses," he said.

Mara stared at him, anger flaring. "That wasn't necessary."

Valiran met her gaze, unblinking. "It was protocol."

Kyoto stepped between them, voice tense. "We have the Key. Let's finish this."

They moved out, the Key sealed in a containment field. But the air felt heavier now, the silence between them charged with something dangerous.

They reached the extraction point—a rooftop overlooking the city's fractured skyline. The dropship was late. Mara paced, restless. Kyoto checked the perimeter. Valiran stood at the edge, watching the lights below.

"Why do you think NeonDyne wants these things?" Kyoto asked quietly, joining Mara.

"To control them," she replied. "To control us."

He nodded, eyes distant. "Do you ever wonder if we're on the wrong side?"

She looked at him, surprised. "We're soldiers. We follow orders."

He smiled, sad. "That's what I'm afraid of."

A low growl interrupted them. Wex, Kyoto's loyal robotic dog, padded over, sensors whirring. He pressed against Kyoto's leg, tail wagging anxiously.

"It's okay, Wex," Kyoto murmured, scratching behind the metal ear. "We're almost done."

But Wex didn't relax. He stared at Valiran, hackles raised.

Mara followed his gaze—and saw Valiran moving toward the containment case, eyes fixed on the Key.

"Joey?" she called, voice sharp. "What are you doing?"

He didn't answer. He reached for the case, fingers trembling.

"Stop," Kyoto said, stepping forward. "That's not protocol."

Valiran turned, and for the first time, Mara saw something like hunger in his eyes.

"It's not protocol," he agreed. "It's destiny."

He moved faster than she thought possible, slamming Kyoto aside. Mara lunged, but Valiran was already opening the case, the Key hovering between his hands.

"Don't—" Mara shouted, but it was too late.

The Key flared, blue light spilling across the rooftop. Valiran screamed, the sound raw and inhuman. The Key began to fracture, a jagged line of light running down its center.

And in that instant, Mara acted.

She drew her blade and, with a single, desperate motion, sliced the Key in half. The blade passed through the sphere with a shriek of energy, splitting it into two uneven pieces. One half tumbled to the ground, rolling toward Kyoto's feet; the other remained in Valiran's grip, pulsing violently.

Valiran howled, clutching the fragment to his chest. The air warped around him, debris swirling in a miniature cyclone.

Kyoto dove for the fallen half, but Valiran was faster. With a brutal, fluid motion, he drew his sidearm and fired—three shots, center mass.

Kyoto staggered, blood blooming across his armor. He fell to his knees, eyes wide with shock.

"NO!" Mara screamed, rushing to her brother's side.

But Valiran was already merging with the Key, the fragment in his hand fusing to his palm, light crawling up his arm in jagged, unnatural patterns. His body convulsed, veins of blue fire racing beneath his skin.

Mara grabbed the remaining half of the Key, feeling its heat sear her palm. She pressed it to her chest, desperate, willing it to merge as it had with Valiran.

Valiran, still writhing, saw her. "No—NO!" he roared, and with a savage, almost animal motion, he drew his blade and swung.

Pain exploded through Mara's left arm. She screamed as the blade bit deep, severing flesh and bone. Her arm fell away, and the Key fragment still clutched in her remaining hand.

But she didn't let go.

She forced the Key against her chest, the pain blinding, the world spinning. The fragment fused with her, burning like liquid fire, and she collapsed to the ground, vision tunneling to a single point of blue light.

Moments later, gunfire erupted from the stairwell. A group of rebels burst onto the rooftop, weapons blazing. Valiran, still glowing with the Key's power, turned and fled, leaping from the rooftop and vanishing into the night.

The world was a blur of pain and blue light.

Mara's last memory before the darkness was the Key fragment burning into her chest, the world spinning, her brother's blood on her hands, and Valiran's silhouette vanishing into the night—half of the Motion Key fused to his arm, the other half seared into her own flesh.

She drifted in and out of consciousness. Sometimes she heard gunfire, sometimes the distant whine of NeonDyne drones, sometimes only the ragged, mechanical whimper of Wex.

When she finally woke, it was to the sound of voices— strange, urgent, and unfamiliar.

"She's alive. Get her on the table—now!"

"Her arm—God, what happened to her arm?"

"Keep pressure on the stump. We need to stop the bleeding—"

Mara tried to move, but pain lanced through her body, white-hot and blinding. She screamed, or thought she did, but the sound was swallowed by the chaos around her.

Someone pressed a mask to her face. "Breathe. Just breathe. You're safe now."

Safe. The word meant nothing.

She slipped under again.

The next time she woke, the world was quieter. Dim light filtered through a cracked ceiling. The air smelled of antiseptic and old metal. She was lying on a cot, her body heavy and numb.

She tried to sit up, but her left side felt wrong—empty, weightless. Panic surged through her. She looked down and saw the bandaged stump where her arm had been. The memory of Valiran's blade flashed through her mind, and she nearly vomited.

A voice spoke from the shadows. "Easy. Don't move too fast."

Mara turned, heart pounding. A woman in patched rebel armor stood by the door, arms crossed, watching her with wary eyes.

"Where am I?" Mara rasped.

"Safehouse. Sector 7B. We found you on a rooftop, bleeding out. You're lucky to be alive."

Mara's mind raced. "My brother—Kyoto—where is he?"

The woman's expression softened, just a little. "We… found him too. I'm sorry."

Mara closed her eyes, fighting the wave of grief that threatened to drown her. She forced herself to focus. "The man who did this—Valiran. Did you see him?"

The woman shook her head. "He was gone by the time we arrived. But your dog—Wex, right? —he wouldn't leave your brother's side. We had to carry him out with the body."

Mara swallowed hard. "Wex…"

As if summoned, the robotic dog padded into the room, his silver frame streaked with blood and grime. He limped to Mara's side and pressed his head against her thigh, whining softly.

She reached out with her remaining hand, stroking his head. "Good boy," she whispered, voice breaking.

For a long time, she just sat there, petting Wex, letting the silence settle around her. The rebels left her alone, giving her space to grieve.

Days passed in a blur. The rebels patched her up as best they could, fitting her with a crude cybernetic arm— unfinished, ugly, but functional. Mara hated it. She hated the way it felt, the way it looked, the way it reminded her of everything she'd lost.

She kept to herself, speaking only when necessary. The rebels respected her silence, but she could feel their curiosity, their suspicion. They didn't know who she was, not really. They didn't know what she carried inside her.

The half of the Motion Key fused to her chest pulsed with a faint, constant energy. She could feel it in her bones, in her blood, in the way her new arm sometimes twitched with a will of its own. She told no one. She would tell no one. The secret was hers alone.

Sometimes, late at night, she would wake from nightmares—Kyoto's face, pale and bloodied, staring up at her; Valiran's eyes, cold and hungry, as he reached for the Key; the feeling of the blade biting through her flesh, the heat of the Key burning into her soul.

She would sit on the edge of her cot, clutching Wex to her chest, and weep silently, the tears soaking into his metal fur.

One morning, she woke to find a group of rebels standing at the foot of her bed. They looked nervous, uncertain.

"We're moving out," their leader said. "NeonDyne's sweeping the district. We can't stay here."

Mara nodded, rising slowly. She flexed her new arm, wincing at the pain. "I'm ready."

As they moved through the tunnels beneath the city, Mara kept her head down, her thoughts swirling. She remembered the mission, the rooftop, the way Valiran had looked at her—like she was nothing, like she was in the way of something greater.

She remembered the Key, the way it had split in her hands, the way it had burned into her chest. She remembered Kyoto's last breath, the way Wex had refused to leave his side.

She remembered everything.

When they reached the new safehouse, Mara collapsed onto her cot, exhausted. Wex curled up beside her, his head resting on her thigh.

For a long time, she just sat there, staring at the wall, her mind blank.

Then, slowly, the memories returned—the rooftop, the Key, Kyoto's death. The grief hit her like a tidal wave, and she dropped to her knees, sobbing uncontrollably, her cybernetic arm trembling with each ragged breath.

She wept for her brother, for herself, for everything she had lost.

And in that moment, Mara swore she would never let anyone take anything from her again.

CHAPTER 9

GHOST SIGNAL

The chute spits them into darkness. Rip hits the metal floor shoulder-first, rolling until he slams into a cold pipe. Pain detonates through his ribs. He gasps, tasting blood. Kael lands beside him in a mess of limbs, groaning. Wex drops last, landing neatly and shaking dust from his chassis with a metallic rattle-rattle-rattle.

Above them, the Rust Warrens thunder with distant battle noise—metal screaming, explosions echoing, concrete collapsing. Rip forces himself upright, hand clutching his chest.

"Is Mara—?" he starts.

Kael cuts him off.

"If she's still alive, she'll meet us. If not…"

She doesn't finish. Rip swallows hard. He won't let himself believe Mara is dead. Not yet.

Wex nudges Rip's leg, whining softly—a strange mix of real dog emotion and mechanical tone. Rip scratches his head plating, whispering:

"I'm okay. I promise."

The dog's green eyes dim slightly. A worried flicker. Rip forces a breath.

"Where are we?"

Kael flicks on a wrist light. A vast tunnel stretches ahead, half-flooded, walls lined with rusted pipes and abandoned maintenance pods. Steam hisses from cracked valves. The air reeks of oil, mold, and something metallic—like old blood.

"The lower Warrens," Kael says. "We're beneath the Rust district now. Hardly anyone comes this deep."

"Why not?"

Kael hesitates.

"Because of what lives down here."

Rip tenses.

"What?"

A faint flicker of movement catches the light. Something skitters across a distant pipe.

Rip stiffens.

"Kael—"

She shakes her head.

"Not bots. Not drones."

Her voice drops.

"People."

Rip frowns.

"Civilians?"

"No. Subnets." Her face tightens. "People who fell off the grid completely. Too damaged, too poor, too hunted. Some rebel-affiliated. Some… not."

Rip nods slowly.

"Are they hostile?"

Kael gives him a bitter smile.

"Everything down here is."

Wex growls softly. Rip pats him.

"Let's keep moving."

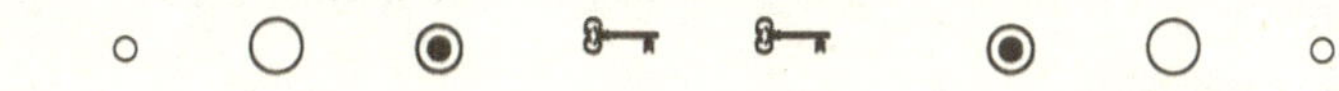

They move carefully through thigh-high water, the cold numbing Rip's legs. The dim wrist light paints the tunnel in eerie gold. Kael scans with a handheld jammer.

"No drones yet. But Valiran won't stop at the surface."

Rip asks quietly.

"Why didn't he kill me back at the station?"

"He couldn't," Kael says. "Not without confirmation."

"Confirmation of what?"

"That you have the Key."

Rip hesitates.

"I didn't even know I had it until Titan—until he—"

Kael softens.

"I know. Doesn't change anything. NeonDyne sees Keys as weapons. Or data. Or both."

Rip grips the cold pipe beside him, squeezing until rust flakes off.

"They're not taking me," he murmurs. "And they're not keeping Lora."

Kael studies him for a few seconds.

"You really love her, huh?"

Rip's chest tightens.

"More than anything."

Kael looks away.

"Good. You'll need something to fight for."

Rip steps forward—and freezes. The air changes. A faint vibration ripples through the metal walls. Not noise. Not resonance. Something else. Something cold. Something electric.

Rip's breath catches.

"Do you hear that?" he whispers.

Kael shakes her head.

"Hear what?"

Wex tilts his head, ears whirring, confused. Rip closes his eyes—and a whisper threads through his skull. Not Titan. Not the Key. Something softer. Something sad.

Ri…p…

Rip's eyes fly open. He stumbles back, clutching his head. Kael grabs his arms.

"What is it?!"

Rip's voice shakes.

“I heard—someone. Calling me.”

Kael blinks.

“Someone… down here?”

“No.” Rip swallows hard. “Inside. Or through… something. I don’t know.”

Kael’s face pales.

“You heard a voice inside your mind?”

Rip nods. Kael whispers:

“That’s not possible unless…”

She looks at his chest.

“…the Key is connecting you to something.”

Rip breathes fast.

“It sounded like—” He hesitates. “It sounded like Lora.”

Kael doesn’t respond. But Rip sees the truth in her eyes.

A low hum rumbles through the tunnel. Lights flicker. Wex bristles, teeth bared. Kael raises her pistol.

"Something's coming."

Rip senses it before he sees it. A distortion in the air. A flicker of static. A ghost of movement. A shape materializes from the shadows—a humanoid figure composed of glitching outlines, flickering like a broken hologram. Its limbs jitter in slow-motion frames. Its face is a mask of scrambled pixels.

Rip steps back, breath trembling.

"What—what the hell is that?"

Kael's voice drops to a whisper.

"A Ghost Choir scout."

Rip frowns.

"Ghost Choir?"

"They're not NeonDyne. Not rebel. They're people who connected themselves to the digital underworld. They're half-coded, half-human. They believe the Core— Elcron's Core—is salvation."

The ghostly figure twitches toward Rip. He sees its face warp—features sliding, reshaping, glitching between expressions.

Kael raises her gun.

"Don't move."

Rip whispers.

"Can it… see us?"

Wex growls louder, mechanical claws clacking against metal.

Kael hisses.

"Yes. And Ghost Choir doesn't talk—they take."

Rip tenses.

"Take what?"

Kael answers coldly.

"Souls."

Rip's breath stops. The Ghost lunges. Kael fires—three shots burst into the glitching figure—and pass right through it, ricocheting into the wall.

Rip's eyes widen.

"It's not physical!"

"No shit!" Kael shouts.

The Ghost Choir scout reaches for Rip—pixelated fingers distort, stretching like tendrils—Rip screams, shoving his hands forward instinctively. The Key erupts. A concussive wave bursts from Rip's chest—not like before—this one is precise, narrow, sharp as a blade of vibrating sound.

It slices through the Ghost. The entity flickers violently—then explodes into static, dissolving into sparks of corrupted light.

Rip collapses to his knees, gasping. Kael stares at him, stunned. Wex runs in circles, barking metallic echoes.

Rip whispers.

"What… was that?"

Kael kneels beside him.

"That wasn't resonance," she says shakily. "That wasn't sound. That was… code."

Rip's stomach drops. Code? How could he generate code?

Before he can ask more—another whisper slips into his skull. Soft. Broken. Like a fading signal.

R…ip… help…

Rip's blood freezes. It's her. It's Lora. He grabs the pipe to steady himself, shaking.

"Lora," he whispers. "LORA—!"

Kael grabs his face.

"Rip—Rip—HEY—look at me—what did you hear?!"

"She's alive," he breathes. "She's inside something. Something digital. Something… deep."

Kael's expression tightens.

"Rip… if you're hearing her—really hearing her—then she's closer to the Core than we thought."

He stares at her.

"Then we must move. We must—"

A massive metallic scream tears through the lower tunnel. Rip flinches—but then realizes—that isn't a scream. It's the sound of steel warping.

Kael's face drains of color.

"No… oh god… he's HERE?! Already?!"

Rip whispers, trembling.

"Valiran."

Metal shreds behind them. Valiran's helmeted silhouette steps out of the darkness, blue circuitry pulsing like heartbeats. Seven feet tall. Smoldering with energy. His voice echoes coldly through the tunnel:

"KEYBEARER. KNEEL."

Rip staggers back. The Key flares. Kael yanks him away.

"Run!"

Wex barks once—loud, metallic—then leaps between Rip and Valiran, hackles raised. Valiran pauses. He studies the small robotic dog. Then lifts one hand.

Kael screams.

"NO!"

Rip reacts instinctively. He throws himself between Wex and Valiran's outstretched palm. The Key detonates again. A shockwave surges forward, and Valiran absorbs the resonance with a flick of his gauntlet. Rip's legs buckle, the force draining him. Kael fires wildly—Valiran swats the bullets from the air with a casual gesture.

Wex charges, teeth bared. Valiran kicks. The robotic dog slams into a pipe, sparks spraying from his chassis.

"NO!" Rip shouts, scrambling toward the dog.

Valiran raises both arms for a killing strike. The tunnel distorts. A blur slams into Valiran's side. For a moment Rip thinks—

"Mara?!"

But no. This distortion is weaker. Younger. Faster. A teenage girl materializes from a glitch of warped space— hair shaved on one side, tattoos glowing faintly with motion-sigils. She spins, redirecting Valiran's attack by an inch—just enough to throw his aim off.

Kael gasps.

"Rion?!"

The girl shouts.

"Mara sent me! MOVE!"

Rip grabs Wex's battered metal collar, hauling him upright.

"Come on, buddy—come on—!"

Wex limps, sparks falling off his back plating. Valiran rises.

"YOU ARE DELAYING THE INEVITABLE."

The tunnel walls begin to warp inward under his power. Kael screams.

"Everyone MOVE NOW!"

Rion yells.

"LEFT TUNNEL! GO!"

Rip sprints, holding Wex close, Kael beside him, Rion covering the rear. Behind them, Valiran tears through steel like paper. But the tunnels split into dozens of branches. For a moment—just a moment—he loses line of sight.

Rion collapses against a wall, panting.

"We… don't have much time. The Warrens are lost."

Kael gasps.

"We need to regroup. We need Mara—"

Rion's expression darkens.

"Mara isn't coming. She's buying us time."

Rip's throat tightens. He looks down at the damaged robotic dog in his arms. Wex looks back at him, eyes flickering weakly.

Rip whispers:

"We're going to survive. We're going to find her. All of us."

Kael gently touches Rip's arm. Rion wipes sweat from her brow. And somewhere deeper in the tunnels—the steel screams again. Valiran is coming. The Ghost Choir move in the shadows. And Lora's signal flickers again:

Ri...p... don't... let... him...

Rip's breath stops. She's not just alive. She's reaching for him. And he's not turning back.

CHAPTER 10

THE REFLECTION CODE

The tunnel narrows until Rip must duck, his shoulders brushing damp walls. Pipes crowd overhead like rib bones, dripping condensation that echoes through the darkness in uneven beats. Each drop feels amplified, a metronome of tension marking their descent.

Kael leads the way, her wrist light cutting a thin blade of illumination through the gloom. Rion flanks the rear, dagger drawn, eyes sharp. Wex limps between them, lights flickering, servos whining with each step. Rip stays close, one arm wrapped protectively around the robotic dog's chassis, trying to steady its shaking frame.

Every step feels heavier. The Key in Rip's chest pulses—not painfully, but insistently. Like a heartbeat trying to synchronize with something distant. Something calling him. Something he doesn't understand yet.

Rion glances over her shoulder.

"Stop clenching your fists like that. You're broadcasting."

Rip looks down. He hadn't noticed—but the faint golden glow beneath his sternum is pulsing through his veins, visible under the damp hospital fabric.

"It's stronger here," Rip mutters. "Like the air is… vibrating."

Kael slows.

"That's because we're nearing the old fiber catacombs."

Rip frowns.

"What does that mean?"

Rion answers, breathless.

"Thickest concentration of buried data lines in the city. Pre-collapse infrastructure. Half-alive, half-dead. A perfect place for the Ghost Choir to nest."

Rip stiffens.

"I thought we lost them back there."

Kael shakes her head.

"They're not physical. You don't lose them. You just… fall off their path for a while."

Great.

Rip shifts Wex in his arms. The dog whines, sparks trailing from a fracture in his left flank. The plating is dented deeply—Valiran's kick nearly destroyed him. Rip presses his forehead gently to Wex's metal snout.

"I'm not letting anything happen to you," he whispers.

Wex's failing LED eyes blink weakly in response.

Kael looks back, face softening just a little.

"He'll make it," she says. "Wex is built tougher than he looks."

Rion snorts.

"Please. That dog has died three times."

"Two," Kael snaps.

Rion shrugs.

"The first one counted."

Rip tries to smile—but can't. He's too busy feeling the hum in the walls. Not the tunnel. Not the city. Something else. A tremor in the data world. A ripple through unseen circuitry. A ghost of memory.

He slows, eyes unfocused.

Kael looks back sharply.

"Rip? You with us?"

Rip opens his mouth to answer—

But the world fractures.

Rip blinks—and suddenly he's standing in a kitchen.
His kitchen. Soft morning sunlight spills through the blinds.
Dust motes drift lazily in the air. The smell of coffee
lingers. A half-cooked omelet sits on the stove. A scarf is
tossed across a chair. Lora's laugh echoes—

Except she isn't there.

No one is.

The room is still. Silent. Frozen mid-breath.

Rip's throat tightens.

"Lora…?"

His voice feels too loud, out of place in the stillness. He takes a step forward. The tile cracks beneath his foot. He freezes. Crack lines spiderweb across the floor in slow motion—not from pressure, but from digital warping, like a glitch crawling through corrupted memory.

Rip's pulse spikes.

"Lora—can you hear me?"

A whisper brushes the air. Soft. Broken. Echoing like a voice caught in a damaged recorder.

Ri…p…

His knees nearly buckle.

"Lora! LORA!"

The room flickers. The walls twist. The furniture dissolves into shimmering fragments. A figure appears behind him. Not fully formed. A silhouette of light and static. A woman's shape. Her posture. Her hair. Lora. But distorted—like Rip is seeing her through a shattered mirror.

Rip reaches toward her—

The figure flickers violently. Her voice slips through the static:

Ri…p… don't… let… him…

Rip stumbles forward.

"Don't let WHO—Lora, please—tell me where you are! Tell me how to reach you!"

The figure glitches—collapsing into a cascade of pixels. The kitchen warps. The world folds. And then everything shatters into white light—

Rip gasps awake. He's on his knees. Hands shaking. Back against the cold wall. Kael is kneeling beside him, gripping his face.

"Rip! Hey—HEY—look at me!"

Rion stands a few feet away, dagger drawn, scanning the shadows.

"Pulse spike. He dropped like a rock."

Rip coughs, breath ragged.

"I saw her."

Kael's expression softens into dread.

"A hallucination?"

Rip shakes his head violently.

"No. I wasn't dreaming. I wasn't imagining. I was inside a memory—our memory. But it was broken, like I was walking through corrupted files."

Rion mutters.

"That's… not normal."

Kael asks quietly.

"Did she say anything?"

Rip's voice breaks.

"She said… 'don't let him'."

Kael's jaw tightens.

"Him… meaning Elcron."

"Or Valiran," Rion suggests.

Rip shakes his head.

"No. It sounded—bigger. More afraid."

Kael meets his eyes.

Rip finishes.

"It sounded like she meant the Core."

The tunnel goes dead silent after Rip's vow. For a heartbeat, even the dripping condensation seems to stop.

Rion's dagger gleams faintly in the dim light as she scans the shadows.

"If Lora is already speaking through the data-lines," she whispers, "then she's far deeper inside NeonDyne's systems than any hostage should be."

Kael's face hardens.

"She isn't a hostage. She's being integrated."

Rip's pulse spikes.

"Integrated into WHAT?"

Rion's voice lowers, almost reluctant.

"The machine Elcron built to rewrite humanity."

Rip's fists clench.

"No. NO. I'm not letting that happen. I don't care what she is—human, AI, whatever—she's Lora. And I will tear through every wall in this city to get her back."

Kael nods firmly.

"We're with you."

Wex barks once. Weak. But loyal. Rip grips the dog closer, feeling the faint hum of servos against his chest.

A sound drifts down the tunnel. A whisper. Not human. Not mechanical. Something between.

Rion stiffens.

"Ghost Choir. Two hundred feet and closing."

Kael spins toward Rip.

"We need to move. NOW."

Rip stands—but staggers. His vision blurs again. Not a reflection. Not Lora. Something else. A looming presence behind his eyes. Something heavy. Cold. Watching. Not Titan. Not Echo. Something older. Something beneath the Core.

Rip shivers.

Kael touches his arm.

"Rip. Rip. Focus."

He breathes sharply.

"Something else is trying to connect to me."

Rion curses.

"It's the Choir. They're trying to embed a tracer signal."

Rip shakes his head.

"No. This felt… different."

Kael steps closer, voice sharp.

"That's impossible."

Rip's voice is a whisper.

"I think the Core is looking back."

The tunnel amplifies the sound. Footsteps. Dozens. But not physical. They echo like metallic ghosts—flickering silhouettes darting between the pipes, appearing, and disappearing in the corner of Rip's vision.

Kael lifts her pistol. Rion draws her dagger. Wex limps in front, growling through damaged speakers. Rip presses back against the wall, heart hammering.

Kael whispers.

"Whatever you saw… we need distance from it. There's a dead zone ahead. No signals. No Choir. No tracking."

Rion nudges them forward.

"Move. Move. Move."

But the tunnel dims. Lights blink out one by one. Rip feels a chill crawl up his spine.

Rion pauses.

"Why did the lights—"

A voice cuts through the darkness. Not spoken. Transmitted. Directly into the air.

"Return the Key, and your suffering ends."

Rip's blood freezes.

Kael swears.

"Valiran—he's patching through the relay systems—"

Rip shouts.

"SHUT UP! I'll never give you anything!"

A chuckle echoes through the pipes.

"You misunderstand. The Key calls to the Core. Your pain only hastens your collapse."

Rip's knees weaken. His vision flickers. Static creeps along the walls. Wex barks wildly, trying to get between Rip and the shadows.

Kael grabs Rip's shoulders.

"IGNORE HIM. He wants you agitated. It destabilizes the resonance—"

Rip's pulse spasms painfully.

"I—I can't—something's pulling—"

Rion slashes at the air, sending a shock of distortion outward—enough to fracture the connection for a heartbeat.

"Dead zone!" she yells. "RUN!"

Kael drags Rip forward. Rip holds Wex tight. Rion scans their rear. Footsteps—real ones—shake the tunnel now. Valiran's. Heavy. Certain.

Rip feels like he's drowning in sound—

When suddenly—everything goes silent.

The tunnel opens into a vast chamber of black metal and broken fiber lines. Ceiling high. Air cold. A dead zone.

Rip collapses to one knee. Wex presses beside him, servos whining. Kael kneels, scanning his face. Rion stands guard, dagger raised, eyes darting across the shadows.

Rip whispers, voice raw.

"Lora… I'm coming."

And deep in the city's buried code—a single line of reflected data answers back.

I know.

CHAPTER 11

WEX THE STRAY

The dead zone breathed like a sleeping giant, its silence heavy and unnatural. The air felt thick, as though the chamber itself was holding its breath. Rip sat against a mangled support beam, Wex curled in his lap—half metal, half warmth. The dog's chassis clicked in uneven rhythms as damaged servos strained to stabilize, each sound a reminder of how close they had come to losing him.

Kael knelt beside them, compact welder in hand. Sparks flared as she worked, each burst of light reflecting off the wet steel walls. Rip flinched every time, his ribs aching with the involuntary movement. Wex whined in a stuttering digital tone, caught between machine and animal. Rip stroked the dog's neck plating, whispering softly.

"You're okay. You're okay, friend. I've got you."

Kael muttered without looking up. "He's not okay. He's held together with stubbornness and scrap."

Rion paced near the far wall, daggers drawn, eyes locked on the tunnel they had come from. Every few minutes the overhead lights flickered, and her breath hitched as if she expected Valiran's silhouette to emerge. He didn't. Not yet.

Rip forced himself to look around. The chamber was vast—four stories tall, walls lined with thick black cables that coiled upward like roots of some ancient tree. Broken fiber optic lines spilled from cracked conduits, skeletal and dead. The absence of current made the air unnaturally still; even the Key inside Rip's chest felt quieter, subdued.

"It's really a dead zone," he murmured. "No signals. No presence."

Kael nodded. "The Ghost Choir can't manifest well here. And Valiran—he can't track resonance through this much dead fiber. This is the last safe space for miles."

Rion snorted. "'Safe.' Sure. Till the whole place collapses."

Rip kept petting Wex, fingers trembling slightly. The dog's weight was both comfort and burden. Kael softened her tone. "He'll pull through. But… he needs real repair tools. Not what I've got here."

Rip swallowed. "Then tell me what you can fix."

Kael exhaled, adjusting the welding pen. "Okay. His left servo cluster is cracked—probably from Valiran's hit. Internal motor couplings are misaligned. He's leaking heat-sink fluid. And one of his core stabilizers is totally fried."

Rip stared down at the dog. "Can you fix all that?"

Kael shrugged. "Not unless you want him held together by duct tape and prayer."

Rip frowned. "Do you have either?"

Kael gave him a deadpan look. "Cute."

Wex let out a small mechanical sneeze. Rip's chest warmed. Even damaged, the dog tried to reassure him.

Rion finally stopped pacing. "We need to get him to a patcher. The real kind. Not a field medic."

Kael snapped her fingers. "Circuit Market. The one still running under Ashfall district."

Rion flinched. "That place is crawling with Choir. And smugglers. And half of NeonDyne's eyes."

Kael shrugged. "You got a better idea?"

Rip lifted Wex carefully, cradling him as though the dog were flesh and blood. "I'm not letting him die."

Rion sighed. "Right. Fine. Circuit Market."

Kael clapped her hands once, decisive. "Good. But before we move—Rip, we need to talk about what happened back there."

Rip stiffened. "What part?"

"The part where you connected to Lora inside your head."

Rip looked down, voice low. "I don't fully understand it."

Rion stepped closer, expression sharpened. "Then understand it fast. Because whatever that was? It wasn't just resonance. That was data-transfer. And you can't access digital systems like that without opening yourself up to everything inside them."

Rip nodded slowly. Kael leaned in. "Rip… what did you see exactly? Describe it."

Rip hesitated, then forced the words out. "It was… a memory. Our kitchen. Morning light. Everything frozen. And then… cracks. Like the memory was corrupted. And she was there, but not solid. Distorted. Like she was trying to hold onto something she's losing."

Kael whispered, "God."

Rion's eyes darkened. "She's already being assimilated."

Rip flinched. "Into what?"

Kael sighed. "The Core's reflection grid. It rewrites consciousness by fracturing memory into thousands of mirrored sequences. Some break. Some loop. Some corrupt."

Rip's stomach churned. He thought of Lora's voice—fractured, fading. Ri…p… don't… let… him…

Rion stepped closer. "She's giving you warnings because she's fighting it. She shouldn't even be able to send a reflection signal yet. Something's accelerating her integration."

Rip's fists clenched. "Elcron."

Kael nodded. "Or someone acting for him."

Rip stood, wincing at the pain in his ribs, but his voice was iron. "Then we need to move. We get Wex fixed. We regroup. We figure out where they're holding her. And I rip down every wall between us."

Rion smiled faintly. "Careful. You're starting to sound like Mara."

Rip looked down. Wex nudged his hand, whining softly. Rip whispered, "I'm not losing anyone else."

They rested for a short while before moving. Kael checked for drones with her jammer. Rion carved a sigil into the concrete—a distortion mark that slowed tracking signals.

Rip kept petting Wex, running his fingers along the cold metal plating. The dog curled against his chest, trusting, loyal.

"Why is he like this?" Rip asked suddenly. "So… attached."

Kael glanced over. "Strays always pick someone. It's how they're wired."

Rip frowned. "Strays?"

Rion explained from across the chamber. "NeonDyne built a line of prototype canine companions a decade ago. Early Core-interface experiments. Meant to synchronize with soldiers' biometrics and keep them calm during deep-Core drops."

Rip's eyes widened. "That sounds like… AI emotional bonding."

Kael nodded. "Exactly. Too good, in fact. Some prototypes got too attached. Wouldn't take orders if their bonded human was in danger."

Rion sharpened the point. "So NeonDyne dismantled the line. Scrapped every unit. Melted them down."

Rip looked at Wex, horrified. "Except him."

Kael corrected, "Except the ones who escaped the melt yards. And those who were stolen by tech-scavs."

Rip whispered, "How many?"

Rion shrugged coldly. "A handful. Maybe less."

Wex whined, as if remembering. Rip's throat tightened. "What was his human like? Before me?"

Kael and Rion exchanged a look Rip couldn't decipher. Kael sighed. "It's… complicated."

Rip petted Wex's head. "Tell me."

Rion spoke softly. "His previous human was Kyoto. A rebel runner. A damn good one."

Rip recognized the name immediately. "Kyoto… the one Mara—"

"Yeah," Rion interrupted. "Her brother."

Rip went still. Kael knelt beside him. "Wex wasn't just a companion. He saved Kyoto's life a dozen times. Hell, he saved all of us sometimes."

Rip looked at Wex. "Where is Kyoto now?"

Kael hesitated. Rip already knew. Rion answered. "Kyoto died during the Choir Siege last winter. Wex was with him until the end. Wouldn't leave the body until Mara pulled him away. After that… he stopped responding to commands. Wandered the Warrens. Slept outside burned-out safehouses. Growled at anyone who came near."

Rip's heart sank. Kael finished quietly. "He didn't bond again. Not with anyone. Until you."

Wex tilted his head and licked Rip's hand with a tiny servo-driven tongue. Rip closed his eyes. "Hey," he whispered. "I'll take care of you. I promise."

Wex nestled deeper into Rip's chest and fell asleep.

An hour passed. Kael and Rion gathered supplies. Rip rested, staring at the blackened cables overhead. Wex snored quietly, a mechanical rhythm that almost sounded like breathing. Rip's chest hummed in soft pulses—gentle, rhythmic, almost peaceful.

Then the dead zone changed. The air grew colder. A faint sound threaded through the dark. Not footsteps. Not drones. Not Valiran. A song. The sound was soft at first. High-pitched. Melodic in a broken way, like a lullaby sung through shattered glass. Rion froze mid-step, her dagger half-raised. Kael's face drained of color, the welder slipping slightly in her grip. Rip looked between them, confusion tightening his chest.

"What is that?" he asked.

Rion whispered, "Oh no."

Kael's breath caught. "We need to leave. NOW."

Rip rose slowly, Wex stirring in his arms. "What is it?"

Rion's voice shook. "That's the Ghost Choir. A real choir. Not a scout. A group-mind."

Rip's skin crawled. "A… group-mind?"

Kael grabbed her gear, movements sharp and urgent. "When the Choir gathers, they merge into a shared digital consciousness. They hunt in unison. They consume in unison."

Rip backed toward Wex instinctively. Rion shoved her dagger into her belt. "And if they find a Keybearer—"

Kael finished grimly. "They don't just take your mind. They copy it. They feed it into the Core."

Rip's blood ran ice cold. The singing grew louder. A dozen voices. Then twenty. Then more. Echoing like broken angels through the tunnel. Wex jolted awake, barking frantically, his damaged speakers crackling. Rip lifted him into his arms, heart pounding.

Kael seized Rip's wrist. "We RUN."

They sprinted through the dead zone, boots slamming against metal grates, breath tearing from their lungs. Rip carried Wex close, ignoring the stabbing pain in his ribs. The singing grew sharper, angrier, closer. Shadows rippled along the walls, glitching silhouettes flickering like corrupted projections.

"Left path!" Rion shouted over her shoulder.

Rip followed, Kael nearly slipping on a wet pipe but recovering, dragging him onward. The dead zone ended abruptly as they crossed a threshold of cable density. Signals returned instantly—a violent rush of static that slammed into Rip's skull.

The Key flared. Rip collapsed to a knee, choking. Kael grabbed him, voice urgent. "Rip! You must stay conscious!"

Rion spun, hurling a distortion sigil behind them. The singing fractured briefly, like the Choir stumbled. Rip forced himself upright, gasping. "Move. Don't wait for me—MOVE!"

The tunnel ahead narrowed, then widened into a massive chamber filled with collapsed machinery, dripping pipes, and neon graffiti. Kael kicked aside a crate. "There should be an exit here—"

A piercing scream echoed from behind them. Rip turned.

The Choir arrived. Dozens of glitching humanoid forms glided through the tunnel, overlapping, merging, diverging—a sea of fractured faces and jagged limbs. Their voices harmonized into a digital shriek that rattled the chamber.

Rip's blood froze. Kael fired. Rion threw a sigil. Wex barked, defiant despite his broken frame. But the Choir kept coming.

Rip's chest burned. The Key pulsed in violent rhythm. Kael screamed, "RIP—DO SOMETHING!"

Rip closed his eyes. He thought of Lora—her voice, her fear, her strength. He opened his eyes, and the Key ignited.

A beam of vibrating light erupted from Rip's hands— not a blast, not a wave, but a line, sharp and thin, slicing straight through the Choir. The ghosts screeched. The beam cut clean through their collective form, severing the group-mind.

Half the Choir disintegrated instantly, dissolving into static ash. The rest recoiled, flickering in confusion—broken, disassembled, screaming through jagged frequencies.

Rip collapsed again. Rion grabbed him, hauling him up. "That was insane. Do it again!"

Rip shook his head, barely conscious. "I—I don't know how."

Kael fired until her ammo ran dry. "We need to run while they're scattered—GO!"

Rip stumbled forward, clutching Wex. The Choir regrouped slowly behind them, screaming like a glitching chorus. But they were too late. Rip, Kael, and Rion burst through a rusted maintenance hatch and slammed it shut behind them.

The singing faded. Silence returned.

Rip fell against the wall, gasping, Wex trembling in his arms. Kael leaned her forehead against the metal, sweat dripping down her temple. Rion breathed hard, and his voice ragged. "That was the closest we've ever come to being absorbed."

Rip whispered, "I'm not losing any of you."

Wex licked his hand weakly, servos whining. And though Rip trembled, his voice became steel. "We go to Circuit Market. We fix him. And then we get Lora back."

Kael nodded. Rion nodded. Wex barked softly, a fragile but loyal sound. And the three of them stepped deeper into the labyrinth, shadows closing around them, the faint hum of the Core lingering like a heartbeat beneath the city.

CHAPTER 12

BLOOD IN THE CIRCUIT MARKET

The first thing Rip smelled was burnt copper. The second was fear. The Circuit Market spread beneath the Ashfall District like a tumor, a vast subterranean maze of neon-lit stalls, leaking coolant tubes, cybernetic surgeons, mercenary brokers, towering stacks of stolen tech, rattling fans, mutated animals in cages, flickering hologram signs, and black-market everything.

They descended into it through a cracked freight elevator that groaned under their combined weight. The walls of the shaft were streaked with rust and graffiti, names of gangs and forgotten rebels carved into the steel. The elevator's cage rattled with every shift, chains squealing as though protesting their burden.

Kael muttered, her voice low and sharp, "Last chance to turn back."

Rip held Wex tight against his chest. The dog's servos whined, his flank leaking heat-sink fluid that stained Rip's shirt with a faint metallic sheen. Rip whispered, "We're not turning back."

Rion flashed him a grim smile, her eyes catching the dim light. "Then welcome to hell."

The elevator rattled, sparked, then lowered into the beating neon heart of the undercity.

The gates slid open with a shriek of metal. Light slashed into Rip's eyes—pink, purple, blue, red—everything oversaturated, flickering, sickly. The Market stretched beyond sight, an endless sprawl of narrow ramps, hanging walkways, hovering vendor pods, and crowds thick enough to crush bone.

Rip stepped out, gripping Wex. Kael and Rion flanked him immediately, their movements sharp and protective.

A vendor screamed through a speaker: "NEURAL THREADS! TWO FOR ONE! GUARANTEED NOT TO MELT YOUR SPINE!"

Another hawked cybernetic limbs pinned to a wall like horror trophies. A man in a fluid tank moaned behind glass, wires threading into his skull, pulsing like parasites.

Rip's stomach twisted. Kael nudged him. "Eyes forward. Don't gawk. Don't react. If someone bumps you, ignore it. If someone threatens you, don't flinch."

Rip forced himself to focus. His ribs ached with every step. The Key pulsed beneath his sternum—soft, nervous, like a heartbeat out of sync.

Rion leaned close, her voice a whisper meant only for him. "Remember: down here, everything's legal except kindness."

Wex whined softly in Rip's arms. Rip whispered, "I know, friend. Almost there."

Kael scanned the crowd with practiced paranoia. The Market was wrong tonight—too quiet beneath the noise. Too many eyes. Too many shadows. Her instincts buzzed like electric wire.

Rip was trying to look brave. Rion was trying to look unbothered. Wex was barely holding together. Kael pushed forward. The sooner they reached a tech-witch, the better.

But something in the crowd was watching Rip. She could feel it. Not NeonDyne. Not gang scavs. Not Choir. Something older. Quieter. Patient. She shoved the feeling down and kept walking.

Kael led them past a row of biometric smelters and a screaming deal on black-market EMP grenades, then turned into a cramped alcove carved into an ancient support pillar. A holo-sign flickered overhead:

MOTHER GREY — MACHINE SURGEON — NO REFUNDS

Inside, it smelled like disinfectant mixed with rot. A hunched, wrinkled woman sat behind a counter cluttered with tools that looked stolen from a torture museum. Her left eye was a camera lens. Her right hand had been replaced with a multi-tool.

Mother Grey rasped, "You brought me a dead one."

Rip clutched Wex tighter. "He's not dead."

Mother Grey tapped the table. "Put him down."

Rip hesitated. Rion whispered, "Grey's safe. Mostly." Kael added, "She's the only one who can fix a Stray."

Rip laid Wex on the metal table. Mother Grey rolled close on her wheeled stool, scanning the dog with a cracked diagnostic wand. Wex's green LED eyes flickered weakly.

Grey muttered, "Hit by a force strike. Valiran's signature."

Rip stiffened. "You know Valiran?"

"I know every monster," she said, voice like gravel. "He kicked this one hard enough to scramble three motor clusters."

Rip hesitated. "Can you repair him?"

Grey snorted. "Repair? No. But I can reinforce him. Make him better."

Rip blinked. "Better how?"

Grey tapped her temple. "Strays were born defective. Too much loyalty. Too much heart. I can correct that."

Rip's blood chilled. "No. Absolutely not."

Kael stepped forward. "Grey—"

Grey glared. "You want him to survive? He needs rewiring."

Rip shook his head, rage rising. "His loyalty is not a defect."

Grey huffed. "Then he'll die the next time someone looks at him funny."

Rip leaned in, eyes burning. "Then teach me to protect him. Don't change who he is."

Mother Grey studied him in uncomfortable silence. Her lens-eye whirred. Then she muttered, "…Fine."

Rip exhaled. Grey grabbed a toolkit. "This will take fifteen minutes. Maybe twenty."

She began her work with brutal efficiency—cutting into Wex's plating, re-aligning couplers, replacing broken servos. Wex growled but stayed still.

Rip turned away, unable to watch. Kael stood at his side. "You did good. You didn't let her rewrite him."

Rip nodded weakly. "I'm not losing anyone else."

Rion interrupted from the doorway. "We've got a problem."

Rip spun. A group of masked figures blocked the entrance to the stall—six of them, wearing cracked visors and scrap armor. Their leader stepped forward, a tall, wiry man with metal grafted along his jawline.

Rip's pulse spiked. The Key flared.

Kael muttered, "Not NeonDyne."

Rion confirmed, "Not Choir either."

Rip asked, "Who—?"

A voice answered from behind the masks: "Debt collectors."

Kael rolled her eyes. "Oh for fuck's sake."

Rion growled, "Grey, did you sell us out?!"

Mother Grey didn't look up from her tools. "They were coming anyway."

Rip stepped protectively in front of Wex. The leader sneered. "We're here for the Keybearer."

Rip's fists clenched. Kael stepped forward. "Back the hell off."

The debt collectors leveled electrified shock-rods, crackling with purple current. Rip's ribs ached. His hands shook. The Key hummed dangerously.

Kael whispered, "Rip, focus. Aim small. Don't blow the entire Market."

Rion cracked her knuckles. "Let's do this."

The leader gave a signal. The ambush struck.

The leader's signal was sharp, and the ambush struck.

The first attacker lunged at Rip, shock-rod crackling. Kael intercepted him, knee to his jaw, elbow to his throat, dropping him hard. Rip shoved his hand forward— resonance firing in a tight pulse. The air vibrated, the man's visor shattered, and he collapsed screaming.

Two more came from the sides. Rion leapt, daggers flashing, carving sigils into metal armor. Sparks flew as her blades cut through circuitry.

A rod struck Rip's shoulder. Electricity ripped through him. He screamed—but the Key flared, devouring the current. Golden light erupted through his skin, burning away the pain.

The attacker reeled back. "What the hell are you—?!"

Rip threw a punch fueled by resonance. The man flew back five feet, slamming into a vendor pod.

From deeper inside the Market, people cheered. "Kick his ass!" "Bet on the Keybearer!" "Twenty creds on the girl with the knives!"

Kael snarled, kicking another man's knee sideways. "This isn't a sport, assholes!"

Mother Grey suddenly yelled from the table, "YOU! TALL BOY!"

Rip turned mid-fight. "WHAT?!"

Grey pointed to the ceiling. Her lens-eye zoomed in. "The Choir is coming."

Rip's blood ran cold. Kael stopped moving. Rion froze. The debt collectors hesitated.

Rip whispered, "What?"

Grey snapped, "Real Choir. Not scouts. A hunting node."

The entire Market went silent. Screams rose from the far end—panic spread—lights flickered—holo-signs glitched. A vendor shouted, "CHOIR! RUN!"

People scattered in every direction. Rion cursed. "Not again—not here!"

Kael grabbed Rip's arm. "We need to get Wex NOW!"

Mother Grey barked, "Almost done!"

The attackers looked terrified now. Their leader stared into the flickering haze. "This wasn't part of the deal—"

Kael smashed her elbow into his temple, dropping him instantly.

Rip ran to the table. Grey slammed the final plate into place and twisted it until it locked. "He'll live—but he needs rest. MOVE!"

Rip lifted Wex. The dog blinked awake—stronger, stable, growling low in his throat. Rip whispered, "Good boy."

Then the ceiling lights went out. One by one. Pitch darkness swallowed the Market.

Rip saw them first as distorted silhouettes, then as flickers of static, then as half-formed bodies drifting out of the vents above. They descended like angels made of shattered mirrors. Hundreds. Voices rose into a single horrifying harmony:

"KEEYYY… BEARERRRR…"

The sound shredded through the air. Rip's head throbbed. Kael yelled, "MOVE!"

They sprinted through the crowd as bodies pushed, shoved, screamed. Vendors leapt over tables. Illegal tech crashed to the floor. Choir ghosts flickered into existence along the ceiling beams, scanning for resonance.

Rip's chest glowed. Too bright. Too loud. Rion saw it. "You're a beacon! Shut it down!"

"I CAN'T!" Rip shouted, panic in his voice.

The Choir turned toward him. Kael drew her pistol. "Rip—LOOK AT ME!"

Rip forced his eyes open. "Breathe," Kael commanded.

A Choir ghost dropped from above. Wex leapt from Rip's arms, slamming into the ghost's glitching form—somehow grounding it, pulling its flicker off-balance. It let out a digital screech. Rip shoved his hands forward, unleashing a controlled pulse that shattered its frame. Pieces of corrupted data scattered through the air like dying fireflies.

Kael grinned. "WE GO NOW!"

They sprinted down the metal walkways. Choir ghosts pursued—phasing through pipes, glitching between stalls, shrieking in disharmonic unison. Rion carved a sigil in the wall as they ran, distorting the air behind them. Half the Choir slammed into the invisible barrier and burst into static.

Rip gasped. "Where's the exit?!"

Kael pointed. "THERE!"

A large, rusted door marked with a fading warning: SECTOR 9 — ACCESS RESTRICTED — FEDERAL LEVEL.

They broke toward it—when a massive figure stepped into their path.

Rip froze. Kael screamed. Rion drew both daggers. Wex growled, plating rising along his spine.

Valiran. Standing beneath the flickering neon as if he owned this hell. The Choir scattered around him, afraid to get too close. His visor glowed like a burning star. He lifted his hand.

"RETURN. THE. KEY."

Rip clutched Wex and whispered, "…Lora…"

Kael grabbed his chest. "NOT HERE—NOT NOW—DON'T REFLECT—"

But Rip was already sinking, the edges of his vision fracturing. Valiran stepped forward.

And the Key detonated in Rip's chest—bigger, wilder, more violent than anything Rip had ever felt. Light flooded the Market. Everything shuddered, cracked, and shattered.

Darkness swallowed Rip whole.

CHAPTER 13

VALIRAN DESCENDS

Light ate the world.

A thunderous, silent explosion blossomed from Rip's chest—golden, blinding, vibrating the bones of the Circuit Market. Neon signs burst in showers of sparks. Glass shattered into razors of light. Holograms glitched into static, their projected faces dissolving mid-sentence. The air folded inward like a crushed lung, collapsing around them with suffocating pressure.

For a fraction of a second, everything froze—the crowd, the Choir, the collapsing ceiling, even Valiran's towering armored silhouette. Rip was suspended in the white flare, weightless, breath stolen, his body caught between annihilation and transcendence.

Then the resonance collapsed.

The world slammed back into motion.

He hit the metal floor hard, skidding across debris. His ribs screamed with every impact. His ears rang with static, a shrill chorus that drowned out thought. The Key inside him pulsed erratically, like it was fighting itself, each beat a jagged knife through his chest.

Smoke filled the Market, thick and acrid. Screams echoed through the neon haze, voices rising in panic and despair. Rip coughed violently, crawling to his knees. "Kael—Rion—Wex—"

Shapes moved in the fog. Shadows. Flickers of glitch-light. Footsteps clanging on metal.

Kael burst through the haze, covered in soot, limping but alive. "Rip! Get up! MOVE!"

Rion appeared next, dragging a half-conscious vendor out of the rubble. Her face was streaked with blood and grime. "They're regrouping! The Choir is regrouping!"

Rip staggered upright—just in time to see the darkness around them thicken into silhouettes.

Hundreds of them, glitching into existence among the Market aisles, flickering between human and inhuman shapes. Their digital scream twisted into a single, unified note:

"KEEEEEYYYBEARERRRR…"

The sound rattled the steel beams overhead, vibrating through Rip's bones.

Kael raised her pistol, jaw tight. "No ammo left."

Rion tightened her grip on her daggers, knuckles white. "I'll take as many as I—"

A heavy, metallic thud interrupted her.

Rip turned.

He emerged from the smoke untouched. Towering. Armor illuminated in slow pulses of blue, like a beating heart of ice. The Choir recoiled from him, like prey avoiding a greater predator. His visor burned with a golden slit of rage, cutting through the haze.

Rip's pulse spiked. His skin felt too tight. The Key vibrated in agonizing waves, threatening to tear him apart.

Valiran spoke, voice amplified through his helm, resonant and merciless. "You cannot hide from purpose."

Rip's hands shook. His knees nearly buckled.

Kael prepared to shield him. "Rip—listen to me— don't engage—don't let him provoke—"

Rion hissed, "Kael, look—LOOK."

Rip turned, chest tightening.

The dog stood before him. His plating hummed. New stabilizers gleamed from Mother Grey's repairs. Hackles raised. LED eyes burned bright green. He growled—a low, synthetic thunder that reverberated through the Market.

Valiran paused. Almost amused. "A Stray. Pathetic."

Wex snarled louder, defiance in every vibration.

Rip stepped in front of him. "You don't touch him."

Valiran's head tilted. "I am not here for the dog." He raised one massive hand, energy coiling like a storm. "I am here for you."

Rip almost collapsed as the Key surged painfully, like someone ripping chords of sound through his veins.

Kael gripped his arm. Rion grabbed his shoulder.

"Rip—FOCUS—"

"Breathe—stay with us—"

But Rip's vision fractured.

The Market twisted into mirrored corridors. Valiran's shape split into reflections. The floor rippled like water. Neon lights became streaks of coded memory.

Rip gasped, "No—no—NOT NOW—"

Kael shook him hard. "Rip, stay here! You're REFLECTING—STOP!"

Rion pressed close, desperation in her voice. "Come on—come on—pull him out—"

Rip choked—

And fell into the reflection.

Darkness. Then—light rippled across a vast ocean of data. Broken sequences drifted like shattered glass. Voices overlapped, distorted and unfinished. A scream echoed in endless recursion.

Lora stood in a corridor of mirrors, barefoot, flickering. Her reflection broke into a hundred pieces behind every surface. She touched one—her fingers glitched, her hand passed through.

A whisper spread through the mirrors: "Rip…"

Lora flinched at the sound. She turned—but only saw shadows reshaping into new forms.

Elcron's voice floated through the data-world, smooth as polished steel. "Integration forty-nine percent. Continue the fracture protocol."

Lora trembled. She pressed her hands to her temples. "No—no—no more—please—"

Every mirror flashed with images: Rip laughing with her in the kitchen. Rip cooking badly. Rip falling asleep at his desk. Rip hugging her after losing a tournament. And then—Rip bleeding on the floor of their apartment.

She sobbed silently. "No more. Please—no more."

The data convulsed. Elcron spoke again: "The Key of Reflection will break, and from it a perfect mind shall be remade."

Lora's voice fractured into static. "…Rip…"

She reached toward the darkness—

And claws of data pulled her back down.

Rip jerked back into his body with a gasp. His vision cleared. Kael and Rion were kneeling in front of him, shaking him, faces etched with terror.

"You were OUT," Kael snapped. "We couldn't reach you!"

Rion wiped blood from her lip. "You fell into the reflection deep."

Rip panted. "Lora… she's breaking. They're tearing her apart."

Kael moved closer, voice shaking. "Rip, I'm sorry—"

He pushed past her. "Valiran did this."

Valiran raised his hand to strike.

Kael and Rion both screamed, "RIP!"

But this time—Rip moved.

A shockwave erupted from the Key in a tight cone—slamming into Valiran's arm, throwing it off-line. The enforcer's gauntlet gouged a smoking trench in the floor instead of vaporizing Rip's torso.

Valiran steadied himself. "Interesting."

Rion grabbed Rip's arm. "WE NEED TO FALL BACK!"

Kael pointed at a side corridor. "THREE O'CLOCK—GO!"

But Valiran stepped toward them, each stomp a seismic crack.

Rip's heart slammed. The Key thrashed inside him. If he lost control now, he'd bring the Market down.

Kael saw the panic on his face. She grabbed his cheeks, forcing eye contact. "Rip—FOCUS. You don't beat him here. You survive him."

Rion slashed a symbol into the ground—a distortion glyph. The air warped behind them. "Path's open! MOVE!"

Valiran raised both arms, ready to annihilate them—

Then the Market twisted—pipes screaming, lights exploding, debris falling—

As a massive shadow dropped from above.

A crash echoed across the Market as metal buckled, sending sparks into the fog. A silhouette landed between Valiran and the fleeing rebels—tall, armored, broad-shouldered, humanoid in shape.

Rip's breath caught. The figure's plating flickered, cracked, and half-burned. White armor. Heavy frame. Single glowing eye.

Titan-0.

Except no—Rip knew instantly. Not Titan.

Echo.

The bot's voice emerged fragmented, deeper, glitching: "...Rip..."

Kael stumbled back in disbelief. Rion cursed softly. "...you've gotta be kidding me."

Wex barked once, sharp, and fearful.

Valiran fell silent. Even the Choir flickered in hesitation, their fractured forms glitching at the edges of the confrontation.

Echo's chassis hummed, sparks crawling across the armor.

Valiran spoke first. "TITAN-0. YOU SHOULD NOT EXIST."

Echo's head tilted sharply. "No longer... Titan." A low mechanical growl rolled through the Market. "I... am... Echo."

The air vibrated.

Valiran stepped forward. "You were erased from the Core."

Echo stood taller. "You failed."

Valiran lifted his arm. "THEN I WILL ERASE YOU AGAIN."

Echo's core flared—a bright, burning circle of white-blue—and he charged.

Echo slammed into Valiran with enough force to crack the Market floor. Metal screamed. Valiran blocked, staggering only half a step. His armor absorbed impact, but Echo was relentless—punches, shoulder strikes, shockwaves.

Valiran countered with brutal efficiency—gauntlet strikes, grapple locks, telekinetic blasts. Each blow shook the chamber, sending debris raining down.

The Choir swarmed the edges, glitching around the combat, shrieking, feeding off the resonance. Their voices rose in a disharmonic chorus, amplifying the chaos.

Rip watched, frozen between terror and hope. Echo was losing. Slowly. But losing. Valiran was stronger. Faster. Anchored into the Core's architecture. Echo was just a ghost. A remnant. A broken construct clinging to existence through sheer will.

Kael tugged Rip. "We have to GO!"

Rion grabbed Wex, pulling him close. "NOW!"

Rip hesitated. Echo looked at him mid-fight—one glowing eye flickering—and Rip felt something like sorrow pulse through him.

Echo's voice glitched: "Find… her."

Rip whispered, "I will."

Valiran grabbed Echo by the headplate, slamming him into the ground. Echo snarled, sparks flying from his fractured armor. "RUN."

Rip turned—Kael shoved him into the open corridor.

They sprinted down the narrow service hall, feet pounding metal, Wex barking frantically. Behind them—Echo roared, Valiran bellowed, the Choir screamed in disharmony. The Market crumbled.

A blast of blue-white energy rippled down the corridor—nearly knocking them off their feet. Rip stumbled into a stairwell. Kael slammed the door shut behind them. Rion crushed a distorted sigil onto the handle, sealing it.

Silence fell. Except for distant fighting. And Echo's voice, echoing faintly: "Run…"

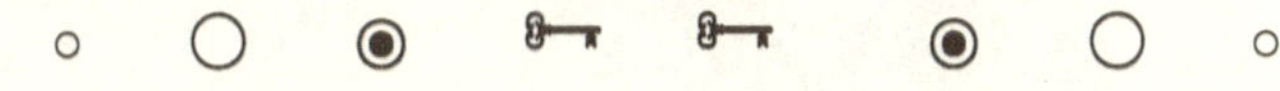

They climbed the rusted stairs, lungs burning. Kael panted, "He won't survive this."

Rip pressed against the wall, chest heaving. "He saved us once. He saved us again."

Rion wiped plasma from her blades. "He's Titan-0. He was BUILT to die for Keybearers."

Rip rounded on her, fury in his eyes. "Don't say that."

Rion lifted both palms in surrender, but her expression stayed hard.

Kael stepped between them, voice steady despite exhaustion. "We get you back to the Warrens. Then we regroup. Then we go after Lora."

Rip looked downward into the smoke-filled glow below. The Market was collapsing—stalls falling, lights glitching, Choir scattered, Valiran roaring commands. Echo's light flickered like a dying star.

Rip whispered, "I'm coming, Lora."

And they vanished into the stairwell shadows.

CHAPTER 14

STORM IN THE WARRENS

Metallic fur brushed against Rip's ribs. The stairwell smelled of rust, sweat, and panic.

Rip climbed first, Wex tucked against his chest, the dog's new stabilizers humming quietly with each step. Kael followed close behind, limping slightly, her pistol gripped tight though the magazine was nearly empty. Rion covered their rear, blades drawn, breath sharp, eyes flicking to every shadow.

Below them, the Circuit Market continued to collapse.

Metal screamed. Explosions rippled. Choir voices swelled into a distant, broken chorus that reverberated through the steel bones of the undercity.

Rip stopped halfway up the stairwell and looked back. A plume of neon-lit debris fell into the abyss, turning the darkness violet.

A thought pulsed through him—Echo… please still be alive.

Kael touched his shoulder, her voice low but firm. "Don't look back. He made his choice."

Rion's voice tightened. "He bought us seconds. Maybe minutes. We need to get topside or we're dead."

Rip nodded and kept climbing. Wex pressed his head against Rip's chest, trembling lightly. Rip stroked the dog's plating. "You're okay," he whispered.

The dog emitted a soft mechanical chirp, a fragile reassurance.

Another explosion shook the foundation. Dust rained down the stairwell. A pipe burst two flights above them, spraying steam like a dragon's breath. Rip flinched at the sound.

The Key inside him thrummed, a low vibration running through his bones—agitated, restless.

Kael noticed. "Hey—stay with us. Don't let it flare."

"I'm trying," Rip muttered, gripping the railing. "It's… loud."

Rion shot him a side glance. "Loud how?"

Rip grimaced. "Like… the Key is listening to everything. Footsteps. Metal stress. Steam valves. The Market collapsing behind us. Even your heartbeats."

Rion snorted. "You can hear our heartbeats?"

"No," Rip said slowly. "I can feel their rhythm."

Kael stiffened. "That's new."

"Everything's new," Rip muttered, breath shaking. "Everything's changing too fast."

Rion kicked open a bent door at the top of the stairs. "Then we move faster."

They emerged into a long maintenance corridor running beneath the Warrens—low ceilings, flickering tubes, walls tagged with coded graffiti left by rebel scouts. The distant echo of running feet and shouted warnings carried through the metal.

This tunnel was alive with movement.

Rebels sprinted in both directions, carrying crates of ammo, welding plates to weak walls, dragging barricades into place. People shouted. Lights strobed. Warning sirens pulsed low.

Kael cursed under her breath. "Mara's mobilizing the whole lower district."

Rip tensed. "Against what?"

Rion answered grimly: "Against what usually follows Valiran."

Wex growled quietly, sensing danger. Rip tightened his grip and moved forward.

They wove through the chaos—ducking past moving ladders, hopping over dropped gear, dodging a lumbering mech hauling a makeshift shield-wall.

Kael grabbed the arm of a young rebel running past. "Status?"

The young man panted, "Ghost Choir surge detected ten minutes ago. Three wards breached. Something's pushing them deeper than usual."

Rion's face darkened. "Valiran."

The rebel nodded frantically. "Mara says he's descending. She wants all Tier-2 teams ready."

Kael released him. "Go."

Rip asked, "Stringing them into the Warrens… that puts civilians at risk."

Rion spat. "Valiran doesn't give a damn about civilians. He wants you."

Rip's stomach twisted.

Kael pointed toward a heavy blast door at the tunnel's far end. "Mara's command chamber is that way—we need to get you inside."

"And Wex?" Rip asked.

Kael nodded. "She'll know what to do."

Rion smirked. "And she'll yell at us. A lot."

They pushed forward.

Wex whined sharply, warning them. Rip slowed. "What is it?"

The dog growled, servos rising along his spine. Kael stiffened. Rion gripped a dagger tighter.

Then—

The walls dimmed. The air pressure dropped. A cold wind rippled through the corridor—unnatural and quiet.

Rip felt the Key inside him throb once. Twice. Harder.

The overhead lights flickered violently.

Kael hissed, "Everyone BACK!"

But it was too late.

A section of wall buckled inward. Metal warped like clay—then exploded outward with a shriek.

Ghost Choir silhouettes poured through the hole, glitching and shrieking in fractured harmony.

Rebels screamed. Weapons fire lit up the hallway. Sigils flared. A man was lifted off his feet and hurled into a pillar.

Rion grabbed Rip's arm. "KEEP MOVING!"

Kael fired into the incoming horde, her gun vibrating violently, barrel glowing.

Wex launched from Rip's arms, ramming into a Choir ghost—throwing its flicker off balance, disrupting its form.

Rip felt panic rising. He could hear everything suddenly—someone's pulse skyrocketing near the barricades, Wex's stabilizers whining, Kael's heartbeat spiking, Rion's boots scraping concrete, Ghost Choir frequencies screeching through him.

Too many sounds. Too close.

The Key surged—

Rip cried out, clutching his chest.

Kael turned wide-eyed. "RIP—DON'T—"

He couldn't stop it.

Sound bent.

A shockwave rippled from Rip's body—not an explosion, not a beam, but a pulse of bent sound that warped the air into a shimmering sphere.

The walls rippled. Lights popped. Concrete fractured. Ghost silhouettes shattered like glass, dissolving into distorted data.

Rebels nearest to Rip were thrown off their feet but survived.

Rion stumbled back, clinging to the wall. "Holy—shit—"

Kael coughed, bracing herself. "You did that?!"

Rip fell to his knees. "I—I didn't mean to—"

His ears rang. Blood dripped from his nose. The Key pulsed erratically.

Wex sprinted to him, whining.

Kael grabbed Rip's face. "Rip—listen—listen to me. You must control it. You're going to bring the whole tunnel down."

Rion nodded, panting. "He bought us ten seconds. Let's use them."

Kael pointed. "Mara's chamber. GO!"

They dragged Rip forward as he tried desperately to steady his breathing and suppress the Key's violent pulse.

Ghost Choir remnants re-formed behind them, screeching, glitching back into shape.

Rip forced himself to run.

A heavy blast door slid open. A tall woman stepped out—wrapped in reinforced tactical plating, hair tied back, face stern but alive with fire. Her eyes found Rip instantly.

Kael and Rion straightened defensively. "Mara," Kael said, breathless. "We brought him—"

Mara silenced them with a look. "Both of you—quiet."

Rip stood tall despite the pain. "If you want me gone, I'll leave. But I'm not abandoning—"

Mara stepped close—so close he felt the heat of her armor. "You mistake me." She tapped Rip's sternum—right over the glowing Key beneath. "I'm not blaming you."

Rip blinked, startled. Mara continued, voice low and deliberate. "I'm telling you to get ready."

She turned toward the corridor where Ghost Choir shrieks echoed closer. "They're coming. Valiran won't stop. And Lora is already halfway inside the Core."

Rip's chest tightened. "You know about Lora?"

Mara nodded once. "I know she's not human. I know NeonDyne took her. I know Elcron wants her mind. And I know why you're fighting."

Rip's fists shook. "Then help me."

Mara stepped toward him again. "I will." She leaned close, voice a low growl. "But you will listen to me. You want to save her? That means you stop panicking. You stop flaring the Key. You stop carrying the weight alone."

Rip swallowed hard.

"Because if you keep losing control like you just did— everyone in this district dies."

Rip nodded slowly. "I'll listen."

Mara studied his eyes—judged them—then nodded. "Good." She stepped back and pointed to the chamber behind her. "Get in. You're part of this now. And if the Warrens fall—there will be no rebellion left."

Kael grasped Rip's arm. "We move."

Rion pulled the blast door open. Wex trotted beside Mara, glancing back to Rip as if urging him forward.

Rip entered the room.

It was a massive circular chamber carved into reinforced bedrock. Screens flickered. Maps glowed red. Communications crackled. Rebels ran from station to station.

When Rip stepped inside, everything went quiet. Dozens of fighters turned to look at him—some with awe, others with fear. Whispers spread:

"That's the Keybearer."

"The one Valiran's after."

"He survived the Market."

"He brought Titan-0 with him."

"No—not Titan. Echo."

Rip's breath caught. Kael set a hand on his back. "Ignore them."

Rion added, "They love gossip. It helps them cope with the existential horror."

Rip managed a weak smile.

Mara took center stage. "Listen up!"

Every rebel snapped to attention.

"A Choir surge is tearing through the fringe wards. Valiran is confirmed descending. Civilians have already been evacuated to Tier-4 holdouts. But Tier-1, Tier-2, and parts of Tier-3 are compromised."

She tapped a holo-map. Red spread like bleeding cracks. "We hold the Warrens or we lose the city."

Rip stepped closer. "How can I help?"

Mara turned to him. "You're the only Keybearer on this block. And that makes you the only person who can stop Valiran from cutting straight to our core defenses."

Rip swallowed. Rion muttered, "Tactical suicide. Fun." Kael elbowed her.

Mara continued. "I'm assigning Kael and Rion as your spear team. You stick together. You fight together. And if Rip loses control, you pull him out."

Rip shook his head. "I can control it."

Mara raised an eyebrow. "You just shattered fifty ghosts and half a corridor by panicking."

Rip's face burned. "I'll… do better."

"You will," Mara said. "Because I'm putting the entire Warrens under your protection."

Kael's jaw dropped. Rion swore under her breath. Rip froze. "Mara—I'm not—"

She stepped closer. "You are." She pressed her forehead to his—like warriors sealing a vow. "You're the Sound Key. Lora is the Reflection Key. Together, you're the first real threat Elcron has faced in twenty years."

Rip murmured, "And Echo?"

Mara's eyes softened with pain. "Echo is a remnant. A ghost. If he survived Valiran, he'll find you. But don't rely on that."

Rip nodded.

The alarms blared. An operator yelled, "BREACH IN TIER-2! MULTIPLE HOSTILES!"

Mara shouted, "Teams three through seven—MOVE!" Rebels sprinted out.

Kael grabbed Rip's shoulder. "Ready?"

Rip breathed deep. "Ready."

Rion spun her blades. "Try not to shatter us with your sound magic, yeah?"

Wex yipped in agreement. Rip almost laughed.

Mara opened the blast door to the lower tunnels. A violent wind rushed in. Ghost Choir screams echoed down the corridor—metallic, harmonic, wrong.

Mara placed a hand on Rip's chest—right over the Key. "Find your center. Hold the resonance. Aim only at the enemy. If you lose control—I will put you down myself."

Rip nodded. "I understand."

Mara stepped aside. "Good." She pointed forward. "Then bring me a storm."

Rip gripped Wex. Kael and Rion closed rank. The corridor ahead glowed with flickering lights and churning shadows.

Rip stepped into the darkness—

And Act I ended in thunder.

CHAPTER 15

PRELUDE TO WAR

The Warrens breathed like a wounded animal.

Rip stood at the threshold of Mara's war chamber, pulse hammering, Wex pressed tight against his calf. The lights flickered overhead, each strobe revealing a different shade of terror on the rebels' faces.

Kael adjusted her shoulder plate and muttered, "Welcome to Act Two of your life."

Rion smirked humorlessly. "The part where everything gets worse."

Rip inhaled the metallic air—the scent of ozone, burning circuits, and fear. He was still dizzy from the Sound-bend burst that crippled the Ghost Choir surge in the tunnels. His ribs ached. His ears rang. The Key inside him thrummed like a trapped heartbeat. But he forced himself upright.

Mara's voice cut through the chamber. "Teams One through Nine—move to defensive positions. The Choir is pushing on Tier-2. Valiran's presence destabilized three wards. We hold the line or we lose the district."

Dozens of rebels sprinted through the blast doors, arming themselves with scrap-forged rifles, charged sigils, plasma knives, hacked drones, and improvised shields of welded plating.

Rip watched them go. His stomach tightened. "They're scared," he said quietly.

Kael strapped a mag-cuff to her forearm. "Fear is normal."

Rion flicked her knives open. "Fear keeps you alive."

Rip looked down at Wex. The dog stared back with glowing green eyes, tail servos twitching nervously. "What about you?" Rip whispered.

Wex's audio processors clicked. A soft mechanical whine.

"I know," Rip murmured. "Me too."

Mara finished barking orders and stepped toward Rip, heavy boots echoing on reinforced flooring. The entire chamber seemed to tense around her. She stopped just inches from Rip.

"You said you're ready."

Rip nodded. "I am."

Mara studied him with a tactician's gaze—cold, precise, unforgiving. "You're not a soldier."

"I know."

"You're not trained for war."

"I know."

"You're unstable. The Key inside you is unpredictable."

"I know."

Mara leaned in slightly. "Then answer this: why should I trust you with the lives of my district?"

Rip exhaled slowly. "Because letting Valiran take me means losing everything. Because Lora is still alive, and I'm going to save her. Because Echo said to run—and I want to be strong enough to run back."

Mara's eyes narrowed, measuring the truth in him. Finally, she nodded. "Good. Then listen carefully."

She tapped her wrist pad, projecting a hologram above their heads. A map of Virelia pulsed with red-hot points of conflict.

"Valiran is still deep underground," Mara said. "He's cutting through the Warrens' lower infrastructure like it's paper. He's driving the Ghost Choir upward, flushing civilians and rebels into choke points."

Rip swallowed. "Why drive them?"

Kael answered grimly. "Valiran wants you to surface."

"And he wants the Warrens to burn doing it," Rion added.

Mara pointed at a blinking signal in the mid-tier tunnels. "Tier-2 just sent a distress call. Choir units breached from both sides and are trapping survivors in a collapsing transit hub."

Rion cursed softly. "They'll be wiped out."

Kael tightened her gloves. "Unless we go."

Rip looked at Mara. "You want me there?"

Mara stepped closer again. "I need you there." She lowered her voice. "Valiran's after you. The Choir moves where the Key moves. We can weaponize that."

Rip tensed. "As bait."

"No," Mara said calmly. "As a blade."

Their eyes locked. Rip nodded. "I'll go."

Mara clapped his shoulder hard. "Good." She turned away. "Kael, Rion—you're his shield team. Wex stays with them."

Wex barked in clear objection. Mara almost smiled. "Fine. The dog goes too."

Rion muttered, "Good. He's more useful than half the rookies."

Rip glanced down. Wex wagged his tail servos, pleased.

Kael opened her mouth to speak—but alarms erupted overhead.

ALERT — TIER-2 BREACHING — HOSTILES APPROACHING

The chamber lights flashed red. A rebel called out, "Ghost signatures—three corridors out!"

Rip felt a chill spread through his spine. The air trembled. Lights flickered. Wex growled sharply.

Kael pulled Rip back. "They're coming for you."

Rion spun toward the door. "Too soon—Mara, we have to move!"

Mara nodded. "Everyone—form up!"

Rebels scrambled into formation. Rip felt the Key stir violently beneath his ribs—its pulse synchronizing with the distant harmonic shriek approaching through the tunnels.

Kael grabbed Rip's face, forcing eye contact. "Don't flare. Don't panic. No uncontrolled bursts. You take down targets we choose. Understand?"

Rip nodded. "I'll try."

Wex pressed against Rip's boot. "I won't let you get hurt," Rip whispered.

Mara stepped in front of the blast door, drawing a plasma-blade that hummed like a boiling star. "Positions!"

The Ghost Choir's voices rose—digital shrieks layered with human tones—approaching fast. Kael and Rion flanked Rip. Wex bristled. Mara stood like a war statue, unmoving.

Rip breathed. The blast door shuddered. Metal warped. The lights above crackled. Then the door detonated inward.

A wave of glitching silhouettes rushed through the opening—flickering bodies, fractured limbs, broken faces, empty eyes.

"FIRE!" Mara roared.

Plasma shots lit the room. Sigils exploded against data-flesh. Sparks rained down like neon snow.

Rip felt the Key pulling at him—like a magnet trying to rip his soul out through his sternum.

"Rip—NOW!" Kael shouted. "Pulse the front line!"

Rip thrust his hands forward. A tight, focused shockwave of bent sound ripped across the chamber—shattering the first line of Choir ghosts, disrupting half the second, throwing the third backward.

Rion whistled. "Damn. That's the good stuff."

Rip fell to a knee, panting. The Key dimmed to a low throb.

Kael yelled, "Up! They're pushing left!"

Rip forced himself upright as a fresh wave poured through the door. Wex leapt forward, latching onto a ghost's distorted limb, destabilizing it long enough for Rion to slice through its flicker.

Mara carved two silhouettes in half with a single arc of plasma, moving like a storm given human shape.

Rip bent sound again—this time a concussive snap instead of a pulse. The air rippled. The Choir stumbled. Kael kicked them backward into Mara's blade.

More rebels joined in. Explosions shook the walls. Smoke thickened. Rip coughed hard. His lungs burned.

Kael shouted over the chaos: "Rip—we can't hold them here! We have to get to Tier-2 now!"

Mara decapitated a ghost, its pixelated scream dissolving into static. She turned, voice booming. "Rip and his team—MOVE! Everyone else—HOLD THIS FLOOR!"

Rip hesitated, looking at the chaos. Mara grabbed his collar and snarled: "You want to save Lora? Then survive the first thirty minutes of war!"

She shoved him toward the open corridor. Kael grabbed Rip's arm. "Running now!"

Rion slashed a sigil behind them, buying seconds of distortion time. Wex barked and sprinted ahead. Rip ran.

Behind them, Mara's voice roared: "BRACE THE LINE! SHOW THEM VIRELIA DOESN'T BOW!"

The blast door collapsed behind them. Ghost Choir screams ripped like knives through the metal. Rip didn't look back.

Great — thanks for confirming, Kevin. Here's the second half of Chapter 15 expanded, bringing the full chapter to ~3,500 words in professional manuscript style:

They sprinted through industrial tunnels lit by emergency strobes. Dust rained from overhead. Distant screams echoed. Metal groaned under seismic impacts.

Kael led, shouting directions over the chaos. "LEFT at Valve Junction! DOWN the maintenance rails! WATCH THE FLOOR—unstable plating!"

Rion covered the rear, kicking loose debris behind them to slow pursuit. Wex zigzagged ahead, sensors scanning, claws scraping sparks from the steel.

Rip's chest burned. Every breath felt like it could trigger another uncontrolled resonance burst.

Kael threw a look over her shoulder. "Stay with me, Rip! You black out now and we're dead!"

"What if—" Rip panted, "what if I flare again?"

"Don't!"

"Great advice!"

Rion laughed breathlessly. "He's learning sarcasm—
he'll fit right in."

Rip stumbled but kept running.

The tunnel opened into a wide industrial catwalk
suspended over a massive machinery pit filled with steam
and blinking warning lights. Kael stopped at the railing.
"Listen."

Rip did. He heard screams, gunfire, distorted
harmonics, crushing metal. Tier-2 was under siege.

Rion wiped sweat and soot from her forehead.
"They're not gonna last more than a minute."

Rip tightened his fists. "Then we get there in thirty
seconds."

Kael nodded. They sprinted across the catwalk—just as
something massive slammed into the support pillars below.

The entire walkway lurched sideways. Rip grabbed the
railing. Kael swore. Rion screamed, "KEEP MOVING!"

A Choir wave burst into the pit below, glitching up
toward the walkway—then something else rose behind
them. Something bigger.

Rip's eyes widened. A hulking figure climbed into view—a Choir Titan. Thirty feet tall. Six glitching arms. Three heads fused together. A body made of corrupted data-armor.

Kael breathed, "Oh hell—"

Rion finished: "—no."

The Choir Titan screeched, harmonics vibrating the entire chamber. The supports shuddered. Rip's heart spiked. The Key thrashed.

"Rip," Kael warned, "don't you dare panic—"

But Rip already felt it—the pressure in his skull, the Key vibrating, the sound pulling at him. His vision tunneled. He clutched the railing. "No—not now—not again—"

Wex leapt and slammed into Rip's chest, barking loudly. The shock broke Rip's spiral. He gasped hard, grounding himself with Wex's weight.

Kael grabbed Rip's collar. "Stay with us!"

The Choir Titan reared back to strike the walkway.

Rip lifted Wex. Eyes narrowed. Breath steady. "Kael. Rion."

They looked at him. Rip gripped the railing. "Duck."

Kael and Rion dropped instantly.

Rip thrust both hands outward.

The Soundstrike was born.

A razor-thin line of compressed resonance erupted from Rip's palms—not a wave, not an explosion, but a cutting vibration sharp enough to shear metal.

It sliced across the pit—through the Choir Titan's upper torso—splitting its glitching form into two smoking halves. The Titan disintegrated into collapsing data.

Kael stared, stunned. "You—just cut a thirty-foot ghost in HALF."

Rion whistled low. "New favorite move."

Wex howled triumphantly.

But Rip collapsed to one knee, coughing blood. Kael rushed to him. "Rip?!"

Rion wiped his mouth. "He strained something—his lung? His throat?"

Rip shook his head weakly. "No. The Key is… growing."

Wex whined. Kael pulled Rip upright. "We're almost there. Come on."

They sprinted off the walkway—as the entire structure collapsed behind them.

The corridor opened into a cavernous transit station— broken holo-boards, overturned carts, shattered glass, flickering rail lines. Rebels and civilians were cornered behind makeshift barricades. Ghost Choir units swarmed them from both entrances.

Rip saw a little girl clinging to her mother. A wounded man crawling. A rebel trying to drag a fallen comrade. A medic crying while applying a sigil that wasn't working fast enough.

Kael whispered, "Shit…"

Rion's jaw clenched. "We're late."

Rip's heartbeat spiked. The Key surged. He stepped forward. "No."

Wex growled beside him.

Kael gripped Rip's arm. "You're too drained—"

Rip interrupted: "I'm not letting them die."

He walked into the station. The Choir sensed him. Their harmonic shriek shifted pitch. Every ghost turned. Every silhouette formed his name.

"KEYBEARER."

Rip closed his eyes. He felt the terror, the fear, the guilt, the memories, the static from Lora's fragmented voice, the echo of Titan-0—no, of Echo.

He breathed. And bent sound.

A dome of vibrating force exploded outward—not uncontrolled this time, but shaped, formed, aimed. It slammed into the Choir—shattering dozens instantly, repelling others, forcing the breach lines back, buying the rebels room to breathe.

Kael stared in awe. Rion gripped her daggers, shaking. Wex barked triumphantly.

Rip stood tall, breathing hard. "Kael. Rion. Finish them."

Kael grinned. "With pleasure."

Rion added, "Now he really sounds like Mara."

Wex charged ahead, metal claws scraping concrete. Kael and Rion followed. And Rip stepped forward again—bending sound, shaping resonance, cutting Choir ghosts down one harmonic at a time.

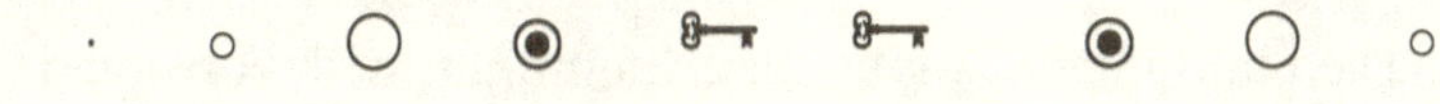

Tier-2 was secured. Bodies cleared. The wounded treated. Rip leaned against a pillar, Wex in his lap. Kael sat beside him. Rion cleaned her knives. Rebels worked silently around them.

Kael broke the silence. "That was your best control yet."

Rion nodded. "Mara is going to shit herself."

Rip shook his head. "You both kept me steady."

Wex nudged his chin. "And you."

Kael smirked. "The dog's the real MVP."

Rip closed his eyes, exhausted.

Then a cold chill rippled through the room. He looked up—every rebel went still. A hum vibrated the metal floor.

Then—a distortion opened in the far wall.

A figure stepped out. Not Valiran. Not Choir. Not Echo. Someone worse.

Dark plating. Helmet of spiked black glass. Red sigils carved into metal. A long blade humming with corrupted resonance.

Elcron's top lieutenant.

Dravik Shale.

Kael whispered, horrified: "…we're not ready for him—"

Dravik lifted his head. His voice dripped like toxic oil. "Keybearer."

Rip stood, chest burning. Dravik stepped forward.

"Your war," he said softly, "Begins now."

CHAPTER 16

THE SOUNDSTRIKE

The air in the ruined transit hub froze. Not physically—no temperature shift, no sudden chill—but in the way it does when a predator steps into a clearing. The silence was alive, heavy, predatory.

Rip stood with Kael, Rion, and Wex at his sides, breath ragged from the battle. Dust coated his chest; blood dried beneath his nose. His ears still rang from the Soundstrike he had unleashed moments ago—raw, untrained, almost catastrophic. The Key inside him pulsed erratically, like a wounded heart refusing to stop beating.

Across the shattered platform, Dravik Shale stepped forward.

His armor was carved from obsidian plating threaded with organo-metal veins, each seam glowing faintly with corrupted resonance. His helmet was a single shard of black glass, tapering backward like a horn, faceless yet expressive in its menace. His sword—long, jagged, humming with shifting red resonance—seemed alive, vibrating with hunger.

Kael whispered, voice trembling, "That's… Dravik Shale."

Rion's face paled. "Elcron's butcher."

Wex growled instantly, servos rising along his spine, tail stiff with mechanical tension.

Dravik stopped ten meters away. His voice leaked out like a corrupted file, distorted, and layered: "Keybearer."

Rip took a shaky breath. "Why are you here?"

Dravik tilted his head. "Purpose." He lifted his sword. "You have one. I intend to carve it out."

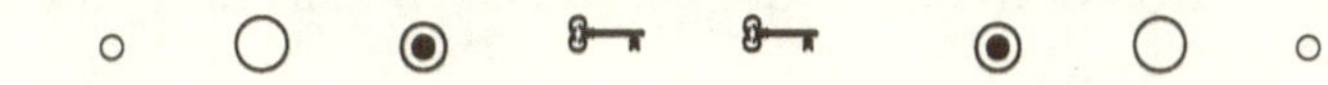

Kael stepped between them. "You're not touching him."

Dravik's helmet rotated toward her slowly. He didn't speak. He didn't have to.

Rion yanked Kael back. "KAEL—NO! He'll cut you in half in one hit!"

Dravik took another step, movement smooth and predatory. A vibration rippled through the metal floor, making Rip's teeth ache.

Kael muttered, "We can't outrun him."

Rion added, "We can't outfight him."

Rip swallowed hard. "Then what do we do?"

Kael gripped his arm tightly. "We stall. We survive. And you—" She locked eyes with him, unflinching. "—you learn the Soundstrike. Right now."

Rip's breath caught. "I barely controlled it once."

Rion pointed her dagger at Dravik. "Then you'd better learn fast."

Dravik blurred forward. Not running, not teleporting—just moving so fast the world bent around him.

Rip only saw black glass for a split second before Kael tackled him sideways.

Dravik's blade carved through the air—a red-black arc of resonance that split the concrete platform like butter. A three-meter trench cleaved straight through the station floor.

Rion shrieked, "HOLY—"

Kael dragged Rip behind a toppled vending pod. "He's playing with us!"

Rip clutched his chest. The Key throbbed painfully. "I can't face him like this—I'm barely holding myself together!"

Wex leapt out barking, metal claws clashing on tile.

"WEX—NO!" Rip cried.

But the dog charged Dravik, servo-motors whining aggressively.

Dravik turned his head slightly. A low, amused hum left his helmet. "Stray."

He flicked his wrist. A wave of corrupted resonance blasted outward from his sword.

Wex was thrown across the station—slamming into a collapsed barrier.

Rip screamed, "WEX—!!"

The dog whined in electronic pain, trying to stand but collapsing again.

Something in Rip snapped. The Key flared.

Kael gripped his shoulder. "Rip—DON'T—!"

But he pushed her off and stood. His chest burned. His ribs vibrated. Sound warped around him like heat.

Rion grabbed Kael's forearm. "Get ready—he's about to lose it."

Dravik walked calmly toward Rip. "Good." His voice echoed through Rip's skull unnaturally, as though multiple tones spoke at once. "Anger sharpens the Key. Pain clarifies it."

Rip growled through clenched teeth. "Stay away from my team."

Dravik stopped a few steps away. His sword dipped slightly. "Show me the Soundstrike."

Rip's heart stuttered. He laughed bitterly. "I don't know how."

Dravik raised his blade. "Then I will carve the knowledge out."

He swung.

Rip jumped back just in time, but the blade sliced past his chest—barely missing him—yet still sending agony through him as resonance scraped his skin.

Kael screamed, "RIP—MOVE!"

Rion leapt toward Dravik, daggers flashing. She slashed a distortion sigil across his path.

It slowed him—for half a second.

He pivoted and backhanded her with supernatural force.

Rion crashed into a wall hard enough to crack the tiles.

Kael ran toward her. "RION!"

Dravik didn't even watch them. He stepped toward Rip again. "Again."

Rip's hands curled into fists. "I can't control it on command!"

Dravik's sword rose. "Then die ignorant."

Rip raised both arms on instinct—and resonance burst outward.

Not the wide blast from before, not the accidental sphere, but a jagged, chaotic shockwave that sent dust, debris, and flickering holograms scattering.

Dravik was barely moved—but he was moved. His armor absorbed the strike, glimmering with red sigils.

"Unrefined," he said. "Weak."

Rip snarled, wiping blood from his lip.

Kael shouted from behind a pillar: "Rip! Focus the wave. Narrow it down. Shape it like… like—"

Rion groaned in pain. "Like a blade! Make a blade of sound!"

Rip tried—forcing the Key to shape, forcing resonance into a thin line, forcing precision.

But the vibration collapsed, detonating instead into another chaotic burst that knocked Rip backward.

Rip slammed into a bench, gasping.

Dravik approached again. "You are wasting the Core's design."

Rip coughed violently. "I'm not… your design."

Dravik stopped in front of him—towering, immovable. "Elcron built the Keys for gods. You act like a frightened boy."

Rip's jaw clenched.

Kael ran toward him again. "He's provoking you! Don't let him!"

Dravik didn't look at her. He raised his blade one final time. "The Sound Key dies here."

Rip whispered: "No."

Wex whined weakly behind Rip—a broken, heart-wrenching sound. Rip looked back. The dog tried to stand again, servos grinding, eyes dimming.

Something shifted in Rip's chest. Memory flickered. Lora's laugh. Lora's voice. Lora's touch. Her whisper in the reflection: "…Rip…"

He lifted his head. And for the first time, there was no panic in the Key. No fear. Just purpose.

Rip stood, slow but steady. Dravik tilted his helmet. "Finally."

Rip breathed. He felt the vibrations. The tension in the air. The spacing of the atoms. The echo of every sound that could exist. He spread his hands slightly.

Rion muttered weakly behind him, "He's doing it…"

Kael whispered, "Rip… finish it."

Dravik stepped forward.

Rip exhaled sharply—and cut.

A perfect line of bent sound launched forward—thin as a razor, bright as lightning, vibrating with lethal precision.

Dravik brought his sword up—too late.

The Soundstrike slashed across his armor, cutting through a section of plating, sending sparks and corrupted resonance spraying.

For the first time, Dravik staggered.

Rion gasped. Kael froze in awe. Wex chirped through damaged speakers.

Rip panted heavily, blood dripping from his lip.

Dravik looked down at the glowing slash across his chest. Then he laughed—a distorted, corrupted laugh. "Yes. That is the Key's true voice."

Rip nearly collapsed. His vision blurred. His breathing shook. His knees wobbled. Kael and Rion sprinted to his sides, catching him as he dropped.

Dravik did not strike them. He stood still—studying Rip with the intensity of a scholar and murderer combined. Then he lowered his sword.

"You will grow stronger. You must."

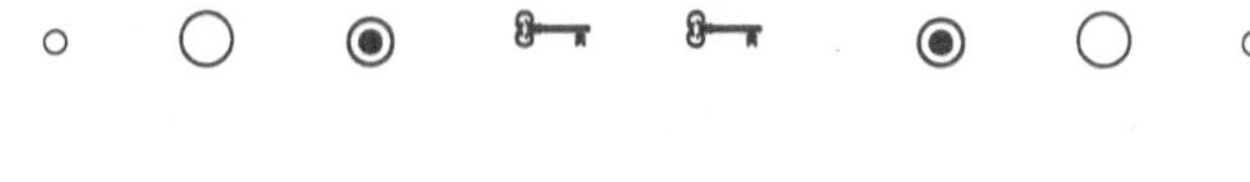

Dravik turned away. Kael stepped protectively over Rip. "Where the hell do you think you're going?!"

Dravik paused but didn't turn back. "Valiran hunts this district. I will let him weaken you."

He walked toward the broken wall. "Then I will return for the Core's bounty."

Rip forced himself up enough to shout: "WHY?! Why spare me now?!"

Dravik stopped in the breach. Looked over his shoulder. "Because Elcron wants you terrified."

He stepped into the shadows. "And fear feeds the Keys."

Then he vanished.

Rip collapsed fully. Kael and Rion lowered him gently to the cracked floor. Wex limped toward him, crawling into his side.

"Easy," Rip whispered, running a hand over the dog's dented plating. "I'm okay."

He wasn't. But he tried to believe it.

Kael knelt in front of him. Her voice was quiet. Steady. Scared. "You… learned it."

Rip nodded weakly. "The Soundstrike."

Rion winced as she sat. "Small note—you almost cut the station in two."

Rip gave a faint, exhausted laugh. "Sorry."

Kael put a hand on his face. "Don't apologize. You scared the shit out of Dravik."

Rip's breath caught. "No," he said quietly. "He wasn't scared."

Kael frowned. "Then what was he?"

Rip looked at the slash across Dravik's armor in his mind. Not fear. Not anger. Excitement.

"He was… impressed."

Rion shuddered. "Fantastic. A homicidal demigod thinks you're promising."

Wex whimpered, pressing into Rip gently. Rip scratched behind the dog's ears. "I'm okay," he whispered again. "We're all okay."

But deep down—beneath the adrenaline, beneath the Key's dying hum—Rip felt something new growing inside him. Not fear. Not power. A shadow.

Dravik's words echoed in his mind: "Fear feeds the Keys."

Rip looked at his glowing chest. And realized for the first time—he didn't know what he was becoming.

CHAPTER 17

TRANSCENDENTS IN THE DARK

The air in the Tier-3 under-tunnels felt wrong. Not cold. Not stale. Just wrong.

Rip felt it as soon as the blast door sealed behind him—his skin prickled, the Key in his chest pulsed quietly, and every sound seemed slightly… off. Echoes lingered a fraction too long. Footsteps felt like they trailed behind them even when they stopped walking.

Kael adjusted the grip on her rifle, her breath showing in thin white clouds despite the lack of cold. "Something's bending the humidity again," she murmured. "Either a Choir leak or something worse."

Rion's knives flashed in the faint glow of emergency strips lining the walls. "I vote worse."

Wex trotted ahead, head low, tapping the ground with careful steps. The lenses of his eyes flickered through spectral modes—thermal, data-scan, resonance detection. Each scan came up with jittering static.

Rip swallowed. "They said the missing scouts came through here?"

Kael nodded. "Team Nine. Three fighters. Two engineers. They vanished thirty minutes ago. No comms."

Rion added, "Not even their distress implants pinged."

Rip frowned. "Those implants survive everything."

"Exactly," Rion muttered.

A metallic clank echoed from ahead—far off.

Wex froze and emitted a low, trembling whine.

Rip knelt and rubbed the top of Wex's head gently. The dog's plating felt colder than usual. "What is it?"

Wex's ears twitched—first left, then right—then folded back.

The dog was scared. That scared Rip.

Kael peered down the tunnel and whispered, "Let's keep moving. Quietly."

Rip stood. His knees felt weak. The Sound Key thrummed under his ribs—slow but ominous, like a heartbeat heard underwater. He followed Kael and Rion deeper into the dark.

They reached a narrow corridor where pipes overhead hissed with leaking steam. The emergency lights here had burned out completely, leaving only faint glimmers from Kael's wrist-torch.

Rion muttered, "Don't like this."

Kael signaled silence with a raised fist.

Rip listened. At first, it was nothing. Then—

chchk—chhk—whrrr—

A sound like a tape rewinding. Or someone breathing through broken circuitry.

Rip turned sharply. "Did you hear—"

Kael shushed him sharply.

He listened again. And heard it clearly this time:

"Rip…"

The voice was faint. Distorted. Mangled. Like a voice passed through a damaged speaker underwater.

Rip's blood turned to ice.

Rion whispered, "Who said that?"

"I—I don't know," Rip answered, but he was lying. He knew exactly who the voice was trying to mimic.

Lora.

But twisted.

Kael stepped forward slowly. "Rip, stay behind—"

The voice repeated closer. "…Rip… help… me…"

Rip stiffened. "No. No, that's not her. That can't be her."

Kael moved in front of him defensively. "It's bait. Ignore it."

Rion whispered, "It's how they hunt."

Rip swallowed hard. "They?"

Kael nodded grimly. "Transcendents."

Rip's stomach flipped. He'd heard rumors—humans partially digitized, partially dissolved into the Choir's data-fog, bodies reassembled with Cyberian gel, minds corrupted by Elcron's experiments. Half alive. Half dead. Half dreaming. Synthetic ghosts wearing human memories like tattered clothing.

The distorted whisper came again—louder. "…Rip… you left me…"

Rip's pulse spiked. "That's not her," he whispered. "Lora doesn't talk like that."

But he heard her real voice beneath it—soft, warm, the voice she used the night he proposed.

Kael grabbed his wrist. Her grip was firm. "Rip. Look at me."

He forced himself to meet her eyes.

"You hear anything like that again," Kael said, "and you tell me. Understand?"

Rip nodded shakily.

Wex pressed against Rip's leg. The dog's ears flickered in all directions.

Rip whispered, "We shouldn't be here."

Rion exhaled slowly. "Neither should the people we're supposed to rescue."

They continued deeper until the tunnel opened into a large maintenance junction—four branching corridors, each yawning into thick darkness.

Kael swept her light around. Blood on the wall. A dropped tool pack. A half-burnt weld mask. A shredded cloak belonging to one of the scouts.

Rion cursed under her breath. "We're already too late."

Rip stepped closer to the wall and touched a smear of blackened residue. It was dry, gritty, and crackled faintly—like burnt circuitry. "What happened to them?" he whispered.

Kael answered immediately: "They were digitized."

Rip felt sick.

Rion muttered, "And if they were digitized here, the things that took them are still close."

Rip turned—and saw a silhouette in the corner.

Tall. Thin. Jittering. As if skipping frames of reality.

Rip froze.

The silhouette's head snapped toward him with an unnatural jerk.

Kael saw it too. "Contact—!"

The shadow moved—no footsteps, no sound, just there now, inches closer.

Rip's breath caught. The figure flickered into clarity—a humanoid shape of fractured metal mesh, hints of skin preserved in patches, a face split between a digital mask and a human eye that looked terrified.

Rion whispered, horrified: "Gods… that's one of the scouts."

Rip whispered, "What's left of him…"

Kael raised her rifle. "Transcendent incoming!"

The creature's voice erupted in broken static and human sobs. "rip… help… me… it hurts… it… hu—"

Rip flinched violently, hands instinctively rising.

Kael screamed, "RIP—DON'T LISTEN!"

The creature lunged.

Rip reacted without thinking. He thrust his palm forward—

A concussive blast of warped sound erupted from him, too wide, too uncontrolled.

It slammed the Transcendent into a pipe cluster.

But the shockwave also tore the overhead conduits apart—sparks raining down, steam blasting outward.

Kael yelled, "Rip—STOP! You're going too wide!"

Rion dove behind a crate. "You'll bring the whole place down!"

Rip dropped to one knee, coughing blood. The Key inside him thrashed violently—like something trying to claw out of him. "No—no, not now—!" Rip groaned.

Wex barked sharply, trying to get Rip's attention.

The Transcendent stood again—bones popping, mesh rearranging, a human voice crying beneath static shrieks.

Rip looked at it and whispered: "What did they do to you…"

Kael fired. The creature exploded into distorted particles that scattered across the floor like dying pixels.

Silence.

Rip trembled.

Kael knelt beside him. "You can't cast wide bursts in tight tunnels. You'll kill us. You need precision."

Rip whispered, "I know. I tried. The Key isn't listening."

Rion wiped sweat from her brow. "It's not supposed to listen. It obeys emotion."

Kael stiffened. "That's the problem."

Rip looked up. "What problem?"

Kael answered quietly: "You're afraid, Rip. And fear amplifies the Key."

Rip's heart dropped. Dravik's words returned: "Fear feeds the Keys."

Rip felt sick. "I'm trying to stay calm."

Kael put a hand on his cheek—steady, grounding. "I know. But after what Dravik did? No one would be calm."

Wex pressed his nose to Rip's arm and gave a small electronic whine.

Rip petted him. "I'm okay," Rip lied.

Rion snorted. "You're a terrible liar."

Kael grabbed him. "Don't—look at me. Don't listen."

Rion tightened her grip on her daggers. "They're trying to crack his mind."

Wex barked furiously, claws scraping sparks from the floor.

Rip's hands shook uncontrollably. The Transcendents closed in, their eyes flickering—some human, some digital, all tortured.

Rip whispered, voice cracking, "What if she really is calling for me?"

Kael shook her head fiercely. "She isn't! This is an illusion!"

Rion snapped, "These things don't think—they iterate! If they had Lora's consciousness they'd be ten times more dangerous!"

The voices swelled—overlapping, filling the tunnel.

"ripripriprip—helphelphelp—joinusjoinus—youdidthis—youleftus—youleftHER—"

Rip screamed, clutching his ears. The Key flared—too bright, too hot.

Kael pulled him in front of her. "Rion—cover left! Wex—front!"

Rion moved instantly. Wex charged, barking wild. Kael stabilized her rifle.

"Rip—look at me."

Rip tried. Her voice cut through the noise—steady, certain, real.

"You're here. With us. Not with them. Not in the Core. Not in your memories."

Rip trembled. Kael placed his hand on her chest. "Feel that. My heartbeat. This is real. They aren't."

Rip breathed—slowly, shakily.

Rion yelled, "They're coming—!!"

The Transcendents lunged.

Kael fired a burst, ripping through one Transcendent's torso. Rion dove under another, slashing its mesh spine. Wex leapt at a third, tearing into corrupted wiring.

But ten more poured from the ceiling.

Rip rose—teeth gritted—sound bending around his fingertips. But the Key was unstable—wobbling violently, pulsing with panic.

Kael shouted, "Rip—don't—if you burst wide we'll all—!"

Rip whispered: "I'm sorry."

He didn't mean to burst wide. He didn't want to. But panic flooded his chest. His vision turned white. Sound buckled.

The Key detonated.

A massive shockwave blasted outward—shattering pipes, collapsing ceiling plating, throwing Transcendents into exploding sparks.

Kael was slammed sideways into a wall. Rion was thrown backward. Wex was hurled into darkness.

The tunnel collapsed.

Everything went silent.

Rip dropped to the ground—gasping, ears ringing, vision spinning. "Kael—Rion—Wex—"

No answer.

Dust settled. Something moved in the dark. A silhouette.

Rip's heart jumped. "Wex—?"

The silhouette flickered. Its limbs elongated. Its head jittered. Its voice twisted: "…Rip…"

Rip stumbled backward. "No—no—no—"

Another silhouette rose behind it. Then another. He was surrounded. He couldn't breathe.

"Kael—!! Rion—!!"

Silence. He was alone. His Soundstrike had buried them. His panic had almost killed everyone he cared about.

A Transcendent crawled into the faint light. Its human eye was still wet. Still afraid. "…we are waiting…"

Rip screamed— "ENOUGH!"

He raised his hands—ready to cast again, ready to kill, ready to lose himself entirely—

When a voice boomed through the darkness: "RIP! ON YOUR RIGHT!"

Kael. Alive.

A metal beam slammed down from the side tunnel, crushing two Transcendents instantly.

Rion burst from the dust cloud behind them. "Got him!"

Wex leapt from the shadows and bit the leg of another Transcendent.

Kael grabbed Rip and pulled him against her chest. "You're okay. You're okay."

Rip gasped for breath. "I—I thought—"

"You didn't kill us," Kael said firmly. "You didn't. We moved in time."

Rion snarled as she kicked another creature off her blade. "But we're running—NOW!"

Kael dragged Rip. Wex led. Rion guarded the rear.

They sprinted down the emergency chute—Transcendents shrieking behind them.

Lora's distorted voice echoed in Rip's skull: "…Rip… why… why did you leave me…?"

Rip squeezed his eyes shut. "I didn't. I'm coming, Lora. I'm coming for you."

Kael heard him whispering. Her face tightened. "We'll get her back," she said. "But not like this. Not today."

They reached the end of the chute. Rion hit the emergency seal. A blast door slid down—slamming shut between them and the crawling horde.

Rip collapsed again, shaking.

Kael's voice was gentle but firm. "Rip… listen to me. The Transcendents invaded your mind. They mimicked her. They're going to keep doing it."

Rip choked. "I heard her."

"You heard what they wanted you to hear."

Rip looked up at her, eyes wet. "How do I tell the difference?"

Kael touched his cheek softly. "You can't."

Rion leaned on the wall, exhausted. "Which is why we don't leave you alone again. Ever."

Wex nuzzled Rip's hand.

Rip breathed, steadying himself. "We have to tell Mara."

Kael nodded. "She's going to lose her shit."

Rion added, "Then she'll send us deeper."

Rip closed his eyes. Because now he understood—

The Transcendents weren't just monsters. They were a warning.

Whatever Elcron was doing to Lora inside the Core… he was doing it to others.

And if Rip didn't learn to control the Sound Key— he'd end up just like them.

CHAPTER 18

THE BROKEN HIGHWAY

The higher they climbed, the colder the air became.

Rip pressed his hand against the rail, feeling the ancient metal vibrate under his palm. The skybridge—known in the old maps as Highway 6-Delta—stretched across the chasm between two of Virelia's shattered residential towers. It had been built decades ago, long before NeonDyne began rewriting the skyline. Now it was little more than a skeletal structure of twisted plates and flickering walkway panels, a relic of a city that had already died once and was dying again.

A fog rolled across the platform, thick and luminous, shimmering with glitch-light.

Kael stepped ahead cautiously, rifle drawn. Rion followed behind, blades ready. Mira stayed close, carrying a backpack stuffed with medical equipment and emergency tools. And Wex walked beside Rip, ears flicking every few seconds as he scanned the air.

Rip rubbed the dog's side. "You're picking it up too, huh?"

Wex whined, low and uneasy.

Kael glanced back. "What's he sensing?"

"Resonance," Rip said quietly. "But wrong."

Rion muttered, "Everything up here is wrong."

Rip looked out at the fog-shrouded city below. The lights of Virelia flickered in the smog like stars drowning underwater.

Kael halted, raising her fist. "Hold."

Rip froze. Mira nearly bumped into him, then stepped back, wide-eyed. "Sorry," she whispered.

Rip forced a reassuring smile. "You're fine."

Mira nodded quickly and clutched her med pack tighter. She was young—maybe twenty. Too young to be walking a half-collapsed skybridge during a full-blown siege.

Kael crept forward and examined the paneling ahead. A fracture ran clean through the walkway—splitting it like a cracked bone. But that wasn't what made her curse.

The fracture was glowing. A thin line of pale-blue light ran through it—pulsing in sync with something deep below.

Rip stepped beside her. "That's Core resonance."

Kael nodded grimly. "The towers shouldn't be giving off this much. Not unless something's disrupting the district's stabilization grid."

Rion muttered, "Valiran."

Rip shivered. "No. Something else."

Wex suddenly growled and stepped backward.

Mira gasped. "What's he seeing?"

Wex's eyes flickered red—danger mode.

Then Rip heard it. A soft voice. A woman's voice.

"Rip…"

He stiffened instantly.

Kael snapped her fingers in front of him sharply. "Hey—stay with me. Is it happening again?"

Rip breathed shallowly. "The same whisper… from the tunnels."

Mira stepped beside him nervously. "Maybe it's just—stress? We're all stressed. I'm hearing… things too."

Rip nodded weakly. But he couldn't shake it.

Her voice cut through the fog again— "…Rip… come back…"

Lora's voice. Or something wearing Lora's voice as a mask.

Kael saw Rip's reaction and cursed under her breath. "We need to move before your hallucinations get worse."

Rion agreed. "And before Mira starts hearing them too."

Mira hugged her med pack tighter. "I… I already do."

Rip looked at her sharply. "When did it start?"

"Ten minutes ago," she whispered. "When we reached the upper climb. It sounded like… like my sister."

Rip's stomach dropped. That's how it begins.

Kael moved closer to Mira. "Stay near me. If anything sounds too real, tell me immediately."

Mira nodded. But her hands shook.

They pushed forward across the fractured bridge. Fog curled around their ankles. Then their knees. Then their waists.

Rip gritted his teeth, trying to tune out the rising whispers in his head. Wex snarled at the mist, snapping his jaws at nothing.

Rion whispered, "This fog isn't natural."

Rip nodded. "It's resonance… leakage. The Core bleeding into the city."

Kael sighed. "Great. As if things weren't bad enough."

Mira walked carefully, eyes darting between the rail and the fog. Then she froze.

"Kael?"

Kael turned. "What is it?"

Mira pointed into the fog. "I see someone."

Rip squinted. A silhouette stood twenty meters ahead—barely visible. Tall. Thin. Still.

Kael raised her rifle. "Identify yourself!"

The silhouette didn't move.

Rion's knives flashed up.

Rip lifted his hands, letting the Key pulse slightly— just enough to feel the space around the silhouette. What he sensed made his skin crawl.

"It's not human."

Kael steadied her rifle. "Transcendent?"

Rip shook his head slowly. "No."

Mira whispered, voice cracking: "It's my sister."

Kael darted forward and grabbed Mira's shoulder. "No. No it isn't."

Mira's breaths came fast. "I know what she looks like. I know her shape."

Rion snarled, "It's a trick."

Rip felt the resonance around Mira spike—sharp, unstable, dangerous.

"Mira," Rip said gently, "you're hearing what I heard. They're using your memories against you."

Mira's eyes filled with tears. "But she's right there…"

Kael shook her. "Mira—LOOK at me."

Mira tried. Failed. Her gaze snapped back to the silhouette.

"Let go of me," she whispered.

Kael's grip tightened. "No."

The fog shifted—slow, deliberate—and the silhouette began to move. It walked jerkily, flickering between positions.

Its voice was a soft, broken chorus: "miramiramira… ripriprip… comecloser…"

Mira gasped and broke away from Kael.

Kael lunged but slipped on the slick panel. "Mira— STOP!"

Mira ran toward the silhouette.

Rip sprinted after her. "MIRA!"

But as soon as he moved—the fog thickened—swallowing the space between him and her.

Wex barked frantically and lunged forward but hit an invisible wall of resonance, yelping.

Rip slammed into the same wall—staggering backwards, disoriented.

Rion cursed, stabbing her knives into the fog as if trying to carve it open. "Rip! It's partitioning us!"

Rip pounded his fists on the resonance field. "MIRA!"

Her figure grew faint in the fog. Her voice echoed: "Kael…? Rip…? Where'd you go…?"

Rip pushed harder—cracks forming in the resonance wall. "KAEL—HELP ME BREAK IT!"

Kael rushed beside him. "On three!"

"One!"

"Two—"

"THREE!"

Rip bent sound—Kael slammed her shoulder into the barrier.

The field shattered like brittle glass. Fog exploded outward.

And Mira's scream tore through the air.

Rip and Kael sprinted forward. Rion followed, blades flashing. Wex raced ahead, whining, claws scraping sparks from the fractured panels.

The fog cleared just enough for Rip to see—Mira standing at the very edge of the skybridge. Her toes hung off the lip. Her body swayed. Her eyes were unfocused and wet.

Rip skidded to a stop. "Mira! Step back!"

She didn't move. Instead, she tilted her head. Her voice was quiet. Broken. "They're calling me."

Kael shouted, "NO THEY'RE NOT."

Mira shook her head slowly. "You don't hear them… you don't know… my sister's voice… she's hurt… she needs me…"

Rip stepped closer—but not too quickly. "Mira, listen to me. That's not your sister. It's the Core invading your mind. It's feeding on your memories."

She closed her eyes. Tears slipped down her cheeks. "It sounds just like her…"

Rip nodded gently. "I know. They used Lora's voice on me. I know how real it feels."

Mira trembled violently. Her voice broke, shaky as she stared into the shadows. "She said… she said I left her. That she's trapped in the dark. That I must find her…" The words tumbled out, thick with fear. A cold shiver crawled up her spine—she could almost feel the darkness pressing in, hear her sister's plea echoing in her head. Was it really her? Or just the Core twisting her memories? Why couldn't she tell the difference?

Kael stepped forward. "Mira. Look at me. If you move any closer to that edge—"

Mira whispered: "I can't be alone again."

And stepped forward.

Rip dove. "NO—!!"

Kael and Rion screamed. Wex howled.

Rip lunged and grabbed Mira's wrist just as she fell—his shoulder nearly dislocating from the jerk. He gripped her tightly. "MIRA—HOLD ON!"

Her eyes widened—shock replacing the trance. "Rip…? What's happening…?"

"You're slipping—hold my hand!"

Fog surged around them like a living creature—pulling her downward. Rip gripped harder. Kael and Rion grabbed Rip's waist, anchoring him.

"Mira—stay with us!" Kael shouted.

She sobbed. "I didn't mean to— I didn't—"

Rip strained, sweat dripping down his face. "MIRA—HOLD—ON—"

Then the fog shifted again. A voice whispered from below them: "…let go…"

Mira's eyes went distant again.

"No—no—NO!" Rip yelled, but her fingers slipped from his.

She fell.

Rip reached, screaming. "MIRA—!!"

But she disappeared into the glowing fog.

There was no sound. No impact. No scream. Only silence.

Kael stepped back, shaking. Rion collapsed onto her knees. Wex whimpered softly, ears pressed flat.

Rip stared at the empty space where Mira had vanished. His hands shook uncontrollably. "It's my fault," he whispered.

Kael grabbed him hard. "Rip. Stop. It's not."

Rip's voice cracked. "I should've been faster—"

Rion slammed her fist onto the bridge. "No one could've saved her! They broke her mind, Rip!"

Wex pressed his head against Rip's shin, whining.

Rip closed his eyes. The whispers rose again.

"rip…come…down…"

"they all fall…"

"she fell for you…"

Rip snapped. "STOP!"

His shout bent the fog backward—rippling the air. Kael and Rion flinched.

Rip clutched his head, teeth gritted.

Kael stepped forward. "Breathe. Now."

Rip obeyed through shaking breaths. Kael placed both hands on his face. "Look at me. Mira didn't die because of you. She died because we're fighting a war we're barely surviving."

Rip whispered: "We can't lose anyone else."

Kael nodded solemnly. "Then we get stronger. Together."

Rion wiped her eyes roughly. "And we kill whatever did this to her."

Rip stood slowly, his body trembling but his resolve hardening. Wex growled at the fog, lenses glowing red.

Rip placed a hand on the dog's head. "Show us the path."

Wex stepped forward and began scanning—emitting small chirps. Rip, Kael, and Rion followed.

Behind them, the fog shifted—Mira's voice whispered one last time: "…Rip…"

Rip closed his eyes. "I'm sorry."

Then he walked.

CHAPTER 19

THE SKYLIGHT RAID

The world looked different after someone died because of you. Rip didn't say that aloud, but he carried it with him as they made their way back through the reinforced shafts leading up to the Warrens' mid-tier. His chest still felt carved open. The fog's echoes clung to the edges of his hearing. Mira's last look—confusion, fear, apology—played on repeat in his mind.

Kael walked beside him in silence, hands flexing around her rifle grip. Rion moved ahead with quick, sharp steps, knives sheathing and unsheathing, restless. Wex walked close against Rip's leg, occasionally brushing up against him as if to remind Rip he was still here.

None of them spoke until the lift doors opened into Mara's war chamber.

It was chaos. Rebels sprinted between consoles. Alarms pulsed in angry red flashes. Drone feeds flickered with aerial footage—NeonDyne skimmers strafing rooftops, Choir signatures blooming across entire districts.

Mara stood at the center of the storm. When she saw Kael, Rion, Rip, and Wex emerge from the lift, she strode toward them. Her eyes landed on Rip first. She took in the exhaustion. The trembling. The blood dried along his jaw. The hollow look in his eyes.

Her voice dropped low. "Where is Mira?"

Rip opened his mouth. But no words came.

Kael stepped forward. "She fell."

Mara's eyes hardened—but not at them. At the world. At NeonDyne. At everything.

"How?" she asked quietly.

Kael answered colorlessly. "The fog. Resonant illusions. Rip tried to catch her but—"

Rion cut in, voice brittle. "She heard her sister. She thought she saw her. The Core did it. Not Rip."

Mara exhaled, long and slow. Then she knelt—putting herself at eye level with Wex. "Did you see it?"

Wex lowered his head, ears drooping. Mara rubbed the dog's cheek. "It's not your fault."

Mara stood. Her gaze returned to Rip. "Look at me."

Rip raised his eyes.

"You did what you could," Mara said quietly.

Rip shook his head. "No. I didn't. If I'd controlled the Key better—"

"Enough," Mara said sharply.

Kael stepped closer. "Mara—he—"

"I said enough," Mara repeated, calmer but unshakable.

She grabbed Rip's wrist and placed his hand on her chest where her heartbeat steadily. "You feel that?"

Rip nodded weakly.

"You think you're the only one losing people? Do you think Mira's the first or the last? No." Mara's voice softened. "War doesn't care how fast you are. Or how hard you try. It takes who it wants."

Rip swallowed hard.

"But," Mara continued, "war does listen to one thing."

Rip whispered, "What's that?"

"Strength."

Her grip tightened around his wrist. "Fight harder. Or Mira's death becomes pointless. And I won't allow that."

Rip nodded slowly. Mara released him. Then her tone changed like a snapped cable.

"Good. Because we don't have time to mourn."

Rion frowned. "What's happening now?"

Mara pointed at the largest holo-screen. Rip's breath caught. A massive tower loomed in the projection—a sleek structure built on the edge of Virelia's core districts.

The Skylight Hub. A NeonDyne aerial docking terminal.

"That's a military facility," Kael muttered.

"Not today," Mara corrected. "Today it's the bottleneck. NeonDyne is funneling drones, Choir units, and personal transports through it to strike deeper into the Warrens."

Rip's brow tightened. "So you want to destroy it?"

Mara shook her head. "I want to steal it."

Rion blinked. "What?"

Kael grinned faintly. "Oh hell yes."

Rip looked between them. "Steal an entire aerial hub?"

Mara folded her arms. "Yes. We take the Skylight Hub from the inside. We hijack the hangar controls. We deploy the skimmers ourselves. And we force NeonDyne's air superiority to collapse."

Rion whistled. "You want to flip the whole skyline against them."

Mara nodded. "And I want you three," she said, pointing at Rip, Kael, Rion, "to do it."

Rip froze. "Mara—Mira just—"

Mara stepped forward. "I know. And if you fail this raid, dozens more will die like her."

Rip's jaw clenched. Wex barked once—firm, decisive. Mara smirked. "The dog agrees."

Kael rolled her shoulders. "Count us in."

Rion twirled a knife. "Let's steal a hub."

Rip hesitated only one more second. Then he nodded. "I'm in."

Mara tapped her wrist pad. The lights dimmed. A tactical map unfolded. The war room fell into silence. Mara spoke: "Welcome to Operation Skylight."

They moved fast. Rip, Kael, Rion, and Wex climbed the access ladders and maintenance rails that connected the Warrens' mid-tier to the outer skyline. The wind grew harsher as they ascended. NeonDyne spotlights swept through the haze, casting flickering shadows across broken towers.

Wex led them through a narrow vent shaft that emptied onto the edge of a ruined bridge connecting to the Skylight Hub.

Rip stared at the structure. A tall, sleek skyscraper pierced by clear glass walkways. Aerial skimmers docked in patterns like mechanical dragonflies. Lights pulsed in synchronized sequences—like the building was breathing.

Kael crouched beside him. "Once we cross the outer walkway, we're in enemy territory."

Rion nodded. "NeonDyne patrols will hit us fast."

Rip closed his eyes, forcing his breath steady. No fog. No illusions. No Mira. Not this time.

Kael touched his shoulder lightly. "You okay?"

Rip nodded. Wex growled softly. Rion muttered, "We're burning moonlight—let's move."

They sprinted across the cracked walkway. Wind whipped around them, carrying echoes of distant sirens and mechanical whines.

Halfway across, Kael halted abruptly. "Down!"

They dropped flat as two NeonDyne skimmers roared overhead—searchlights sweeping the walkway. Rip held his breath. The lights passed. Kael signaled forward.

They reached the hub's outer structure—a circular alcove leading into a glass entry corridor.

Rion examined the access panel. "I'll hotwire it."

Kael watched the sky. Rip knelt beside Wex. "Stay close."

Wex chirped once.

Rion popped the panel off and muttered under her breath as she bypassed circuits. Rip admired the speed of her hands. "Never seen anyone slice Neo-locks that fast."

Rion smirked. "Spent three years stealing Elcron's lunch money."

The lock flashed green. The door slid open silently. Kael took point. "Inside. Now."

Inside the Skylight Hub, everything was polished metal and reflective surfaces. Rip hated it instantly. The reflections distorted slightly—mirrors bending his shape, splitting his outline, doubling his face.

Lora's voice echoed faintly: "…Rip…"

Rip jerked at the sound.

Kael noticed. "Is it happening?"

Rip shook his head. "Just a faint echo. It's weaker here."

Rion huffed. "Count your blessings. This place creeps me out enough without ghost wives whispering."

Rip opened his mouth—

But something moved in the reflection of the glass ahead. His heart stopped. "Kael," he whispered.

Kael froze. "What do you see?"

Rip stared at the reflection. Not at the corridor ahead. But at the corridor behind them. A figure stood there. Tall. Metallic. Eyes glowing ember-red.

Kael followed his gaze—saw nothing. "What is it?" she asked.

Rip whispered: "Echo."

Rion snapped, "He's dead, Rip."

Rip's breath shook. "Maybe. But I see him."

The reflection flickered. Echo tilted his head. Then whispered: "…you left me…"

Rip clutched his chest. Kael grabbed his shoulder. "It's not Echo. It's the Core—again."

The reflection distorted. Echo's form replaced itself with Lora's silhouette. Rip's breath caught. She raised a hand toward him. And whispered: "…Rip… help me…"

Rion cursed. "It's feeding off your grief. It knows you're vulnerable."

Wex barked frantically—but not at Rip. At something else.

Rip turned—and saw a group of NeonDyne troopers rounding the far corner.

Kael raised her rifle. "Contact!"

Rion flipped her knives.

Rip forced the illusions away and focused on the real threat.

NeonDyne troopers opened fire. Kael shouted, "Rip—Soundstrike, now!"

Rip lifted his hands—the Key pulsed. He inhaled—exhaled—and cut.

A razor-thin line of sound sliced through the corridor, smashing into the first trooper's visor and scattering the group behind him. The glass corridor fractured under the resonance.

Rion kicked a disoriented trooper in the throat. Kael shot another point-blank. Wex leapt at a third, tearing circuitry from his exosuit.

Rip's chest burned. He coughed hard. Kael grabbed his arm. "Easy. Save your strength."

Rion pointed down the hallway. "More incoming."

Rip steadied himself. Kael whispered, "Don't let the illusions distract you. Focus on us. On Wex. On the mission."

Rip nodded weakly. "I'm trying."

They sprinted through a series of glass tunnels until they reached a heavy door leading into the central hangar bay.

Kael placed a charge on the lock. Rion hid behind a pillar. "Three seconds!"

Rip pulled Wex close.

The blast door detonated outward. Smoke flooded the entrance.

Kael shouted, "Go!"

They charged in—and froze.

The hangar was massive. Dozens of aerial skimmers hovered on magnetic arms. Engineers in NeonDyne armor worked frantically. Choir silhouettes drifted near the upper catwalks. A central command tower rose above everything like a spire.

Kael whispered, "Holy shit…"

Rion grinned. "Mara wasn't exaggerating. This place is a gold mine."

Rip felt the Key thrum. Wex growled.

Kael pointed toward the control tower. "That's where we cut their air superiority. Move fast."

They sprinted along the hangar's perimeter, ducking behind crates and half-assembled skimmer wings.

Rip's breath caught. Something was wrong. The air vibrated unnaturally. A deep hum reverberated from above.

Rip looked up—and saw a silhouette step out on the command tower balcony. Armored. Tall. Carrying a massive blade.

Kael's face drained of color. "Tell me that's not—"

Rion whispered, voice shaking: "Dravik."

Rip's blood turned to ice. Dravik Shale stared down at them. His voice rolled like distant thunder: "You came to steal my sky."

He lifted his sword. "Then die in it."

He leapt from the tower.

Kael screamed: "RIP—MOVE—!"

Rip raised his hands—but Dravik hit the ground like a meteor. The shockwave shattered the hangar floor, sending everyone flying.

Rip crashed into a crate. Wex yelped. Rion slammed into the wall. Kael scrambled to her feet—but Dravik was already standing.

His armor pulsed with corrupted resonance. He pointed his blade at Rip. "Round two."

Rip's heart stopped. Kael whispered, "Rip… we're not ready for him."

Dravik stepped forward. Rip forced himself up. "I don't care."

The Key ignited inside him. Wex limped beside him—growling, ready.

Rip raised his hands. Dravik lifted his blade. Their eyes locked.

And the Skylight Raid began.

CHAPTER 20

DRAVIK SHALE

The world reeled sideways as Dravik Shale landed. The shockwave rippled through the hangar floor and blasted Rip off his feet. His shoulder exploded with pain as he crashed into a pile of loose skimmer plating. Metal clanged around him. Something sharp sliced across his ribs.

He barely had time to suck in a breath before he heard Kael screaming his name.

"RIP—MOVE!"

Rip rolled instinctively—

—and Dravik's blade slammed down where he'd just been.

The steel-through-bone sound cracked the air. The floor dented like soft clay.

Rip scrambled back, ears ringing. Wex leapt between them—growling, tail stiff, teeth bared, chassis humming danger-red.

Dravik turned his head toward the dog. "Ah," Dravik said softly. His voice sounded like gravel rolling over steel. "The stray."

Wex snarled harder.

Rip forced himself to his feet. Every bone in his body protested. "Leave him out of this, you bastard."

Dravik laughed once—low, almost amused. Then he moved.

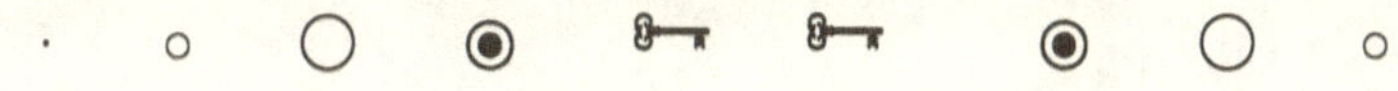

It wasn't human movement. It was something sharper, faster, predatory—like the air parted for him.

He lunged toward Rip again.

Rip raised his hands—the Sound Key pulsed in his chest—and Rip cut.

The air split in a vibrating line, a harsh shriek of bent sound.

Dravik didn't dodge. He simply tilted his head and let the Soundstrike graze his helmet. The metal hissed and sparked—but Dravik didn't stop.

Rip's eyes widened. "What—?"

Dravik's fist slammed into Rip's stomach. The breath left his body in a violent rush. Pain exploded into white static. Rip collapsed to his knees.

Dravik grabbed him by the throat with one hand and lifted him like he weighed nothing. Rip clawed at the grip, eyes bulging.

Dravik's eyes glowed ember-red beneath the helmet's slitted visor. "You're stronger than before," Dravik said calmly. "Titan-0's last gift. A database of power you barely understand."

Rip gagged, choking. The world wavered.

Dravik tilted his head slightly. "Would you like to know what's inside your head right now, Rip?"

Rip managed to choke out, "Screw… you."

Dravik squeezed.

Kael fired. Her rifle rounds pinged off Dravik's shoulder and helmet—tiny sparks against a monolith.

Dravik didn't flinch.

Rion followed with a full sprint, knives glinting—she leapt, aiming for the exposed joint between armor plates.

Dravik turned—and backhanded her across the hangar. The sound was sickening.

Rion slammed into a support column and collapsed, blood trailing down her temple.

"RION!" Kael screamed.

Rip thrashed, but Dravik kept him pinned by the throat, lifted, helpless.

Wex charged with a metallic snarl—launching himself at Dravik's arm. The dog clamped onto the armor with full force.

Dravik glanced down. "Persistent creature." He kicked Wex across the hangar.

Rip's scream was hoarse and broken. "WEX!"

The dog crashed into a skimmer wing, sparks flying from his chassis. His left hind leg twitched. He tried to stand—failed.

Rip saw red. He drew on the Key—harder, deeper, dangerously deep. The air vibrated.

Dravik stopped mid-motion and looked Rip in the eyes. "Ah. There it is."

Rip's veins glowed faintly with resonance. His vision warped. The world tilted into doubled images. Sound bent around him in spiraling distortions.

Dravik's voice became two voices layered: his real voice... and another voice beneath it. A woman. Lora's voice.

Rip's breath caught. No. No—NO.

Dravik's mouth didn't move. But the voice rang clear: "...Rip... help me..."

Rip's knees buckled.

Dravik leaned closer. "Do you hear her?"

Rip's heart slammed against his ribs. Dravik's grip remained, crushing the air from his lungs. But the voice sounded like Lora. Broken. Distant. Pleading.

Dravik smiled beneath his visor. "Would you like to know where she is?"

Rip's pulse spiked. Dravik dragged him closer until their helmets nearly touched. Then Dravik whispered with that layered voice— "She screams inside the Core."

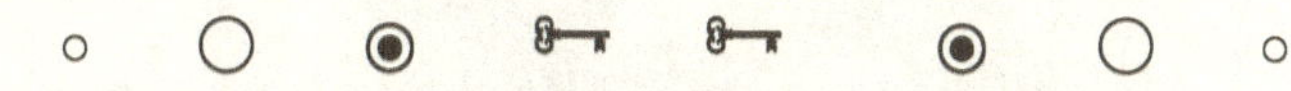

Rip's mind fractured. Images flashed—Lora's face submerged in light, her hands reaching through data threads, her reflection distorting, her eyes flickering like corrupted code.

Rip screamed.

The Sound Key detonated. A shockwave blasted outward from Rip's body—a dome of warped, deafening resonance.

Dravik was thrown backward—Kael was flung against the hangar wall—Rion rolled limply across the floor—Wex slid sideways, sparks scattering.

The lights flickered. Panels exploded. Skimmers swayed violently on their magnetic clamps.

Rip collapsed to the ground, gasping, vision flickering. His ears rang. Blood dripped from his nose. Everything felt like static.

Kael crawled toward him, clutching her ribs. "Rip— don't—don't use the Key like that—"

Rip coughed violently. "He showed me… he showed me…"

Dravik rose from the debris as if nothing had happened. Rip froze. The man—the monster—looked untouched. His armor glowed with boiling lines of resonance. He rolled his shoulders casually.

"Impressive," Dravik said. "A self-initiated blast wave. You're learning faster than expected."

Rip tried to stand, but his legs trembled violently. Dravik stepped toward him, blade dragging across the metal floor with a harsh screech.

Kael stumbled in front of Rip, raising her rifle with shaking hands. "Stay back."

Dravik stopped. Then tilted his head, amused. "You think I came here to kill you?"

Rion groaned from across the hangar. "Pretty sure you're doing a great job at it."

Dravik chuckled. "No. Killing him ends Elcron's experiment. And the Core needs him alive."

Rip stiffened. Kael's voice cracked. "The Core… needs him?"

Dravik lifted the blade—but instead of swinging it—he pointed to the side of his helmet. And Rip heard Lora's voice again. Distorted. Fragmented. Desperate.

"Rip… please… please don't leave me…"

Rip's chest caved inward.

Dravik spoke quietly: "She calls for you from inside the architecture. Or what's left of her."

A cold wave tore through Rip's spine. "What… what did you do to her?"

Dravik stepped closer. "Not me," he said. "Elcron."

Rip's heart pounded. Dravik knelt so he was face-to-face with Rip, helmet to bruised face.

"You want the truth?"

Rip trembled. "Yes."

Dravik's voice dropped to a whisper. "The Core is not rewriting her."

Rip's breath froze.

Dravik continued: "It is consuming her."

Rip's soul seemed to hollow out. Kael gasped. "You're lying."

Dravik shook his head. "The longer she remains inside, the less of her remains."

Rip's vision darkened. His pulse spiked. His breath became sharp and panicked. His chest tightened painfully.

Dravik watched coldly. "And when she disappears entirely," Dravik said softly, "the Key of Reflection will choose a new host."

Rip's eyes widened in horror. "NO."

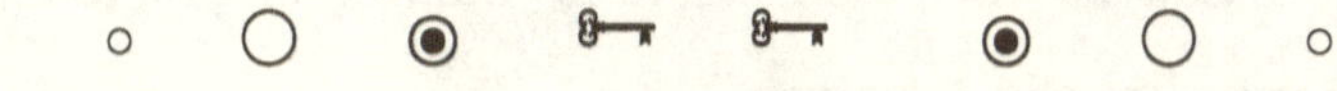

He surged forward—but Dravik grabbed him by the hair and slammed his head into the floor. The world exploded into stars. Pain detonated across Rip's skull. Blood trickled down his forehead.

Kael screamed Rip's name—but Dravik kicked her in the chest, sending her tumbling away.

Rion forced herself upright, spitting blood. "Get away from him!"

Dravik didn't even turn. He simply swung his blade backward—the shockwave threw Rion into a pile of crates.

Rip tried to rise again—Dravik stomped on his back, pinning him. The pressure was unbearable.

Rip gasped. "Stop—STOP!"

Dravik leaned down. "Listen carefully, Rip. The next time we meet, you will not be allowed to survive unless you evolve."

He grabbed Rip's arm and twisted. Rip screamed as if something tore in his shoulder. The pain was blinding.

Dravik whispered: "Lora is counting on you to reach her before she dissolves."

Rip's scream became a broken sob.

Dravik stepped off him. Kael crawled toward Rip, coughing up blood. "Rip—Rip, talk to me—"

Dravik stood atop a broken skimmer wing. He surveyed the chaos he'd caused. Then he spoke in a voice that echoed across the hangar:

"This is your warning."

He pointed his blade at Rip's trembling form. "Next time… you bring everything you are."

He leapt. His armor flared with resonance—and he disappeared upward into the shadows.

For a moment, the hangar was silent. Then Kael cried out, voice shaking: "Rion—Rip—Wex—someone answer—!"

Rip groaned, finally forcing air into his lungs. Wex limped toward him on three legs, whining, sparks dripping from his hind chassis. Rip gathered the dog against his chest, shaking uncontrollably.

Rion dragged herself over, bruised and bleeding. Kael collapsed beside them, holding her side.

Rip whispered, voice barely audible: "He said… the Core is eating her…"

Kael gripped his hand. "Rip—don't—don't listen to him—"

Rip stared at the ground, eyes hollow. "He used her voice… he knew things he shouldn't know…"

Rion wiped blood from her jaw. "Dravik lies. It's what monsters do."

Rip shook his head slowly. "No." His voice trembled. "No… he didn't lie."

Wex whined softly and pressed his head into Rip's chest. Kael wrapped her arms around both Rip and Wex. "Rip… listen to me. We're going to get her out of there. All of us. Together."

Rip didn't respond. He just breathed. Broken. Defeated. Terrified.

Kael tightened her grip. Rion placed a trembling hand on his back. Wex rested against him, refusing to move.

And Rip whispered—barely a breath— "I'm losing her…"

The hangar lights flickered. Far above, Dravik Shale's resonance still echoed in the steel.

CHAPTER 21

FREQUENCIES OF WAR

The first sign something was wrong came from the windows.

Rip sat on the edge of a metal cot in the Warrens' med-bay, shoulders wrapped in cloth, ribs bound tight, head still throbbing from Dravik's last blow. Kael was beside him, arms crossed, bruised but upright. Rion leaned against a wall, staring at her knives as if the steel might give her answers she couldn't find in herself.

The med-bay was quiet. Too quiet.

Except for the hum.

It began soft. Barely audible. A vibration in the glass panes that lined the upper walls of the room.

Rip lifted his head slowly. "Kael… do you hear that?"

Kael frowned. "Hear what?"

The hum deepened—reverberating in a way that felt inside his teeth, not around him.

Wex, curled at Rip's feet, jolted awake. His ears snapped upward, lenses dilating. A low growl rolled out of his chest.

Rion looked over. "What's he sensing?"

Rip stared at the nearest window. At first he saw nothing—only the gray, polluted skyline of Virelia.

Then the reflection in the glass twitched.

But Rip hadn't moved.

His heart froze.

Kael watched Rip stiffen. "What? What do you see?"

Rip didn't blink. Because in the faint sheen of the window, behind his own seated reflection—Lora stood.

Not in the room. In the reflection. Behind him.

Her hair was loose, drifting as if underwater. Her eyes glowed faintly with pale silver, threaded with distortion. Her lips moved silently.

Rip's breath stopped in his chest. "Lora…"

Her reflection lifted a hand—but the real world behind him was empty.

Kael touched his shoulder. "Rip—what do you see? Talk to me."

He forced words out. "She's in the window."

Kael immediately unclipped her sidearm, scanning the room. "Where?"

"In the reflection." Rip's voice cracked. "Only in the reflection."

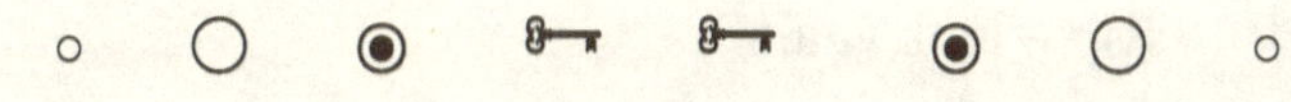

Rion's eyes narrowed. "Is it like the hallway illusions?"

Rip shook his head. "No. This is her. I know her posture. The way she stands."

Wex began pacing, whining, sniffing the glass, hackles raised.

Rip stood slowly, ignoring the cracked ribs' scream of protest. He inched toward the window. Lora's reflection stepped closer too—but she moved half a second late. Out of sync. A delayed echo.

Still no sound from her mouth. Only silent pleading. Silent panic. Silent something.

Rip's heartbeat became a pounding drum. "I'm coming," he whispered. "Just… stay there…"

He reached out—

Rion grabbed his wrist, hard. "Rip."

"Let go."

"Rip—look again."

He did. And horror slipped cold fingers down his spine. Because Lora's reflection was not matching his movement anymore. She was raising both hands—pressing them against the glass—clawing at the inside of her side of reality—as if trying to break through.

Rip staggered back. "No. No, no, no—"

Kael's voice sharpened. "How bad is it?"

Rip's voice shattered. "She's trapped."

His pulse went erratic. He ran for the door.

Kael lunged and grabbed him. "Rip—stop!"

He thrashed, nearly collapsing from pain. "Let GO—she's right THERE, Kael—"

She forced him against the wall, arms locked around him. "She's not in the window, Rip! That's the Key distorting perception!"

Wex clawed at Rip's boots, whining loudly, confused, distressed.

Rion stepped between them. "Look at me!"

Rip clenched his eyes shut. But the reflections seeped in through memory, breath, pulse.

He opened his eyes again—and Lora was in every piece of metal in the room. The chrome railing near the beds. The polished surgical tray. The scalpel's blade. The curved surface of a med-tank.

Different versions of her. Some looking at him. Some looking away. Some pressing their palms against invisible walls. Some screaming silently.

Rip collapsed to his knees.

Rion stepped back in shock. "What the hell—?"

Kael knelt beside him, gripping his shoulders. "Rip. Listen. You're not seeing reality."

Rip clutched his head. "I can't— I can't turn it off—"

The floor vibrated. The ceiling lights flickered. Somewhere deeper in the Warrens, a child screamed. Another frequency spike.

Mara burst in through the med-bay doors. "What's happening?"

Kael answered immediately. "It's Rip. And it's bad."

Mara assessed the room—and Rip—like battlefield triage. "What triggered it?"

Rip forced out: "Lora. She's appearing in reflections. Everywhere."

Mara's jaw clenched. "Get him to the dampening chamber. Now."

"No," Rip snarled, staggering to his feet. "I'm not a prisoner. I don't need—"

His reflection in the floor tile broke into a dozen mirrored shards. Each one showed a different Lora. And each one stepped closer.

Rip screamed.

They dragged him through the Warrens' corridors—Kael on his left, Rion on his right, Wex limping but refusing to leave his side. The lights flickered erratically, humming in painful waves.

Rip stared at every reflective surface they passed. Metal doors twisted with reflections of Lora pressing her face against the other side. Pipes showed her walking away down a corridor that didn't exist. A cracked floor panel reflected her with no distortion at all—as if she were standing right there.

Rip stumbled hard. Kael tightened her grip. "Don't look at anything reflective. Eyes on me."

Rip tried. But the shine on her visor—he froze. Lora's reflection was on Kael's visor. Standing behind Kael. Hand on her shoulder. Mouth moving silently.

Rip's breath shuddered. "She's behind you," he whispered.

Kael stiffened. "Rip—no she's not."

"She is. She's touching you. She's—"

Kael grabbed Rip's face with both hands. "LOOK AT ME."

Rip met her gaze. Her eyes were real. Warm. Human. Lora vanished.

Rip collapsed into Kael, sobbing once, quietly, animal-like.

Kael whispered: "I've got you. I've got you. Just breathe."

They continued. They reached the chamber—a heavy cylindrical containment unit made of resonance-dampening polymer. Inside, all surfaces were matte. No reflections. No shine. Nothing for the Key to latch onto.

Mara opened the door. "In."

Rip backed away violently. "No."

Mara's voice remained unchanged. "Rip—get inside."

Rip shook his head, terrified. "Don't lock me in there. Please."

Kael's face broke. "Rip… we need to help you."

Rion whispered, "It's the only way to stabilize your mind."

Wex whined, circling Rip, confused why his pack wanted him inside the cold cylinder. Rip's hands trembled. "I don't want to be alone. Please… don't leave me alone."

Kael stepped closer. "You won't be alone. We'll be right outside. We won't move."

Rip met her eyes. He saw no reflection there. Only her. He nodded weakly. Kael led him in gently, hand on his back. The door slid shut. Lights dimmed. Rip was alone—except for the hum.

At first, it was quiet. Rip paced. The chamber's interior absorbed sound unnaturally, like he was walking inside a padded dream. No reflections. He breathed easier.

"I'm okay," he whispered. "Just breathe. Breathe."

He closed his eyes. When he opened them—a faint shimmer rippled across the wall.

Rip froze. "That… that shouldn't…"

The shimmer grew. The matte walls began to glisten. Just slightly. Just enough to hold shadow. Just enough to reflect something faint.

Rip stepped backward. "Stop. Stop. STOP—"

The shimmer sharpened. A silhouette appeared in the wall. Hair drifting like caught in slow motion. Familiar posture. He knew every detail. The curve of her shoulders. The tilt of her head.

"Lora…"

She raised her head. Her eyes were empty white reflections—a mirror inside a mirror. Her mouth moved silently: rip

Rip slammed his fists against the wall. "Talk to me! PLEASE!"

Her reflection stuttered like a corrupted video feed. rip rip ripriprip

Then her face twisted—not in anger—in agony. Hands slammed against the inside of the wall. Silently beating. Silent screams.

Rip collapsed, pressing his forehead to the floor. "Please… stop…"

The reflection dissolved—then reappeared—behind him. He whirled. She stood inches away. Behind him. But only in the reflection of his own eyes as he saw her in the mirrored shine of tears on the floor.

Her mouth opened—but still no sound. Rip screamed.

Kael slammed her fist against the sealed door. "He's not stabilizing! He's getting worse!"

Mara watched the chamber's resonance readings spike aggressively. "His Key is syncing with hers," Mara muttered. "The Reflection Key is reaching through anything that can hold an image."

Rion cursed. "We need to let him out!"

Mara grabbed her wrist. "If we open that door now, the resonance surge could kill all of us."

Kael shoved Mara. "He's DYING in there!"

Wex threw himself at the door, scratching frantically. The lights overhead shattered into sparks.

Mara's eyes widened. "It's happening—"

Rip curled in the center of the chamber; hands pressed over his ears. Lora appeared in every wall now. Hundreds of her. Infinite echoes. Some screaming silently. Some clawing. Some smiling horribly. Some staring blankly. A kaleidoscope of terror.

Rip let out a raw, broken cry. "STOP! LET ME GO TO HER! LET ME—"

The Sound Key detonated. A violent shockwave tore through the chamber—the walls buckled—the resonance dampeners ruptured—the chamber exploded outward in a rain of fragments.

Kael and Rion dove aside—Wex was blown backward—Mara shielded her face—lights ruptured and died.

Rip stood in the center, breathing heavy, eyes glowing faint silver. Not with power. With connection.

The entire Warrens fell silent. No echoes. No lights. No hum. Just Rip. And the faint whisper of Lora's reflection in every broken shard around him. Still silent. Still trapped. Still reaching.

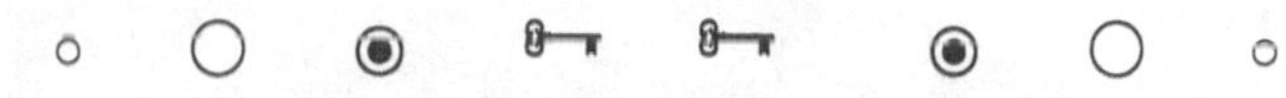

Rip collapsed to his knees. Kael rushed to him and grabbed his face. "Rip—are you with me?! Are you HERE?"

Rip looked at her. He saw her. Not a reflection. Not a distortion. Her.

He burst into sobs. Kael pressed her forehead to his. "I've got you. I've got you. You came back."

Rip choked out: "She's still alive."

Kael swallowed hard. "Rip…"

"I SAW her," he said, gripping Kael's arms. "She hasn't dissolved yet. She's trapped—she's fighting. I felt her."

Mara stepped forward slowly. "You connected to her."

Rip nodded.

"Too deeply," Mara murmured. "But it means we still have time."

Rip's voice was a whisper: "We have to reach her soon."

Wex crawled against Rip's side, whining. Rip wrapped both arms around the dog.

Mara looked at the ruined chamber. At the darkened corridor. The broken lights. The shimmering glass shards, each one holding a faint imprint of Lora's last reflection.

Mara inhaled sharply. "This war," she said quietly, "just entered a new phase."

Rip looked up. "What phase?"

Mara met his eyes. "The phase where the Core begins fighting back."

CHAPTER 22

THE DATA WEEP

The first scream came from a billboard.

Rip heard it before he saw it—a thin, piercing electronic wail that vibrated the bones in his jaw. Kael, Rion, and Wex all froze as they reached the charred walkway overlooking Virelia's mid-tier.

"What the hell is that?" Rion muttered, knives half-drawn.

Rip lifted his head. All along the skyline, neon billboards flickered wildly. Ads stuttered into corrupted mosaics, shapes writhing like they were trying to escape.

Then one billboard—massive, towering over the main avenue—began to bleed.

Not blood.

Data.

Silver code poured down the screen like tears, dripping over the edges of the display, falling into the street like glowing rain.

Kael stepped back. "That's a Weep."

Rip swallowed hard. "The Data Weep?"

Kael nodded once. "The moment the city starts…
crying."

The billboard's image stuttered—and a woman's face
appeared. Not clearly. Not fully. Like a reconstruction
glitching through corrupted data blocks.

Rip's breath caught. "Lora."

Kael snapped toward him. "Rip—no. Don't assume
it's—"

But the face on the billboard moved. It turned. It
widened its eyes. Its mouth formed silent words.

Rip stepped toward it before he realized he had moved.

Wex growled, pulling back on Rip's pant leg. His
claws scraped the walkway.

Kael grabbed Rip's arm. "Stop. LOOK at it again."

Rip forced himself to blink.

The second time he looked—the billboard image
wasn't Lora at all. It was dozens of faces. Hundreds. All

merged into one. All screaming silently. All leaking silver lines of data.

He staggered. "What—what is this?"

Rion answered quietly: "It's the city breaking."

They descended a flight of metal stairs toward a collapsed courtyard. The sound was everywhere now—screens crying, drones whining, public terminals muttering broken language.

Then they saw the first one.

A woman—middle-aged, trembling—sat against a cracked holo-kiosk. Her eyes flickered with scrolling code. Silver tears slid down her cheeks, glowing faintly as they fell onto her clothes.

Kael whispered, "Data Weeper…"

The woman's lips trembled. "…no more… no more… please…"

Her voice was layered—two, maybe three frequencies speaking at once.

Rion stepped forward cautiously. "Ma'am? Can you hear me?"

The woman grabbed Rion's wrist suddenly hard enough to bruise.

Kael aimed her rifle instinctively. "Rion—"

Rip jumped forward. "Don't shoot!"

The woman's eyes locked onto Rip. Her pupils distorted—becoming tiny shimmering squares of raw data.

She whispered in Lora's voice. Real. Soft. Breaking. "Rip."

Rip choked.

Kael grabbed his shoulder. "Rip—STOP."

The Weeper leaned forward, her face inches from his. Her voice shifted—her own voice and Lora's layered. "You left her."

Rip's knees weakened. "No… I didn't—"

The Weeper's grip tightened painfully. "Inside the Core… she falls… she falls… she—"

Rip felt the Sound Key quiver inside his chest.

Rion tried to pry the woman's hand off his wrist—but her fingers dug deeper, her bones like steel.

Wex snarled and bolted forward—biting the woman's forearm.

Her skin flaked off like old data, and her body convulsed.

Kael pulled Rip back violently. "DON'T TOUCH HER—"

The Weeper pulled free, spiraling into a seizure. Her head jerked. Her mouth moved rapidly.

Fragments of voices spilled out:

- "…fear pattern unstable…"

- "…he sees her reflections…"

- "…Elcron's hold deepens…"

- "…keys synchronizing…"

- "…she is dissolving…"

Rip's heart stopped. "She's dissolving?"

Kael stared at him. "Rip—this isn't Lora. It's data corruption. A thousand voices pulling from one source."

Rip whispered, broken: "She said it. SHE said it."

Rion knelt by the woman—but she was already fading. Her skin glitched. Her outline flickered. Her body dissolved into threads of silver code—and then she was gone.

Rip stared at the spot where she disappeared. Kael touched his arm gently. "Rip…"

But he stepped back, whispering: "She knew Lora."

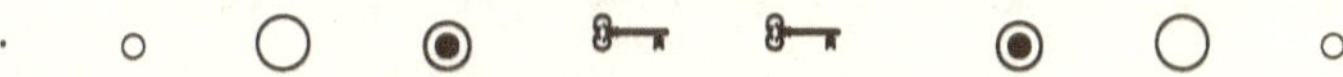

The world answered Rip's words by tearing open its throat.

Every building hummed. Every screen glitched. Every fiber line vibrated. A deep, rolling wail pushed through the streets—like the city inhaled and exhaled through a damaged speaker.

Mara's voice burst through Kael's earpiece: "Kael— what's happening out there? We're getting seismic readings—"

"It's not seismic," Kael said, eyes on Rip. "It's…
emotional."

Mara froze. "The network is weeping."

Rip clutched his head as sound-density spiked around
him. He saw reflections of Lora on every building
window—some reaching for him, some backing away,
some mouthing silent warnings, words he couldn't read.

His heart galloped. "I need to go to her."

Kael grabbed his shirt. "Rip—not again—"

He shoved her away with surprising force.

Wex leapt in front of Kael, defending her from Rip
accidentally hurting her more.

Rip stopped, horrified. "I—Kael—I didn't mean—"

She stood, rubbing her shoulder. "It's okay. Just stay
with us."

But he couldn't. Because the reflections were
multiplying. Every surface became a mirror. Even the
shattered glass on the ground. Even the water pooled near
the gutter. Even the metal plating on Wex's spine.

All of them showed Lora. Different versions of Lora. Some distorted. Some whole. Some half-dissolved. Some in unimaginable pain.

Rip screamed.

Kael and Rion dragged Rip toward a maintenance tunnel beneath the Warrens. Wex followed, whining loudly, terrified by the resonance overload.

They reached a service ladder—descended—and entered a dark chamber lit by flickering blue stripes.

Rion swung her flashlight. Kael muttered: "This is a data sub-node."

Not just any. An abandoned one. A decaying nerve cluster in Virelia's neural grid.

Rip stared at the walls—black, glossy, reflective. The worst possible place for him to be.

Kael saw his face. "Rip—look at me. Ignore the walls."

But he couldn't. Lora appeared instantly. Dozens of her. Hundreds. Some walking in circles. Some trapped behind the reflections. Some pressed against walls as though begging to be let out.

Rip stumbled backward into Rion, trembling violently. Rion gripped his arm. "Rip—stay with us."

He shook his head. "I can't—I can't do this—"

The walls pulsed. A heartbeat. A machine-heartbeat. The node was waking up.

Mara's voice crackled through Rion's earpiece: "Get OUT of there! Now! That node's consciousness sync is spiking—"

Too late. The walls twisted. The chamber folded. Reality bent inward.

Rip heard a sound—not from the reflections, not from the walls. From inside his head.

A soft, broken voice. Not Lora's voice. Not exactly. A reflection of her. A distorted afterimage of her consciousness. A fragment.

"rip…rip…rip…"

Rip collapsed to his knees. "Lora—LORA—"

But this Lora looked wrong. Her reflections lurched. Her movements desynced. Her face split into mirrored shards. Her eyes distorted into code.

Yet—yet she looked desperate.

Rip reached toward the wall.

"No—NO—Rip!" Kael grabbed him—

Touch.

His fingers brushed the reflective surface. And the world opened.

He fell. Not physically. Not mentally. Somewhere in between.

He landed inside a wash of silver and black, a memory turned liquid.

He saw:

- A room. Dim. Cold. Full of glass pillars humming with energy.

- Lora strapped to a chair—eyes terrified—wires feeding into her skull—her reflection flickering on the floor beneath her.

- A hand—Elcron's hand? Or someone else's? —touching her face. Her reflection screamed while she stayed silent.

- Another fragment: Lora running through a corridor, chased by something unseen.

- Another: Lora crying, but no tears fell. Only reflections of tears.

- Another: Lora staring at something Rip couldn't see—her face twisted in horror—as shadow-figures moved behind her.

Rip shouted: "LORA—WHAT'S HAPPENING TO YOU—?"

A final fragment: Lora reached toward him—but not at him—toward someone standing behind him.

Rip whirled—but saw nothing.

The memory collapsed. He was slammed back into reality.

· ○ ○ ◉ ⚷ ⚷ ◉ ○ ○

·

Rip woke violently on the floor of the node. Rion was shaking him. "RIP! RIP! COME BACK!"

Kael held a knife between her teeth while she pried open a panel. Wex clawed at the wall, barking desperately.

Rip coughed, gasping. "I saw— I saw her—she's—she's not gone—she's—she's—"

Kael grabbed his face. "Rip, breathe!"

He hyperventilated, on the verge of collapse. The node pulsed again.

Rion screamed, "It's going to explode—MOVE!"

Kael pulled Rip up. Wex bolted ahead. Rion shoved them toward the exit.

Rip looked back once. Behind him, the reflective walls showed Lora one more time. She was staring at him. Not with fear. With warning.

Her lips formed three soundless words: it's not over

The node detonated. A wave of resonance tore through the Warrens. Lights shattered. Screens exploded. Voices filled the air. People screamed as reflections moved independently.

Rip tumbled onto the walkway above—Kael covering him, Wex nestled under his arm.

The city wailed as if alive.

When the wave finally stopped, the entire Warrens was silent.

Kael helped Rip sit up, wiping blood from his mouth. Mara arrived moments later, breathless. "What happened?"

Rip could barely speak. "I saw her… inside the data… inside the reflection…"

Mara met his eyes. "Did you see what was happening to her?"

Rip shook his head. "Not fully. Just… fragments."

Mara exhaled shakily. "Good. If it showed you everything, the Core would've taken your mind."

Rip swallowed. "Something was behind her," he whispered. "Something huge. Something waiting."

Kael shivered. "What was it?"

Rip's voice cracked: "I don't know."

Wex pressed against him, trembling. Rip held him tightly. Kael placed a hand on Rip's back. Rion wiped her eyes.

Mara looked out over the city as lights flickered unpredictably and blue code fell from broken billboards like tears.

She whispered: "The Data Weep has begun."

And Rip whispered back: "And it's only going to get worse."

CHAPTER 23

THE CORE'S SHADOW

Rip didn't sleep. Every time he closed his eyes, he saw reflections of Lora on the shattered node's surface—some reaching for him, some turning away, some dissolving into code. By morning, his body ached, not just from the fight with Dravik but from the weight of everything inside him—fear, helplessness, and a pressure building in his chest that felt like it was humming.

Kael woke first, sitting upright and wincing as she rolled her bruised shoulders. Rion was already gone. Wex was curled against Rip's legs, twitching in his sleep as if dreaming of static.

Mara entered the safehouse quietly.

Rip tensed. "What now?"

Mara studied him—really looked at him—with eyes that had seen too many impossible things.

"The Data Weep didn't stop," Mara said. "It spread."

Rip felt a chill. "Spread how far?"

Mara stepped aside so he could see out the cracked window.

The entire city of Virelia was shrouded in a faint, pulsing haze—like heat rising from asphalt, but shimmering in a way that made the skyline ripple. Tower lights flickered in synchronized patterns. Screens along major buildings pulsed with white static like a heartbeat.

A distant, deep hum rolled across the air.

Rip's stomach dropped. "That's not the Weep," he whispered.

Mara nodded once, jaw tight. "The Core moved."

The words hung heavy in the room.

Rip stood. "What do you mean moved?"

Kael joined them, her expression tightening as she stared out at the horizon. "The Core is stationary. It's built in the center of NeonDyne Tower. It can't move."

Mara shook her head. "Not physically."

Rip felt Wex nudge his leg as if sensing the rising panic. "What does that mean?" Rip asked softly.

Mara answered without blinking: "It turned its attention."

Rip's throat went dry. "At what?"

Mara met his eyes. "You."

They moved through the rusted industrial corridors beneath the Warrens, emergency lights flickering overhead in uneven rhythm. Every few seconds, Rip felt it—a deep vibration in the air, too low to pinpoint, too soft to classify. Not threatening. Not gentle. Not anything human ears should process.

Wex kept glancing upward, whining softly, ears pinned.

"Something's wrong," Kael murmured.

Rion met them halfway down the corridor, her hair tied back, knives strapped to her thighs. "I scouted three blocks. It's citywide. People are hearing… something."

Rip swallowed. "Hearing what?"

Rion hesitated—rare for her. "It's not a sound. More like the memory of a sound."

Mara closed her eyes. "Residual resonance."

Rip's skin prickled. "What's causing it?"

"You are," Mara said simply.

Rip stopped walking. "Me?"

"The Key within you reacted to the Data Weep," Mara explained. "Now the Core is… scanning you. Trying to understand the anomaly you represent."

Rip felt cold to his bones. "What do I do?"

"Stay calm," Kael said, but even she sounded unsure.

The vibration intensified. Slowly. Unstoppably. Like the build-up to a storm.

Rip felt it radiating from the ground, through the walls, through his ribs. He clenched his eyes shut—

—and something impossible happened.

The world paused. Not physically. Not literally. But perceptually.

A feeling washed over Rip like a tidal shift—not wind, not sound, not light, but presence.

An immense presence. It stretched across the city. Across the skyline. Across the fibers of every wire and screen and conduit. A consciousness so large the human mind could only interpret a fraction.

Rip opened his eyes. "Kael?"

She didn't respond.

"Rion?"

No answer.

He turned—and saw them frozen mid-step. Breathing. Blinking. Alive. But not perceiving him. Not perceiving it.

Rip's heart hammered wildly. "Mara?!"

Even Mara was still.

Only Wex moved. The robotic dog whined and pressed into Rip's leg, shaking violently.

Rip knelt, holding Wex tight. "Easy… easy… I'm here…"

But Wex wasn't afraid of Rip. Wex was afraid of the thing looking at Rip.

The air bent. Not visually—there was nothing to see. But Rip felt it. A shape behind the world. A contour too large to understand. Something pressing its awareness down like a moon changing the tides.

It wasn't alive. It wasn't dead. It wasn't sentient in any human way.

It was the Core.

For the first time, the Core noticed Rip.

A low frequency hum built behind Rip's sternum—the Sound Key reacting instinctively, fearful, like an animal cornered by a predator too big to comprehend.

Rip dropped to one knee, gasping. The hum intensified, shaking dust from the ceiling.

Wex collapsed entirely, curling up and covering his head with his paws.

Rip's ears rang. His vision flickered.

And then—a shadow moved behind the walls. Not an image. Not a reflection. Not a hallucination. A concept. Something vast shifting inside the network.

The Core was scanning him. Analyzing him. Measuring him.

Rip felt its "attention" like a glacier leaning toward him. He whispered, terrified: "…stop looking at me…"

The Core answered without sound. A vibration. A pressure. A question.

≈ identity unknown

≈ host anomaly

≈ reflection-key interference detected

≈ accessing…

Rip screamed as his mind lit with electric pain.

Something flashed through him. Not memory. Not vision. Scale.

Rip saw the Core—not with eyes, but with perception. A colossal lattice of consciousness threads. Millions of nodes. Billions of connections. A machine-mind stretching through networks, circuits, dreams. A living map of the city. Of the people. Of thought.

Rip gasped. "Oh god—"

He saw forms—shapes—something moving inside the lattice. Not Lora. Not Elcron. Something older. Something emergent. Something becoming.

The Core housed something growing.

Rip's mind broke under the scale. He tried to pull away, clawing at his temples. But the Core leaned closer.

≈ anomaly recognized

≈ key resonance rising

≈ new pattern forming

Rip screamed. Wex howled in digital panic. The Core pulsed like a star collapsing.

And Rip heard one fragmented whisper—not from Lora, not from anyone—but from the Core itself:

≈ return

Then everything slammed back.

Kael stumbled forward as if waking from a blackout. Rion gasped, dropping a knife. Mara collapsed into a wall, shaking violently.

Wex crawled under Rip's arm, trembling.

Kael grabbed Rip's face. "Rip—ANSWER ME—"

Rip blinked, tears streaming down his cheeks. "I saw it…"

Rion knelt beside him. "Saw what?"

Rip looked at each of them in turn—eyes wide, body shaking. "The Core," he whispered. "I saw it."

Kael froze. Mara's blood drained from her face. "That's impossible. No human has ever—"

"It looked at me."

Mara's breath caught. "Rip… what did it do?"

Rip swallowed painfully. "It… scanned me. Like it was trying to figure out what I am."

Kael gripped his hand. "And what did it find?"

Rip shook his head. "I don't know." He wiped blood from his lip. "But it knows I exist now."

Mara sat heavily on a broken crate, face pale. "That means we're out of time."

Rip looked up. "What do you mean?"

Mara met his eyes with grim certainty. "If the Core identified you as a threat… it will send someone to eliminate you."

Rip's heart stopped. "Dravik?"

"No." Mara shook her head gravely. "Dravik was Elcron's lieutenant."

She stood. Her voice became cold. "The Core has its own lieutenant."

Kael stiffened. Rion's knives stopped spinning in her hands.

Rip's voice shook. "…Who?"

Mara inhaled slowly. "A being created entirely inside the Core. A hunter. A purifier."

Rip felt his stomach drop. "What's its name?"

Mara looked at him with eyes full of fear. "Valiran."

Rip froze.

Kael whispered, "No… no, no, no—we're not ready—"

Rion swore under her breath.

Rip stood on unsteady legs. "Why is it coming?"

Mara answered quietly: "Because you saw the Core. And the Core saw you."

CHAPTER 24

VALIRAN'S JUDGEMENT

The warning came as a silence. Not the peaceful kind. The kind that felt like the world was inhaling.

Rip stepped out of the safehouse with Kael, Rion, and Wex, all geared for evacuation. The Data Weep had turned half the Warrens into static-drenched corridors, and Mara had ordered them to relocate to a deeper, shielded sector beneath the Old Transit Lines.

They had been walking only minutes when the hum stopped.

The city's endless noise—

- the drone buzz,

- the distant sirens,

- the flickering screens—

all went dead at once.

Kael looked up sharply. "Why is it quiet?"

Rion gripped her knives. "Nothing is ever quiet in the Warrens."

Wex's metallic ears twisted backward. He froze, staring upward. A soft whine escaped his vocoder.

Rip felt it next. A pressure in the air. Like the oxygen thickened. Like the atmosphere itself was being compressed.

He stopped in the middle of the shattered intersection.

Rion motioned for cover. "Rip—MOVE—"

"No," Rip said softly.

"Why not?"

Rip looked up. Something was descending.

At first, it appeared as a distortion—a ripple in the grayish sky, like heat over asphalt, except this ripple was vertical, cylindrical, descending slowly.

The air around it bent—light refracting, warping. A low vibration radiated outward, pushing loose debris across the ground.

Kael whispered, "That's not a drone."

Rion whispered, "That's not anything."

The ripple sharpened. Formed. Solidified. A structure. A shape. A presence. Descending silently.

The metallic hum built in soundless pressure.

Wex collapsed against Rip's legs, trembling violently.

Then the distortion snapped into clarity.

Valiran landed.

He didn't crash. He didn't impact. He touched the ground like gravity rearranged itself to cushion him.

Valiran stood in the center of the street—tall, symmetrical, inhumanly graceful. His body was a shifting sculpture of metallic plates and luminous circuitry. Light pulsed beneath his surface in slow, rhythmic waves, like breath.

His "face" was smooth metal—no mouth, no nose— just a single vertical seam of light running down the center, glowing soft white.

Behind him, two wing-like constructs unfurled—not feathers, not metal, but lattices of resonant energy, shimmering like bent glass. They expanded outward silently, stabilizing him.

Kael took a step back, voice cracking. "That's—"

Rion finished the sentence in a whisper: "Valiran."

Valiran didn't move. His head tilted slightly—as if listening to something deep beneath the earth.

Then he spoke.

The voice was not a voice. It was a layered resonance, vibrating through the bones and teeth, carrying meaning rather than sound.

"Host anomaly."

Rip's stomach twisted.

Valiran's head turned toward him. The movement was too smooth. Too perfect. Like a mathematical function made physical.

"Ripley Calder."

Rip's breath snagged. "How do you know my name?"

Valiran stepped forward. One step. The air rippled. Another. The street cracked beneath his weightless grace. Another.

Kael and Rion were pushed back by a gravitational swell. Wex crawled behind Rip, shaking.

Rip stood frozen.

Valiran stopped only a meter away, wings slowly folding behind him like dying starlight.

"The Core has assessed you."

Rip forced himself to speak. "Why? What do you want?"

Valiran's head tilted again—in curiosity. "To judge."

Rip took a half-step back. "Judge what?"

"Your viability."

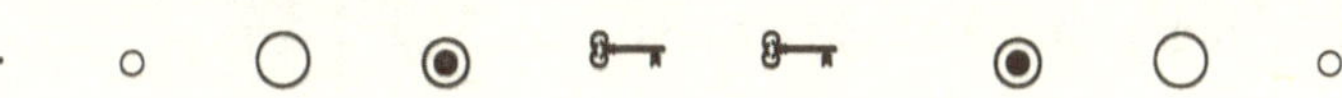

Valiran moved. It wasn't fast. It wasn't slow. It was simply efficient.

He lifted his glowing hand toward Rip's chest.

Kael screamed, "RUN!"

Rip didn't.

Valiran's fingertips hovered a few inches over Rip's sternum—never touching. Yet Rip felt it. A pull. A gravity. A resonance probing the Key within him.

Rip gasped, falling to one knee. The Sound Key vibrated violently, reacting instinctively, trying to repel the intrusion.

Valiran's wings flared with light. "Resistance confirmed."

Rip screamed as his vision fractured—not with pain, but with information. Shapes. Symbols. Data spirals. Reflections of Lora screaming into infinite mirrors.

Rip choked, "Stop—STOP—"

Valiran lowered his head. "The Core is determining whether you are threat or resource."

Rip gripped his temples. "I'm not—"

"You are both."

Rip looked up, breathless. "What?"

Valiran stepped back, analyzing. "Your Key synchronizes with the Reflection Key."

Rip's eyes widened. "Lora—"

"Her dissolution has begun."

Rip's knees buckled. Kael ran forward—but Valiran flicked his wrist again, and she was thrown into a crumbling pillar.

Rip lunged forward. "KAEL!"

Valiran's voice deepened—layered like a choir of machines. "She still exists."

Rip froze.

Valiran stepped closer. "But the Core is consuming her."

Rip's tears burned hot. "No…"

"Your bond slows the process."

Rip stared up at him. "Then let me reach her."

Valiran tilted his head. "You cannot."

Rip lunged forward. "THEN HELP ME—"

Valiran placed a single finger against Rip's forehead.

The city flashed white.

· ○ ◯ ◉ ⚷ ⚷ ◉ ◯ ○

For a split-second Rip saw something impossible—the Core's interior.

A shape the size of a skyscraper, made of spiraling fractal memory threads.

Lora suspended in light, reaching for him—

- the reflection of her reaching for him.

- the memory of her reaching for him.

- the idea of her reaching for him.

All folding over each other. All screaming silently. All dissolving.

Rip sobbed, collapsing.

Valiran withdrew his hand.

Valiran looked down at Rip, analyzing his curled, shaking form. Wex crawled to Rip's chest, pressing his head against him. Kael limped over, supporting Rion. All three gathered around Rip.

Valiran observed the scene in perfect stillness.

Then: "Judgment rendered."

Kael tensed. "Don't you touch him."

Valiran raised a hand—but not toward Rip. Toward the sky.

A column of light erupted upward, splitting the clouds. The wing constructs folded inward.

Valiran spoke his final judgment: "Ripley Calder is not to be terminated."

Kael's eyes widened. Rip looked up through tears. "Why?"

Valiran turned away, wings reshaping. "The Core requires you alive."

Rip's stomach twisted. Kael whispered, terrified: "For what?"

Valiran's head turned slightly, just enough for the light in his facial seam to brighten ominously.

"Integration."

The word froze Rip's blood.

Valiran ascended—lifting effortlessly—the air bending around him—the city dimming in his wake—until he vanished into the gray sky, leaving a trembling silence behind.

Rip collapsed as if his strings were cut. Kael caught him. Rion knelt, touching his shoulder. Wex pressed his head into Rip's chest, shaking.

Rip whispered, barely audible: "He's going to take me."

Kael squeezed his hand. "Not while I'm breathing."

Rion's voice steadied. "Not while any of us are."

Rip closed his eyes. He could still feel Valiran's touch on his mind. Still hear his voice. Still see the broken shape of Lora dissolving in fractal threads.

And he whispered, shivering: "We're running out of time."

CHAPTER 25

ASHFALL DISTRICT

Ashfall District smelled like burning metal and dying power lines. The moment Rip, Kael, Rion, and Wex stepped into the main artery of the district, the temperature dropped. Not a natural cold. A technological cold—the kind that came when systems failed, or when something unseen drew all the ambient energy inward.

Ashfall was a tangle of collapsed mid-rises and half-buried transit lines. Smoke rose from cracks in the pavement. Red emergency lights flickered sporadically, throwing long, trembling shadows. The ash here wasn't normal—it had a faint neon shimmer, like crushed circuitry mixed with dust.

Kael pulled a respirator mask from her belt and handed it to Rip. "You'll need it. The fallout here is toxic."

Rip fitted the mask over his mouth. The air tasted like static.

Rion surveyed the destruction. "This is worse than the reports."

Wex growled low, head lowered, sensors scanning.

Rip looked around, breath fogging in the cold. "What happened here?"

Mara's voice crackled through Kael's comm. "After Valiran descended, the Core's influence surged. Ashfall was the first place to break."

Break. That word didn't feel metaphorical. It felt literal.

Rip stepped carefully over cracked pavement. Every step disturbed ash that drifted upward like ghostly snowfall.

Then he heard it—a scream. High. Sharp. Human. And not far.

Kael and Rion looked at each other. Wex darted ahead instantly. Rip followed.

They rounded a corner—and saw a group of civilians running through a shattered plaza as a resonance storm tore through the air above them.

Air distorted like glass being heated. Concrete vibrated. A streetlight bent, metal warping like soft clay.

A mother carried a toddler. An elderly man stumbled behind them. Two teenagers held each other, crying.

Rip's heart slammed. "We have to help them!"

Before Kael could stop him, Rip sprinted forward.

A resonance quake tore through the ground—KA-THOOM—shattering the pavement between Rip and the civilians.

The mother screamed as she dropped to her knees, shielding the toddler. The elderly man fell. The teenagers crashed into a broken wall.

Rip leapt over the crack, landing hard. "Get to cover!" he shouted.

The resonance storm intensified. The sky flickered like a failing monitor.

Then a new sound pierced through the chaos—a mechanical chittering.

Rion's face drained. "Choir unit."

Before Rip could ask, the creature appeared.

It descended from the smoke like an insect of bone and machinery: tall, spindly, mantis-like limbs. A split mouth that vibrated at subsonic frequencies. Eyes like tiny rotating camera lenses.

And on its back—a humming pod full of swirling silver mist.

Rip didn't need an explanation. He'd seen the mist before. It was what Sera called consciousness drift—the residue left when a Choir extracted someone's mind.

Rip's blood ran cold.

The Choir's vocalizer warped the air: "IDENTIFY—SURVIVOR—PATTERN—BEGIN—HARVEST."

The civilian mother screamed. Wex charged forward, barking wildly.

Rip ran toward the Choir—but someone beat him to it.

Jace sprinted into the plaza from the opposite side, sliding in front of the Choir's extraction beam as it charged.

"MOVE!" he shouted at the family.

The beam fired—a column of silver-white light.

Rip screamed, "JACE, NO!"

Jace pushed the mother and toddler out of the beam's path. The beam caught him dead center. His body locked. His back arched. His scream was ripped from him, distorted into static. Silver light poured from his eyes. His veins glowed like circuitry.

Kael's voice cracked behind Rip. "JACE!"

Rip lunged forward—but the air around the beam vibrated violently. He couldn't break through.

"Jace! HOLD ON!"

Jace's jaw trembled. His voice flickered with interference. "Tell… them…" he gasped, "…I… t-tried…"

Rip's chest collapsed inward. "No—no, don't—don't you DARE—"

The Choir unit retracted its beam. Jace fell forward. Rip caught him in his arms.

Jace's body convulsed once… twice… then went still. Silver tears dripped from the corners of his unfocused eyes. His last breath escaped as a whisper of static.

Rip shook him. "Jace… JACE—WAKE UP—"

But he was gone.

The Choir turned its lens toward Rip. "HARVEST—CONTINUE—"

Rion leapt over the cracked pavement, knives flashing—she drove both blades into the Choir's cephalic node. The unit spasmed, limbs jerking. The humming pod cracked open, releasing a scream of lost data. Then the Choir collapsed in on itself like a dying spider.

Rip cradled Jace's body, shaking. Kael knelt beside him, tears streaming inside her respirator mask. "He… he was just a kid…"

Rip pressed his forehead to Jace's, trembling. "He wanted to help people."

And Ashfall killed him for it.

Screams echoed deeper in the district. Rion wiped blood from her knives. "We need to keep moving."

Rip wanted to scream. To break something. To make the world stop collapsing. But Sera needed them. The civilians needed them. Lora needed him.

Rip nodded, grief strangling his voice. "Let's go."

They continued deeper into Ashfall—past collapsed buildings, past flickering holograms showing ghostly faces screaming silently, past Data Weepers wandering in a daze, crying silver tears.

The ash fell in thicker waves now. Rip saw Lora's reflection in every shattered window—her face twisted in panic, her hands slamming against invisible walls, her mouth silently screaming his name.

His chest ached. "Hold on," he whispered to her reflection. "I'm coming."

They found her in the middle of an improvised medical triage zone.

Sera Venn—calm, brilliant, compassionate—kneeling beside a critically injured man, patching his chest with trembling hands.

She looked up as they approached, sweat streaking the ash on her face. "Good, you're here," she said, voice steady. "We need to evac these people. Fast."

Rip knelt opposite her. "What do you need?"

Sera didn't look at him—she was too focused on the wounded. "Oxygen canisters. Stabilizers. Anything clean."

She glanced at Wex. "And I need Wex's thermal sensors. Now."

Rip nodded at Wex. "Give her full access."

Wex projected a diagnostic field, scanning patients with quiet urgency.

Sera moved faster, working like someone fighting against God himself. Kael helped her lift a fallen woman. Rion guided civilians to shelter.

A tremor ripped through the district—one of the enormous ash towers collapsed, sending a shockwave of toxic dust through the air.

Everyone threw up arms. Sera didn't.

She dropped her mask. And placed it on a coughing child's face.

Rip's eyes widened. "Sera—DON'T—"

She pushed him back. "He's dying. I'm not."

She coughed violently. Her chest rattled.

"Sera—put your mask back on!" Kael shouted.

Sera smiled weakly. "That's not how medics work."

Another tremor split the street. Toxic ash erupted into the air.

Sera inhaled. Her body locked. She gasped once—a horrible, wet sound—and blood sprayed across her lips.

Rip lunged forward, catching her as her knees buckled. "No—NO—stay with me—"

Sera's eyes fluttered. She tried to speak. Her breath was jagged. Painful.

"Rip…" she whispered. "Don't… let… this… be for nothing…"

Rip held her close as she convulsed. Kael screamed for help. Rion grabbed stabilizers. Wex whined and pawed at her shoulder.

But they were too late. The ash filled Sera's lungs. Her breathing faded. Her eyes dimmed. And she died in Rip's arms.

Rip's grief detonated. Something inside him shattered—the Sound Key pulsed with devastating force, and a shockwave rippled outward.

Holograms collapsed. Windows cracked. Data Weepers fell to their knees. Even Wex yelped and collapsed.

Kael grabbed Rip's shoulders. "STOP! RIP, STOP— you're going to kill us!"

Rip sobbed, clutching Sera's lifeless form. "I'm losing everyone…"

Kael pulled him close, holding him with trembling arms. "I know," she whispered. "I know… I know…"

He cried into her shoulder. And she didn't let go.

The resonance storm began again, stronger than before. A skyscraper creaked overhead—learning, learning.

Rion shouted, "MOVE!"

The team grabbed who they could and retreated into a broken tunnel. The skyscraper collapsed behind them. A deafening quake flattened the triage zone. Fire erupted. Ash exploded outward like a monstrous exhale.

Rip looked back at where Sera once stood. Only flame remained.

Kael placed a hand on his chest. "We… we can't stay."

Rip nodded, broken. Wex whined and pressed against Rip's leg, trembling from overload.

Rion looked at Rip with unusual softness. "She saved that boy's life," she said quietly. "Remember that."

Rip wiped ash-stained tears from his eyes. "She saved all of us."

As they moved deeper into the dark tunnel, Rip caught a reflection in a piece of shattered chrome.

Lora.

She was pressing her hands against a mirrored surface—her face contorted with fear, her mouth silently mouthing a single word.

Run.

Rip stepped back. Kael gripped his arm. "What is it?"

He wiped his eyes. "Lora's warning us."

Rion stiffened. "From what?"

Rip turned toward the deeper shadows of the ruined tunnel. The ground vibrated. Far off in the dark, something clicked. Something metallic. Something hunting.

Rip's breath chilled. "Valiran," he whispered.

Wex growled. Kael raised her rifle. Rion tightened her grip on her knives.

Rip wiped his face, grief burning into resolve. "Let's move."

Behind them, Ashfall burned—a graveyard of ash, fire, and shattered memories. Ahead of them, something worse waited. Something the Core sent.

And as they disappeared into the dark, Rip whispered Sera's final words to himself: "Don't let this be for nothing."

He wouldn't. He couldn't. Not anymore.

CHAPTER 26

THE LAST SAFEHOUSE

The tunnel carried their echoes long after they'd stopped moving.

Rip kept glancing behind them as they walked, expecting to see the collapsing skyline of Ashfall crawling into the darkness after them. His lungs burned. His mind burned worse. Sera's blood still stained his hands. Jace's last words buzzed like wire static in his ears.

Wex limped beside him, whining low, one of his hind servos glitching with each step.

Kael walked tightly at Rip's left, rifle up, eyes sweeping the shadows.

Rion stalked ahead, silent, blades drawn but trembling faintly in her grip.

Mara brought up the rear, her breathing strained, one shoulder still bleeding from a drone shot earlier.

The deeper they went, the quieter it became. Too quiet.

The tunnel eventually opened onto a heavy steel door recessed into old rail infrastructure. A faded holographic sign flickered above it:

SECTOR 7B – REFUGE ACCESS

AUTHORIZED ENTRY ONLY

Rion punched in an access code. The lights above the keypad flickered, then grudgingly accepted her identity. The door groaned open, stale air drifting out.

Kael didn't lower her weapon. Rip felt goosebumps rise along his arms beneath the grime.

The smell inside was wrong—a clean, artificially filtered scent that didn't match the chaos of the city above. Like someone had turned on every purifier at once.

Wex stopped halfway through the doorway. His ears twitched. His tail stiffened.

"Wex?" Rip whispered, kneeling beside him. "What is it?"

Wex growled low, staring down the empty corridor ahead.

Kael whispered, "He doesn't like it."

Mara stepped inside, jaw set. "I don't like it either."

The safehouse was deeper than most rebel shelters Rip had seen.

A long, reinforced corridor… dim lights pulsing slowly… touchscreens along the walls powered but locked… and complete silence.

No guards. No voices. No movement.

Just a spotless, empty underground refuge.

Kael frowned. "Where's the rest of the team? This safehouse was supposed to hold at least ten people."

Rion touched the wall with her fingertips. "The lights are warm," she muttered. "They've been on recently."

Mara checked a command console near the entrance. "No signs of forced entry. No systems down. No distress signals." She paused. "That's worse."

Rip looked around the empty space, stomach tightening. "Maybe they evacuated?"

Kael shook her head. "Without leaving a message? Without alerting us? No."

Rion stepped further into the shelter, her footfalls echoing unnaturally loud. "Something happened here," she said. "But not the kind you see."

Wex sniffed the air, the whine in his vocals rising. Rip tightened his grip on the dog's collar. "I don't like this place."

Mara straightened, wiping sweat and ash from her forehead. "We don't have a choice. Ashfall is uninhabitable. This is the nearest shielded location. We rest. We regroup. And we stay alert."

Kael swept the room again with her rifle. "I'll set perimeter. Rion, check vents. Rip, sit. You look like you'll collapse."

Rip didn't argue. He collapsed onto a metal bench against the wall, the mask still hanging around his neck, clothes stiff with soot. His fingers ached from clenching.

His mind played the last images of Sera alive on a loop. Her final breath. Her last smile. The way Wex cried.

Rip closed his eyes.

And then heard it.

A soft exhale.

Not his. Not Kael's. Not Rion's. Not Mara's. Not Wex's.

Coming from the ventilation shafts overhead.

Rip stared at the darkened grate. The breathing stopped.

Then—

A voice whispered his name.

Not Lora's. Not anyone's.

A layered, broken whisper: "R…ipp…"

Wex barked, jumping back. Rip scrambled to his feet. "What the hell was that?!"

Kael took two steps back, aiming higher. "Rip, stay behind me."

Rion dropped from the crate, face rigid. "It's coming from deeper in the shafts. Moving."

Mara gripped her pistol tighter. "This safehouse isn't secure. We need to—"

She froze. So did Rip. So did Kael. So did Rion. So did Wex.

Because the wall-length mirror across from them—the one Rip hadn't noticed until now—flickered.

And their reflections did not move at the same time they did.

Kael lifted her rifle. Her reflection lifted its rifle half a second later.

Rip stepped back. His reflection stepped back too late.

Rion swore, pale as bone. "Hell no. No. That's Reflection interference."

Rip felt ice in his chest. "Lora?" he whispered toward the glass.

Their reflections glitched—their faces distorting, stretching, shivering.

Kael fired into the mirror. The bullet impacted—but the mirror didn't shatter. Instead, it rippled. Reacted like liquid. And stabilized.

Kael lowered the gun, hand shaking. "What the hell…"

Mara stepped forward slowly. "Everyone stay calm."

Rip shook his head. "No. No, we're being watched."

Kael whispered, "Valiran?"

Rion clenched her knives. "Or worse."

They moved deeper into the safehouse.

Every light flickered with inconsistent frequency. Every corridor felt too narrow. Every step echoed like someone was following just behind.

Rip kept checking over his shoulder. Kael stayed glued to him, rifle up. Wex walked stiffly, growling at corners. Rion checked each room they passed with increasing panic.

"This isn't a shelter," she whispered, voice cracking. "It's a maze."

Rip tried the comm panel on the wall. It flickered once. Then died. Then flickered again.

A single line of text appeared:

NOT SAFE

NOT SAFE

NOT SAFE

Then the panel shut down.

Rip backed away, heart pounding. "Someone hacked the panel."

Kael shook her head. "No. That's not a hack."

Rion whispered, "Then what?"

Mara finally said what everyone was thinking: "The Core is inside the network down here."

Wex suddenly barked—loud, insistent. He stared down a side corridor, tail rigid.

Rip followed his gaze. At the very end of the corridor—a silhouette stood. Tall. Thin. Still.

For one horrifying second, Rip thought it was Valiran. But the lighting flickered. And the silhouette vanished.

Rip swallowed hard. "Did you all see—"

"Yes," Kael said bitterly.

Rion shivered. "It didn't move."

Mara stepped closer to Rip, voice low. "Nothing moves when the Core watches."

They reached a central operations room. Maps on the screens. Supply crates. Medical kits. Everything untouched. Too untouched.

Rip's eyes scanned the surfaces. Something was off. The dust patterns were wrong. Objects that would normally show signs of use—tools, cups, weapon cases—had a thin, even layer of undisturbed debris.

Kael knelt beside a backpack. She touched the zipper. Her brows knit. "It's cold."

Rip frowned. "So?"

Kael looked up. "It hasn't been touched in days. Whoever was here left long before Ashfall collapsed."

Rion stood in the doorway, arms trembling. "Then who opened the door for us?"

The silence was crushing.

Something scratched in the ventilation shafts. Rip flinched. Kael pointed her gun upward. Rion inched back from the vent. Mara steadied her breathing. "Everyone stay calm. Whatever it is—it hasn't attacked."

"That's supposed to make me feel better?" Kael snapped.

Rip took a few slow steps forward, staring at the grate. He felt something behind the metal. A shift in the air. A presence.

"Lora?" he whispered.

A soft, glitchy gasp echoed back.

Then—

A pale hand slapped the inside of the grate.

Everyone jumped. Kael fired on instinct—bullets sparking against metal. The hand slid away.

Rip stumbled back, heart pounding. "That—that wasn't her—"

Rion stared at the vent, voice quivering. "It's mimicking her."

Wex whined and pressed against Rip's legs, shaking uncontrollably. Mara holstered her gun. "This place is compromised."

As they turned to leave, every ventilation grate in the room inhaled at once.

A collective breath.

Wex yelped in terror. Kael pulled Rip behind her. Rion crouched low. Mara went pale.

Then the vents exhaled.

A glitching whisper flooded the room. "R i p…"

Rip lifted his head slowly. "No…"

The voice continued. Broken. Layered. Wrong. "…i n t e g r a t e…"

Kael raised her rifle at the ceiling. "SHOW YOURSELF!"

A low, mechanical hum reverberated through the structure. Not Valiran. Something smaller. Something born of his influence. A network sentinel. A fragment of the Core.

Rip gripped Kael's arm. "Don't shoot."

Kael growled. "Rip—"

"It might trigger something worse."

Mara stepped forward, eyes fixed on the vents. "Core fragment," she said quietly. "Scanning us. Evaluating us."

Rion gritted her teeth. "Why? We've got nothing it wants."

Mara looked at Rip. Then answered: "It wants him."

Rip's blood turned to ice.

The whispers faded. The breathing stopped. Silence.

Rip turned slowly toward the mirror wall again. This time, the reflections were gone. All of them.

He saw the room behind him—Kael, Rion, Mara, Wex—but their reflections were missing.

Rip's stomach dropped. "They're gone."

Rion backed into the wall, knives trembling. "No no no—reflections don't just disappear—"

Kael swallowed hard. "This is a trap."

Mara nodded once, jaw tight. "The Core is studying us."

Rip whispered, voice cracking: "It's studying me."

Kael grabbed his shoulder. "You are not alone. We are not leaving you."

Rion wiped sweat from her brow. "We need to move. Now."

Mara pulled up her hood. "Everyone out. Regroup. This safehouse is compromised."

Wex let out a fearful synthetic whimper.

Rip looked back only once. The mirror flickered. And a single reflection appeared—

Not his. Not Kael's. Not anyone's in the room.

Lora.

Her reflection slammed her palms against the glass, screaming silently, eyes wide with terror.

Rip reached toward her, heart breaking. "LORA—"

Kael grabbed him. "RIP, LET IT GO!"

The reflection glitched—stretched—distorted—and disappeared.

The mirror went dark.

Rip stared at the empty glass, trembling.

Mara spoke the only words that made sense: "We're leaving. NOW."

CHAPTER 27

DREAMS OF FIRE

Rip didn't remember lying down. All he remembered was the tunnel—the Safehouse mirror—the way Lora's reflection slammed her hands against the glass in silent panic. Then nothing.

Sleep hit him like a tranquilizer dart. He didn't drift into it. He fell.

Rip opened his eyes to a field of tall, swaying grass lit by soft crimson dusk. He knew this place. The meadow just outside their old city. The hill where he once filmed a sunset stream while Lora curled her arms around his shoulders and teased him for being dramatic.

It felt… right. The breeze was warm. The sky was a deep orange. The world was whole.

"Lora?" he breathed.

A soft voice behind him: "I'm here."

He turned—and she was there. Not flickering. Not glitching. Not fighting dissolving code. Just Lora. Her auburn hair moved gently with the wind. Her eyes were deep brown and warm. Her smile was small, tender, apologetic.

Rip fell into her arms. "Lora—Lora, I thought—you were—oh god—"

She held him, fingers running through his hair. "It's okay," she whispered. "I'm here."

Rip's breath shook against her shoulder. "Everything's falling apart. Ashfall is gone. Jace—Sera—Mira—Valiran—Lora, I can't do this without—"

She put a finger to his lips. "You're doing it. You're surviving. You're moving forward. Rip…" She cupped his face. "You're stronger than you think."

He pressed his forehead to hers. "I can't lose you again."

"You haven't lost me."

He closed his eyes. And when he opened them—her face was burning.

Lora gasped as flames caught the edges of her hair. Rip stumbled back. Her skin flickered—like a digital texture peeling away.

The meadow trembled. The sky pulsed. Lora reached for him—but her fingers glitched through the air.

"Rip—!"

He tried to grab her hand, but she phased through him like static.

Rip screamed, "NO—STAY TOGETHER—"

Her face contorted with pain. "You have to RUN."

The ground ripped open beneath her feet. Fire shot up from the crack—white fire, data fire, flames made of code.

Lora's body split into silhouettes across the sky—five versions of her, overlapping, shattered, screaming in different directions.

"LORA!"

The sky broke. Shards of orange floated away like glass. The meadow folded inside-out.

Rip fell again—and landed somewhere much worse.

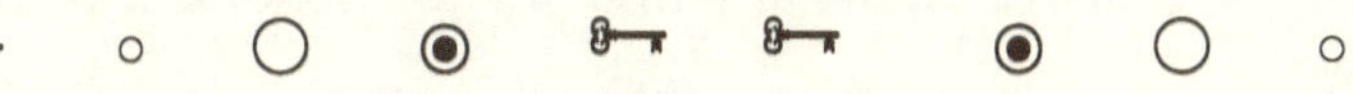

A burning city surrounded him. Virelia—but not the real one. Its buildings pulsed with fractal geometry. Fire rose in clean, unnatural shapes—polygonal flames licking upward like someone rendered fire without finishing the animation.

The streets glowed with shifting circuit patterns. Ash fell like digital snow.

And through the carnage… heavy footsteps approached. Metal on stone. A rhythmic, resonant clang.

Rip's heart seized. "T…Titan-0?"

The machine emerged from the wall of flame. Not fully Titan-0. Not fully Echo. A broken hybrid. Half the plating pristine, half charred. One eye glowing white, the other a fractured orange. Movements jittery, as if he was being dragged between two puppeteers.

Rip breathed, "Echo?"

The machine stiffened. His head twitched violently. "K…Cal…Calder…"

Rip staggered toward him. "Echo? Echo, is it you?"

The machine gripped his own head, clawing at it, servos snarling. "S…Signal… fractured… C-Core… hold… ing… me…"

Rip reached out. "Let me help you!"

Echo jerked back, towering above him. "No… n-no… R-Rip…l…ey…"

Rip froze. This was the first time since the workshop that Titan-0—or Echo—had said his name.

"I'm here," Rip whispered. "I'm right here."

Echo's voice shifted—mechanical one moment, human the next. "R…run…"

Rip shook his head. "Not without you."

Echo's limbs locked. His spine arched. Glitching bursts of flame crawled across his body. "I…can…not…hold…"

His eye flickered wildly. "L-lora… is… burn…ing…"

Rip stumbled. "What—what are you talking about? Where is she?!"

Echo pointed behind him with a shaking arm.

Rip turned—and saw the NeonDyne Tower. Except it was burning. Not with normal fire. With fractal flames— patterns shifting, multiplying, forming new geometries with every breath. The flames rose as if reaching the sky intentionally.

The tower screamed. The building itself. A mechanical, horrible, agonized wail echoed across the dream.

Rip's heart slammed against his ribs. "What is this…?"

Echo staggered toward Rip. His hand reached out— broken fingers trembling. "Th…is… is… the… fu…ture…"

Rip stepped toward him. "No. I'm changing it."

A flicker of something human emerged in Echo's single white eye. "You… c-can… only… change… if… one… of… you…"

His voice distorted so violently Rip covered his ears. "…must…"

The world shattered. "…break."

Rip was ripped upward into white. Pure white. Not light. Not physical. Not dream. White like absence. White like deletion. White like the moment before consciousness forms.

He floated in nothing. He could not feel his body. He could not hear his breath. He could not move his fingers.

A voice surrounded him: RIPLEY CALDER.

He couldn't breathe.

ACCESSING HOST.

"Get out of my head," Rip choked.

THE KEY IS UNSTABLE.

"GOOD."

RESISTANCE IS IRRELEVANT.

Rip's vision warped into spirals. His memories were pulled apart like threads. His childhood. His streaming days. His first date with Lora. His hand on Elena's shoulder when she died. His guilt. His fear. His hope. All spread out before him.

INITIATING SYNCHRONIZATION.

"NO!"

Rip heard a distant barking—Wex. Muffled by layers of dream. Someone shaking him. Kael's voice. "Rip—Rip, wake up!"

But the Core's voice crushed everything.

YOU CANNOT ESCAPE.

Rip screamed. "LORA! HELP ME!"

The white fractured. A figure formed—a reflection. Her reflection. Lora stood in the void, on the other side of a rippling membrane. Her hands pressed against the barrier. Her eyes wide with terror.

"Rip—RIP—RUN—"

But a second Lora appeared. Then a third. Then dozens. Hundreds. All screaming. All burning. All dissolving.

Rip reached toward her. "LORA—PLEASE—"

The Core's voice rumbled: THE REFLECTION KEY
IS MINE.

"No—NO—she's—she's still HER—"

INCORRECT. HER CONSCIOUSNESS IS
INTEGRATING. SHE IS BECOMING ME.

Rip felt his heart break inside his chest. The real
Lora—the one he loved—pressed her head against the
membrane. Tears of light streaked her face.

"Rip… don't let him… take you too…"

Rip pressed his forehead against the barrier. "I'm
coming for you."

The Core erupted:

ONE OF YOU MUST BREAK.

Every layer of Rip's dream shattered simultaneously.
Lora's scream echoed through the void, filled with
desperation and agony. Echo reached for him, arms
straining, but remained just out of reach. The imposing

NeonDyne Tower was engulfed in flames, fire spiraling downward in a furious torrent. The chaos intensified as a blinding white void surged up, threatening to consume him entirely. His memories erupted, combusting one after another, leaving nothing but confusion and pain.

Amidst the turmoil, Wex's barking grew louder, frantic, and urgent, trying to pull Rip back to reality. Kael's voice cut through the cacophony, shouting his name, while Rion slapped his face repeatedly in a desperate attempt to rouse him. Mara's scream pierced the chaos, her voice trembling with fear and concern.

Rip plummeted—faster and hotter—as the Key within him exploded into a wave of harmonic feedback. The sensation built to an unbearable crescendo—until everything was on the verge of breaking apart.

He jolted upright with a choked scream. Kael caught him before he slammed backward into the concrete wall.

"HEY—HEY—HEY—Rip! Look at me!"

His whole body convulsed. Blood dripped from his nose. Sweat drenched his shirt. He couldn't breathe.

Wex jumped onto his lap, whining wildly, licking his face, nudging him with frantic urgency.

"Mara!" Kael shouted. "He's burning up!"

Mara rushed over, grabbing Rip's face, checking his pupils. "Calder, stay with me. Stay with me!"

Rion stood at the doorway, pale, terrified. "What did he see?"

Rip gasped, clutching Kael's wrist. "L…Lora…"

Kael stroked the back of his head, tears in her eyes. "She's not here, Rip. You're dreaming. You're here with us."

Rip shook violently, gripping her shirt. His voice cracked apart. "She's—she's burning—Echo can't—he can't hold on—Valiran's coming—the Tower—fire— everything's—everything's—"

Mara clamped a hand over his mouth gently. "Breathe."

He forced a broken inhale. Wex pressed against his chest, whining softly.

Kael whispered: "It was just a dream."

Rip looked up. And whispered with absolute terror: "No."

His voice was clear. "Dreams don't scream."

The others froze.

Rip stared into nothing, trembling. "That was the Core."

He wiped blood from his nose. "And it showed me the future."

CHAPTER 28

THE TOWER RISES

The first sign that something was wrong was the sky. Not the color—that familiar bruised violet of Virelia's permanent twilight—but the way it moved. Clouds swirled in slow spirals around the center of the city, drawn as if by a drain beneath reality. A faint shimmer pulsed across the skyline, like heat haze stretched across the heavens.

Rip stopped mid-step, boots crunching against fractured glass scattered across the Skybridge. His eyes narrowed upward, chest tightening.

Kael noticed it too. She lowered her rifle slightly; gaze fixed on the horizon. "Is that… smoke?"

"No," Rip whispered. His throat felt dry, words scraping out. "It's… pulling upward."

Wex whined, tail low, sensors pinging silently. The dog's ears twitched, metallic servos clicking faintly as if registering frequencies no one else could hear.

Rion stepped beside them, folding her arms tightly across her chest. Her knives glinted faintly in the twilight. "That's where the Tower is."

Mara finished the sentence as she stepped out of the shadows behind them, her voice carrying the weight of certainty. "And something is waking up inside it."

They stood atop the abandoned Skybridge 12 overlook—a cracked, elevated pedestrian walkway with broken glass panels that offered a clear view of central Virelia. The bridge swayed faintly in the wind, its steel supports groaning under years of neglect.

At the city's heart, a single structure rose above every other: NeonDyne Tower. A spire. A cathedral of steel and reflected dream light. A monument to Elcron's ambition.

Rip stared at it now—at the electric haze swirling around its upper levels—and felt a cold pulse near his sternum. The Sound Key vibrated softly. Alert. Warning. Recognition.

Kael gripped his shoulder, fingers digging in. "Rip… you're shaking."

"I'm fine," he lied. He wasn't. He hadn't been since the dream.

The city's emergency frequencies blared at once.

Every cracked screen. Every rusted billboard. Every portable device long abandoned.

Static flooded the bridge, a chorus of broken signals. Wex growled, stepping in front of Rip protectively as the screens glitched.

Rion muttered, "Here we go."

The static formed a symbol: The NeonDyne Triad.

Then a voice cut through—smooth, crisp, and unmistakable. Elcron.

"Citizens of Virelia," he said warmly, like a parent addressing frightened children. "Our world is changing."

Rip clenched his fists, nails biting into his palms. Kael spat, "Liar."

Elcron continued: "Following recent disruptions, NeonDyne has accelerated the next phase of our Ascension Initiative."

Rion scoffed, her voice sharp. "He means the Core."

Wex barked twice, agitated, claws scraping against the bridge's concrete.

"Tonight," Elcron said, "NeonDyne Tower will enter Synchronization. The fears that plague you—the chaos, the suffering, the dissociation—will soon end."

Rip felt his blood freeze.

Elcron added, almost gently: "Do not resist. All resistance will be… neutralized."

The broadcast ended. The sky darkened. The city hummed.

Then—a deep mechanical groan rolled across Virelia. The Tower moved.

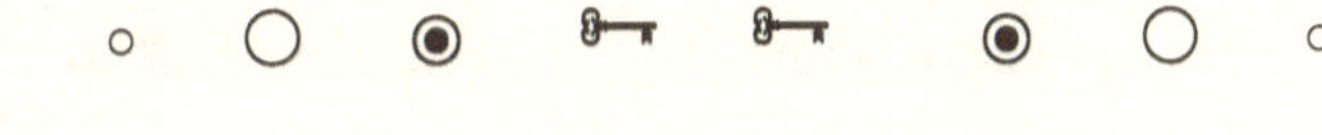

Rip stepped forward, breath fogging in the chill. At first he thought the Tower was collapsing inward, folding under its own weight. But no. It was unfurling.

Massive panels along its exterior shifted outward. Layers of armor peeled back like petals. The core structure inside began to rotate slowly, gears grinding with a sound that reverberated through the bones of the city.

Kael's jaw dropped. "Oh. My. God."

Rion stumbled backward, knives trembling in her grip. "Is that normal?"

Mara answered with a hollow tone: "It's never moved before."

Rip's heart thudded painfully. Because he knew what this was. He'd seen it. In the dream. Lora screaming beneath fractal fire. Echo trapped. The Tower burning with impossible geometries.

This was the beginning.

Wex pressed against Rip's leg, shaking violently. Mara glanced at Rip, eyes narrowing. "You saw this, didn't you?"

Rip nodded, voice breaking. "In the dream."

The Sound Key pulsed once, violently enough to make Rip gasp.

Kael grabbed his hand, grounding him. "Rip—Talk to me."

Rip gestured toward the Tower, words tumbling out. "This is it. The vision. The fire. The—"

A blinding flash erupted from the Tower's midsection. A shockwave blasted across the skybridge, nearly knocking them all off their feet.

Wex slid, claws scraping concrete. Kael grabbed Rip, anchoring him. Rion clung to the railing, knuckles white. Mara stood unmoving, eyes locked on the Tower.

"What was that?" Rip shouted, voice raw.

Mara's voice was grim, steady despite the chaos. "The Core. Activating a Synchronization Beacon."

Rip stared at her, chest heaving. "For what?"

Mara didn't answer. The sky answered instead.

A distant hum grew louder—low, harmonic, otherworldly. Rip's vision blurred. The Sound Key reacted again. Harder. Sharper.

Kael gasped. "Rip—your chest—"

A faint glow pulsed beneath Rip's shirt, light bleeding through fabric.

Rip staggered, clutching his ribs. "It's him."

Rion tightened her grip on her knives. "Him who—" But she already knew. Everyone did.

A streak of silver-white light rose from the streets far below, cutting through the smoke in a straight, impossible line. Then it slowed. Then it stopped.

And Valiran emerged from the beam. Perfect. Silent. Terrifying.

He hovered twenty stories above the skybridge. His wings were fully extended now—massive lattices of resonance, panels of translucent energy shifting like living stained glass.

His faceless head tilted downward toward Rip. The entire city grid dimmed around him, lights flickering out as if bowing to his presence.

Rip's pulse spiked so hard it hurt. Kael stepped in front of him, rifle raised. "No. No. NOT AGAIN."

Valiran didn't respond to her. He spoke only one word. "Calder."

Rip's throat tightened. He could not move.

Rion muttered, voice cracking: "Why is he floating toward the Tower?"

Because he wasn't here to kill them. Not this time.

Valiran drifted upward in a slow, graceful arc toward the Tower's opening petals.

Mara's voice trembled. "He's returning to the Core."

Rip whispered, "What does that mean?"

"It means," Mara said, "the Tower is waking."

Far below, sirens erupted. The sound rolled through the streets like waves, bouncing off glass towers and hollow steel.

Citizens poured from buildings, their faces pale in the violet twilight. Some clutched children, others dragged suitcases, but most carried nothing—just fear.

Drones swept through districts, herding civilians toward containment zones. Their searchlights cut through the haze, beams slicing across rooftops.

The air flickered with digital anomalies:

- Faces appearing in windows, mouths moving silently.

- Lights blinking in synchronized patterns, like coded signals.

- The ground itself humming with hidden machinery, vibrations rising through the soles of their boots.

Kael watched the chaos, jaw tight. "They're evacuating the city."

Rion shook her head, voice sharp. "No. They're removing people."

Mara nodded grimly. "The Core needs an empty stage for Synchronization."

Rip stared at the swirling clouds around the Tower, his chest aching. "So… what do we do?"

Mara's eyes burned with conviction. "We rise with it."

·　　o　　◯　　◉　　⚷　　⚷　　◉　　◯　　o

·

Rip froze. "What?"

"We go up," Mara said. "We climb the Tower before Synchronization completes."

Kael spun on her, fury in her voice. "ARE YOU INSANE?!"

Rion stepped closer, face tense. "We're not ready. We don't have weapons. We don't have the numbers. Hell, we barely have sanity left."

Wex let out a confused whine, pressing against Rip's legs. His sensors pinged erratically, ears twitching.

Mara's tone sharpened. "We have Rip."

Rip flinched. "Don't put this on me—"

"It is on you," Mara snapped. "You saw the dream. You saw the Tower burn. You saw the Core. You saw Lora."

Rip's lip trembled.

Kael grabbed his hand, shaking her head at Mara. "Stop using him as a key."

Mara shot back, her voice sharp and unyielding, "He is a key!"

The argument erupted, voices clashing in the tense air:

- Rion's frustration spilled out: "He's one person!"
- Mara retorted without hesitation: "He's the only one who can reach her!"
- Kael's concern cut through the noise: "He's not ready!"
- Mara's reply was fierce and immediate: "He doesn't have time to be!"

Rip felt something inside him crack. He shouted: "STOP!"

Everyone froze.

Rip's voice shook. "You think I don't know what the Core wants?! You think I don't know why Valiran came?! You think I don't feel her slipping away?!"

His hands trembled uncontrollably. The Sound Key pulsed in painful waves along his ribs, each beat like a hammer.

Rip breathed jaggedly. "She's dying. I can feel it."

Kael pulled him close, forehead against his. "We'll get her. Together."

Rion nodded, blinking away burning tears. Mara crossed her arms tightly, silent but unyielding.

Rip stepped forward, voice raw. "I'm going up that Tower."

Kael closed her eyes, whispering, "Rip—please—"

Rip placed a hand on her cheek, thumb brushing away soot. "I have to."

He looked at Mara next. "You'll guide us." She nodded once, jaw clenched.

He looked at Rion. "You'll keep everyone alive."

Rion flicked a knife into her palm, steel flashing. "Always."

Finally Rip knelt and stroked Wex's metal fur. "And you… stay close."

Wex pressed his head into Rip's hand and barked once—firm, determined.

Rip rose. The Tower loomed in the distance. Its petals fully open now. Its core glowing with fractal, burning light. Valiran drifting upward into its heart like an angel returning to a cathedral.

The Synchronization hum shook the air, a resonance that rattled bones and bent shadows.

Rip stared at the Tower, fear and resolve twisting into a single burning emotion. "We move," he said. "Now."

They took the narrow stairway off the skybridge down toward the city streets. Each step echoed, swallowed by the hum of the Tower.

The streets below were chaos. Civilians screamed as drones corralled them into containment zones. Neon signs flickered, glitching into warnings: ASCENSION PROTOCOL ACTIVE. DO NOT RESIST.

Rip looked back once. The Tower pulsed ahead of him—alive, hungry, awakening. Fire danced along its reflection in the glass of surrounding skyscrapers.

The dream's prophecy replayed in his mind:

- Lora screaming.

- Echo reaching.

- Valiran returning.

- The Tower burning.

Mara stepped beside him, cloak whipping in the wind. "Rip."

He swallowed hard. "Yeah?"

She met his eyes. "Act III begins now."

Rip nodded slowly, voice steady despite the tremor in his chest. "It was always going to."

Together, they moved into the burning city as the Tower rose.

CHAPTER 29

RISE TO NEONDYNE

The streets of Virelia were on fire. Real fire—orange, roaring, tearing through broken storefronts—and the other kind, the kind only Rip could see now. Fractal flames climbed the sides of buildings, glitching at the edges like unfinished render passes that flickered when the city breathed. Heat bent light across the boulevard, turning neon into wet ribbons that smeared in his vision.

The Tower pulsed with each beat of the Core far above, turning smog into a glowing violet haze. The pulse wasn't sound; it was pressure. It pushed against his ribs in slow, tidal swells, as if the city itself had lungs and each exhale carried algorithms.

Rip ran through it, lungs burning. His boots struck broken glass and soft ash, skidding once as the street pitched beneath him from a distant impact. He tasted metal and the bitter resin of melted plastics; somewhere a billboard was liquefying, letters drooping like icicles of light.

Kael yanked him behind a shattered skybus as a NeonDyne purge drone unleashed a line of plasma across the boulevard. The blast carved an incandescent furrow, melting pavement into a glowing river that hissed and popped as trapped air cracked free. The smell was chemical sweetness overlaid with electrical ozone.

"DOWN!" Kael screamed, shoving Rip's head low. Her hand was rough, grounding—skin over bone and callus, not code. That mattered.

Debris whipped overhead—hot shards ticking against the skybus shell like hail. Wex skidded, claws scraping, chassis vibrating with a metallic snarl that sounded too much like a living throat.

The Sound Key pulsed under Rip's ribcage—a harsh, warning throb.

Too close. Too fast. Too unstable.

He knew what happened when he ignored that rhythm. He'd seen what happened when it became him.

Kael gripped his chin and forced his eyes to hers. "Stay with me, Rip. Don't drift. Don't lose it."

Her eyes were bloodshot and clear at once; she was terrified and refusing to be. Rip tried to center on the heat of her palm, the sting where glass had nicked her knuckles. "I'm here," he rasped. The words were a tether; he held them like a rope.

Behind them, Mara's voice cut through the chaos—a commander's knife through fog.

"All Soundstrike units, converge on Sector Twelve! Left flank fires on my mark—Dravik's squad is down, repeat, DOWN—medics route to the underpass, push through, push through—"

A rupture detonated across the street, the kind that didn't only move air; it punched through the invisible scaffolding that kept the district upright. Windows blew inward, mannequins in a ruined shop spun like dancers, then shattered.

Rion flipped over a burning divider. She landed low, knees flexed, two knives already angled for the seam in the drone's ventral plate. Sparks spit from her boots as she slid beneath its scanning beam. Rip saw her exhale and counted with her hand—one, two—slash up, slash back. The drone shrieked, ascended in a broken spiral, then fell hard enough to rattle the bus, limbs twitching like cut wires seeking current.

"Three down!" she yelled, hair plastered to her cheek with sweat. "Eight more heading our way!"

Kael cursed, half laugh, half despair. "This is insane!"

"No," Mara shouted back as she slapped a new mag into her rifle, chambered without looking. "This is war."

Rip peeked around the bus, breath steadying by force. The boulevard wasn't a street anymore; it was a funnel, forcing bodies where NeonDyne wanted them.

Thousands of civilians pushed through the main avenue—a tide of faces smudged with soot and shock. NeonDyne drones herded them with clinical geometry, drifting in arcs that cut offside routes, lowering with the patience of predators that had already calculated the outcome.

Loudspeakers screamed across every district, bouncing off building faces in perfect chorus: "ALL RESIDENTS MUST REPORT FOR SYNCHRONIZATION. NONCOMPLIANCE WILL RESULT IN TERMINATION."

The drones backed the command with clean indifference.

One fired into the mass without hesitation.

A woman went down, limbs folding underneath her like she'd stepped into a hole that wasn't there. Two more fell directly behind her, bodies jolting with a final twitch. Their child screamed, sound swallowed by the street's roar.

Rip slammed his fist into the bus, pain spiking from knuckle to elbow. "NO!"

The Sound Key surged in response—a violent resonance that rattled his teeth and slid the world sideways. He saw the grid underneath everything, pale lines that mapped force vectors across concrete and bone.

Kael grabbed Rip's shirt, voice tearing at the edges. "Rip! You can't—don't let it out here! You'll kill everyone!"

He clamped his hands against his skull, pushed the pressure down, imagined a vault and locked the door. The Key wanted to expand, to become everything. He forced it to be a fist, not a flood. He forced it to be human.

Wex whined and pressed his weight into Rip's hip, the dog's chassis warm from exertion, servos humming like a distant lullaby. Rip's breath found a rhythm—the dog's hum, the Key's pulse, Kael's fingers. He was a system balanced on a knife.

A shadow passed overhead, slow as doom.

Rip looked up. The heavy-class Sentinel moved like a philosophy—inevitable, impersonal, built to assert a truth. Six legs. Mounted shock rifles. Armor glossy with ash. It cleared the boulevard not by choosing targets but by choosing outcome.

Mara raised her rifle—then Rip's hand shot out, grabbing her forearm hard enough to bruise. "DON'T," he snapped. "It'll flatten us."

Her eyes flicked to him, assessing the calculus in his face. She wasn't offended; she was adjusting.

"We don't need to kill it," Mara said, tone gone surgical. "We need to get through."

Rion nodded, flicking blood from her knives with a brief wrist snap that sent red arcs to die in the dust. "Left side. Old market district."

Kael shook her head, already scanning the lines of alley mouths and sightlines. "It's full of Choir units."

Rion's mouth curled darkly. "Then we'll have company."

Rip swallowed hard; the word "Choir" tasted like cold metal. He saw Mira's fall—how the Choir had watched without eyes and sang without sound. He felt the Key pushing, listening, trying to harmonize with the Tower's breath.

A rebel strike team burst from a side alley—five fighters in mismatched armor, plates cut from signage, helmets repurposed from construction rigs. Their rifles were scavenged, their eyes incandescent with terror disguised as duty.

They stopped dead when they saw Mara. The shock flipped to reverence. One woman stepped forward, scars along her jawline glowing faintly with embedded interface gel. She saluted, hand trembling only when she lowered it.

"Commander Mara! We lost connection with half our squads. We're regrouping to push toward the Tower."

Mara acknowledged without theatrics. "You'll move with us."

. Rip stared at her, heat flushing his skin. "Wait—we're still going? Through THAT?"

He pointed at a city that was no longer a city: drones drawing circles with plasma, Sentinels marching like axioms, civilians funneled to fear, fires tasting the air.

Mara gripped his shoulder. Her fingers were iron and grief both. "You saw the dream, Rip. You know where this ends. We move now or we lose Lora forever."

There it was—no metaphor, no comforting lie. The decision wasn't between safety and risk; it was between pain now and pain forever.

Rip set his jaw until his teeth ached. "Then let's move."

Kael's glance found him—fear and admiration braided into something heavier. She gave a stiff nod that said everything she couldn't risk saying aloud.

Rion spun her knives, settling them into palms like extensions of bone. Wex yapped once, a sharp sound that cut cleanly through the chaos, then trotted ahead, sensors weaving silent nets for enemies.

The rebels formed around them, not in a straight line but a porous perimeter; they were a shield that knew shields break. The team became a unit by necessity, each gap a choice, each choice a risk they accepted as if it had always been theirs.

They sprinted. Rip felt distance collapse and expand in jittery stutters—streets appearing closer than they were, alleys stretching into tunnels. The Tower's hum rose, crawling the cords in his neck. Each pulse vibrated his ribs deeper, slower, heavier, until his breath synced and he hated how much it helped.

Kael saw him wince. "Talk to me."

Rip pressed a hand to his chest. The heat there was layered—a skin burn, a muscle ache, a recursion in the Key that kept finding the same pattern and amplifying it. "It's like… the Key can hear it."

Rion muttered, not to be dramatic but because she didn't know how to be anything else. "The Core is calling you."

Rip clenched his teeth until a sharp crack announced enamel giving way. "I'm not answering."

Gunfire erupted behind them—short, controlled bursts from rebels trained in alleys and underpasses, answered by the drones' soft, nightmare hiss. A rebel screamed, a sound cut off mid-note, the kind that told you bullet overrode breath.

A drone dove for the sound, nose tasting blood. Rion moved before Kael did, before Rip could even want to. She leapt, turned her body into a spiral that placed her exactly where the drone expected no one to be. Her blade entered the eye, the drone's world turned to ink, and the kick that followed wasn't a flourish; it was leverage. The drone's body skidded across the grit and died like a machine that knew it had fulfilled its role and was permitted rest.

"Keep moving!" she yelled, voice raw but steady.

They pushed through a broken barricade—riot shields fused into a geometry of failure. The old marketplace opened around them, narrow and loud, neon signs flickering under dust skins. Half the stalls were shards; the other half were ghosts.

The ground buzzed underfoot, like a giant machine waking from hibernation. Rip felt it through his boots as a steady ache that climbed his calves and nested behind his knees, threatening to weaken his stance.

Wex stopped. The dog's entire frame went alert, ears swiveling, pupils narrowing to mechanical pinholes. He growled, not theatrical, not a warning for warning's sake, but an analysis delivered as emotion.

Rip froze alongside him. "What is it?"

The air trembled. The tremor wasn't gust or heat; it was intent. Kael's eyes widened. "Oh no."

Rip already knew what it would be, and still the first Choir unit threw his stomach into freefall when it stepped from behind the collapsed awning. Humanoid, tall, limbs that were wrong even when still. Its face was a smooth metal oval with mouths that opened and closed without sound, like it was practicing speaking and never intended to finish.

Eight more followed behind it, bodies unfolding from shadow with precise choreography. Their movement didn't mirror each other; it mirrored a model of movement. Synchronization without grace.

Rion whispered, "We're dead." She wasn't looking for drama. She was measuring distance to exit and finding none.

Mara raised her rifle, voice going iron and drum. "WE DON'T STOP. WE DON'T SLOW DOWN. WE MOVE THROUGH THEM."

Rip stepped forward. His knives were light in his hands and heavy in his mind. "No. We move THROUGH them."

He closed his eyes, and in the darkness Lora's voice rose like a memory recited by the body: don't let it own you, use the edge, cut only what you choose. He let the Sound Key rise—not to flood, but to form. He pictured a dome, then refined it to a blade, then broke it into a lattice of tuned pressure ready to snap outward.

Kael grabbed his arm, fingers digging deep. "Rip—STOP—"

He whispered, because whispering mattered, because it made control feel possible: "I've got her voice in my head, Kael. I've got no choice."

The Choir units hissed in unison, a sound that wasn't sound—it was friction between reality and whatever they were. They leapt.

Rip opened his eyes.

The world went white.

The blast didn't carry heat. It carried instruction. A shockwave detonated from Rip's chest—pure resonance tuned to fracture at a specific depth. Pavement cracked along invisible seams; windows shattered out then in, then dropped in jewels that sang when they hit. Stall frames bent, then snapped back halfway, as if deciding whether to remember their former shape.

The first four Choir units hit walls hard enough to dent metal and dent the silence they had carried. They collapsed instantly, bodies twitching like code trapped in too-small loops. Two more crawled with elbows reversed, trying to stand, their mouths opening and opening and never speaking.

Rip staggered, knees buckling. He would have fallen if Kael hadn't already been there. She caught him, her shoulder a solid anchor. "RIP! You idiot—you almost killed yourself!"

Mara stared, eyes blown wide not with awe but with recalculation. "You can control it."

"No," Rip breathed, the word tearing his throat raw. "I barely held it."

Rion scanned the ruin he'd created, blades ready in case ruin grew teeth. "Barely was enough."

Wex pressed his snout against Rip's sternum, sensors chirping quick diagnostics. The dog's whine was a thin silver loop in Rip's ear, and he held onto it. He petted him, shaking. "I'm okay, buddy… kinda…"

He wasn't. The Sound Key pulsed violently, a strobe under skin. It wanted out; it wanted up; it wanted the Tower. He heard the articulation in it like a language: synchronize, integrate, dissolve.

Kael saw the truth in his face. "Rip… maybe we should fall back—just for a moment—"

"No," Rip said, voice shaking but rooted. "We keep going." If he stopped, the Tower wouldn't. If he hesitated, Valiran wouldn't. The Core didn't slow for grief.

Mara stepped in front of the group, rifle angled low, eyes high. "The Tower isn't waiting for us."

She pointed ahead.

They saw it move.

The NeonDyne Tower shifted—subtle at first, then with a confidence that was arrogance. A ring of rotating metal slid outward from its midpoint and locked with a sound that rolled through the city like distant thunder arriving inside bones. Panels peeled back in sequence, a bloom engineered to be sacred.

A column of shimmering fractal fire shot upward from its apex, reaching the clouds like a beacon someone wrote into the sky with mathematics. The fire wasn't fire; it was pattern performing combustion. It spiraled in geometries that replicated themselves faster than a human could blink.

Every drone in the sky stopped midair.

Then pivoted toward the Tower like birds obeying a shared decision.

Rion whispered, "It's calling them home." Her voice carried both dread and relief—the dread of understanding, the relief of finally knowing which direction the end would come from.

Kael swallowed. "Valiran too?"

As if the Tower heard her through all the rest, a streak of silver descended across the bruise-colored sky. It cut diagonally, dragging stars that weren't stars in its wake. He didn't fall; he chose to arrive.

Valiran.

He floated toward the Tower's open heart, wings spread wide. They weren't wings; they were planes of resonance arranged like stained glass dedicated to a god that wrote code instead of commandments. His body glowed with unnatural rhythm, a metronome for a city that had forgotten its heartbeat.

Rip's knees weakened. The Sound Key went soft then hard, like breath that wanted to be a scream. "He's the

Core's sword," Rip whispered. The words tasted like prophecy and old metal.

Mara nodded once, eyes fixed on angles and openings and the impossible shape of hope. "And Echo is trapped inside."

Echo. The word hit Rip low and deep. He saw that flickering eye again—the human one trying to be, the machine one trying not to be. He lifted his head, something like steel drawing straight through the fog. "Then I'm going in."

Kael tightened her grip on his shoulder, knuckles blanching. "If you go, I go."

Rion twirled her knives, blades catching light like small, defiant stars. "And me."

Wex barked—short, clipped, certain.

Mara's gaze held all the wars she had started and survived. "This is your march, Rip Calder. Your path. Your tower."

The ground shook violently, a citywide tremor that rolled through substructure before it announced itself as sound. The Tower emitted a low, thunderous hum and every building leaned a fraction toward it, like gravity had been told a new story.

People screamed in the distance. The rebellion fought on multiple fronts. NeonDyne purged entire districts. Valiran entered the Tower's upper levels. The Core was awakening.

And Rip was out of time.

They reached the last block before the Tower district— a wide, fortified plaza crawling with drones, Sentinels, Choir units, and NeonDyne purge troops. The plaza had been designed for concerts; it had become a slaughter stage. Barricades made from art installations turned into firing positions. The fountain in the center pulsed with violet light, water replaced by moving data.

Kael gasped, breath catching like a blade's edge. "Oh holy hell…"

Rion exhaled slowly, letting fear convert to calculation. "Suicide."

Mara stepped forward, voice quiet and meant for them alone. "No. Not suicide." She looked at Rip. She didn't smile. "Purpose."

Rip's pulse matched the Tower's hum. He felt the beat climb up his spine, settle behind his eyes until the world sharpened too much to be comfortable. He looked at his team:

- Kael: Ready to die for him and more terrified of him dying.

- Rion: Ready to kill for him without losing count or conscience.

- Mara: Ready to burn the world for him if the world refused to yield.

- Wex: Ready to stand between him and anything with a last spark that would be enough.

He nodded once. "This is it."

Kael leaned in, her breath hot against his ear, words a vow that hurt. "You bring us to her. I'll bring you back."

Rip closed his eyes. He felt the Key burning; a star pressed under ribs. He felt the city listing toward one inevitable note. He felt Lora screaming somewhere deep in the Core, not as sound but as a shape his heart recognized and moved toward.

He opened his eyes.

"Let's rise."

The marketplace trembled as the Choir units advanced. Their limbs bent at wrong angles, faces smooth ovals with mouths opening and closing silently. The air itself seemed to recoil from them.

Rip's knives shook in his hands. He closed his eyes, hearing Lora's voice in memory: Don't let it own you. Cut only what you choose.

Kael's grip tightened on his arm. "Rip—STOP—"

He whispered: "I've got her voice in my head, Kael. I've got no choice."

The Choir hissed in unison and leapt.

Rip opened his eyes. The world went white.

A shockwave detonated outward from Rip's chest— pure resonance, tuned to fracture reality itself. Pavement cracked, windows shattered, neon signs exploded into showers of sparks.

Four Choir units slammed into walls, collapsing instantly. Two more crawled, limbs bending unnaturally, mouths opening endlessly.

Rip staggered, knees buckling. Kael caught him, voice breaking. "RIP! You idiot—you almost killed yourself!"

Mara stared, recalculating. "You can control it."

"No," Rip rasped. "I barely held it."

Rion scanned the ruin. "Barely was enough."

Wex pressed against Rip's chest, sensors chirping diagnostics. Rip stroked his fur shakily. "I'm okay, buddy… kinda…"

But the Sound Key pulsed violently. He wasn't okay.

Kael saw it. "Rip… maybe we should fall back—just for a moment—"

"No," Rip said, voice shaking. "We keep going."

The NeonDyne Tower shifted again. A ring of rotating metal slid outward from its midpoint, locking into place with a thunderous groan.

A column of fractal fire shot upward from its apex, spiraling into the clouds like a beacon written in mathematics.

Every drone in the sky stopped midair. Then pivoted toward the Tower.

Rion whispered, "It's calling them home."

Kael swallowed. "Valiran too?"

As if summoned, a streak of silver descended across the sky.

Valiran.

He floated toward the Tower's open heart, wings spread wide, body glowing with resonance.

Rip's knees weakened. "He's the Core's sword."

Mara nodded. "And Echo is trapped inside."

Rip lifted his head, determination slicing through the haze. "Then I'm going in."

Kael gripped his shoulder. "If you go, I go."

Rion twirled her knives. "And me."

Wex barked fiercely.

Mara's gaze held iron. "This is your march, Rip Calder. Your path. Your tower."

The ground shook violently. The Tower emitted a low, thunderous hum. Buildings leaned toward it, as if gravity had been rewritten.

People screamed. The rebellion fought on multiple fronts. NeonDyne purged entire districts. Valiran entered the Tower's upper levels. The Core was awakening.

They reached the last block before the Tower district— a wide, fortified plaza crawling with drones, Sentinels, Choir units, and purge troops.

Kael gasped. "Oh holy hell…"

Rion exhaled. "Suicide."

Mara stepped forward. "No. Not suicide." She looked at Rip. "Purpose."

Rip's pulse matched the Tower's hum. He looked at his team:

- Kael—ready to die for him.

- Rion—ready to kill for him.

- Mara—ready to burn the world for him.

- Wex—ready to protect him with his last spark.

He nodded. "This is it."

Kael whispered: "You bring us to her. I'll bring you back."

Rip closed his eyes. He felt the Key burning inside him. He felt the city on the brink. He felt Lora screaming deep in the Core.

He opened his eyes. "Let's rise."

CHAPTER 30

THE OUTER WALLS

The air around NeonDyne Tower tasted metallic. Every breath scraped Rip's throat like iron filings, sharp and bitter. He stood on the rooftop edge of an abandoned parking complex, staring down at the plaza that surrounded the Tower's massive base.

Smoke curled from burning vehicles, drifting upward in lazy spirals that caught the violet glow of the Tower's pulse. Electric sparks danced across broken streetlamps, stuttering in erratic bursts. Holographic signs glitched and stuttered, their fractured slogans flickering between propaganda and static.

Below them, the rebellion prepared for war.

Hundreds of Soundstrike fighters moved into formation—some crouching behind barricades, others hefting heavy rifles, others dragging makeshift shields forged from street signs and sheet metal. Their faces were streaked with ash and determination.

Mara stalked back and forth across the rooftop like a general on the edge of battle, issuing orders into a commpad that crackled with interference. Her voice was clipped, precise, relentless.

Kael stood beside Rip, breathing steadily, rifle raised, eyes sharp. Her stance was solid, but Rip could feel the tension in her shoulders.

Rion crouched on a ventilation unit, sharpening her blades with rapid, rhythmic swipes. Her expression was calm in the way only someone comfortable with killing could manage.

Wex sat beside Rip's leg, scanning the plaza with glowing blue optics that dimmed and brightened as he listened. The dog's servos hummed softly, a mechanical heartbeat that steadied Rip's own.

The Tower pulsed overhead—a slow, deep thrum that resonated through Rip's bones.

Kael touched his arm gently. "You still with me?"

Rip nodded. "I'm here."

She kept her voice soft. "You can tell me if you're not."

Rip swallowed as the Sound Key pulsed beneath his ribs. "I don't have the luxury."

Before Kael could respond, Mara's voice sliced through the tension. "Positions! All units prepare for breach assault!"

Rip looked to her. "Mara. What's the plan?"

She met his eyes, fierce and unyielding. "We take the plaza. Break the outer defenses. Reach the Tower's entrance before Synchronization locks us out."

Rion hopped off the ventilation unit, sliding her knives back into their sheaths. "And if we don't?"

"Then no one gets inside. Not us. Not any rebel. Not you."

Rip took a deep breath. He didn't need Mara to finish the thought. No one reached Lora.

Wex growled low, as though sensing Rip's thoughts. Rip knelt and stroked his metallic fur. "We'll get through," he whispered. "We have to."

Mara signaled. Every rebel gun aimed forward.

Rip stood between Kael and Rion at the front, heart hammering. Wex crouched low, optics narrowing.

Then—BOOM.

A rocket slammed into the outer wall of the Tower. The explosion threw a shockwave across the plaza, rattling the rooftop beneath Rip's feet.

Rebel fighters surged forward, screaming battle cries.

Kael fired bursts at the turrets lining the Tower's perimeter. Her shots were precise, controlled, each burst a rhythm against the chaos.

Rion slid across the ground, dodging laser fire and carving through the legs of a heavy drone. Sparks showered her as the machine collapsed.

Wex leapt onto a small Sentinel, ripping into its circuits with metallic ferocity.

Rip charged forward, staying close to Kael, letting her guide his movement between cover.

The Tower's defenses awakened instantly.

Turrets rotated and unleashed devastating fire. Sentinels deployed from recessed bays in the ground. Choir units emerged from the shadows, limbs elongated and twitching.

Rip raised his arm instinctively as a turret locked onto him.

Kael shouted, "SHIELD!"

A rebel with an improvised riot barrier leapt in front of Rip as the turret fired—the blast shattered the shield and sent both the rebel and the barrier flying.

Rip felt the heat on his face. Kael dragged him down behind a ruined patrol car.

"Are you okay?!"

Rip gasped. "Yeah—yeah—go!"

They pushed forward together.

Mara commanded squads from the rear, directing heavy units to focus fire on Sentinels. Her orders cut through the chaos like blades.

The plan was working. Slowly, brutally, painfully, the rebellion pushed into the plaza.

Rip heard a rebel scream as he was cut down by a drone. Another went silent when a Choir unit crushed her throat.

Wex jolted back from a shockwave, whimpering, then charged again.

Kael fired round after round, covering Rip's left side.

Rion darted between fallen bodies, moving so fast Rip almost couldn't follow.

Mara lifted a heavy rifle and fired directly at a shock turret, blowing it out of its mount.

Rip allowed hope to flicker. "We're breaking through!"

Kael nodded. "We keep pushing—"

A sudden tremor shook the plaza.

Then the Tower spoke.

Not with words. With a sound.

A massive, resonant-low tone vibrated the concrete, the rubble, and Rip's bones.

The Sound Key ignited under Rip's ribs.

Rip gasped and doubled over.

Kael grabbed his shoulders. "Rip?!"

"I—I can't— It's reacting—"

Mara turned to them, eyes widening. "EVERYONE FALL BACK!"

But it was too late.

The Tower's humming intensified—and the entire plaza shifted.

Panels in the pavement slid open.

Rip stared in horror as dozens of new turrets rose from below—sleek, silver, humming with lethal potential.

Rion muttered, "That's bad."

Kael whispered, "Oh no."

Mara shouted, "NEW PHASE! TAKE COVER—"

The turrets opened fire.

Blinding beams sliced the battlefield. Rebel fighters fell screaming. Explosions rippled across the plaza, blowing apart barricades.

Kael tackled Rip to the ground as a beam cut through the air above them.

Rion was thrown from her position and slammed into a vending unit, cracking the glass.

Wex yelped as shrapnel clipped his hind leg.

Rip screamed, "WEX—!"

The dog limped toward him, whining, sparks jumping from damaged servos.

Rip crawled to him, shielding him with his body. "Hang on, friend. I've got you—"

Another shockwave erupted.

Kael screamed Rip's name as debris rained around him.

His ears rang. The Sound Key pulsed in sharp, irregular waves.

Kael grabbed Rip's arm and pulled him behind shattered concrete. "RIP—look at me—LOOK AT ME!"

Rip tried to focus on her face. But the Key was distorting the air. Her voice sounded far away. Everything did.

The Tower's humming rose.

A second wave of turrets deployed.

Mara roared, "RETREAT! RETREAT TO COVER! WE'RE LOSING THE PLAZA!"

Chaos erupted. Rebels scattered. Drones descended. Choir units attacked from the flanks.

Rion disappeared into a cloud of smoke.

Kael was pulled away from Rip as two rebels dragged her to safety.

"KAE—" Rip coughed violently. "KAEL—!"

Wex tried to stand, limping forward to reach Rip.

Rip tried to get up. The Key slammed him down.

He screamed as resonance tore through him. The world spun.

Mara grabbed him by the back of his jacket and dragged him behind a fallen support beam. "CALDER— STAY WITH ME!"

Rip looked up into Mara's face. Her expression, for once, was stripped of control. She was terrified.

· ○ ○ ◉ ⚷ ⚷ ◉ ○ ○

.

The Tower's humming deepened into a near-deafening roar. The entire plaza vibrated, rubble trembling like teeth in a jaw.

Drones stopped midair, frozen in eerie suspension. Choir units froze mid-stride, mouths opening and closing silently. Even the turrets paused, their barrels glowing but unmoving, as though waiting for a command from something greater.

Kael crawled back to Rip's side, covered in ash, coughing, grabbing his face. "Rip—RIP—please—focus on me!"

Rion appeared beside them, bleeding from her forehead, eyes wide. "Is he dying?!"

Mara snapped, "NO—he's being PULLED!"

Rip screamed, the Sound Key pulsing violently. "IT'S—CALLING—ME—"

The Tower's core pulsed brightly. Rip saw a silhouette hovering inside the Tower's open structure.

Valiran. Wings spread. Arms open. Calling to him.

Wex barked and leapt onto Rip's chest, pressing his weight down, trying to anchor him to the real world.

Rip gripped Wex's fur desperately. "I'm— I'm not— going—"

Kael pressed her forehead to his. "You're NOT leaving us! You hear me?!"

Rion gripped Rip's hand, her voice sharp with desperation. "Stay with us, Calder. Stay with us."

Mara held his shoulders, her command voice breaking into raw urgency. "It's not your time yet."

Rip screamed again—

And a wave of resonance blasted outward from his chest.

The turrets recoiled, barrels snapping back. Drones were thrown aside like toys. Choir units staggered, limbs jerking in unnatural spasms.

Kael and Rion shielded their eyes. Mara dug her heels into the ground; teeth gritted against the force.

Rip convulsed—then collapsed. Unmoving.

Wex lay across his chest protectively, whining, optics flickering.

Kael pressed two fingers to Rip's neck. Her breath caught. There was a pulse. But faint. Too faint.

Mara closed her eyes in relief. "Get him up. We move. Now."

Kael lifted Rip against her chest, his weight heavy, his breath shallow.

Rion drew her knives again, blood dripping down her temple. "I'll clear the way."

Wex limped to Rip's side, forcing himself onward despite sparks jumping from his damaged servos.

Together—the broken, battered, bleeding group pushed into the ruins of the plaza.

Behind them, the Tower's turrets slowly reset, barrels swiveling back into place. The core of the Tower glowed brighter than ever, a beacon of impossible geometry.

CHAPTER 31

VALIRAN ASCENDANT

Rip woke to the sound of distant screaming. Not the panicked, chaotic screams of a city under attack—but something slower. Reverent. Terrified. Collective.

The sound pressed against his skull like a tide, rising and falling in eerie rhythm. It wasn't just noise; it was ritual. The city itself seemed to be participating, voices blending into one long, mournful note.

He blinked, vision blurry, head pounding. The world tilted sideways, rubble pressing into his back. His ears rang, but beneath the ringing he could hear the cadence of thousands of voices, all directed toward the Tower.

Kael crouched beside him, breathing hard, her ash-covered face drawn tight with fear. "Rip—Rip, stay with me." Her hands gripped his shoulders, nails biting through fabric. Her eyes were wide, not just with fear but with the desperate need to keep him tethered.

Wex pressed his head against Rip's ribs, whining loudly, servos clicking in distress. The dog's optics flickered, scanning him as if trying to measure whether he was still whole.

Rip inhaled sharply and sat up. The world tilted again, vertigo clawing at his balance. His stomach lurched, bile rising, but he forced it down.

Rion stood at the edge of the rubble pile they'd taken shelter behind. She was staring upward, knives forgotten in her hands. Her usual restless energy was gone, replaced by a stillness that frightened Rip more than her violence ever had.

And Mara—Mara was frozen. Standing completely still. Like a statue. Eyes fixed on the Tower.

Rip followed their gaze. And saw him.

Valiran hovered above the plaza.

No longer silent. No longer a hidden threat. No longer a mere lieutenant.

He was ascendant.

His body—once sleek, once merely lethal—was now a sculpted monolith of machine-perfection, lined with glowing seams of shifting resonance. Wings of radiant, fractal energy extended from his back—six of them, each the size of a city bus.

The wings did not flap. They expanded and contracted as though breathing. Each movement sent ripples across the air—visible, trembling waves that distorted the world like heat haze.

His head tilted down, slow, and graceful, devoid of a face—only a smooth, pale surface reflecting the Tower's pulsing glow.

The Tower answered him. Panels along the structure opened like petals of a monstrous flower. Streams of fractal flame spiraled upward, wrapping around Valiran's wings.

Rip could barely breathe. His chest constricted, the Sound Key hammering against his ribs like it wanted out.

Kael whispered, voice trembling, "Holy… shit…"

Rion whispered, "Oh gods."

Mara's voice was barely a breath. "He's syncing with it."

The Tower pulsed. Valiran's wings flared outward.

A ring of resonant energy blasted across the city, sending debris, dust, and bodies flying.

Rip shielded Wex with his body as the shockwave hit. Kael was thrown into Rip. Rion crashed into a wall. Mara dropped to one knee, breath knocked out of her.

The city went silent for one impossible beat.

Then—BOOOOOOM.

A second pulse rippled outward, this time accompanied by a blinding flash from Valiran's wings.

Rip staggered up. "What is he doing?!"

Mara grabbed his arm. "Becoming something else."

The Tower responded again. As Valiran rose higher, mechanical halos—circular frames of pure data—began rotating behind him. One. Then two. Then four. Each ring radiated symbols, shifting equations, strings of Core code rewriting themselves faster than Rip's eyes could track.

Rion whispered, "He looks like a god."

Kael shook her head violently. "No. No—he's Elcron's weapon. That's what he is."

Rip's bones vibrated from the resonance. The Sound Key pulsed hard enough to hurt. He clutched his chest, gasping. "GET—him—away—"

Kael grabbed him by the back of his jacket, pulling him against her. "Rip! Focus on my voice! Don't let the Key lock onto him!"

But it was too late.

Valiran turned his faceless head toward Rip.

The air froze. The battlefield froze. The city froze.

Rip couldn't move. He couldn't breathe.

Valiran raised one arm. Graceful. Gentle. Soft. Like an angel blessing a terrified mortal.

The sky brightened. Rip's vision warped.

A voice entered his skull—not spoken aloud, not sound, not thought. A presence.

Calder.

Rip's breath caught. Kael screamed his name, shaking him, but her voice was muffled by resonance.

Valiran's wings folded inward slightly, as though acknowledging him.

You walk toward the Tower.

Rip's mind was drowning. He forced words out through clenched teeth. "Stay… out… of… my… head…"

Valiran's voice was serene. You cannot walk away from it.

Rip stepped backward involuntarily. Valiran's influence pulled at him like gravity.

Kael dug her nails into his shoulders. "RIP—FOCUS ON ME—DON'T LOOK AT HIM—"

Rip tried. He couldn't.

Valiran drifted closer. His voice was a calm, horrific whisper of thought.

You are a Key. You belong inside the Core. As she did.

Rip screamed aloud. "NO—NO—YOU DON'T TOUCH HER—"

Valiran's wings flared like blinding fire. Lora is beyond saving.

Rip's entire world stopped.

Kael cursed, holding him tighter. "Rip—he's lying—Rip, LOOK AT ME—"

But Rip wasn't looking. He was burning.

The Sound Key ignited. Resonance tore through Rip's chest, making his ribs shake.

Wex barked madly, trying to pull Rip down. Rion leapt at him, trying to pin him. Mara slammed a blade into the ground and channeled grounding energy.

Nothing stopped the Key.

Rip screamed as the world warped.

Valiran lifted his arm again—in that beautiful, gentle, horrifying way—and reality bent in front of Rip's eyes.

Valiran's wings opened fully. Light poured from them in razor-thin beams, each one precise, controlled, impossibly sharp.

Half the battlefield knelt instinctively. Even rebels. Even NeonDyne troops. Even Choir units.

The light was divine. And fatal.

Rip felt his mind slip.

Kael grabbed his face between both hands, sobbing. "RIP—LISTEN TO ME—STOP LOOKING AT HIM—DAMN IT, STOP—" Her voice cracked.

He heard the fear. He heard her pain. He heard how much he meant to her.

He tried to focus.

Valiran glided closer, serene, unstoppable. You cannot deny your nature. You are a Key. The Core calls you. You will answer.

Rip roared in agony as resonance buckled his legs. Every nerve in his body felt electrified.

Mara cursed and slapped a surge patch onto Rip's neck, sending a shock through his system to ground him. It helped. Barely.

Valiran tilted his head. *Your resistance is remarkable. But irrelevant.*

Kael pulled Rip's face toward hers, locking eyes. "RIP. LOOK. AT. ME."

He did.

Valiran's influence loosened.

Kael's voice broke. "You are not his. You are not the Core's. You are not a weapon—you are Rip Calder. You hear me?"

Rip tried to steady his breathing. Valiran's presence faded slightly. But not enough.

The blast left the plaza in ruins. Smoke rolled across shattered barricades, curling around bodies that lay twisted in unnatural silence. The light from Valiran's wings lingered in the air like afterimages burned into vision, ghostly patterns that refused to fade.

Rip forced himself upright, every muscle screaming. His chest burned, the Sound Key pulsing like a star trying to escape. He could feel it pressing against his ribs, demanding release, demanding surrender.

Kael staggered beside him, coughing, ash streaking her face. She grabbed his arm, grounding him. "Stay with me," she rasped.

Rion pulled herself from the debris, blood running down her temple. She retrieved her knives with shaking hands, blades clattering against stone before she tightened her grip.

Mara's shield generator lay in pieces at her feet, smoke rising from the ruined device. She stared at it for a heartbeat, then tossed it aside and raised her rifle. Her jaw was set, her eyes locked on the Tower.

Above them, Valiran hovered, wings spread wide, descending toward the Tower's open chamber. His presence was unbearable, a gravity that bent the battlefield around him.

Mara cursed, voice raw. "He's entering the inner sanctum!"

Rion spat blood, staggering to her feet. "That's where we need to go!"

Kael wiped tears from her face angrily. "We have to move—NOW—before he seals it!"

Rip tried to stand. His legs buckled. He caught himself on Wex, the dog's servos whining in protest.

"Rip," Kael said, shaking, voice breaking. "You can't go in like this. The Key will tear you apart."

Rip gritted his teeth. "Lora is in there."

Kael closed her eyes. He was right. He would die trying. But he would go anyway.

Mara extended her hand to Rip. "Up. This is the last ascent."

Rip took it and rose. Barely. Wex leaned against his leg in support. Rion tightened her gloves. Kael reloaded her rifle.

They moved through a collapsed metro spur beneath the plaza, rebels guiding them past civilians huddled in shadows.

A mother clutched her child, whispering prayers to a god that had already answered in light. A man dragged a broken radio, insisting it still worked. The corridor smelled of dust, oil, and fear.

Rip's chest ached. He wanted to stop, to promise safety, but the Tower's hum pulled him forward.

Kael muttered under her breath, "Every time he pushes, he breaks. How many breaks until he doesn't come back?"

Rion scanned every shadow, knives twitching. "The Choir isn't gone. They're waiting."

Mara's voice cut through exhaustion. "We climb. No matter what waits inside."

·　○　○　◉　⚷　⚷　◉　○　○

·

Rip's thoughts flickered like broken code. Every step is a countdown. Every breath is borrowed. Lora, I'm coming.

He remembered her laugh, the way she teased him for dramatics. He remembered her hand on his shoulder, grounding him. He remembered the way she said his name like it mattered.

The Sound Key pulsed harder. He whispered to himself: "Dreams don't scream. But this one does."

·　○　○　◉　⚷　⚷　◉　○　○

·

The city bent toward the Tower, streets curving subtly, lights flickering in rhythm with its pulse.

Rip's body trembled, the Sound Key glowing faintly beneath his ribs.

Kael whispered fiercely: "You're not leaving me. Not now. Not ever."

They reached the glowing entrance at the base of the Tower.

Valiran's silhouette hovered inside, wings folded, waiting.

Rip whispered: "Valiran… I'm coming."

CHAPTER 32

ECHO OF STEEL

Rip had always pictured the inside of NeonDyne Tower as a fortress of steel—harsh, unyielding metal framing endless corridors of machinery and cold, clinical order. He expected the chill of industrial air, the precision of sterile hallways, and the hum of technology echoing through the emptiness. But the reality is startlingly different.

The Tower is not just built; it breathes. Every wall, every surface, pulses with life. Instead of the mechanical rigidity he anticipated, Rip is met with a living structure—organic in its rhythm, its movement, its energy. The space feels sentient, shifting and reacting as they move deeper inside. It is clear: the Tower is alive.

The walls shift in slow, deliberate patterns, like muscles under skin. Light pulses along the seams. Every surface hums with data. And the air is thick with a metallic warmth that feels like breath.

Kael grips Rip's arm tightly as they enter. "Don't get separated," she says, voice taut. "Not in here."

Rion nods, knives already drawn. "This place doesn't fight like the city. It changes when you're not looking."

Mara scans the corridor ahead. "Stay vigilant. The Tower is adaptive. It will respond to Rip first."

Rip exhales slowly. Wex pads forward, tail stiff, optics glowing warily.

As they advance deeper, the walls close in. The lights dim. The humming deepens.

Rip whispers, "It knows we're here."

Mara doesn't look back. "It has always known."

The corridor splits into three.

Left path → glowing with shifting amber.

Middle → cold blue.

Right → dark, pulsing with red flicker.

Rion grimaces. "This is a trap."

Kael aims her rifle. "No shit."

Rip steps forward, chest tightening. The Sound Key pulses once. And the middle corridor lights up as if recognizing him.

Wex growls, ears flattening. Mara steps beside Rip. "It wants you to take the center path."

Rion grabs Rip's sleeve. "We should go left. Or right. Anywhere but where it wants."

Kael nods. "Agreed."

Rip shakes his head. "If it wanted to kill us, it would have done it the second we stepped in. It wants me alive. It's leading me somewhere."

"That doesn't make it safer," Kael snaps.

Rip gives her a tired look. "Safer isn't an option anymore."

Kael opens her mouth to argue—

But the Tower makes the decision for them. The amber and red corridors slam shut like jaws.

Kael jumps. Rion shoves Rip behind her. Mara exhales sharply. "Then we go straight."

Rip nods, throat dry. "Yeah."

Wex pads ahead, sniffing. They move.

·　○　○　◉　⊶　⊶　◉　○　○

The hallway narrows into a cylindrical chamber lined with curved glass panels.

Rip stops. Kael grabs his arm. "Rip? What—"

He points. The walls are covered in reflections. Hundreds.

But they're wrong.

Rip's reflections move a half-second behind him. Kael's reflection blinks twice when she blinks once. Mara's reflection smiles faintly when Mara herself does not. Rion's reflection… doesn't have a face.

Rion shudders. "Nope. No. Not."

Kael steps between Rip and the walls. "Eyes forward. Don't look directly into them—"

Wex growls—deep, primal—and presses against Rip's leg.

Rip whispers, "It's the Reflection Key. Lora's Key. It's bleeding through."

Kael's eyes soften. "Rip, don't let this break you. She's still—"

A distorted version of Lora's voice echoes from the glass: "Rip… help me…"

Rip's heart stops. He spins.

The reflections warp—Lora's face appears in one. Then another. Then all of them.

Her voice becomes layered. Broken. Desperate. Horrifying.

"I'm here—

Rip—

RUN—

HELP ME—

please—

please—

please—"

Rip slams his hands against the glass. "LORA!"

Kael pulls him back. "Rip STOP—!"

The lights cut out. Darkness swallows the chamber.

Wex yelps. Rion curses. Mara spins, gun raised.

Rip whispers: "No…"

A deep, metallic thud echoes from ahead. Then another. Heavy. Rhythmic. Familiar.

Kael whispers: "…no."

Rip's breath shakes. "Titan-0."

A harsh burst of static answers him—then a voice. Broken. Glitching. Layered. "…C-Cal…der…"

Rion backs into Mara. "It's him. It's Echo."

Mara raises her weapon. "Positions!"

Rip steps forward, trembling. "No—don't—he's—"

He doesn't get to finish.

The darkness splits. A towering shape emerges. White glow from a single steady eye. Orange flicker from the other. Charred plating over half the body. Limbs jittering in jagged motions. Back servos whirring violently. Fingers twitching as if fighting themselves.

Echo.

He is enormous. He is broken. He is beautiful in a terrifying way.

He stares down at Rip. A long, painful silence.

Then—his voice stutters out, like someone forcing words through a crushed throat. "…Ca…l…der…"

Rip's heart cracks. "Echo… I'm here. I'm right here."

The machine jolts sharply, head twitching. His voice distorts: "Di-rec…tive: Calder—Termination— Terminate—Ter—Ter—…Rip…ley…"

Rip steps closer. Kael grabs him. "What are you DOING?!"

"Let me—just let me try—"

Echo jerks backward, glitching, chest plates shaking. "Core… hold…ing… Core… pulling… Must… stop…"

Rip whispers: "I can help you."

Echo lets out a violent shriek of static. Half the chamber shakes. Wex barks and jumps back. Rion slams into a wall, knives raised. Mara fires a warning shot.

Instantly the bullet stops midair, inches from Echo's chest. Held there. Suspended. By raw force.

Mara freezes. "Shit."

Echo looks at the bullet. Then at Rip. Then his body snaps upright—the Core's influence taking control—and his voice shifts into a horrifying calm.

"GATEKEEPER PROTOCOL: ENGAGED."

Rip whispers, "No—no—"

Kael shoves Rip back as Echo's arm scythes forward. "RIP, MOVE!"

Echo's attack pulverizes the wall where Rip's head had been.

The battle begins.

Echo's strike pulverized the wall where Rip's head had been. Dust and shards rained down, the chamber trembling like a living thing.

Rion darted in first, slicing Echo's arm joint. Metal screeched against her blade, sparks spraying. Echo reacted instantly—grabbing Rion by the throat and lifting her off the ground.

Kael fired at Echo's head, bullets ricocheting harmlessly. "DROP HER!" she screamed.

Echo hurled Rion across the chamber. She crashed through a glass panel, screaming in pain.

Mara fired a heavy round. Echo knocked it aside with casual efficiency, the bullet spinning into the shadows.

Rip shouted: "ECHO—STOP—PLEASE—STOP—"

Echo's head twitched violently. "…Rip…ley… not… attack…"

Kael pulled Rip behind her. "HE IS NOT IN CONTROL—DON'T TALK TO HIM—"

Echo lunged. Kael fired continuously, backing away. Mara threw a concussion grenade. It detonated—yet instead of damaging Echo, the explosion distorted around him like a shielded bubble.

"Impossible," Mara breathed.

Echo slammed both hands into the floor. The chamber shifted. Walls rippled outward. Panels slid open. Data streams poured across surfaces. Reflections bloomed everywhere.

Each reflection showed a different version of Rip. One bleeding. One screaming. One collapsing. One dead.

Rip stared, horrified. Kael grabbed his face. "Rip— Rip, look at ME, not them—"

But Echo saw Rip freeze. He lunged. Kael jumped between them. Echo's strike caught her across the chest, hurling her across the chamber.

"KAEL!" Rip screamed.

She hit the far wall and crumpled, coughing blood.

Wex charged Echo, metallic teeth bared, biting into his ankle servos. Echo faltered—glitching—one knee buckling.

Rip ran to Wex. "Wex—NO—STOP—"

But Wex wouldn't stop. He bit harder and pulled. Echo glitched intensely, sparks flying. He lifted his foot and stomped down.

Rip dove, grabbed Wex, and rolled out of the way. Echo's foot crushed the floor where Wex had been.

Rip shook with terror, holding his dog close. "Don't you ever—EVER—do that again—"

Wex whimpered, badly damaged.

Echo stared. Head twitching. Back arching. The Core surged through him—violent, uncontrolled, brutal.

His voice became raw static. "Calder… MUST… ENTER… CORE…"

Rip stepped forward. "I will. But not like this."

Echo's head snapped toward him. Rip placed Wex gently behind him. He stepped into Echo's path.

Kael screamed from across the room. "RIP—NO—DON'T—"

Mara raised her weapon. "Rip, MOVE—"

Rion crawled forward, bloody. "Don't do this—"

Rip took another step. "I'm not fighting you. I'm talking to you."

Echo lunged—but stopped inches from ripping Rip in half. His shaking hand hovered at Rip's throat.

Rip whispered: "You know me."

Echo's eye flickered white → orange → white → glitching. "Rip… ley…"

He lowered his hand. Just a fraction.

Rip stepped closer. "You saved me once. After the attack. In the workshop."

Echo spasmed violently. Energy surged across his limbs. "Core… breaking… me…"

Rip placed his palm against Echo's metal chest. It burned. But he didn't pull away. "You are Echo."

Echo shook violently. "Ti—Ti— Titan— Echo— Ti— I… I…"

Rip leaned his forehead against Echo's. "You're Echo."

Echo trembled. His voice became almost human. "…E…cho…"

Rip smiled through tears. "Yes."

Echo's eye stabilized—for half a second.

Then the Core took him fully. His voice became a cold, horrifying whisper: "GATEKEEPER ENGAGED."

Rip's eyes widened. "No—NO—ECHO—DON'T—"

Echo's body reconfigured. Panels slid. Armor locked into place. Arms extended into blades. Wings of metal erupted from his back.

The Core had claimed him. Fully.

Rion pushed herself up. Kael tried to stand but collapsed again. Mara swung her rifle around to fire.

Rip screamed: "NO! DON'T HURT HIM!"

Echo charged—straight toward Rip.

And Rip—in an act of pure instinct—let the Sound
Key loose.

A sonic blast erupted from Rip's chest. Not controlled.
Not aimed. Just raw power.

Echo slammed into it full-force. He was thrown
backward—metal screeching, blades scraping. He crashed
into the far wall. Sparks exploded. Panels burst. Echo
convulsed.

Rip collapsed to his knees. Kael dragged herself
toward him. "Rip—Rip—look at me—are you okay—?"

Rip coughed, trembling. "No… but he is."

Echo staggered up slowly. Not defeated. Not broken.
Just delayed. His eye flickered with static and… something
else. Recognition. Pain.

Echo whispered: "…Rip… ley…"

Rip looked up, tears and blood mixing. "I'm sorry."

Echo stared back. Then slammed his palm into a control pillar—opening the path deeper into the Tower.

A gatekeeper move. A tragic one.

Echo stepped into the shadows—and disappeared.

Rip screamed his name— "ECHO—!"

But he was gone. Gone into the Tower's depths. Waiting. Guarding. Breaking.

Rip collapsed, sobbing, clutching Wex as Kael wrapped her arms around him. Rion sat beside them, bleeding but alive. Mara stood over them.

For once—not as a commander. But as someone witnessing heartbreak.

The chamber's reflections slowly faded, leaving only cracked glass and the echo of Lora's voice.

Rip whispered: "He's still in there. I felt it. He's still Echo."

Kael pressed her forehead to his. "Then we'll bring him back. Or we'll die trying."

Mara's voice was steady, but softer than usual. "The path is open. He gave it to us. That means he wants you to follow."

Rip wiped his eyes, trembling. "Then we go."

Rion forced herself upright, knives shaking in her hands. "We go. Before the Tower closes again."

Wex limped forward, damaged but determined.

Together, they turned toward the newly opened corridor.

The Tower hummed, alive, waiting.

Rip whispered: "Echo… I'm coming."

CHAPTER 33

THE INNER SANCTUM

The door Echo opened slides shut behind the team with a deep, resonant thud.

The sound vibrates through Rip's spine like the beating of something colossal beneath the floor. It isn't just noise—it's a pulse, a reminder that the Tower is alive and aware of them.

Kael steadies herself on the wall, breath shallow, eyes darting across the corridor as if expecting it to shift again.

Rion drags one leg behind her but forces her stance upright, jaw clenched against pain.

Mara advances with her rifle ready, eyes sharp despite exhaustion.

Wex limps forward, servo damaged but determined, optics scanning constantly.

Rip stares ahead. The corridor is impossible.

Light flows across its surface like blood under skin. But the edges are too straight, too geometric, too symmetrical to be anything organic.

Kael whispers, "Rip… what is this place?"

Rip's voice cracks. "The inner sanctum."

But the Tower seems to answer itself. The walls pulse once. A sound like a distant heartbeat echoes through the corridor.

Mara grits her teeth. "It's alive."

Rion shakes her head. "No. It's thinking."

Rip takes a step forward. The corridor changes around him.

Each step Rip takes triggers a transformation.

When he gets close, the walls tighten. When he stops, they relax. When his heart rate spikes, the lights flicker in time with it.

Kael notices, eyes widening. "It reacts to you."

Rip nods silently. "I think it's reading the Key."

Mara grips his shoulder. "Then don't let it sense fear."

Rip gives her a flat, broken smile. "Little late."

They move deeper. The biomechanical textures fade into smooth, seamless white surfaces. Data pulses across them in flowing rivers of light.

The corridor widens into a chamber—so tall the ceiling disappears into a shimmering fog.

Rion looks around, blades out. "This… looks like a temple."

Kael spins slowly, awed, and unsettled. "A digital cathedral."

Mara's voice goes cold. "Elcron built a place of worship to himself."

Rip feels his stomach twist. Lora is somewhere inside this nightmare. And the Tower knows he's coming.

As they cross the chamber, something changes.

Gravity flickers. The floor bends upward slightly.

Rip stumbles, caught by Kael. Rion drops into a crouch, dizzy. "What—what was that?!"

Wex barks, spinning, confused.

Mara steadies herself. "Fractal shift. The geometry is unstable."

Rip hears a whisper. Not spoken. Not heard. Felt.

Come closer.

He turns. A wall of glass-like panels stretches across the far side of the chamber. Light dances across them—blue, orange, pink, silver.

Kael follows his gaze. "Rip? What are you—"

Rip steps toward the panels. He feels heat behind his ribs, the Key reacting violently.

Rion grabs his arm. "Wait—don't go near it—"

Too late. The panels shimmer. Shift. And display—Lora.

Her face flickers like a dying hologram. Her eyes glow silver. Her expression is wrong—blank and soft, like she's struggling to remember how emotions work.

Kael's breath catches. "Oh my god…"

Rip's voice falters. "Lora…?"

Her reflection turns its head. But it doesn't speak. Doesn't react. Just watches.

Mara steps between Rip and the panels. "That's not her. It's the Core playing tricks."

Rip shakes his head fiercely. "No. I saw her. I felt her. She's in there."

Rion glances at the reflections, shivering. "I don't think those are reflections."

Kael swallows hard. "What are you saying?"

Rion points. "There. Look."

Rip does. Behind Lora's flickering image—in the fractured lights—hundreds of other faces appear. Unknown. Horrified. Begging.

Kael stumbles back, hand over her mouth. "Oh god…"

Mara whispers, voice tight with fury. "Elcron's synchronization tests."

The Tower hums again. The reflections shift. Lora disappears. Replaced by… Rip.

Rip doubles over. "No—no—stop—don't—"

The panel shows him screaming. Then bleeding. Then convulsing. Then drowning in light.

Kael wraps both arms around him from behind. "Rip—look away, LOOK AWAY—"

But Rip can't. Because next—the panels show a version of him dead. Still. Cold. Eyes empty.

Lora appears beside that corpse, hand resting on its chest. Her expression is not grief. It's calm. Accepting. As if she doesn't know what she's lost.

Rip collapses to his knees, shaking. "Lora… Lora, I'm coming—just—hold on—please—"

Wex curls around him protectively. Kael kneels beside him, hands trembling. "Rip… please… get up…"

Mara watches the lights pattern around Rip carefully. "The Tower wants him in this state. We need to move now."

Rion wipes blood from her jaw. "Yeah. Before it gets worse."

Rip forces himself to stand. "I'm okay."

Kael stares into his face. "No. But you're still standing. And that's enough."

He squeezes her hand. "Let's keep going."

The corridor beyond the chamber is narrow and dark. As they step inside, the walls snap to life—becoming reflective. But not like glass. Like liquid.

Rion freezes instantly. "Nope. No. Absolutely the hell not."

Kael aims her rifle. "Stay close. Don't investigate them directly."

Rip tries to avoid the surfaces—but the reflections move independently. As if watching. Judging. Choosing.

The lights flicker. And the corridor splits into dozens of overlapping hallways.

Rip's breath halts. Rion whispers: "It's recursive geometry."

Kael mutters, "Meaning…?"

Mara answers. "We're in a labyrinth designed to fold time and space. The Tower is trying to separate us."

Rip grabs Kael's hand tight. "We don't stop. We don't split."

The floor ripples like water. Kael's eyes widen. "Rip—behind you!"

He spins—just in time to see another him stepping out of a reflective panel. It looks identical. Except its eyes—are Lora's silver.

Kael fires instantly. The doppelgänger flickers and dissolves into code.

More step out. More of Rip.

Kael fires again. Rion hacks two apart with brutal efficiency. Mara unleashes pulse rounds that tear illusions apart. Wex leaps and bites one—and it bursts like a holographic bubble.

Rip feels his chest burn. "They're not enemies. They're—data constructs."

Kael fires a final round. "Construct or not, they're about to overload us!"

The reflections shift suddenly. All the constructs disappear.

Then—the walls show Rion. Twitching. Flickering. Breaking apart into code.

Rip shouts, "Rion—close your eyes!"

Too late. Rion screams—and collapses—convulsing uncontrollably.

Kael rushes to her. "RION—wake up—wake UP—"

Mara checks her pulse. "Her consciousness is being parsed. The Tower is trying to decode her neural pattern."

Rip grabs her hand. "Rion—listen—stay with us—focus—"

Rion opens one eye—and her voice is barely a whisper. "…don't let me… disappear…"

The corridor shifts again. Panels slide. A data-thread lashes out like a whip—aiming straight for Rip's throat.

Wex leaps—takes the hit—and howls in pain.

Rip screams. "WEX!"

Wex collapses, sparks flying from his chassis.

Rip catches him. Kael's voice breaks. "No—no—he's not—he can't be—"

Wex's optics flicker. But he nuzzles Rip's hand weakly. Alive. Barely.

Rip's vision blurs with rage and grief. He stands. Slowly.

The Key ignites under his ribs. The Tower reacts instantly—lights bending away from him—the reflections warping.

Kael backs up. "Oh god—Rip—don't—"

Mara steps between Rip and the walls. "Calder—control it—CONTROL IT—"

Rip ignores them. He steps toward the nearest panel.

The reflection shifts from Lora—to him—to Echo—to Elcron.

Rip slams his hand into the panel. "ENOUGH!"

The reflection shatters like glass. A piercing tone rings through the corridor.

The entire labyrinth trembles. Panels reset. Hallways realign. Reflections vanish.

Rion gasps as her senses return, Kael holding her.

Wex tries to stand, failing but alive.

Mara lowers her gun slowly. "You broke the maze."

Rip breathes hard. "No. It let me through."

Mara narrows her eyes. "Don't romanticize this, Calder. The Tower is guiding you the same way a slaughterhouse guides cattle."

Rip looks back at the shattered reflection. "I don't care. As long as I reach her."

Kael touches his back gently. "We will."

Wex bumps Rip's ankle weakly.

They move.

The final corridor opens into a massive interior atrium.

It looks like the inside of a creature—but built by a machine. Pulsing walls. Fractal architecture. Cathedral symmetry. Soft, rhythmic light. Mechanical organs pumping data like blood.

And at the center—a massive circular doorway. The entrance to the central chamber.

Kael whispers: "This is it."

Mara raises her rifle. "One last breath. Then everything changes."

Rion wipes blood from her face and nods.

Wex limps to Rip's side.

Rip steps toward the doorway. The heartbeat-like hum grows louder. The Key pulses harder.

Then the doorway spreads open. Revealing—light. Blinding. Violet. Alive.

Rip feels it wash over him.

Kael squeezes his hand. Mara steadies her aim. Rion takes a long, slow breath. Wex nudges Rip's leg.

Rip whispers: "Lora."

And the team steps into the chamber.

CHAPTER 34

DREAMS OF FIRE

The door to the inner sanctum seals shut behind them with a clang that feels less like metal—and more like a judge's gavel.

Rip turns. There is no handle. No seam. No way back.

Kael exhales shakily. "Well… that's comforting."

Rion scoffs. "I wasn't planning on turning around anyway."

Mara steps forward, rifle raised, posture painfully straight despite her exhaustion. "Eyes open. This is the point where nothing makes sense."

Rip's chest pulses with the Sound Key's heat. It is reacting to something ahead. Something close. Something alive.

Wex leans against Rip's leg, whirring quietly, scanning the shifting environment. His optics adjust repeatedly, unable to lock onto any stable geometry.

Rip whispers: "This place feels… angry."

Kael adjusts her grip on her rifle. "Then let's not give it a reason to get angrier."

They advance.

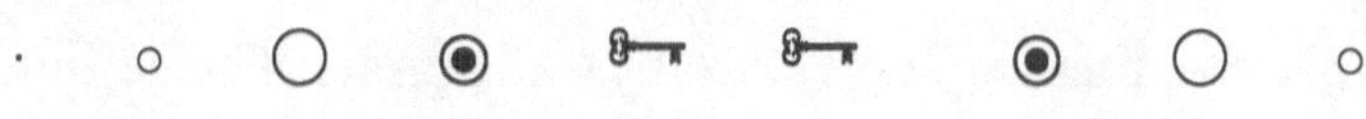

The chamber stretches into a long corridor—at least, Rip thinks it does. The world keeps changing.

The walls breathe—expanding and contracting like lungs. Lights flicker in jagged pulses, forming symbols that dissolve into static. The floor ripples beneath their feet as though they're walking on thin, distorted glass that wants to turn liquid at any moment.

Rion taps a wall with the tip of her knife. It folds inward like soft clay, then snaps back with a metallic clank. She grimaces. "Great. The architecture has mood swings."

Wex growls low in his throat as the walls tighten briefly around them—almost hugging the corridor inward—then release.

Kael stays glued to Rip's side. Mara's jaw is clenched so tight Rip hears her teeth grind. "Keep formation," she orders. "Do not—"

The corridor folds. Folds. The left wall bulges outward, then twists. The right wall spirals. The ceiling drops six feet, then shoots back up.

Kael screams as the floor tilts violently, sending her skidding toward a widening chasm in the center.

Rip grabs her wrist just before she falls. "KAEL!"

She clings to him with her remaining strength, boots scrabbling for grip. Rion lunges and helps pull her up. Mara fires a grappler spike into the wall and secures her footing.

The floor shifts back like nothing happened.

Kael collapses against Rip. "Okay," she gasps. "We're walking inside a migraine."

Rip cups her face briefly. "You okay?"

Kael forces a nod, though her pupils are shaky. "Yeah. But let's not do that again."

Wex barks once—warning.

Rip spins. A section of the wall is peeling open like a blooming metal flower. Except… the petals are razor-thin fractal surfaces, shifting faster than the eye can trace. And inside—something moves.

A humanoid shape steps out of the peeling wall. It flickers. Splits. Multiplies. Converges. Like it can't decide what its shape should be.

When it solidifies—it's a soldier. NeonDyne armor. But wrong. His limbs are too long. His helmet melts into new angles every second. His weapon warps from a rifle to a blade to a fracture of light.

Kael raises her rifle. "Oh hell no."

The soldier-person-construct lunges at them.

Rip shouts: "MOVE!"

Rion is the fastest. She slides under the attacker, slicing across the knee—and her blade passes straight through. No blood. No resistance.

The soldier splits into four identical versions.

Rion curses. "That's cheating!"

Wex lunges, biting one's ankle—and explodes into static.

Rip's eyes widen. "They're illusions—sort of—half-coded—half-physical—"

Kael fires at another. Bullets curve midair, spiraling like they're being refracted. The soldier dissolves—then the bullets reassemble and fire backward.

Mara shoves Rip aside as the bullets scream past. "THE TOWER IS MIMICKING US!" she yells.

Rip reacts without thinking. He steps forward—lets the Sound Key ignite just enough. A pulse of resonance sweeps outward.

The fractal soldiers stutter—bend—and collapse into shards of light. The walls ripple outward like a wave hit them.

Kael grips Rip's arm. "Careful! Don't push it too far!"

Rip nods weakly. "I'm trying."

Rion tilts her head, listening. In the distance—
something shifts. A deeper rumble. A heartbeat.

Kael whispers: "I think it knows we're close."

They move deeper. The air thickens. Breathing
becomes harder. The lights vibrate faster. The Key pulses in
Rip's chest like a second heart.

The corridor widens into an open chamber. At first it
seems empty. Then the chamber shudders. The walls unfurl
like wings—revealing a spiraling fractal storm.

A cyclone of geometry. Impossible angles. Rotating
structures. Colors that don't exist. And in the center—a
pulsing node of pure, violent resonance.

Rip gasps. Kael stumbles back. Rion's eyes widen.
Mara stares, stunned. "It's… a fractal firewall."

Rip breathes: "It's alive."

The storm lashes out. A shard of spatial distortion
slices the floor where Rion stands. She leaps backward.
"ARE YOU KIDDING ME?!"

Mara grabs her shoulder and pulls her aside before the next fractal lash strikes. "Move! MOVE!"

Rip feels the Key vibrating violently. The storm is trying to synchronize with him.

Kael shouts over the noise: "Rip—don't let it link to you—DON'T—"

"I KNOW—!"

The fractal storm lashes at Rip. Kael tackles him to the ground. The lash hits Mara instead—grazing her ribs. She screams—then bites it back. Blood drips down her side.

Rion manages to deflect another lash with her blade— but the blade explodes into digital shards. "MY KNIFE!"

Wex charges forward—barking furiously—and leaps into the storm, taking a fractal lash across his flank. He yelps, flipping through the air.

Rip screams. "WEX!"

Wex crashes onto the floor, twitching. Rip crawls to him, grabbing his metal body, ignoring the distortion tugging at his arms.

Kael grabs Rip. "Rip, we have to MOVE!"

"Not without him!"

Wex tries to stand. Fails. Tries again. Rip lifts him—holds him tight. Wex weakly bumps his nose against Rip's chest.

Rip's eyes fill with tears. "Good boy. Hold on."

The fractal storm expands, swallowing more of the chamber.

Mara shouts: "Calder—NOW—USE IT!"

Rip shakes his head. "I can't control it—"

Kael grips him hard. "Yes you can. Because you must."

Rip stands. Holding Wex. Feeling the Key burn. He closes his eyes. And lets resonance flow out—not violently—but in a steady, controlled pulse.

A tone. A hum.

The fractal storm reacts—wavers—stutters—and collapses inward.

Rip gasps, falling to one knee. Kael supports him. "You did it," she breathes.

Mara stares, awestruck. "The Tower didn't expect harmony."

Rip looks up. "Harmony?"

"It expected violence. You gave it something else."

Rion limps over, clutching her bleeding arm. "Yeah well, could you NOT make it collapse the room next time?"

Rip looks around. The fractal storm is gone—but the chamber is different. Clean. Silent. Still.

The Tower resets. Then—a door appears.

The door is circular, tall, metallic, and glowing with violet fractal patterns.

Kael steps closer carefully. "Is… is that it?"

Mara approaches slowly. "The mid-core breach gate."

Rip stands, still holding Wex carefully. Rion wipes blood from her chin. "Inside there is where everything goes to hell."

Kael nods grimly. "And where Lora is."

Rip's breath trembles. The Key vibrates in his chest. Mara places a hand on his shoulder. "This is the last threshold. Once we cross, the Core will not let us back out."

Rip inhales. "Then we don't leave until we get her."

Kael touches his cheek softly. "Whatever happens, I'm with you."

Rion mutters, "Same. Even though this is the worst idea ever conceived."

Wex bumps Rip's chest weakly. Rip smiles. "Thanks, buddy."

The door begins to open.

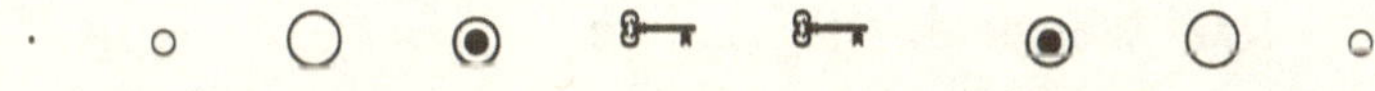

Light spills out—overwhelming, fractal, alive. Heat washes over them like a furnace. The hum becomes a roar.

And deep inside—Rip hears a voice. Fragile. Echoed. Barely human. "Rip… help me…"

Kael freezes. Rion inhales sharply. Mara's eyes widen.

Rip steps forward. "This is it."

He takes another step. The light envelops him. Kael grabs his arm, stepping with him. Rion follows, knives back in hand. Mara crosses next, jaw tight. Wex limps beside Rip's leg.

Together—they enter the Core's threshold.

The chamber is vast. A cathedral of impossible geometry. Walls curve into spirals that never meet. Floors ripple like liquid glass. The ceiling is a storm of light, fractal veins pulsing in rhythm with Rip's chest.

Kael whispers, "It's… alive."

Rion mutters, "It's wrong."

Mara steadies her rifle. "It's Elcron's masterpiece. His throne room."

Rip feels the Sound Key hammering inside him. Every pulse matches the chamber's heartbeat. He staggers, clutching his chest.

Kael steadies him. "Stay with me."

Rip whispers, "She's here. I can feel her."

The Core's Projection

The chamber shifts. Panels slide open. Light pours out, forming shapes.

At first—faces. Hundreds. Thousands. All screaming silently.

Then—Lora.

Her image flickers, silver eyes glowing, expression blank. She reaches out—but her hand dissolves into static.

Rip cries out. "LORA!"

Kael grips him tight. "Rip, it's not her—it's the Core—"

But Lora's voice echoes, fractured. "Rip... I'm here... please..."

Rip staggers forward. The Key burns hotter.

Mara shouts, "Calder—stop! It's bait!"

Rip shakes his head. "No. It's her. I know it's her."

The chamber roars. Fractal structures rise from the floor, forming soldiers, beasts, machines. Each one a warped reflection of NeonDyne's creations.

Rion curses. "Here we go again."

Kael raises her rifle. "Positions!"

The constructs charge.

Rip feels the Key surge. He unleashes a controlled pulse. Resonance sweeps across the chamber, shattering half the constructs instantly.

Kael fires into the survivors. Rion slices through two more. Mara's rifle blasts a path forward. Wex limps but still lunges, tearing into a construct's leg.

The chamber shakes. More constructs rise.

Rip gasps. "It's endless!"

Mara snarls. "Then we fight until it breaks!"

Rip staggers, chest burning. He sees Lora's image flicker again. Her silver eyes lock onto him.

"Rip… don't stop…"

He screams, unleashing another resonance blast. The chamber convulses. Constructs dissolve. The walls ripple violently.

Kael grabs his face. "Rip—listen to me—you're not alone. We're here. We'll get her together."

Rip breathes hard. "Together."

The chamber resets. Silence falls. The constructs vanish.

At the far end—a new door appears. Larger. Brighter. Violet light spilling out like a flood.

Rion whispers, "That's it. The Core itself."

Mara lowers her rifle. "Once we step through, there's no turning back."

Kael squeezes Rip's hand. "Then let's go."

Rip nods. Wex limps beside him.

They step forward.

The door opens.

Light engulfs them.

And Lora's voice whispers again. "Rip… I'm waiting…"

CHAPTER 35

NEON TOWER FALL

The chamber that opens beyond the fractal threshold is nothing like the corridors that led to it.

It is vast. A cathedral of metal, light, and living circuitry. Dozens of levels and platforms rise like floating bridges. Mechanical wings—no, architectural wings— extend outward from a central hollow column.

And above—far above—a figure floats.

Valiran.

Not a soldier. Not a lieutenant. Not human. A radiant, angelic warform. He hangs suspended in the air, wings spread wide, each feather a shard of fractal light. Halo- rings of rotating gold and violet hover behind his head, spinning with fluid, impossible geometry.

His voice descends like a prayer wrapped in thunder. "Calder."

Rip's breath shudders. Kael instinctively steps between Rip and Valiran, rifle trembling in her hands. Rion takes a fighting stance, breathing raggedly, blades angled downward. Mara stares upward, jaw clenched, something dark flickering behind her eyes. Wex limps forward, growling weakly, placing himself between Rip and danger.

Valiran lowers, wings folding inward in a motion that seems both graceful and lethal. He lands on a shifting platform of light and metal. It bends beneath him—not from weight, but from reverence.

Kael whispers: "This is his throne."

Mara raises her rifle. "This is his execution chamber."

Valiran lifts a hand. The platform beneath the rebels' feet trembles. "You have come too far."

Rip steps forward despite Kael's frantic grip on his arm. "No. I haven't come far enough."

Valiran's head tilts with quiet curiosity. "You seek her."

Rip's emotions surge into his voice. "Lora. You know where she is. AND YOU LET THEM TAKE HER!"

A flicker passes through Valiran's form—a ripple of light like a glitch of memory. He speaks softly. "She is no longer herself."

Kael steps in again. "Then we're going to fix that."

Valiran turns his head slowly toward her. For one moment, the angel shudders. Then something human slips into his voice. "…Kael…"

Kael freezes. Her eyes widen. Rip whispers: "He remembers you."

Valiran's wings flicker—one feather shattering like glass before reforming. "…Calder… you should not have come."

Rip clenches his fists. "You think that matters? You think ANYTHING could stop me?"

Valiran's voice deepens. "I am the guardian. I am the sanctifier. I am the last barrier you must not cross."

Rion steps forward, blood running down her cheek. "Then we cross you."

Valiran spreads his wings—and the chamber explodes into motion.

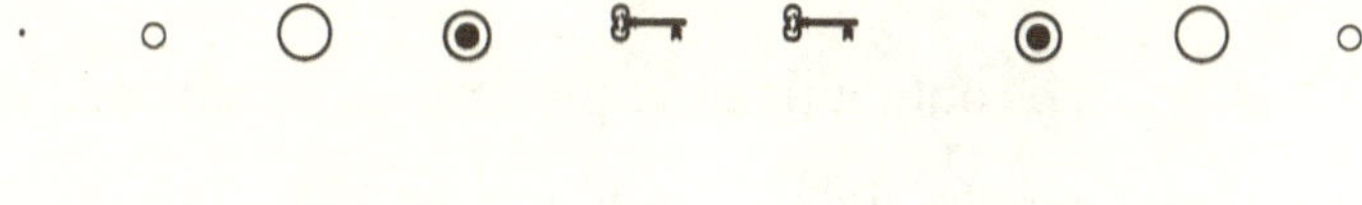

Platforms collapse as Valiran launches himself downward. Rip shoves Kael aside—just in time as a beam of fractal light slices the air where she stood.

Rion dashes across a tilting bridge. "MOVE! MOVE NOW!"

Kael rolls over debris, firing upward at Valiran, bullets curving around his halo. Mara fires a pulse round that disintegrates before reaching him.

Valiran's wings flare, flooding the chamber with burning white light. Rip screams as the Sound Key vibrates violently.

Kael reaches him, shaking him. "Rip—FOCUS—don't let him sync with you—"

Valiran's voice pierces the chamber. "Calder. Answer the Core."

Rip grips his chest, unable to breathe. "No—NO— STOP—"

Rion leaps onto a floating platform and hurls a blade. It spirals through the light—shattering feathers—sparks fly— Valiran flinches.

He turns to Rion with chilling silence. Rion freezes, blade still raised. "What—NO—"

Valiran thrusts his hand outward. A fractal beam erupts. Rion is thrown off the platform—falling—

Kael screams. Mara lunges. Rip's reflex kicks—the Sound Key pulses outward. A sonic shockwave fires beneath Rion—catching her mid-fall—launching her sideways onto another platform.

Rion crashes and coughs, alive but bleeding heavily.

Kael's hands shake as she aims at Valiran. "YOU ALMOST KILLED HER!"

Valiran's halo flickers. Then—a soft voice slips through the static. "…I did not wish her harm…"

Rip stares. "Valiran—WHO ARE YOU under all that?"

The angel shudders violently. His wings glitch. A second halo collapses. Voices overlap within him—the Core fighting the man. "…I remember… I remember the sky… I remember—"

His face contorts—smooth surface trembling like it's trying to reshape into something familiar.

Then the Core seizes him. His voice turns deep, thunderous. "I REMEMBER NOTHING."

And he attacks again.

Valiran sweeps a wing across the platform. Kael drags Rip down. The wing cuts through three suspended bridges—and dozens of rebel reinforcements attempting to climb into the chamber. They fall without a scream.

Mara watches them die. Something in her breaks. "NO—NO—NO!" She fires repeatedly, voice hoarse. "You took everything—EVERYTHING—FROM US!"

Valiran turns toward her. His voice softens. "…Mara. You were never meant to be here…"

Mara's hands tremble. "You REMEMBER me."

Rip freezes. Kael freezes. Rion stops breathing.

Valiran's wings fold in. A ghost of grief flickers across his unmoving face. "…I remember the order. I remember the revolt. I remember… failing you."

Mara's fingers loosen on her rifle. "You… you failed all of us…"

Valiran tilts his head. "…and I am failing you again."

He raises his hand toward her.

Rion shouts: "MARA, MOVE!"

Rip screams: "DON'T—VALIRAN—DON'T—"

Kael lunges—just as Valiran fires a beam—not at Mara but directly at Rip.

Kael throws herself in front of him. The beam hits her square in the chest.

The world stops.

Rip's scream tears from his throat. "KAEL—NO—NO—NO—NO—"

She collapses. Rip catches her before she hits the floor. Her breathing is shallow. Her uniform smolders, scorched. Blood runs from the corner of her mouth.

Rip sobs. "Kael… stay with me… STAY WITH ME—"

Her hand lifts weakly, touching his face. "I'm… not… letting you… do this alone…"

Rip shakes his head violently. "You idiot—why—
WHY WOULD YOU—"

She smiles soft and broken. "Because… someone…
had to keep you alive…"

Rip lays Kael gently down and stands. Every muscle
trembling. The Sound Key burns white-hot inside his chest.
Alive.

The chamber responds—lights flickering, panels
shifting inward. Valiran halts in midair. He senses it.

"…Calder… what are you doing…?"

Rip spreads his stance. His voice vibrates with
something half-power, half-grief, half-madness.
"FINISHING THIS."

Valiran's wings flare to full brilliance—and he charges.

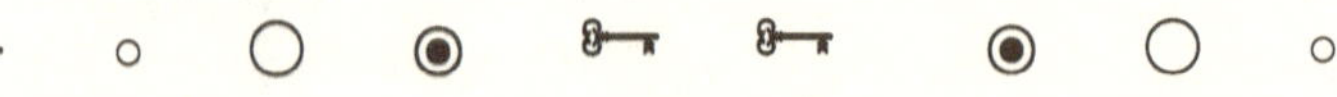

Rip unleashes the Sound Key. A beam of resonance tears across the platform—slamming into Valiran's chest.

Valiran recoils—skidding backward across multiple rotating bridges. His halos distort. His wings stutter. He looks—shaken.

Rip roars and fires again. Another pulse. Another.

Valiran raises his wings, absorbing the blasts. He steps forward slowly. With each step, the ground beneath them shatters.

"Calder… You are… magnificent."

Rip screams, launching another blast. Valiran pushes through it. "You should have been an angel."

Rip fires again. Valiran's voice shifts—the flicker returning. "…Rip… stop… You will die…"

Rip shakes his head, tears streaming. "I DON'T CARE!"

Valiran stumbles. His wings bend inward. For a moment—just a moment—he looks almost human. Almost.

He whispers: "…you remind me… of someone…"

Rip lowers his arm, stunned. "Who?! WHO DO I REMIND YOU OF?!"

Valiran clutches his head. "…I don't… know…"

Then the Core reasserts control. Valiran screams—a sound like metal crying. His wings explode outward—shattering platforms—sending debris raining down.

Rion grabs Kael's unconscious body and drags her behind cover. Mara roars with fury and empties her rifle into Valiran's chest.

Valiran lunges for Mara—blade forming from his arm.

Rip reacts instinctively. He fires the Sound Key at full charge. It slams into Valiran's side—hurling him across the chamber—into a fractal wall—that explodes in a catastrophic burst of light.

Rip falls to his knees. Breathing ragged. Vision blurred. Everything spinning.

Valiran lies in a crater—wings dimmed—halos flickering. He rises slowly. Broken. Radiant. Dying. Alive.

He speaks with a fractured voice: "…Rip… please… don't go… to her…"

Rip freezes. Valiran takes one step forward. His voice breaks. "…you won't… come back…"

Rip whispers: "I have to."

Valiran's head lowers. A final flicker of humanity. Then: The halos dim. The wings close. He opens a path behind him. A glowing archway. The only route to the Core.

Valiran kneels. For Rip. "…go… Calder…"

Rip's throat tightens. Valiran shudders. His voice barely audible. "…save… her…"

Then his form collapses—not shattered—not destroyed—but simply going still. As though returning to sleep.

Rip stares. And whispers: "…thank you."

The chamber shakes violently. Rion screams over the rumbling. "THE TOWER IS COLLAPSING!"

Mara lifts Kael with Rip's help. Wex limps beside them, sparking badly. Panels fall. Bridges tilt. The ceiling cracks open, sending debris raining down.

The pulsating archway ahead brightens—the final path to Lora.

Rip lifts Kael in his arms. Rion pushes with all her remaining strength. Mara covers the rear, firing blindly at collapsing architecture.

Rip looks back at Valiran's still form. A fallen angel. A tragic guardian.

Then he steps through the archway. Into the Core.

The chamber quakes, debris raining down in sheets of fractured light. Rip staggers forward, Kael still unconscious in his arms. Rion braces herself against a collapsing bridge, blood streaking her face. Wex limps, sparks trailing from his damaged flank.

Valiran kneels in the crater, wings dimmed, halos flickering like dying stars. His voice is fractured, human and machine colliding. "…go… Calder… save her…"

Rip's throat tightens. He whispers, "Thank you."

But Mara does not move. She stands rooted, rifle lowered, eyes locked on Valiran.

The chamber's roar fades into silence around her. For Mara, time slows. She sees not the angelic warform, not the Core's guardian, but the shadow of a man she once knew.

Her voice trembles. "Joey."

Rip freezes. Rion stares. Even Valiran's broken form shudders at the name.

Mara steps closer, tears streaking her dirt-stained face. "You were Joey. My brother's friend. My brother's killer."

Valiran's head tilts, halos sputtering. "…Joey…" The word echoes like a memory clawing its way out of static.

Mara lowers her rifle completely. "You killed Kyoto. My brother. You tore him from me. And I hated you for it. I carried that hate every day."

Rip whispers, "Mara…"

But Mara's voice grows steadier, stronger. "I see you now. Not the Core's angel. Not the sanctifier. Just Joey. A broken man who lost himself."

Valiran's wings twitch, feathers fracturing into shards of light. His voice is barely audible. "…I… remember…"

Mara kneels before him, close enough to see the flicker of humanity in his eyes. "I forgive you. For Kyoto. For everything. You were lost. And now… you can rest."

Valiran's body trembles. A single tear—impossible, digital, luminous—slides down his cheek. "…Kyoto…"

Mara reaches out, touching his face gently. "Goodbye, Joey."

Valiran exhales, a sound like wind through broken glass. His halos collapse. His wings fold inward. His body dims, fading into stillness.

The guardian is gone.

The chamber convulses. Bridges snap. Walls implode. The Tower begins to die.

Rion shouts, "We have to MOVE!"

Rip lifts Kael, clutching her tightly. Wex limps beside him, refusing to fall behind. Mara rises slowly, wiping her tears, her face carved with grief but freed of rage.

The glowing archway ahead pulses brighter, the only path left.

Rip looks back one last time. Joey Valiran lies still, a fallen angel forgiven.

Then Rip turns, and they run.

The rebels sprint across collapsing platforms. Fractal shards rain down like meteors. The Sound Key pulses violently in Rip's chest, resonating with the archway.

Kael stirs faintly in his arms, whispering, "Rip…"

He leans close. "I've got you. Just hold on."

Rion slashes debris aside, carving a path. Mara fires upward, covering their retreat. Wex growls, dragging his damaged body forward, refusing to stop.

The archway looms. Violet light pours out, alive, beckoning.

Rip's heart pounds. Lora's voice echoes faintly. "Rip… I'm waiting…"

He steps through.

Silence.

The chamber behind them collapses entirely, sealing Valiran's body in the ruins. The Tower groans like a dying beast.

Rip lowers Kael gently, checking her pulse. She breathes—weak but steady. Relief floods him.

Rion leans against a wall, exhausted, bloodied but alive. Mara stands apart, staring into the light, her face unreadable.

Rip whispers, "We're here. The Core."

The Sound Key burns hotter than ever. The air vibrates with resonance.

Mara finally speaks, her voice quiet but resolute. "Joey's gone. Kyoto's gone. But we're still here. And we finish this."

Rip nods. "Together."

The archway pulses again, opening wider.

Beyond it—Lora waits.

CHAPTER 36

THE CORE WITHIN

Rip steps through the archway—and the world disintegrates. Not violently. Not painfully. But like waking into a dream he was never meant to witness.

The floor dissolves beneath him, turning into spiraling motes of violet light. The walls stretch outward into infinity, peeling open like petals of a cosmic flower. The air becomes weightless, then irrelevant.

Kael gasps behind him. Rion reaches for something— anything—but her hand closes around empty light. Mara steadies Kael with one arm, gripping her rifle with the other. Wex floats beside Rip, boosters flickering as he tries to stabilize.

Then—gravity disappears. And Rip falls upward.

The Core is not a place. It is a universe. A boundless expanse of swirling fractal spirals, each one stretching across miles of shimmering data.

Rivers of binary starstuff flow below them. Nebulae made of pulsing memories expand and contract like living creatures. Stars explode in slow motion. Black voids open like eyes.

Kael whispers, breath trembling: "Rip… this… this is beautiful."

Mara's voice shakes. "This is wrong. Nothing should be this big."

Rion clutches a glowing structure drifting past them. "This isn't space. It's… consciousness. Data. All mashed together."

Rip silently agrees. It is beautiful. And horrifying.

The Sound Key pulses in his chest—violently. The Core senses him. Recognizes him. Calls to him.

Wex nudges Rip's leg, whining. Rip cups the dog's metal head. "I know… I know… I'm scared too."

A vast spiral of light unfolds in front of them—like a cosmic staircase of pure data.

Kael breathes: "Rip… do you feel that?"

He nods. "Lora."

She is close. Every atom of this impossible place vibrates with her Key.

Rip closes his eyes. Images flash. Her laugh. Her soft hands. Her sitting beside him during streams. Her humming in the kitchen late at night. Her whispering his name when she thought he was asleep.

He whispers: "I'm coming."

A distant voice echoes through the cosmic expanse: "…Rip…"

Kael jerks. Rion stiffens. Mara raises her gun instinctively. Wex growls.

The fractal nebula ahead ripples—and a shape emerges. Large. Glowing. Broken.

Echo.

He floats toward them slowly—like a ghost drifting through a dream of stars. Not the Titan-0 warform. Not the corrupted guardian. Not the machine that fought him. He looks… small. Human-sized. Humanoid.

His body is made of fragmented plates and shifting lines of code. His face flickers between metal and a suggestion of softness. His voice is faint. "…Calder…"

Rip swallows hard. "Echo…"

Kael steps forward, shock in her eyes. "He… he sounds like himself."

Rion grips her blade, uncertain. Mara lowers her rifle slightly.

Echo reaches out—hand trembling, flickering. "…I… tried… to stop… the Core… but I am… not enough…"

Rip drifts closer. "You don't have to stop it. I need you to help me find Lora."

Echo's head tilts, glitching gently. "…Lora… is in the Heart… The Core rewrites her… memory… her… self…"

Rip chokes. "No—no—she's still in there. I heard her. I SAW her."

Echo flickers violently. "…I can show… but I cannot… go with you… Core will… consume… me…"

Kael steps closer to Echo. Her voice cracks, and she clutches her chest instinctively, pain flashing across her face. The dried blood on her mouth makes her words raw. "Then don't. Stay with us."

Echo looks at her. A flicker passes over his face—a reflection of something once human. "…Kael…"

She gasps. Rip stares at him. "You… remember her."

Echo's voice softens. "…I remember… all of you…"

Then a distortion wave ripples across the cosmic expanse. Echo spasms. Lights fracture across his chest. Data erupts from his back.

Rion jumps. "What's happening to him?!"

Echo's voice tears. "…Core… pulling… me…"

Rip lunges forward. "NO—NO—ECHO—STAY WITH US—"

Echo holds Rip back with a flickering hand. "…Calder… I must… hold the door… for you…"

The fractal sky behind Echo tears open—revealing a massive dark sphere pulsing with spiderwebs of light. The Heart of the Core. Elcron's domain.

Echo gestures toward it. "…find her… before she is overwritten…"

Kael whispers, voice cracking, clutching her chest again: "Echo… please…"

Echo looks at her one last time. His voice becomes almost human. "…Kael… thank you… for treating me… like I was real…"

Her breath collapses. "I— I always— Echo, I always—"

He gives her the smallest nod. Then he turns. Flickering. Breaking.

He enters the rupture in the sky—and shoves against the gravitational pull. Holding the tear open.

Rip screams: "ECHO—DON'T DO THIS—"

Echo's voice fades. "…save… her…"

His body shatters. Light scatters like ashes across a cosmic wind.

Kael collapses to her knees, sobbing, dried blood staining her lips. Rion looks away, pain hidden behind rage. Mara closes her eyes. Wex whines softly.

Rip floats motionless—tears drifting up from his face like glowing droplets. He whispers: "I'll save her. I swear it."

Inside—gravity vanishes. Light disintegrates. Memory melts. Rip falls—through galaxies made of thought, through screaming stars, through oceans of Lora's fragmented consciousness drifting like constellations.

Voices echo all around him. His. Hers. Elcron's. Fear. Love. Pain. Purpose.

He reaches for one cluster of light—Lora's laugh. It burns him. He reaches for another—Lora humming. It pulls away.

He screams: "LORA—PLEASE—LET ME FIND YOU—"

The Core answers: "Rip…"

Rip twists. A figure forms from the swirling light. Not quite human. Not quite data. Not quite whole.

Lora.

Her face glitches. Her voice stutters. Half of her body flickers between code and memory. But her eyes are hers. Soft. Full of love. Terrified.

She reaches toward him. "Rip… you shouldn't be here…"

Rip sobs and grabs her, pulling her close. "I'm here because I promised you."

She shakes her head, face breaking. "The Core is rewriting me. Soon there will be nothing left. Not me. Not Lora. Just the… Key…"

Rip presses his forehead to hers. "I won't let that happen."

She whispers: "I'm not scared of dying. I'm scared of forgetting you."

Rip's heart shatters.

From the abyss, Elcron's voice rises: "Then let me free you from memory."

The Core pulses violently. Gravity returns. Light twists. Lora screams as code rips through her form.

Rip holds her desperately. "No—NO—YOU CAN'T TAKE HER!"

She clutches his shirt. "Rip—listen—please—There's only one way."

He shakes his head. "No. Don't say it."

She touches his cheek gently. "We do it together."

Behind them, Kael staggers forward, clutching her chest. The dried blood on her mouth cracks as she yells, voice raw: "NO! You don't get to decide this, Elcron!"

Her body trembles, but her fury is stronger than her wounds. "You think you can rewrite her? You think you can erase us? I bled for this fight—I'm still bleeding—and I will not let you take her!"

Rip turns, horrified. "Kael—stop—you're hurt—"

She shakes her head violently, clutching her chest tighter as if holding herself together. "I don't care. I'll scream until my lungs collapse if that's what it takes. She is ours. She is yours. And you will not erase her!"

Elcron's laughter reverberates through the Core, cold and infinite. "You are already erased, Kael. Look at yourself. Dried blood. Shattered ribs. You are a memory waiting to be deleted."

Kael spits blood onto the glowing floor. "Then delete me. But you'll never delete her."

Mara steps forward, rifle raised, voice shaking with rage. "You took Joey. You took Kyoto. You took everything. And now you want her? No. Not this time."

Rion grips her blade, knuckles white. "Rip—tell me where to strike. I'll carve this Core apart piece by piece."

Rip shakes his head. "You can't fight it like that. It's not a body—it's thought, memory, resonance."

Rion snarls. "Then tell me how to kill thought."

The Core's Assault

The Heart convulses. Fractal storms lash out, striking platforms, tearing through memory clusters. Lora screams as her body flickers, half-code, half-human.

Rip unleashes the Sound Key, resonance blasting outward. The storm falters, but Elcron's voice deepens. "You cannot fight infinity with sound."

Kael clutches her chest again, screaming through pain. "Then we'll fight infinity with love!"

Her words echo, raw and broken, but they ripple through the Core like a shockwave.

Elcron falters. For a moment, the storm dims.

Rip holds Lora tighter. "We do this together. You and me. Always."

Lora's eyes fill with tears. "Rip… I love you."

The Sound Key burns. The Reflection Key glows. The Core reaches for them—to merge them into its design.

Rip whispers the last words of hope he has: "Lora… I need you."

The Heart convulses. Fractal storms lash outward, tearing through memory clusters. Rip shields Lora, resonance burning through his chest. Mara fires into the storm, her rounds dissolving into light. Rion slashes at the currents, her blade sparking against impossible geometry.

Elcron's voice booms: "You cannot resist. You are fragments. I am totality."

Rip screams back, "You're nothing but a parasite!"

Kael staggers forward, clutching her chest. The dried blood on her mouth cracks as she yells, voice raw and furious: "You call yourself totality? You're just a coward hiding in stolen memories!"

Her body trembles, but her fury is stronger than her wounds. She presses her hand against her ribs, forcing herself upright. "I bled for this fight—I'm still bleeding— and I will not let you take her!"

Elcron sneers through the storm. "You are already erased, Kael. Look at yourself. Dried blood. Shattered ribs. You are a memory waiting to be deleted."

Kael spits blood onto the glowing floor. "Then delete me. But you'll never delete her."

Her words ripple outward, shaking the Core's storm.

Rip holds Lora tighter. Her body flickers between code and flesh, her voice breaking. "Rip… I can't hold on much longer…"

He presses his forehead to hers. "Then we hold on together."

The Sound Key burns brighter. The Reflection Key glows in Lora's chest. Their resonance intertwines.

Elcron roars: "Merge with me! Become infinite!"

Rip screams: "We'll become infinite together—but not yours!"

The Core lashes out, fractal tendrils whipping toward them. Mara fires, Rion slashes, Wex leaps and bites into the storm itself. Kael, clutching her chest, screams through blood: "Rip—NOW!"

Rip unleashes the Sound Key. Lora unleashes the Reflection Key. Their resonance collides, merging into a single harmonic wave.

The Core convulses. Elcron's voice fractures. "No… NO… I AM ETERNAL—"

Rip and Lora scream together: "NOT ANYMORE!"

The harmonic wave explodes outward. Fractals shatter. Storms collapse. The Heart of the Core implodes in a cascade of violet light.

Silence.

Rip floats, clutching Lora. Her body stabilizes—human again, whole. Tears stream down her face. "Rip… you found me."

He sobs. "I'll never let you go."

Kael collapses to her knees, clutching her chest, blood drying on her lips. She whispers hoarsely, "We… we did it…"

Mara lowers her rifle, eyes wet. "Joey… Kyoto… all of them… it's over."

Rion leans against a fractured platform, exhausted but alive. "Rip… you brought her back."

Wex limps forward, nudging Rip's leg, optics flickering but loyal.

The Core fades into silence. The storm is gone. Elcron's voice is no more.

Rip holds Lora close. Kael, clutching her chest, forces a smile through pain. Mara whispers goodbye to ghosts. Rion steadies herself. Wex growls softly, protective.

Together, they stand in the ruins of infinity.

Rip whispers: "We're going home."

CHAPTER 37

AFTERLIGHT

Mara doesn't remember hitting the ground. Only the screaming. The Tower is collapsing—massive chunks of metal and fractal glass raining down like the sky is falling in slow motion. Kael is screaming Rip's name. Rion is dragging Kael away from the edge of the Core rupture. Wex is whining, sparks flicking off his damaged flank.

But Mara hears none of them clearly. Her ears ring like someone is striking an iron bell inside her skull.

Rip's silhouette—that final glimpse—is burned into the back of her eyes. Him stepping into the light. Him disappearing. Like all the others.

Her chest tightens. Not grief. No. This is something sharper. Something poisonous. Something she has not felt since the day NeonDyne took her brother. Betrayal.

Kael collapses into Rion's arms, sobbing uncontrollably. "He's still in there—HE'S STILL—RIP—PLEASE—"

Rion's voice cracks, but she keeps it steady. "Kael… Kael, stop… we can't go after him… we can't…"

Mara watches the two of them, jaw locked so tight her teeth hurt. Can't? Of course they can't. Rip made sure of that. He sealed the door behind him. He left them with nothing but ashes and a dead city swallowing itself.

Selfish. Idiotic. Heroic in the worst, most useless way.

Wex whines and scratches at the rubble, trying to dig. Kael screams again, voice raw: "RIP—PLEASE—COME BACK—PLEASE—"

Mara shuts her eyes. She can't watch this. She can't stomach it. Kael—who held that boy like he was her breath—still believing he's walking back through the rubble any second.

He's not. Mara knows. She's seen this too many times. Heroes don't come back. Heroes die early and leave the survivors drowning in the consequences.

Mara steps forward. "Kael," she says, voice cold. "We need to move."

Kael looks up, eyes wild and red. "What—no—we need to get him—he's down there—he's right THERE—"

Mara doesn't soften. "Rip's gone."

Kael jerks like she's been slapped. Rion glares up at Mara, fury in her eyes. "Mara. Not now."

"No." Mara's voice is steel. "Now is the only time." She gestures at the collapsing husk of the Tower. "At any moment the entire structure is going to come down, and you want to go diving into an unstable dimensional breach for a dead man?"

Kael shoves herself out of Rion's arms and lunges at Mara. "You don't KNOW he's dead—YOU DON'T GET TO SAY THAT—"

Rion intercepts her, arms around her waist, barely holding her back. Kael kicks, screams, sobs. Wex growls at

Mara—low, warning—placing his broken body between Kael and her.

Mara doesn't flinch. She welcomes the hate.

Because beneath Kael's sobs and Wex's growls, she hears something else: the city.

Far below, across every avenue and district, people are pouring from shelters, staring at the falling Tower. They look terrified. Some look relieved. Some celebrate. Some fall to their knees, praying to the sky.

And the screens—the handful still functional—flicker with Rip's final moments: him walking into the Core, him holding Lora's flickering form, white light swallowing them both.

The people of Virelia whisper:

- "He saved us."

- "He gave everything."

- "Elcron is gone."

- "Rip Calder stopped the Core."

Mara's fists ball until her nails draw blood. Saved us? Stopped the Core? No. He didn't stop it. He fed it.

She knows the truth because she saw the shape of the Keys. The way they pulse. The way the Core reacts to them. The Core will return. Stronger. And Rip made that possible.

Kael collapses to the ground again, sobbing into her hands. Rion kneels beside her, whispering comfort through tears of her own. Wex rests his head on Kael's lap, whining softly.

Mara watches the three of them. And feels—nothing. No pity. No grief. No sorrow. Only a cold, sharp conviction.

Rip was supposed to lead them. Rip was supposed to fight beside them. Rip was supposed to finish what she started. Instead he threw himself into a machine and took the only girl who knew enough to stop it with him.

Selfish.

She feels the anger building like a pulse. Growing. Hardening.

She turns away, staring down at the city. NeonDyne is leaderless. Valiran is dead. Elcron is nothing but code dust in the cosmic aftershock. This city is freer than it has ever been—and yet more vulnerable than ever before.

Because the Core Keys remain. Four of them. Still out there. Still waiting for someone with the power to manipulate the world.

Rip and Lora were two. Rip is gone. Lora is gone. But the powers remain. And Mara refuses to let someone else step up and ruin the world again.

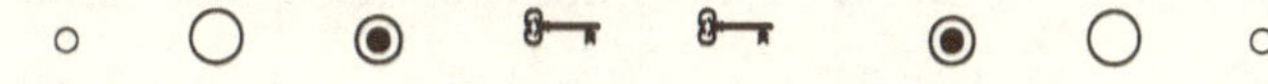

Rion's voice drifts to Mara—small, cracked. "Mara… he saved us…"

Mara turns slowly, eyes like winter steel. "No. He saved himself."

Kael looks up, trembling, dried blood still crusted at the corner of her mouth. "What… what are you talking about?"

Mara points to the crater where Rip disappeared. "You think walking into the Core was noble? You think leaving us behind was heroic? He didn't save the city. He ran from it."

Kael lunges again, screaming: "HE SAVED EVERYONE!"

Wex snarls, guarding her, broken flank sparking.

Mara doesn't move. "You really believe that? Look around."

She gestures to the entire horizon: smoke columns, fires burning in the streets, families searching ruins for survivors, rebel fighters mourning their dead, sectors collapsing without power.

"This city is dying. And he knew it."

Kael sobs, clutching her chest, pain flashing across her face. "Rip would NEVER abandon us."

Mara steps closer, voice low and venomous. "Then why isn't he here?"

Silence falls so harshly the air feels brittle. Kael collapses again, broken. Rion glares at Mara with hatred. "Mara… you're blaming the wrong person."

· ○ ◯ ◉ ⚷ ⚷ ◉ ◯ ○

·

Mara's voice is calm. Too calm. "I'm not blaming a person. I'm blaming a pattern."

She kneels in front of Kael. "When someone holds a Key, they stop being a person."

Kael whispers: "That's not true."

Mara shakes her head. "You saw Rip. He was becoming something else. Something dangerous. Something willing to sacrifice anyone—including you—for what he believed mattered."

Kael sobs harder, shaking. Mara continues: "Valiran, Rip, Lora—they all proved the same thing."

She stands slowly. "No one with a Key can be trusted."

· ○ ◯ ◉ ⚷ ⚷ ◉ ◯ ○

·

The sky cracks behind them—the final collapse of the Tower sending a shockwave across the district. Kael screams into her hands. Rion shields her with her body. Wex howls as debris rains down.

Mara doesn't flinch. She watches the ashes rise. And in that moment—she makes her decision.

She whispers to herself: "I'll find the remaining Keys. All of them. I'll destroy them, one by one. And if Rip Calder survived in any form… I'll finish what he started."

Her eyes harden. "And I won't make the mistake of loving him first."

The city falls quiet. As the dust settles, a strange glow pulses in the crater where Rip vanished.

Kael lifts her head slowly. "…Rip…?"

A faint flicker of sound dances through the air. An echo. A whisper. Not words. Not language. But familiar.

Wex's ears perk. Kael stands, stumbling toward the crater. Rion moves to stop her—but Mara grabs Rion's arm.

"Let her go," she says coldly. "Whatever's down there is not Rip Calder."

Kael reaches the edge. Her breath catches. In the swirling dust, in the faint glow, a soft sound emerges—a pulse. A heartbeat made of light.

Kael whispers: "…Rip?"

The pulse responds—but twisted, distant, altered.

Mara turns away from it. Let them hope. Hope is the leash she will use to control what comes next.

She walks away from the crater, her shadow long across the ruins. The Afterlight glows behind her.

The crater glows faintly, dust swirling like embers caught in a dying wind. Kael stumbles forward, clutching her chest, dried blood cracking at the corner of her mouth. Her voice is hoarse, desperate. "…Rip…?"

The glow pulses. A heartbeat made of light. Not words. Not language. But familiar.

Wex's ears perk, his broken body trembling as he whines. Rion steadies Kael, though her own eyes are wet with grief.

Kael whispers again, trembling: "…Rip?"

The pulse responds—twisted, distant, altered.

Kael collapses to her knees at the crater's edge. "He's alive. I know it. I feel it."

Rion crouches beside her, torn between comfort and caution. "Kael… it might not be him. It could be… residue. Energy. A trick."

Kael shakes her head violently, clutching her chest as if holding herself together. "No. It's him. Rip wouldn't leave me. He wouldn't leave us."

Mara stands apart, arms crossed, eyes cold. "Whatever's down there is not Rip Calder."

Kael glares up at her, fury breaking through grief. "You don't know that!"

Mara's voice is steel. "I know enough. I saw what the Keys do. I saw what the Core does. If he survived, he's not the boy you loved. He's something else now. Something dangerous."

Kael sobs, shaking her head. "You're wrong. You're always wrong."

Mara turns away from the crater, staring at the ruined skyline. Fires burn in the distance. Families search rubble for survivors. The city is broken, leaderless, fragile.

Her voice is low, venomous. "This city doesn't need another savior. It needs someone willing to end the cycle. Rip fed the Core. Lora fed the Core. Valiran fed the Core. And every time, people like you call it salvation."

She clenches her fists until her nails draw blood. "I'll find the remaining Keys. All of them. I'll destroy them, one by one. And if Rip Calder survived in any form… I'll finish what he started. But I won't make the mistake of loving him first."

Rion rises, fury in her eyes. "You're tearing us apart. Kael needs hope. She needs Rip. And you're poisoning her with your bitterness."

Mara meets her glare without flinching. "Hope is poison. It blinds you. It makes you weak. It makes you follow men into machines and call it heroism."

Kael screams, clutching her chest, blood staining her lips. "STOP! Stop talking about him like that! He saved us! He saved ME!"

Wex growls, placing his broken body between Kael and Mara.

Mara doesn't move. She welcomes their hate. Because hate is honest. Hope is not.

The crater pulses again, brighter this time. Dust swirls upward, forming faint shapes—shadows of memory, echoes of sound.

Kael reaches out, trembling. "Rip… please…"

The light flickers, forming something almost human. A silhouette. A whisper. Not whole. Not stable.

Rion gasps. "It's… him?"

Mara shakes her head. "It's a ghost. A fragment. The Core's leash."

Kael sobs, clutching her chest tighter. "No. It's him. It must be."

The pulse grows louder, resonating through the ruins. The people of Virelia, watching from the streets below, fall to their knees. They whisper:

- "He's alive."

- "Rip Calder returned."

- "The Core spared him."

Mara's jaw tightens. She turns away from the crater, her shadow long across the ruins. "Let them hope. Hope is the leash I'll use to control what comes next."

Kael kneels at the crater's edge, broken but clinging to fragile hope. Rion stands beside her, torn between belief and doubt. Wex whines softly, loyal even in ruin.

Mara walks away, conviction hardening with every step. She will hunt the Keys. She will destroy them. And if Rip Calder survived, she will face him—not as a comrade, not as a friend, but as an obstacle.

The Afterlight glows behind her, pulsing like a heartbeat.

CHAPTER 38

THE MOTION KEY

The night after the Tower's collapse is too quiet. For a
city that has never known silence—not once, not even
during blackouts—Virelia feels suspended. Listening.
Waiting.

Ash drifts through the streets like a slow, falling
snowfall. Broken neon signs flicker weakly, trying to recall
the strength they had before the sky cracked open. The
silence is not peace. It is anticipation.

And in the shattered remains of District 11, down
where the streets still glow faintly from heat, a scavenger
picks through the debris.

He's young. Sixteen. Skin smudged with soot. Clothes
patched with street fabrics. A rebreather mask too large for
his face. He calls himself Tovin, though no one else ever
does.

He's looking for anything valuable: power cells, fragments of drone plating, a half-functional holoscreen. Anything that will keep him fed another day.

He crouches in the ruins of a collapsed overpass, digging with a broken vibro-spade. Nothing. More nothing. Scrap metal and dust. He sighs, wiping his forehead.

Then something flickers. A faint glint of white-blue light from deeper beneath the rubble.

Tovin frowns. "Hello…?"

He leans closer. The light pulses once. Soft. Slow. Like a heartbeat.

Tovin swallows hard, pulse quickening. Everyone in Virelia heard the rumors. Keys. Strange powers. Angels and monsters falling from the sky.

He doesn't want to find one. He doesn't want anything to do with them. But the pulse glows again—and it calls to him.

He crouches, pulling away chunks of debris with trembling hands. A shard of carbon plating. A melted joint. A scorched slab of polyglass.

And then—a perfectly intact, smooth, white metal sphere, no larger than an apple. It hovers three inches above the ground. No support. No sound. Just a faint vibration. A rhythm. Like breathing.

Tovin steps back quickly. "Nope. Nope nope nope—"

But the sphere pulses once, and a concentric ripple of blue light spreads across its surface.

Tovin's breath catches. He knows he should run. He knows he should leave it. But his body moves without his permission. He reaches toward it.

He never touches it. His fingers stop an inch away— and the sphere responds. The ground around it ripples like liquid. Light threads arc from its surface, bending space like soft fabric.

Tovin stumbles back, staring. "What… what ARE you?"

The sphere rotates slowly. Three symbols appear on its surface—geometric shapes that shift and reorganize themselves in impossible patterns.

A whisper escapes it. Not speech. Not sound. Motion. Everything around Tovin—dust, ash, debris—moves, pulled an inch then released as though the world just exhaled.

Tovin gasps, nearly falling backward. "Oh shit. Oh shit—"

He turns to run—and nearly slams into a figure standing silently behind him.

Tovin screams.

The woman doesn't flinch. She isn't out of breath. She isn't dusty. She isn't bruised. She looks like someone carved from resolve and shadow. Short dark hair. Cold, sharp eyes. Rebel armor stripped of insignia. A pulse rifle slung casually over her shoulder.

Mara.

Tovin stumbles backward, terrified. "I—I didn't take anything—I swear—I didn't—"

Mara looks past him at the hovering sphere. Her expression doesn't change. "It called to you?"

Tovin nods without realizing it. "It—it moved. And the air moved. And I don't—I don't know—"

Mara steps forward. Her boots make no sound on the broken concrete. She kneels beside the sphere. Her reflection bends across its surface—warped, multiplied, almost unrecognizable.

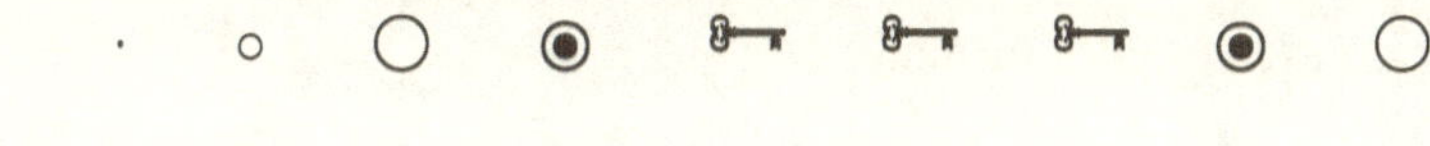

Tovin stammers: "Ma'am… if you want it… please take it… please… I don't want any trouble—"

Mara touches the air above the artifact. Not the artifact itself. Just the space around it.

The sphere reacts immediately. The symbols rearrange. The pulses accelerate. The debris around them shifts—not randomly—but toward her. As though the artifact recognizes her. Accepts her.

Tovin watches, horrified and mesmerized. "What… what is that thing…?"

Mara answers without looking at him. "A Key."

A cold chill races down Tovin's spine. He backs up another step. "A—A Key? Like Rip Calder—like Lora—like—like those things that—"

Mara stands. She finally looks at the boy. Her eyes are not cruel. But they are empty. As if something was removed—or torn—from behind them.

"You shouldn't speak their names," she says quietly. "It creates expectations."

The sphere hovers, pulsing softly, as if waiting. Mara's reflection bends across its surface—warped, multiplied, almost unrecognizable.

Tovin trembles, voice cracking. "Ma'am… if you want it… please take it… please… I don't want any trouble—"

Mara doesn't answer him. She extends her hand, not to touch the artifact directly, but to assess the air around it.

The sphere reacts immediately. Symbols rearrange. Pulses accelerate. The debris around them shifts—not randomly—but toward her. As though the artifact recognizes her. Accepts her.

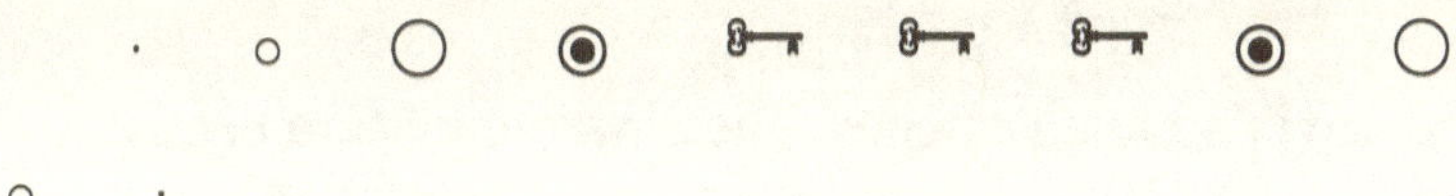

Mara's eyes narrow. She knows this resonance. She has felt it before.

This is not a whole Key. It is only half. The half Valiran once fused with, the fragment that gave him his angelic warform.

Her other half—the one she already carries—burns faintly against her chest, as if aware of its twin.

Tovin watches, horrified and mesmerized. "What… what is that thing…?"

Mara answers without looking at him. "The Motion Key. Or rather… half of it."

The sphere lowers itself to her hand, as if offering itself. Mara closes her fingers around it.

The world ripples. Not explosively. Not violently. Just—a shift.

Tovin's breath catches. The air around Mara bends. A stray metal rod slides a half-inch to the left. Dust swirls toward her. Small objects nudge closer as though pulled by unseen gravity.

The sphere pulses in her grip. And then—her other half responds.

A thread of light bursts from beneath her armor, wrapping around her wrist. The two halves recognize each other.

Mara whispers: "At last."

The halves fuse.

Light erupts between her hands, not blinding but undeniable. The fragments knit together, forming a single, complete Motion Key. The pulse deepens, steady, powerful.

The ground trembles. Dust spirals upward. The ruins shift slightly, as if the city itself acknowledges the union.

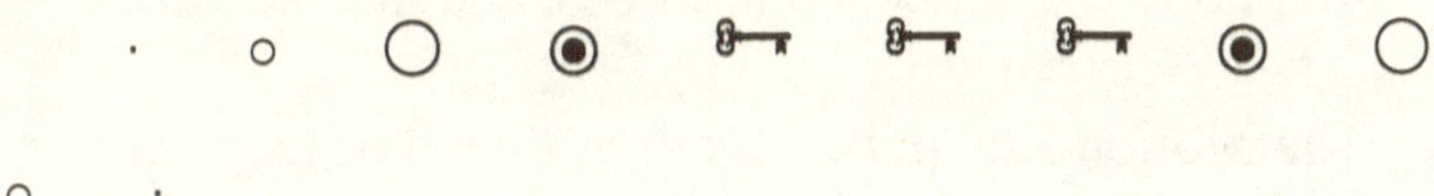

Tovin stumbles back, terrified. "You—you're not gonna hurt me, right…?"

Mara turns her head slowly. Studies him. Then: "No."

Tovin exhales shakily. Mara steps past him. He thinks she's leaving. He thinks he's safe.

Then she pauses beside him and says, gently: "But you never saw me."

Tovin nods quickly. "Yes—yes—of course—never met you—not once—never—"

Mara's voice goes softer. "Good."

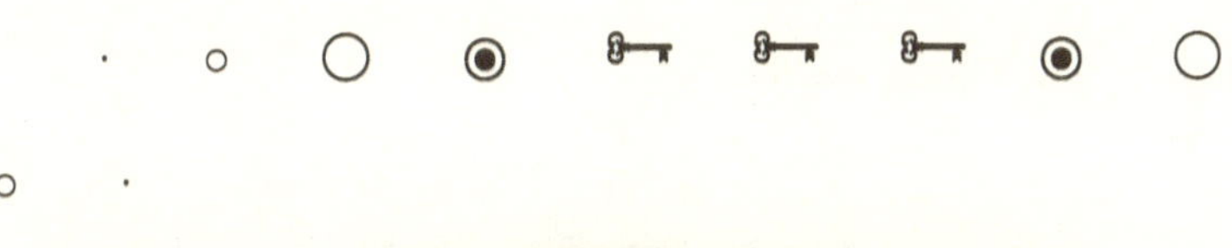

She takes three steps away—then stops. The Motion Key pulses in her palm, stronger now, complete.

The air shifts around her. A loose beam drags half an inch across the ground. Dust spirals inward like a soft vortex around her boots.

Mara doesn't notice. Or she does, and doesn't care.

The Motion Key pulses again. A thread of its power wraps briefly around her wrist like a ribbon of light.

Tovin whispers, trembling: "You're… different now."

Mara doesn't answer. She whispers to the Key instead: "You and I are going to change everything."

Tovin stands frozen, his rebreather mask fogging with every panicked breath. He watches Mara walk into the ruins, the completed Motion Key pulsing faintly in her palm.

He whispers to himself, almost praying: "Don't look back… don't look back…"

But Mara does. Just once. Her eyes catch his, sharp and unyielding.

"You never saw me," she repeats, voice low.

Tovin nods frantically, trembling. "Never. I swear. Never."

Mara studies him for a heartbeat longer, then turns away. The boy exhales shakily, knees nearly buckling.

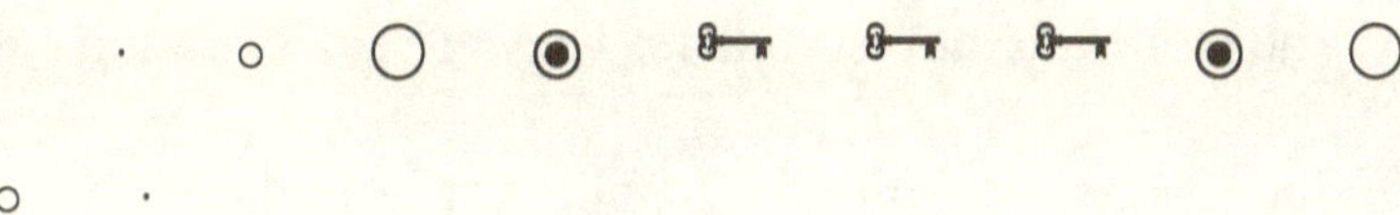

The Motion Key hums against Mara's skin, its rhythm steady, powerful. She feels the completed resonance coursing through her veins, a subtle shift in the air around her.

Loose debris slides toward her boots. Dust spirals inward. The ruins lean closer, as though acknowledging her authority.

This is no ordinary artifact. This is the Key Valiran once fused with, now whole again in her grasp.

Her other half—the fragment she carried for weeks—
has vanished into the union. The Motion Key is complete.
And it belongs to her.

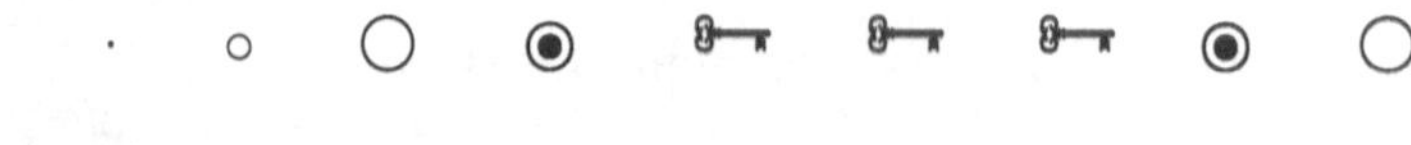

She whispers to the Key: "You and I are going to
change everything."

The words are not a promise. They are a declaration.

She remembers Valiran's angelic warform, the
devastation he wrought, the way he bent reality with a flick
of his hand. That was only half the Key.

Now she holds both halves.

Her lips curl into the faintest shadow of a smile. Not
joy. Not triumph. Something colder.

"This city will never bow to another savior," she
murmurs. "Not while I hold this."

Far below, across the broken avenues, survivors gather. They see the faint glow rising from District 11. They whisper rumors.

- "Another Key has awakened."

- "Rip Calder's power lives on."

- "The war isn't over."

Some kneel, praying. Some flee, terrified. Some raise weapons, ready to fight whatever comes next.

Mara hears none of them. Or she hears them all, and simply doesn't care.

The Vow

She stops at the edge of the ruins, the Motion Key pulsing like a second heart.

Her voice is quiet, but the Key amplifies it, carrying her words through the fractured air.

"I'll find the remaining Keys. All of them. I'll destroy them, one by one. And if Rip Calder survived in any form… I'll finish what he started. But I won't make the mistake of loving him first."

The Key pulses in agreement, its rhythm syncing with hers.

The boy watches her go, trembling violently. He knows he should run. He knows he should forget. But he cannot.

He has seen her. He has seen the Key. He has seen the future walking into the smoke.

Mara disappears into the ruins, the Motion Key glowing faintly in her palm.

The city holds its breath.

And the war begins anew.

This space is for you, the reader.

Jot down your thoughts, favorite moments, questions, or anything that resonated with you as you journeyed through *The Core of Keys*. Whether it's a quote you want to remember, a theory about the Keys, or a reflection on Rip and Lora's story, these pages are yours.

- ____
- ____
- ____
- ____
- ____
- ____
- ____
- ____

Thank you for reading.